"Who are you?" Cathy asked breathlessly....

He was so close to her, she could see the way his dark eyes came back into focus.

"I have told you," Laurence answered slowly, not quite understanding.

She drew away from him a little. "You must have a Huron name."

"It is Tohin-ontan."

"What does it mean?"

He had difficulty interpreting the question.

"In English?"

"Ah. It means—" he searched for the word "—Bird of Fire. Firebird."

Cathy's eyes were drawn to the old copper scars at his neck that slid into the collar of his shirt. "You are not an angel, are you?"

Laurence had no difficulty with that one. He shook his head. "No, I come from Hell...."

Dear Reader,

When author Julie Tetel first introduced the character of Laurence Harris in *Sweet Sensations*, the second book in the North Point series, he was a half-wild teenager. Now, in *Sweet Surrender*, Laurence has grown into a handsome young man who charms small-town busybody Cathy Davidson into letting go and enjoying herself in this tale of laughter and love.

Also this month, we are pleased to have another Western by Mary McBride, *The Gunslinger*. Set in Glory, Kansas, it's the story of a reclusive gunfighter who finally discovers someone who sees him as a man, not a legend, yet can't escape from his dangerous reputation.

Our other titles for February include *Lord Liar*, a medieval tale of secrets and deception by Laurie Grant, and from Deborah Simmons, *The Vicar's Daughter*, a frothy Regency about a nobleman who meets his match when he agrees to shepherd a naive vicar's daughter through a London Season.

We hope you will enjoy all four books this month and keep an eye out for all our titles, wherever Harlequin Historicals are sold.

Sincerely,

Tracy Farrell
Senior Editor

Please address questions and book requests to:
Harlequin Reader Service
U.S.: 3010 Walden Ave., P.O. Box 1325, Buffalo, NY 14269
Canadian: P.O. Box 609, Fort Erie, Ont. L2A 5X3

Julie Tetel

Sweet Surrender

Harlequin Books

TORONTO • NEW YORK • LONDON
AMSTERDAM • PARIS • SYDNEY • HAMBURG
STOCKHOLM • ATHENS • TOKYO • MILAN
MADRID • WARSAW • BUDAPEST • AUCKLAND

ISBN 0-373-28855-7

SWEET SURRENDER

Copyright © 1995 by Julie Tetel Andresen.

JULIE TETEL

has always loved both history and romance, making it easy for her to love reading and writing historical romances. She is from a suburb of Chicago and currently lives in Durham, North Carolina. She has two sons, two careers, at least two points of view and one husband.

For Charm

Acknowledgment

I would like to thank Lee Calhoun of Calhoun's Nursery in Pittsboro, North Carolina, for his generous help in providing me with information concerning the fascinating, and now-forgotten, history of apple-growing in the South.

Chapter One

Hillsborough, North Carolina
May 1825

Perched on a thick, midlevel branch of one of her flowering apple trees, Cathy Davidson was examining a pretty brooch of pearl pink blossoms with a well-trained eye.

For no reason at all, she sighed once, deeply, and looked up from her study, across the tops of the trees in her small orchard. From her perch on the rise of a gentle slope, she surveyed the expanse of thick pine forest rippling below her and away to the west. Suddenly her gaze blurred, and she was dazzled by the vision of a vast apple orchard, rich in rows of magnificent trees of all her favorite varieties. She must have unconsciously shifted her position for, just as suddenly, something happened that had never happened to her before.

Her world turned on a sharp angle, and she was scattering fragile apple-blossom petals as her body crashed downward. Before she could grasp a branch, before she could curse herself for her carelessness, before she could imagine broken bones, she landed with a cushioned thud.

In that first flash of a second after the fall, she felt relieved but perplexed. She realized, dimly, that she had fallen atop some body, and it must have been the body of a man, to judge from the noseful of buckskin she inhaled and the hardness of the chest against which her cheek and breasts were flattened. The man was sprawled beneath her on the ground, and he was cradling her in strong arms, suggesting that he had been trying to catch her in her fall.

After a stunned moment, she lifted her head to look at him. From her severely foreshortened angle, the man's face appeared to be all chin, and his eyes were shut. Even so, and despite the fact that her senses were swimming, she was sure that she had never seen him before.

Surprised now and vexed, she disentangled herself from his heavy, haphazard embrace and shifted awkwardly to her knees. She blinked, shook her head and hastily arranged her apron and skirts for modesty when she saw that the man had opened his eyes. He was staring, unblinking, into the tangled clouds of branches overhead, which were gently showering their blossom petals. Then he craned his neck, keeping the rest of his body immobile. Because Cathy had succeeded in struggling to her feet, his eyes were attempting to come into focus on the hem of her skirt and her bare toes.

A swarm of words buzzed on her tongue, but all she could manage at first was a gusty ''Ooff!''

The man propped himself up on his elbows. He, too, blinked and shook his head. Then his eyes traveled up from her toes to her face. When his gaze met hers, his eyes widened briefly in combined awe and surprise, but she was still too dazed to register the fact. The next moment, it was gone, and his expression was impenetrable, his features impassive.

Not bothering to mask the array of her own shifting emotions, she said the first thing that came to mind. "What are you doing here?"

"Saving you . . . from a . . . fall," he croaked, short of breath.

The blossoms were still drifting around them. She brushed aside an impertinent petal that had landed on her nose, then fisted her hips. She demanded again, "No, I mean what are you *doing* here?"

He thumped his chest, drew a deep breath and pushed himself up from his elbows. "Saving you," he repeated. He rose fluidly to his feet and his full height. "Although I did not know that it would be from a fall."

"I don't need saving," she retorted, looking up at him.

"You did from the fall," was his solemn reply.

"I've never fallen from a tree before," she answered with bruised dignity.

"I could not have known that," he answered in turn.

"Indeed, you could *not* have know that, could you?"

He shook his head. "No, we have never met."

She smiled archly. "I did not *think* we had ever met, and so I ask you again, sir, what you are doing here on my property, lurking beneath one of my apple trees."

One black brow quirked at the word lurking, but otherwise his face betrayed nothing. He said evenly, "I am putting myself at your service, ma'am."

She made an attempt to collect her wits. "I have not advertised for help," she said, still a little dazed. "Why would you want to put yourself at my service?"

"To repay my debt to you."

"Your debt to me?"

"From this morning," he said, "at the market-place in town."

"At the marketplace? This morning—?" she echoed, then broke off. Her eyes widened, and she glimpsed the odd fragment of a memory from the morning. She recalled that the rough-and-tumble Watts brothers, come to market from next door in East Orange County, had looked to be harassing some poor Indian who had wandered into town. They were shoving him a little, taunting him a little and bullying him a lot. She had had no hesitation in confronting those stupid, unkempt Watts brothers, in facing them down and sending them off with fleas in their ears.

Now, she had seen the poor Indian only from the back, but her impression of that back clashed with the image of the man who stood before her. The Indian of this morning had been tall and lean, like this man. However, the black hair that hung below his poor Indian's shoulders had seemed to be stringy and greasy, not clean like his. She saw that this man was wearing the same clothes as the Indian, namely a buckskin vest and breeches stuffed into calfskin boots. However, from the back, the poor Indian had looked dirty, even ragged. She saw that this man's buckskins were well seasoned, but the clean white shirt he wore was crisp, if somewhat crumpled now, and almost new. Furthermore, from the way the poor Indian had withstood so stoically the challenging shoves and jeers of the Watts brothers, she would have guessed him to be quite old and sadly experienced at this sort of harassment. The man before her could not be much beyond his midtwenties.

And she was not even certain that he *was* an Indian, now that she had a good look at his face. Sure, he had black hair tied back at the nape, black eyes, high cheekbones and skin the color of new copper. She noted as well that fingers of an older copper color climbed up from his collar and clutched his neck. Nevertheless, at first glance, he did not have the look of an Indian, and it was only at second glance that she discerned an Indian cast to his strong, expressionless features. It was certainly an unusual face. At the moment it held a touch of incongruous beauty, given that several blossom petals had fallen to flock the glossy black tresses disordered from his encounter with her.

After a moment's silence, and apparently sensing her confusion, he reminded her with a minimal nod, "You were carrying a basket this morning and wearing a different dress. It was blue." His dark eyes roamed her hair. She had no doubt that it was now as disheveled as his. "You were also wearing a bonnet."

She strained to reconcile the two images: one of the poor Indian at the market and the other of the healthy young man before her. She gave it up when the thought occurred to her that, if they were one and the same man, her intervention on his behalf might have been unnecessary.

Never liking to think herself *superfluous*, she attempted to turn the tables on him by scolding, "I suppose you are well served for thinking that I needed saving from a fall—which, of course, is something I never do, except in this rare instance—and ended up by being knocked down! What gave you the fool idea to try and catch me?''

He answered gravely, ''I had not realized you were so heavy.''

In the space of a few, short minutes, she had been, by turns, relieved, perplexed, surprised and vexed. Now she was feeling mighty indignant. Although what he said was entirely true, for she was not some featherweight thing, she was of no mind now to *thank* him for having spared her the greater part of the pain of her fall.

Instead, she said with what dignity the ridiculous situation allowed, ''I cannot be pleased that you took it into your head to sneak along behind me and to follow me home.''

''I did not sneak along behind you.''

''You walked out in the open, I suppose.''

''Yes, out in the open,'' he confirmed. ''I left the market about half an hour after you did.''

Her earlier surprise returned. ''How did you find me, then? By asking someone where I lived?''

He shook his head. ''That was not necessary. The trail you left was plain enough.''

She did not recall leaving any trail. She harrumphed. ''Well, I still don't think I needed saving,'' she insisted, ''and I must say, sir, that you went to a lot of trouble for nothing.''

He did not respond to that. To her further displeasure, she noted that for a man with such an expressionless face, he looked pretty smug. A clever retort darted into her head, then darted out again when her thoughts were interrupted by a familiar voice calling, ''Miss Cathy! Miss Cathy! Halloo! Where are you?''

Her attention diverted, she answered back, "Over here, Clive. What do you have for me today?"

"Ah, there you are!" Mr. Clive Smith exclaimed happily as he emerged from behind a row of trees. "When you weren't on your porch or inside the house, I suspected that I'd find you out here. I see I was right! But I have to tell you that having to hunt you down like this puts me off schedule! Way off!"

"In that case, you could have left my mail in the mailbox," she suggested practically.

"And so I could have, Miss Cathy, but then I would not have been absolutely sure that it came into your hands, and I like the satisfaction of hand delivery, which, as you know, ranks only slightly above my desire to stay on schedule!"

While uttering several more comments along this and other lines, Hillsborough's most efficient, and only, postman dug deep into the leather bag slung across his shoulder and withdrew a letter that he presented to Cathy with a flourish.

Instantly recognizing the crabbed handwriting on the envelope, Cathy thought, What's this, now? She did not immediately pursue the question, for her attention was caught by the tail end of one of Mr. Smith's various remarks. She asked, a little breathlessly, "Who did you say has returned today?"

"Why, his nephew!"

She tapped the unopened letter against her palm and queried cautiously, "Old Hitch's nephew?"

"That's what I've been telling you, Miss Cathy!" Clive Smith confirmed cheerfully. "Young Hitchcock MacGuffin has come back to town. Saw him today. With my own eyes! Nearly threw my entire day off schedule, too, but I resisted the impulse to stop to talk to him, for it's obvious why he's returned. Plain as day!''

Cathy held up the letter. ''Anything to do with this?''

Mr. Smith shrugged good-naturedly. ''Looks to be from Old Hitch,'' he said in the manner of an unashamed busybody. ''Got one like it myself. Got several more in my bag.'' He patted his pouch affectionately. ''Old Hitch took an unaccountable maggot into his head before he died, I would say! But the truth is, the old man dies one day, and who wouldn't have predicted that Young MacGuff would return the next?''

Cathy had not predicted it. She knew that Young Hitchcock MacGuffin, who had left Hillsborough the year before to live in Raleigh, had not responded to his uncle's last letters, calling him to his bedside. Word was that Young MacGuff had been out of town on a business trip, and so Cathy had thought that he might not make it back for his uncle's funeral. At this news of his return, she felt the old flutter in the region of her heart. Trying to ignore it, she said, ''Of course, it stands to reason that Young MacGuff would return to pay his last respects to his uncle.''

''Last respects? Is that what you call it?'' Mr. Smith replied with the hint of a malicious wink. He did not explain himself, for he was looking off to one side, over Cathy's shoulder. He asked abruptly, ''Eh? Who's that?''

Cathy glanced in the direction of Mr. Smith's gaze and saw the quiet man standing not more than ten feet away. She was surprised all over again by his presence, for he had melted into the background at Mr. Smith's arrival. He was looking away from them, too, and although he undoubtedly heard Mr. Smith's question, he gave no sign of having done so.

Cathy spoke of him as if he were not there. "That's a man who followed me here from town this morning," she replied.

"Followed you here from town?" Mr. Smith echoed, alarmed.

"Well, he didn't follow me precisely, or at least he said he didn't have to follow me," Cathy said, adding uncertainly, "since I left a clear trail. In any case, he showed up here, under the tree where I was working."

"What does he want?" Mr. Smith demanded.

"I don't know."

"Who is he?"

"I don't know."

Mr. Smith peered at the man. "Is he an Injun?"

"I don't know," she said a third time.

Mr. Smith concluded his scrutiny. "Me neither. Doesn't look like anyone I know. Is he from around here?"

"I don't think so," Cathy said to this. "He talks strange."

Mr. Smith's mobile face scrunched in deep disapproval. Not lowering his voice, he asked, "Do you mean he says things that oughtn't to be said to a lady—a young lady, I might add—who isn't married?"

Cathy glanced toward the quiet man and noted that his expression had still not changed. "No," she said quickly. "I mean that he has an accent."

"An Injun accent?" Mr. Smith pressed.

"Not quite." Her gesture implied ignorance. "I can't place it, but he's not from around here."

"How long was he below the tree while you were up in it?"

Cathy had no idea, and the question had not even occurred to her. She had been climbing around in the tree for a good while, examining the quality and quantity of the pollen and pistils of the Nickajack blossoms. She glanced back at the quiet man, standing still and straight. Since he had a way of not making his presence felt, he could have been below her for a quarter hour without her knowing it.

Mr. Smith looked over at him, too, and spoke his thoughts aloud. "He doesn't look dangerous, but you never know." He patted his mail pouch again, then said, "I must get back to my rounds. Come, Miss Cathy, I'll accompany you to the house, where I'm sure you have other things to do."

Cathy didn't think the quiet man looked dangerous, either, and she was sure he did not mean her any harm. Still and all, she had nothing further to say to him, and so she accepted Mr. Smith's broad hint and the offer of his protective escort, which she neither needed nor wanted. She fetched her shoes and stockings from the base of the tree and followed Mr. Smith's lead, suppressing the thought that she was readily accepting the chatty postman's escort in the hopes that he would yield more information about Young Hitchcock MacGuffin.

Mr. Smith obliged. As they walked together through the orchard, skirting the chickens and guinea fowl, and past the hog pen and the garden, the postman fed Cathy's secret heart with the details of Young Mac-Guff's return. So absorbed was she that she absently slipped Old Hitch's unopened letter into the front pocket of her apron and forgot it. Presently they were walking down the grassy slope that led to the back of her neat blue clapboard house with red shutters, wrapped on three sides with fine porches.

They followed the stone path banked by drifts of azaleas aflame the month before in magenta and crimson, now emerald with leaves that circled the house. "And wouldn't you just know it," the postman was saying, "that Young MacGuff would show up, turned out bright as a shiny silver dollar? Ooh, he looked fine!"

"Nicely dressed, you say, Clive?" she pursued.

"My, my, yes!" the postman answered. "Everything store-bought, right down to his shoelaces, I reckon! Ever the one for personal appearance, our Young MacGuff!"

Cathy frowned a little. She recalled that some of the townspeople had called Young Hitchcock MacGuffin a "vain puppy" and that his uncle had always called him a "silly whippersnapper." She thought rather that he was misunderstood, for anyone that handsome would be thought vain by those endowed with plainer features.

"I'll be looking forward to seeing him again," she said as conversationally as she could.

"You'll no doubt see him tonight at the dance—and you done good to have organized the Apple Blossom Festival once again, Miss Cathy! But most likely you'll see him before, since he's strutting the streets! Why, he's just as likely to come down Queen Street as any other this afternoon, and why not? Here we are, then." They had arrived at the front gate of Cathy's picket fence, and Mr. Smith looked up and down Queen Street. "Don't see him at the moment, but that don't mean he won't be coming by later."

"Perhaps he's already been by," Cathy suggested mildly.

"Don't mean he won't be by a second time!" Mr. Smith answered cheerfully. "Or even a third. The town ain't that big!" He squinted. "Is that Miss Ginger I see coming down the street? Now, *that's* a happy coincidence. I have one of Old Hitch's letters in my bag for her today, as well! That's it, then. I must be off!"

The postman let himself out of the gate and turned down the street. Cathy was left to contemplate her old, brown work dress and to wonder whether she should hurry to change it and repin her hair in the chance that Young MacGuff would choose to pass by. She turned toward the house and went up the brick walk, which was lined on either side by a row of flowering pink dogwoods past their pink-and-white bloom and thick with young leaves.

In any event, she did not get an opportunity to repair her toilette. She was no farther than the bottom of the steps to the front porch when Miss Ginger Mangum burst—if such a dainty lady could ever be said to "burst"—through the gate that Mr. Smith had lately used.

"Cathy!" Ginger wailed, as she flung herself up the walk. "Oh, Cathy! I must talk to you, really I must!" She was fluttering her arms and clutching in one hand an unopened letter delivered to her just now by Clive Smith. It was similar to the one in Cathy's apron pocket, and Ginger was evidently as uninterested in the letter as Cathy was. "It's awful! Hopeless!" she cried. "And I'm so glad you're home!" Her sweet voice caught on a sob.

"Yes, I'm home," Cathy returned, completely prosaic despite her visitor's heartfelt emotion.

Ginger Mangum's exquisite emotion was fully matched by her face. She had pretty blue eyes, a pert nose, and a Cupid's bow mouth. With the whole framed by perfect golden curls, Miss Ginger was considered the loveliest young lady in Hillsborough—in all of Orange County, in fact, since neither Chapel Hill nor Pittsboro could boast such a beauty. She had a figure to match her face and knew how to dress. To anyone looking at the two women standing together, Cathy could only have been considered round-faced plain and ungainly by comparison.

Next to her visitor, however, Cathy felt not so much plain and ungainly as competent and effective. To her, Ginger Mangum was a silly if beautiful twit, but Cathy loved her for her beautiful twittiness and was happy to lend her friend a sympathetic shoulder to cry on.

Forgetting her own untidiness, Cathy smiled wisely and invited, "Set a spell with me on the porch. Would you like something to drink?"

Ginger accepted the offer of the porch but declined the drink, being too distracted, she said, to even think of swallowing anything. "Not that my sorrow isn't enough to swallow in the present instance," she said with another sob. "If only a drink *could* wash it all away, but it can't!"

Cathy ignored this tearful refusal, installed Ginger on the porch swing and deposited her own shoes at the front door. Then she walked out to the side yard toward the stone well that stood under a cluster of towering southern oaks, whose thick, leafy branches generously shaded the house, as well.

To her continuing surprise, the quiet man from the orchard was now standing in front of one of these trees. Cathy checked her step, debating whether to say something to him, but then continued on to the well, saying nothing. He was gazing into the middle distance and made no sign that acknowledged her passing next to him. He stood in full view of the street, so she could not think that he was hiding. On the other hand, he was so still and contained that she doubted whether any passerby would notice him, just as she had not.

She scooped a ladleful of water, then returned to Ginger's side, saying, "I don't expect it to wash away the sorrow, my dear, but you'll be able to speak better after a refreshing drink."

Ginger forgot her earlier refusal and gulped the water gratefully. Once Cathy was seated beside her on the swing, she began her sad tale, nearly choking on a sob, but recovering her breath when Cathy delivered several no-nonsense raps on her back. A series of half sentences followed, accompanied by some disjointed commentary that ended on the half-tearful, half-fearful exclamation, "It's all *her* fault!"

"You mean Mrs. Travis, don't you, my dear?"

Ginger turned to Cathy, her beautiful, watery blue eyes now lit by a militant spark. "Of course I mean George's mother! Pray, who else could I be speaking of?" she asked bitterly. "She makes mean, mean comments about me every day, and poor, poor George believes every word that wicked, wicked woman says!"

"Did George tell you such?" Cathy asked with mild surprise.

"Not in so many words," Ginger replied, "but when it comes to the fact that he must dance with Sylvia Lee *twice* tonight, I can only imagine what that wicked woman has said about me."

"Ah!"

"And George is in love with *me,* and his mother is too...too—" she paused, searching for the right word "—*wicked* to permit her son to marry the woman he loves."

Cathy's tender heart went out to Ginger in her distress. She wanted nothing more than to see her friend happily united with the man of her choice. She understood the obstacles that lay in Ginger's way and so chose a soothing approach. "We are not speaking about marriage, but about dancing, my dear." She stretched the truth by adding, "You must not read too much into George's dances with Miss Sylvia, for Mrs. Travis has already discussed with me how she desires that her son oblige any number of ladies by dancing with them this evening."

Ginger's gaze turned reproachful. "I am not stupid, Cathy," she said with a little sniff. She dabbed a pretty lace handkerchief to her eyes and touched her nose with it. "Sylvia Lee's father is rich, and mine is not. To my sorrow! But not to George's! He doesn't think of it and I just *know* that he wants me to be his wife, even though I can bring nothing but myself to the marriage! But he is too much of a good son to his mother to bring himself to ask me to marry him against her wishes."

From there Ginger launched into a poignantly loving recital of the virtues of her thwarted lover, from his noble features to his even more noble disposition. The discourse ended somewhat anticlimactically, with the heartfelt wish that he display a little more backbone in his dealings with his mother. Then, having exhausted a large measure of her emotion, Ginger rose from the swing and crossed the porch to the front walk. Cathy put a motherly arm around her friend and accompanied her to the bottom of the steps.

Ginger dabbed her eyes several more times, sniffed, and was about to depart when she saw a strange man standing near the walk. Her eyes widened, and she asked, "Who's that?"

Cathy's answer was unoriginal. "I don't know."

Apparently far less curious than Clive Smith, Ginger uttered a tiny "Oh!" She dabbed her eyes again, gave a soul-rending sigh, then took her leave.

Cathy turned to the quiet man, who had come to stand next to her.

Chapter Two

The man was watching Ginger Mangum's retreat. Cathy had to suppress her desire to laugh at the trace of disgust she caught on his otherwise impassive face. She suppressed as well a quick, wry comment on what she supposed was his masculine distaste at this lavish display of feminine emotion.

Instead, she demanded imperiously, "Well?"

The man's eyes were still following Ginger Mangum. "Yes, I begin to see," he said, somewhat cryptically to Cathy's way of thinking. "Breaking your fall—" he made a dismissive gesture with his hand "—that was nothing. A small service only."

She insisted, impatient now, "Who *are* you?"

His eyes cut back to her. He said solemnly, "I am the man who will rid you of this tiresome woman's troubles."

Cathy laughed and said, "I hardly need saving from that! I am used to attending to Miss Mangum's troubles."

He nodded. "Yes, I imagined so."

Inferring reproach, she added quickly, "Well, not only her troubles, of course. Miss Mangum is a friend of mine, and when one is a friend, one listens in both good times and bad.'' A thought struck her. ''And just what makes you imagine that I am used to attending to Miss Mangum's troubles?''

''It is not usual for a young, unarmed woman to confront three big men who are challenging a fourth man unknown to her. Such a woman must be used to attending to other people's troubles.''

Cathy's mouth almost fell open, but she was not going to be diverted from her purpose. ''All right, then, who are you? And don't,'' she said swiftly, ''tell me that you're the man who's come to rid me of a very dear friend! Instead, let's begin simply. What's your name?''

''Laurence Harris.''

She was surprised. ''Laurence Harris?''

His silence confirmed her understanding.

''Well, why didn't you say so in the first place?''

''You did not ask.''

Exasperated, she continued, ''Where do you come from?''

''Maryland.''

Now she was amazed. ''Maryland?''

This time his silence seemed to suggest something else.

She slanted him a glance. ''No, I am not in the habit of repeating everything anyone says,'' she said. ''If I seem surprised, it's only that I had not thought you would have such an ordinary name or come from such an ordinary place.'' With an edge of disbelief, she queried, ''So you were born in Maryland?''

''Born in Massachusetts.''

''Born and bred in Massachusetts?''

''No, bred in Quebec.''

''Oh. Does that make you French?''

"No."

She waited expectantly, then had to ask, "What are you?"

"Half Iroquois, half Welsh-Breton."

She regarded him frankly, and he accepted her assessing gaze without a flick of an eyelid. To a young woman who had lived her entire life in Hillsborough, North Carolina, and who was of standard Scots-Irish stock, Mr. Laurence Harris's life and lineage struck her as alien. Still, she found no reason to fear him, and she was reassured by the fact that he responded to direct questions with direct answers. Given that, she was tempted to ask him how he had gotten the old copper scars crawling up his neck, but decided against taking unfair advantage of his directness.

She asked next, "What are you doing in North Carolina?"

"Passing through, heading west."

"Now then what, may I ask, are you doing on my property?"

"You have asked me not to repeat my reason."

Although his rejoinder was seemingly polite, something in his manner made her begin to suspect that he felt not so much indebted but rather more amused by the incident at the market. She regarded him keenly. Was that a smirk she detected in the depths of his black, black eyes? Really, it was so hard to tell when the man had such an expressionless face!

"Oh, that's right," she said with gentle irony, "you've come to repay your debt to me. To put yourself at my service."

He bowed slightly. It was a respectful gesture.

"Since I don't currently stand in need of anyone's services, can you tell me exactly what you propose to do for me?"

"I do not yet know."

"Nor will you ever discover it, in fact! Please understand that you owe me no debt."

"No one has ever helped me in the way you did this morning."

She scanned his features again. A hint of inflection in his voice made her wonder again whether he was laughing at her. Yet she could read little humor, or any other emotion, in the steady gaze of his eyes or in the straight set of his finely cut mouth.

"Let's agree that you have already repaid the debt you imagine you owe me by having broken my fall out of the tree—which is something I never do, you know."

"There is always a first time. How did it happen?"

Cathy was not sure. "I must have lost my concentration. One moment I was examining an apple blossom. The next moment I was tumbling through space."

To this he said nothing, merely nodded.

His silences, she noticed, were highly nuanced. "I know you think that trying to catch me was a small service and, well, I don't mean to be rude, but I need to go inside." She was becoming anxious to freshen up in the event that Young Hitchcock MacGuffin should choose to stroll down Queen Street. "So I was wondering whether, if I was to say thank-you for catching me, you might be on your way, and we could leave it at that?"

Before he could answer, a second person burst through her front gate, and this one could be said to have truly burst through it. The force of his shove left the gate clattering behind him as he strode dramatically up Cathy's front walk.

Though not in his first youth, the man was young, of medium height, and had a pleasant face that held a hint of weakness around the chin. He was dressed to receive customers at the front counter of Travis's Dry Goods, and he was waving in his hand an unopened letter similar to the one in Cathy's apron pocket. He seemed no more interested in its contents than anyone else in Hillsborough who had received one that day. Other matters were evidently on his mind, for his brow was deeply furrowed and his expression was one of extreme agitation.

Cathy's greeting was nevertheless mild. "Hey, George."

"Miss Cathy! I must speak with you!"

"Of course, George," she said, gesturing toward the front porch and the swing. "I can't say that I was expecting you, but seeing you now, I am sure we have much to discuss."

"I was on my way back to the store, having taken a break to go home to check on Mama," he explained, "and you must know whom I have just seen!"

Cathy glanced at the letter in his fist. "Mr. Smith?"

George looked at the letter and frowned. "Yes, I've just seen Clive, but that is not to the point!"

Cathy led the way up the front steps. "Then I must guess you have seen Miss Mangum, as well."

George followed her. "Indeed, I have!" he affirmed, as if a tragedy had occurred that he had met the love of his life on Queen Street. "And that is exactly what I wish to speak to you about! I need your advice!"

"Will you sit with me here," she inquired calmly, as she desposited herself on the whitewashed swing, "or take the rocker?"

George wanted neither. He wished to pace the porch. He took several turns, heavily treading the clean, gray-painted boards and swatting at imaginary flies with the letter in his hand. He was mumbling under his breath, working himself up to actual speech, when at one end of the porch he looked abstractedly into the side yard. Then he stood up straight, as if at attention.

Flinging an arm dramatically before him, he asked loudly and rudely, "Who's that?"

Cathy looked in the direction of George's gesture. This time she had the answer. "Mr. Harris."

"Who's Mr. Harris?"

"A man from Maryland."

"What's he doing here?"

"Heading west."

"So is everyone else is this country," George commented, "and if he's from Maryland, he didn't get to North Carolina by heading west, but by heading south. What's he doing *here?*"

"He was with me in the orchard."

"Is he an apple grower, too? He doesn't look like an apple grower."

Cathy had no desire to explain the incident in the marketplace or Laurence Harris's strange notions of indebtedness. Although she was not by nature a fibber, she decided that the occasion called for some ready invention. "Miss Martha at the Lindley nursery sent him over to inspect the new grafts."

George considered this information. "The Lindleys have kin in Maryland," he confirmed, "but none by the name of Harris.'' He turned to Cathy. ''He's not kin to the Lindleys, is he?''

''I don't know.''

Like a dog with a bone, George was determined to worry the question of Mr. Harris. ''If he's just passing through and heading west, why'd Miss Martha send him over here to inspect your new grafts? And furthermore, if he's here to inspect your new grafts, what's he doing standing there in your side yard?''

Cathy held up her hands. ''Why don't you ask him yourself?''

George seemed startled by the question. ''Can he hear me?''

''I am sure that he can.''

''He's not deaf or anything?''

''No, he's not deaf.''

George grunted. ''I thought he was part of the tree trunk at first.''

Cathy glanced over at Mr. Harris, standing motionless in front of one of the oaks. She was convinced now that she had been mistaken to think that this quiet man had a sense of humor. If she had been the subject of this absurd conversation, she would have at least cracked a smile by now. Mr. Harris's face was, on the contrary, impressively impassive.

George suddenly lost interest in the subject of Laurence Harris. He turned away from the side porch and took to pacing again. As he strode back toward Cathy, he said, ''It's more than a man can stand, I tell you, to be confronted with a woman's tears day and night!''

''Yes,'' Cathy agreed sympathetically. ''Miss Ginger was upset when she left me a few moments ago.''

George stopped, startled. "Miss Mangum left you *crying?*"

"I thought you said you saw her just now and that you were, er, unmanned by her tears."

"I was referring to my *mother,* if you must know, who has confused herself with a watering pot—never plentiful tears, mind you, but continuous sprinklings! It's more than a man can stand, I say, Miss Cathy! But what's this about Miss Ginger's distress? When I saw her now, she was all loving smiles and beauty! Such a sweet, uncritical disposition!"

Cathy bit her lip. "Miss Ginger was upset about what she perceives—perhaps rightly—as your mother's opposition to your marriage to her."

"Thunderation!" George expostulated. To the porch ceiling, he continued, mightily aggrieved, "And if it isn't enough of a plague on a man to live with an ailing watering pot of a mother whose nerves are delicate, he must have his private affairs broadcast throughout the neighborhood!"

Cathy's response was gentle. "I don't think that Miss Ginger's quiet discussion with me qualifies as broadcasting your private affairs throughout the neighborhood."

"Yes, but anyone traveling Queen Street would have overheard!"

"Fortunately, no one passed, and Mr. Smith had already gone by the time Miss Ginger arrived."

"Well, *he* heard it!" George once again flung his arm dramatically in the direction of Laurence Harris. "And you have just told me that he's not deaf!"

Cathy glanced in the direction of George's outflung arm. She discovered that her billy goat, Smokehouse, who hated strangers, was grazing contentedly in Mr. Harris's shadow and that her tabby cat, Aunt Rachel, who detested the goat, was playing amiably at the quiet man's feet.

Cathy returned her attention to George. "Since Mr. Harris is merely passing through, I doubt he is keenly interested in your affairs or anyone else's." She was of a mind to tell George to keep his voice down if he was so concerned to keep his private affairs private, but doubted that such a suggestion would have the desired effect. "And Miss Ginger came to me only for consolation, not to betray confidences."

"But you said that she was *crying,* so she must have told you what she was crying about."

"She did not have to," Cathy said, matter-of-factly, "because I already knew that it had something to do with Sylvia Lee and the dances you will have with her tonight."

George was incredulous. "You *knew?* How did you know that?"

"Your mother has mentioned Miss Sylvia to me every time I visited her this past month."

George made a noise of disgust deep in his throat. "For some reason, my mother likes you."

Cathy folded her hands primly in her lap. "Thank you kindly, George."

His handsome face fell comically. "Thunderation, Miss Cathy, I never meant—! That is to say—!" He clapped his hand to his heart. "I have no wish to insult you! It is rather that my mother likes so very few people, you know. And I hardly need tell you in what high esteem you are held in all of Hillsborough!"

Cathy smiled her acceptance of George's heavy-handed apology, certainly more amused than offended by his ill-considered remark. "Mrs. Travis's tastes are particular, that's true," she acknowledged, "and I'm aware that those in her favor include Miss Sylvia, while those in her disfavor include—"

"—Miss Mangum!" George finished. "The sweetest woman imaginable! And very beautiful, too." A thought occurred to him, and he frowned. "Perhaps her beauty blinded me to her current distress. What a poor excuse for a lover I am!"

To prevent him from falling into a pit of self-reproach, Cathy said quickly, "You can make it up to her tonight by paying special attention to the delicacy of her emotions."

"But I have to dance with Miss Sylvia," George said with a pout.

"So dance with her."

"Twice!"

"Dance with Miss Sylvia twice, and for good measure I would recommend that you dance with as many other eligible young ladies as you can."

"There *are* no other eligible young ladies," George said mournfully.

Cathy ignored this insult to her person. "Then dance with the older, ineligible ladies," she replied calmly. "Only dance, and dance a lot, and not just with Miss Sylvia and Miss Ginger."

George assimilated this advice, drew in a deep breath, then exclaimed, "It's all Reverend Lee's fault!"

"It is?"

"There shouldn't even be a dance tonight," George said severely, "what with Old Hitch dying only yesterday. The reverend should have called it off!"

"Old Hitch made it very clear to the reverend right before he died that the Apple Blossom Festival was to take place just as it always does. We've all agreed, as you know, George, to honor Old Hitch's last wishes by dancing tonight and burying him tomorrow." She added on a practical note, "And if the dance were canceled, your problems would only be deferred, not solved."

George clapped his hand to his brow. "What am I to do?"

Cathy sighed. She saw no point in attempting to reason with him further. The time had come for diversionary tactics. She ran her eye over George Travis's handsome countenance, ennobled by suffering, then over his well-kept person. Her eye fell on a significant detail.

"To begin with, you could open the letter in your hand," she suggested, as she fished in her apron pocket for her own letter. "You see, I have one just like it, and if I'm not mistaken, it's from Old Hitch."

Cathy's tactic worked. George looked at the letter with exaggerated surprise, and his attention immediately seized on it. "Maybe he's written to tell everyone that he changed his mind before he died and that we're all to stay home tonight, in bereavement," he said, not unhopefully.

Slitting open the envelope with her finger, Cathy replied, "He's just as likely to write the lot of us that we have no more sense than a flea and might as well elect Toodle Tom as mayor, to make our collective stupidity official!"

George laughed at that. He had been present along with Cathy several years ago when Old Hitch had told Mayor Cameron that Tom, the village idiot, could take the mayor's place and no one would notice the difference. Old Hitch's blistering condemnation of some new ordinance proposed by the mayor had caused that official's feathers to be sorely ruffled. Cathy had been able to calm the offended public servant by pointing out to him that Old Hitch's comment had reflected more on the general intelligence of the town's citizenry than on the mayor's leadership abilities.

George had opened his envelope and was spreading the letter out in his hand when he exclaimed, "Thunderation! I don't envy the devil, if he chances to aggravate Old Hitch—for I haven't a doubt about which direction Old Hitch took when he left this world for the next! The man had a scathing tongue, no doubt about it!"

Cathy smiled in fond remembrance of Hillsborough's most crotchety inhabitant, but her smile faded as she read her own letter. She blinked, reread the lines, looked up at George and met his blank stare with one of her own.

"Don't that beat everything!" George exclaimed in disgust. He flicked the page he held in one hand with the backs of the fingers of his other hand. "Don't make a durned shred of sense! And I think I would have preferred a taste of Old Hitch's tongue. At least a scold would have made more sense than *this!*"

"Does your letter say anything about apples?" Cathy asked, bewildered.

"Apples? Why should my letter say anything about apples? All I've got is two lines, and it's about land. Not even a greeting."

"I have two lines, too," Cathy said, "and it's about apples. Mine doesn't have a greeting, either. What does yours say?"

George read aloud:

"Together you'll see, but mostly you'll ask:
What did Old Hitch have but a scrap of land?"

He looked up from the page. "I wasn't going to ask that," he commented, obviously baffled, "and why should I? What does your letter say, Miss Cathy?"

Cathy read aloud:

"Apples don't fall very far from the tree,
Try as you might, say and do what you will."

She shook her head. "This makes no more sense than your lines," she said. "The man was impossible!"

George could only agree, and, since he had been gone from the store longer than he had intended, he made noises to the effect that he should be getting back.

Cathy rose from the swing and linked arms with him companionably. They walked to the porch steps leading down to the front walk. As they descended, they traded letters and puzzled over the meaning of these four incomprehensible lines. George hit on the possibility that this was some kind of practical joke and that Old Hitch had had nothing to do with it.

At the bottom step, they traded letters back again. Cathy stopped there and hugged the white column in her abstraction. "You might be right," she said. "For one thing, Old Hitch couldn't have physically managed to post the letters, since he was confined to his bed this past week. For another thing, he was never mysterious. Ornery always, but never mysterious. Ornery to the end."

A voice interpolated, "Or-ner-ee? What does or-ner-ee mean?"

Cathy looked to the side of the walk to see Mr. Harris. His entourage now included not only the billy goat and the cat but also her old, mangy hound, Black Twig. "It means crabby, I suppose, and contrary," she answered easily, still hugging the porch-steps pillar. "Wouldn't you define it that way, George?"

George had no intention of defining it. He swerved his head toward the quiet man. "Don't they have that word in Maryland?" he demanded, frowning heavily.

"I do not know," Harris answered.

"Of course they do, George," Cathy said. "Mr. Harris is not *from* Maryland originally," she explained, "he's only coming from there now."

Harris asked, "Is the nephew to the man you call Old Hitch also ornery?"

George's frown vanished. "Of the many things Old Hitch's nephew has been called, ornery is not one of them," he answered. Then asked, "Just where did you say you come from, Mr. Harris?"

"I did not say," Harris replied.

Cathy knew that only a direct question would yield a direct answer from Mr. Harris. "If you must know, George, he was born in Massachusetts, but he grew up in Quebec."

George hesitated at mention of Quebec. It might have been that he could not quite place it. He chose to save face by saying knowledgeably, "Well, I'm sure the Lindleys don't have kin in Kaybeck. Don't have any in Maryland, either, by the name of Harris, so far as I know." To the quiet man, he said, "You aren't kin to the Lindleys, are you?"

"No."

Satisfied, George turned to Cathy. "Told you he wasn't kin to Miss Martha and her clan. Didn't think so when I heard he was from Maryland. Stands to reason, now that I hear he's from Kaybeck."

At that juncture, Harris, who was looking beyond George's shoulder, asked, "And is that the nephew-who-is-not-ornery coming down the street now? The one you call Young Cock?"

Cathy straightened from her lounging position and blinked in suspicion at the quiet man's innocent lack of expression.

George stifled a guffaw.

She gave her head a tiny shake. She had no time to waste wondering whether or not Mr. Harris possessed an unpredictable—and indelicate—sense of humor. She turned and groaned at the sight of Young Hitchcock MacGuffin sauntering down the other side of the street, heading in the direction of her house.

Chapter Three

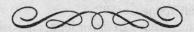

George coughed into his fist. "Old Hitch's nephew goes by the name Young MacGuff."

"Ah," Harris said, with no change of expression.

George was eyeing the quiet man with some curiosity. "Tell me now, just where is this Kaybeck place exactly?"

While the two men thrashed out the fine points of geography, Cathy fretted about the disheveled state of her clothing. She looked from her shabby brown dress to her dirt-smudged apron and fixed her dismay, irrelevantly, on her bare feet. She wriggled her toes in frustration that she was about to be seen at her worst by the handsome Hitchcock MacGuffin.

She silently cursed the visits of the star-crossed lovers, which had prevented her from tidying up. She entertained a few ill thoughts about the practical joker who had sent the nonsensical letters that had frittered even more of her time. And as long as she was laying blame, she decided that, in some mysterious way, it was really Mr. Harris who was the cause of her present predicament.

Looking from her front door to the street, where Young MacGuff was fast approaching, then back to the front door, she rapidly calculated the time it would take to dash into the house and change into her good blue dress. When Mr. MacGuffin crossed the street, angling straight for her front gate, she gave up the idea of any last-minute heroics to improve her appearance and resigned herself to her fate. Tapping the dratted letter against her skirts, she sighed and muttered, "It's too late now."

Harris concluded his conversation with George. "It may seem too late," he said to her, "but you will be able to work it out, if you put your mind to it."

Although Cathy was momentarily puzzled by this comment, it apparently had the effect of reminding George of his various duties and troubles. "It *is* late," he agreed grumpily, "but as for working it out—well! That remains to be seen! Now that Young MacGuff is coming to call on you, Miss Cathy, I'll take my leave, since he and I already had a lengthy howdy-do earlier today down at the store." To Laurence Harris he offered a piece of parting advice: "Now that I've had a chance to think about it, I've got to tell you that the shortest way west from Kaybeck is not through North Carolina. If you're wanting to explore Oregon Country and the like, Mr. Harris, you'll have to quit heading *south.*"

Harris accepted this wisdom in silence.

"I'll see you later at the festival," Cathy called to George. To Laurence Harris, she said quickly, "What do you mean, I'll be able to work it out, if I put my mind to it?"

Harris looked down at the crisp page she held at her side. "Do you think it is a practical joke, then, these letters?"

"What else could it be?"

He did not answer that. "Do you recognize the handwriting?"

"It's Old Hitch's," she admitted reluctantly. "Or at least it looks remarkably like it! But you see, he was bedridden this past week and in no condition to have posted them himself."

"And no one could have done it for him?"

"I'm sure I would have heard about it if Old Hitch had asked someone to post these letters. The only other person to have visited him regularly this week, besides myself, was the Reverend Lee, and he certainly made no mention of any letters to me yesterday afternoon at Old Hitch's bedside."

"Could the nephew have done the service for his uncle?"

Cathy glanced to the front gate, where George had stopped to exchange a few words with Young Mac-Guff. "Clive said that he arrived only this morning."

"Could a passing stranger have done it for the old man?"

Cathy regarded the quiet man frankly. "Did you post them yesterday, Mr. Harris?"

His response was equally frank. "No."

Cathy considered this. "Were you even in town yesterday?"

"No."

"Well, then, the mystery remains. Today is Saturday, and Mr. Smith is delivering all the mail that arrived at the post office during the day on Friday. Since Old Hitch died yesterday afternoon, he would have had to post the letters yesterday morning. If he'd done it earlier, they would have been delivered by now." Cathy shrugged and gestured with the letter in her hand. "This must have been someone else's doing—but, of course, I couldn't say why."

"People often have a final 'good' day before they die," Harris said. "If the old man had such a day on Thursday, he could have posted the letters Thursday night without anyone knowing it."

"It's possible," Cathy acknowledged rather distractedly, for she was keeping half an eye on the street, where George was saluting his goodbye to Young MacGuff. "But it still makes no sense!"

"It makes no more sense as a practical joke," Harris argued, "and don't forget that there are two more letters similar to your own that you have not read."

Since a part of her mind was on Young MacGuff's approach up her front walk, she was not thinking clearly. "Two more letters?"

"At least."

Cathy could devote no more of her attention to what Mr. Harris was saying. She forgot about Old Hitch, his possible final good day and the odd letters. She forgot about Ginger Mangum's tears and George Travis's travails. She forgot about Laurence Harris, the incident in the marketplace and her fall from the apple tree. The only man who had ever made her regret her plainness was strolling up her front walk, twirling his new hat around one finger and wearing a jaunty smile that melted her heart and turned her brain to mush.

In response, she lifted the corners of her mouth, lost in his smile, but not so lost that she was not also conscious that she looked a mess. Only when her mangy old hound Black Twig began to bark at the new arrival did she recall her immediate surroundings. Fortunately, Mr. Harris brought the dog to order. Then, strange man that he was, he wandered off without another word into the side yard, heading in the direction opposite the orchard. In his wake loped the unlikely trio of the dog, the cat and the billy goat, the last finding an interesting tuft of grass to nuzzle here and there.

When he was standing before her, Young Hitchcock MacGuffin—natty in his new suit, his glossy chestnut curls combed to perfection—kept his warm amber eyes on Cathy and his beguiling smile in place. "Miss Cathy," he said in heavy, honeyed tones. Then, with a casual nod at Laurence Harris's back, he asked merely, "New in town?"

Cathy had trouble remembering. Her yes was tentative.

"You still have that menagerie, I see." MacGuff's voice held a hint of derision.

Cathy strained to interpret the note as affectionate teasing. Still, she felt the need to defend her pets. "Smokehouse still eats everything in sight, but you know that I could never get rid of him, no matter how much he eats. Why, only last week it was a pair of shoes. Not new ones, mind you, but good enough for doing house chores! As for Aunt Rachel and Black Twig, why, they might fight like cat and dog—" here she began to feel silly, because Aunt Rachel and Black Twig *were* cat and dog "—but they've been with me forever, so..." She had no idea how to finish such a statement and left it hanging awkwardly.

MacGuff let her flounder a moment before he said softly, almost suggestively, "It's been a long time."

"Oh, yes," she agreed, "a year, in fact." She put her arms behind her back and clasped her right wrist with her left hand. She was acutely conscious of standing in the presence of spit-and-polished, store-bought perfection, and she rushed into a tangled apology for her appearance, knowing that she should restrain the impulse, but feeling at the same time absolutely incapable of doing so. "I was out in the orchard just now, wearing my oldest dress, in case I should get it dirty or snag it on a branch and rip it—which I have done a half-dozen times already, as you can see! And, well, with one thing and another, I haven't had time to change or even replace my apron, or put on my shoes and stockings, or pin my hair, or... or—"

"Or wash your face?" MacGuff suggested helpfully.

Cathy clapped her palms to her cheeks in horror. "That bad?"

His smile broadened, and he filliped her chin lightly with two fingers. "Miss Take-Me-Too-Serious!" he chided.

She let go of her cheeks on a wave of relief. All the same, she felt them redden, but her emotions were too jumbled to be able to identify embarrassment. Nor could she name the curl of humiliation that crimped the edges of her self-esteem.

"Oh! You were joking!" she exclaimed. "But how could I have known, when I haven't been inside yet to repair myself after climbing around in the trees and making my dress very dirty—" She broke off. "But I've mentioned that already, and there's no call to repeat what's plain to see—" She broke off again, knowing that she was overexplaining herself. Something in the come-hither twinkle in his eyes and the slight set to his charming smile caused her to quit dithering. She said, straightforwardly, "I'm sorry about your uncle."

MacGuff took the sympathy in stride. "Thank you. I'll miss him."

"We all will," she added. She ignored the echo of a crotchety voice in her mind saying: "Now don't go inventin' mawkish things to say about the dead, Cathy gal, and no caterwaulin' when I'm gone!" Aloud she said, "I was sorry that you weren't able to see your uncle before he died. He was asking for you."

MacGuff acquired a look of graceful distress. "I had to attend to business all week and wish now, of course, that I had better heeded the news that Uncle was feeling puny. I'm only glad to have been able to return in time for the funeral."

She easily accepted these conventional sentiments, for the fuzz in her brain screened Old Hitch's exact and irascible deathbed words to her on the subject of his nephew: "Business? Says he's tied up in *business?* In Sanford? My care-for-nobody scapegrace of a nephew don't have the business sense God gave a pack of flies swarming a dunghill! I'll be *damned* if that boy has sold a single trowel in Sanford all week, not to mention a shovel or a plow, the devil rot 'im! I'll be damned if he's even seen the main street of Sanford anytime this past month. And I'll be damned if he hasn't been spendin' his time preenin' before some Raleigh tailor's mirror! The devil of it is, I'll be damned anyway!"

Cathy said, "Oh, yes, it's good that you've returned for the funeral tomorrow. When we learned earlier in the week that you had planned an important trip to Sanford, we were worried—Reverend Lee and I, that is—that you would not be back in Raleigh to hear the news, and then you would not make it to Hillsborough in time for the burial. And that would have been a shame!"

"A shame," MacGuff agreed, shaking his head.

Cathy could not resist asking, a hopeful note in her voice, "And the business in Sanford? It went well?"

He smiled a most-winning smile and said in the manner of exaggerated understatement, "The farmers in Sanford had a few orders to make." He added, with a cocky wink, "But I don't like to brag."

Cathy was glad that Young MacGuff was making a go of it, despite his uncle's dire predictions to the contrary.

Then, still smiling at her as if she were the only woman in the world, he said that he had better be off to "take care of things." He added that he had not wanted the afternoon to go by without stopping expressly to see *her* and that he would see her again later that evening at the Apple Blossom Festival. "For it's a fortunate thing, too, that the townsfolk have chosen to continue with the festival, and I'm sure that Uncle would have wanted it that way."

On that note, he smoothly departed.

Cathy remained on the front walk, trying to believe that the fact that Young MacGuff had not reserved a dance with her did not mean he was not going to ask her to dance tonight. Her attempts to convince herself were hindered by the memory of his complete snub of her at last year's festival, just before he had left Hillsborough for good. She felt suddenly depressed and certainly more unattractive than she had at any other time during the past year.

Never one for self-pity, she briskly pulled herself together and looked around, scrutinizing every tree trunk for signs of Mr. Harris. Not finding him any-where in sight, she thought, Well, good, that's one problem off my mind.

Laurence Harris knew the language of dogs well enough to make rapid acquaintance with Black Twig and thus to be able to tame the hound's belligerence at the arrival of Young Cock. He had also sized up the situation well enough to know exactly when to leave Miss Cathy's side.

He neither commanded the three animals to leave with him nor objected to them trailing along behind, but he would indulge their illusion that he was their master no farther than the edge of Miss Cathy's property. He headed toward the grassy expanse that sloped up toward the orchard, then forged a path that sloped down into town. He rolled the word ornery around on his tongue several times and whistled a perfect *jo-reep* in response to a mocking wren's war-ble. He gave Smokehouse a lesson in manners and discussed with Aunt Rachel how better to handle Black Twig.

He fully accepted the idea that he would be spend-ing the next few days in Hillsborough. He guessed, but did not know precisely, the nature of the services he would be offering the Woman Who Fell From the Sky. However, he was confident that his mission would soon become clear to him. As clear to him as the trail that had led from the market and that had ended, in-explicably, at the base of the tree in the orchard. As clear to him as his realization that the young woman must have climbed up in the tree. As clear to him as the sight of her body beginning to fall.

He had never expected to be hit over the head with a sign. In fact, up until the moment he had fallen to the ground with a feminine weight atop him he had denied the very existence of Signs. He denied no longer. He had no idea what this sign meant, but he knew not to question it, for enough of Attean's teaching, forgotten during the past ten years, had surfaced as a result of the blow from above. He did not need to be hit over the head twice to stop and remember all that he had learned as a boy. He was prepared, in true warrior fashion, to perform whatever tasks and tests and trials would be required of him.

As he left Miss Cathy's property, he was uncomfortably aware just how close he had come to ignoring the incident in the marketplace and moving on out of town. It had certainly been trivial enough to ignore. However, he had chosen not to, for the incident had also held a touch of something magical and never-before-experienced. The nature of the magic had nothing to do with the fact that the incident entailed a debt to a woman. He accepted as natural his general debt to women and acknowledged that, beyond the first life he had been given by his mother, his second life had been given to him by women, as well. He owed his body to an unnamed woman who had saved him as an infant from the fiery hell that had killed his mother. He owed his soul to Morgan's wife, Barbara.

No, the magic of the morning's trivial incident had nothing to do with the young woman and everything to do with its triviality. Just as he had been about to take care of the three swaggering braggarts, this young woman—this Miss Cathy—had relieved him of the effort. In being spared his own time and trouble, he had received a small gift from a stranger, which was all the more lovely because it had not been needed. She had walked away then, not asking for thanks, nor needing any. Then came the magical, never-before-experienced part: in having to accept the gift-not-needed, he had felt an odd movement in his breast, as if something heavy had grown lighter or a shadowed space had momentarily brightened. So he had turned his attention to her trail and his feet toward her orchard, where the truly unexpected and extraordinary had occurred.

When he had left Maryland two weeks before and had taken the road to Virginia, he had had no set path in mind, only the desire to explore new territory. At Petersburg he had taken the road to North Carolina, just like that. On a whim. Or so he had thought at the time. Thinking back on it now, he realized he might have predicted that something magical would happen as a result of that whimsical turning at the fork in the road. The sign from above gave him an inkling that some grander scheme for his life was outrunning his conscious intentions, and he began to suspect that a pattern for the future was already within him but had yet to be released. Attean had taught him that signs occurred from without, but originated from within.

Thus he searched inside himself, attempting to discover some glimmer of urgency he may have felt in Petersburg at the moment that he'd turned south to North Carolina instead of west to Kentucky. He found only darkness and was puzzled, for he prided himself on finding what others could not: The four-leaf clover in a sea of green; Barbara's kidnapped baby, taken away by a devious route; Morgan's whereabouts at a distance of fourteen years and five hundred miles. He was unaccustomed to searching for something and finding nothing.

Still, the day's events struck him as much by their unpredictability as by their retrospective necessity. For him, the incidents at the market and in the orchard were both original and inevitable, and he experienced them as he imagined one might experience a good joke. He might even have laughed, if he had only known how. For now, it was enough for him to recognize that the day's events, with their combination of rare possibility and implicit necessity, had produced in him several magical moments of delight. He was convinced that he had taken the first steps down the path of an exalted mission.

As he headed toward town, he surfaced from these deep thoughts. He became aware of nothing beyond the physical pleasures of making his way soundlessly through extravagant gardens, fresh scented with blossoms, luxuriant with leaves, soft quilted with color and alive with birds and squirrels and the earth critters of spring. He sent his mind to hover above the town, where it would secure for him his bearings.

When he had been the boy known as Tohin-ontan, Laurence Harris had studied the qualitative contrasts that marked his mental life, the flow of which could change from moment to moment. He came to understand the contrasts in terms of a bird's life, as alternations of flights and perchings. The perchings he called moments of "paying attention." The transitory flights he called daydreaming or "not paying attention." He set about learning to control the pace of his flights in order to discover whether this control could serve any purpose. He learned that a controlled flight, while not able to render him invisible, could make his presence virtually unnoticeable to others.

As he traveled the backyard gardens of Hillsborough, between Queen and Tryon streets, he controlled the transitory flight of his consciousness to such a degree that Old Lady Witherspoon, on her knees and plucking at weeds, did not even notice him coming within five feet of her on the other side of her flower bed. She was aware only of a mild breeze passing.

Harris reeled his mind back in when he arrived at Churton Street, which cut through the center of town. He turned right and headed toward the intersection of Churton and King streets, spanned by the wooden Market House, with its clock tower and its three archways through which vehicles drove. Stalls for the sale of the week's produce, occupying the ground floor, were closed by the time he passed by. He looked up to the second floor, where he guessed town officials had their offices, and caught a glimpse of the "high sheriff" looking down on him. He made eye contact and nodded minimally. He moved on down Churton Street, past the Orange County Courthouse and the grassy square behind it, where preparations were going forward for the evening's festival. He crossed Margaret Lane which defined the southern boundary of the town.

At that point he shunned the road to Chapel Hill and walked confidently into a thicket of trees. He light-footed it down a scraggly bank until he was at the edge of the waters of the Eno. He turned his back toward the mill and followed the river a ways, stitching his steps between the pebbly banks and the rocks and turtles studding the water's edge. At the wide turning, he left the river, but not before wading out into the water in his boots, where he speared a fish with a likely stick he had found and whittled along the way. With the finny thing quivering on the tip of his stick, he came upon a little clearing, at the edge of which he had stashed his gear.

His horse trotted across the clearing at his whistle, received generous rewards brought from town, sniffed disapprovingly at the fish and pranced off again at the slight tap of his master's hand on his rump.

Harris found the dogwood tree over whose middle branch he had thrown his saddlebags and bedroll, and began to establish camp the way he wanted it for the next few days. Then he built his fire, roasted his fish and savored it. He sanded the fire and applied warm embers to dry out his soaked walking boots. Since he had washed himself head to toe that morning in the river, he had nothing more to do to ready himself for the evening than regroom his hair, exchange his buckskin vest for what he still called his ''Yankee-cut coat'' and don his moccasins.

When he had tended to his horse's needs for the evening, he strapped a slim knife to his calf under his buckskin breeches and secured a broad knife in the sheath under his shirt. He slung his bow and quiver of arrows over his shoulder, just in case. His rifle and pistols he left where they belonged, in his saddlebags.

He dived back into the thickest part of the woods, taking a new trail into town, and threw his mind high into the sky.

Chapter Four

It was not until Cathy was leaving the house for the Apple Blossom Festival that she recalled Mr. Harris's parting words to her that afternoon. She was juggling the front-door handle and a large pan of bread pudding when she said aloud, "Two more letters? There are two more of Old Hitch's letters that I have not read? I remember seeing only Ginger's letter, besides George's and my own."

Aunt Rachel, who had been languidly guarding the entry, skittered out of the way. She sprang up to the porch railing, arched her back and mewled her irritation.

Cathy pulled the door shut. Looking over at her lazy cat, she soothed, "No, I did not mean to scare you, dear Auntie. Good night now, and don't wait up."

At that, she crossed the porch and went down the front steps to the walkway, still puzzling over the matter of the letters. She had recalled no second letter by the time she arrived at her front gate, where she again had to balance the bread-pudding pan on her hip in order to lift the latch. She had hardly taken a step out to the street when she heard voices behind her.

"Miss Cathy!"

"Hey, Miss Cathy!"

"Ken we help you with that?"

"Goin' to the dance, Miss Cathy? We'll escort you!"

She looked around to see four men known collectively as the Boys, usually considered as a mass by the inhabitants of Hillsborough and rarely seen disintegrated into its component parts. The Boys fell into step with her, and the group proceeded down Queen Street.

"Good evening, boys," Cathy replied. "Yes, you can help me, since you see I have my hands full. But don't let's give the bread pudding to Orin here, or there won't be any left by the time we reach Churton Street."

"Aw!" the sound came from Orin, a burly fellow with an easygoing disposition, a huge appetite and an even larger thirst.

Hank, the leader more or less, took the pan from Cathy's hands. "I'll guard it," he said, huddling it away from Orin.

He essayed a gentlemanly smile, which, to Cathy's way of thinking, fell wide of the mark and matched his equally inexpert attempts to slick back his hair.

"And don't you look nice tonight, Miss Cathy!" He referred the question to the group. "Don't she, boys?"

Orin, apparently, had no opinion on that score. Richard, a big Negro man who was generally considered the brains of the group—giving each a quarter brain, according to Old Hitch—agreed. It was left to the skinny, yellow-haired one called simply Boy to say, "She don't look no different than she did this mornin' at the market, Hank, when she gave them Watts brothers what for!"

"It's called a politeness, you simpleton," Hank snapped back. "That's what you say to a lady goin' to a dance. You say, 'My, don't you look nice, Miss Whoever.' You say that whether she looks nice or not!"

"Why, thank you, Hank," Cathy said. "I'm deeply flattered."

Hank graciously accepted her thanks.

"Miss Whoever?" Boy queried uncertainly.

The big Negro offered, "You looked nice just now when you was smilin', Miss Cathy."

"Why, thank you, Richard," Cathy said again, and meant it.

"She weren't smilin' this mornin' when she blistered them Watts brothers with her tongue," Boy said, this time in accents of awe. "Ooohh-eee! Reminds me of Old Hitch, she does!" He shook his yellow head mournfully. "Poor Old Hitch. Dead and gone."

Cathy found it impossible to be offended by anything Boy said, even being compared to Hillsborough's least-liked citizen. Trying not to spoil the effect by laughing, she replied, "Now you truly put me to the blush with such high praise! But I must protest that you do Old Hitch an injustice, for I'm sure he could have hit upon something far more effective to call the Watts brothers than 'addlepated nincompoops'."

"But it was the *way* you said it, Miss Cathy!" Boy insisted.

"Speakin' of Old Hitch," Richard said, "I received a letter from him this afternoon, but cain't make heads nor tails of it. Or, at least, I *think* it was from him."

Cathy's ears pricked up. "Letter?"

"Yes'm, a letter by the post," Richard explained, "and delivered to me this afternoon by Clive Smith. I ain't never received no letter from Old Hitch when he was alive, and I was taken by surprise by the one I received from him now that he's dead!"

Cathy touched her brow at mention of the postman. "Of course!" she said. "*Clive Smith's* was the second letter, and the reason I didn't remember seeing it was because he was carrying it in his mailbag." She flushed when she realized further that she had forgotten about Mr. Smith's letter because she had been so preoccupied to learn what the postman had to say about the return of Young MacGuff.

"Second letter?" Richard asked.

"There now," Orin said, "Miss Cathy looks a dang sight better with a little color in her cheeks. Makes her look more like a fresh peach and less like a dead fish."

"Cain't you think of anything but food?" Hank asked peevishly. "Have some bread puddin', if yer so hungry."

"Hush now, Hank," Cathy scolded. "Don't encourage him. And for the 'dead fish' remark, Orin, I refuse to let you have any of my bread pudding. You'll have to eat Miss Mabel's instead!"

"Awww!"

"See what I mean about politeness?" Hank instructed, sanctimoniously. "It never hurts to turn a purty phrase for a lady whether she looks like a dead fish or not. Especially when she cooks like Miss Cathy."

"We got a letter from Old Hitch, too," Boy piped up, "but we had to show it to Richard so that he could read it to us."

Orin's attention was diverted by this important topic. "It says something about a still," he said. "Old Hitch had one of the best stills in the county, but he had it hid away all these years and was mighty stingy with his 'shine, cussed old coot!"

"One thing at a time, boys," Cathy recommended, finally cutting through the commentary. "I received a letter from Old Hitch today, too, as did George Travis, Ginger Mangum and Clive Smith, if I'm not mistaken. And now you're telling me that Richard received one separate from the rest of you?"

That was exactly what they were telling her.

"And it said something about a still?" Cathy pursued.

Hank, Orin and Boy had no doubt about it.

"The one I received said sump'n about salvation," Richard informed her. "Mighty strange, ma'am, I must say, comin' from Old Hitch!"

"Were your letters composed of two lines each, with no greeting?" Cathy asked.

The ensuing discussion revealed that the Boys and Richard had received letters similar to Cathy's and George's, and Cathy was willing to bet that Miss Ginger's and Mr. Smith's letters had the same format. "Do you remember exactly what your lines said, Richard?"

"I read 'em so many times, scratchin' my head, that I ended by memorizin' 'em," he replied. "They go like this—

"Between time and water, water and time,
The way to salvation, which lies in a box."

He continued, "It don't make no sense, ma'am, and that's for shore." Then he quoted again, his expression dubious, " 'The way to salvation, *which lies in a box'?* Why, it ain't even a real sentence!"

"True," Cathy conceded. "And Orin, Hank and Boy? How do your lines go?"

The three white faces turned toward the black one.

"Richard read 'em."

"He might remember."

"Cain't recall the exact words, but I know Old Hitch was tellin' us about his still!"

Richard put a long finger to his temple and tried to recall the lines but failed. "I read 'em only once out loud, so I don't recall 'zakly, but they did say sump'n about a still."

Cathy asked, "And none of you thinks this could be someone else's idea of a practical joke?"

"It ain't mine," Richard said.

"Makes no sense as someone else's practical joke," Hank opined. "Makes no sense as Old Hitch's, but there you have it!"

"But why would Old Hitch send one letter to Richard and one letter to the other three?" Cathy wondered aloud. "Why wouldn't he send but one letter to the four of you? I can't recall him ever referring to you individually."

"Could be 'cuz I ken read, ma'am, and the rest of 'em cain't," Richard said.

"Nah, it's 'cuz Old Hitch wants to rub our noses in the fact that he's gone to his grave without tellin' us the hidin' place of his *still,* and Richard don't drink," Hank explained, "which is his only flaw so far as I ken see. Ha! Salvation! In a box, no less. Well, that's where Old Hitch finds hisself now! But I'll be danged if he's saved!"

"It's shore strange to think of Old Hitch communicatin' with us from beyond the grave," Boy said in hushed tones.

Orin had fallen silent, momentarily lost in the thick shrubbery of his cogitations. Suddenly he said, "My, don't you look nice tonight, Miss Cathy!"

She fixed the burly man with her clear hazel gaze which bore no resemblance to that of a dead fish. "Nothing doing, Orin. You're not getting any of my bread pudding!"

"Aww!"

She smiled and pressed a finger to Orin's doughy stomach to show she was not mad at him. "Make a fuss over Miss Mabel's instead. She'll thank you for it, and it will give her the satisfaction of being one up on me. Anyway, I've promised my lot to the fiddlers tonight."

They had arrived close enough to the main activity of the festival to be interrupted by enough calls of "Hey!" that further discussion of the letters did not prosper. Cathy had heard enough, anyway, and had concluded that Old Hitch was indeed the author of the enigmatic epistles. Counting her letter along with George's, Ginger's, Clive's, Richard's and the Boys', she totaled six pairs of lines, or twelve lines all told. She had the passing thought to find both Ginger and Mr. Smith this evening and to ask them what their lines from Old Hitch said.

However, her thoughts were completely diverted when she came upon the main square, and she had to assure herself that everything was in order. She asked Hank to put her pudding on one of the tables under the trees, then walked down the long end of the square that bordered the main street, to where the men were putting the finishing touches on the platform they had erected for the musicians. She directed other men to set up the long trestle tables for eating right out on Churton Street and Margaret Lane, for the town was closed to horse-and-buggy traffic for the evening. She moved on around the square, stopping briefly at the roasting pit, where Joe Whitey, head cook and pig picker, was turning the pigs on their spits. She walked back up the other side of the square past the cider butts, where the men were already beginning to gather.

She turned down the fourth side and found some older boys who were eager to begin lighting the lanterns, gaily wrapped in Chinese paper, that had been hung around all four sides of the square. Then she walked back to where she had started, toward the tables set up under the old oaks behind the courthouse, holding food provided by the ladies' auxiliary. The tables were already crowded with platters of ham biscuits, as well as dishes of new butter beans, collard greens, hominy and succotash, set side by side with cakes, creams, puddings and fruit tarts and interspersed with pitchers of tea and lemonade.

At the far end of one table sat Mrs. Travis, George's mother, in a willow-wickered rocker. She was looking delicately crumpled and quite beside herself in an exquisite state of nerves. She beckoned to Cathy with a fluttery wave of her hand and a smile that faded the moment it was born.

"Cathy, dear," the matron greeted her in the accents of a very cultivated Southern lady, "how good of you to come to comfort me."

"Comfort you, Mrs. Travis?" Cathy said, smiling. She squeezed the woman's outstretched hand in greeting, then knelt down beside her chair in the grass.

"You look to have every comfort already, seated as you are in this most marvelous rocker."

"Aren't you sweet," Mrs. Travis replied to this modest pleasantry. "Dear Mr. Lloyd fetched it for me. Yes, and I will have such a fine view of all the festivities. Of course, I will only be watching them, and not participating. Not in my condition." She sighed. "I was feeling most fatigued by the time I walked from home to the courthouse, needing George's strong arm all the way, but I assure you that I carried the tray of my molasses cookies here myself. Oh, yes. I could not bear for George to have to worry about the cookies and about me, all at once, you know, so I insisted that I carry the tray—despite all his most loving protests." Her smile, though brave, was wan. "But I prevailed, because I so dislike imposing on the dear boy."

Cathy had a pretty good idea how the conversation between George and his mother must have gone for the few blocks from the corner of Queen and Churton to King Street and the square. She looked over the array of dishes until she spied Mrs. Travis's well-known molasses cookies and said that she was looking forward to dessert. They talked for a while in this vein until Mrs. Travis brought the conversation around to the topic she had, no doubt, wanted to discuss all along. She introduced it by commenting on the finery of the young ladies, in particular Miss Ginger's pretty dress.

"It *is* pretty," Cathy agreed, playing her part by adding, "and so is Miss Sylvia's. You see that Miss Sylvia has just walked up to the group of young ladies over there."

"Why, yes, so she has. What a lovely group of young ladies, I declare." Mrs. Travis's speech was as slow and sweet as the molasses that went into her cookies. "Now, Miss Ginger may well be the prettiest of the group. I am afraid that she quite takes the shine out of everyone else—and out of Miss Sylvia, too, who, I might add, is a fine-looking young woman."

"Indeed, a fine-looking young woman," Cathy agreed.

"And such an amiable disposition," Mrs. Travis continued. "Even more amiable, perhaps, than Miss Ginger's, although I'm not comparing them. It's as if the Good Lord has compensated Miss Sylvia's slight lack of beauty, with respect to Miss Ginger, that is, with an even more amiable disposition. One that is entirely suitable to what my dear boy George needs in a wife." This time her sigh was soulful. "But I am not one to judge." She smiled faintly. "What do you think, Cathy dear?"

Cathy was more than prepared for the question. "I think, Mrs. Travis," she said firmly, "that you will have to allow George to decide for himself." She took one of the matron's hands in hers and patted it gently. "Now, you have done very well for yourself to be seated here, where you'll have a wonderful view of the dancing. You will be able to see when and with whom George dances, and you will be able to compare the difference between how he dances with Miss Sylvia and how he dances with Miss Ginger."

Mrs. Travis looked taken aback. "Do you think that George will ask Miss Ginger to dance?"

"You and I would be both very disappointed if he did not," Cathy said seriously.

"We would?"

"Oh, yes, for then we would never have the satisfaction of being able to see them together for ourselves, would we?"

"The satisfaction—" Mrs. Travis echoed, unsure of this turn in conversation.

"There, I knew we'd agree," Cathy said with a soft smile. She released Mrs. Travis's hand and stood up. "And now I'm going to the cider barrels," she said, brushing off her skirts, "where I see Orin standing about with an extremely guilty look on his face. I want to make sure that he is not spiking the cider, which is already hard, with anything that he should not."

"Oh, no, you musn't let him do that," Mrs. Travis fretted. "Why, it seems that every year the Boys spoil the Apple Blossom Festival by causing any number of righteous, Christian men to become unbecomingly intoxicated."

Cathy took her leave and crossed the square to where the two large cider butts had been placed. Her object was not to stop the Boys from spiking one of the containers but to prevent them from spiking both, for if she dared keep both barrels free of spirits, many Christian men—Presbyterians, Methodists, Episcopalians and Baptists alike—would complain that the festival was mighty flat.

After that, Cathy tended to other of her duties as the line for the food swelled, then dwindled. Twilight lingered and finally languished, making the lanterns glow brighter. When the eating had progressed far enough for the masculine scent of Brightleaf and Gold Dollar tobacco to begin wafting through the air, Cathy became aware that an ill defined but palpable pall hung over the crowd. She understood the reason, for the townsfolk hardly knew how to reconcile Old

Hitch's death to his cantankerous demand that the festival go on without him.

"Just like Old Hitch to spoil the festival again this year!" Old Lady Witherspoon grumbled.

"Be glad, Ida, that he's not here to complain that you haven't enough vinegar in your coleslaw, as he usually does," Mrs. Kenan of King Street replied, not without her own touch of acid.

Cathy knew what to do. She circulated slowly, dropped a word in this ear and that and recounted some of Old Hitch's more outrageous opinions, which produced in her listeners the strange mix of affection and irritation that only an anecdote about Old Hitch could inspire. Then she got the fiddlers to begin scraping out their tunes and opened the dancing by stepping out first with Old Man Lloyd, then with Mayor Cameron and Reverend Lee.

When folks caught the spirit of the occasion, Cathy retired to the sidelines. She refused to feel sadness at Old Hitch's death, for she had promised herself to defer her mourning to the morrow and the funeral. That stout defense against melancholy was almost, but not quite, able to keep out the hurtful unloveliness she felt at the sight of Young MacGuff flirting with everyond in a skirt, it seemed, but her.

Harris was glad of the fish in his belly when he arrived at the festival. He did not eat pork, not even succulent Carolina barbecue roasted to a turn and picked straight from the pig. He partook sparingly of the side dishes, spoke only when spoken to and knew how to make his presence felt without being threatening. After studying the lay of the land, he knew that his place was at the cider butts.

As he walked toward the masculine preserve, he sized up the four men who were hanging over the barrels, distributing the drink and whooping it up with the other men who drifted to and fro in a steady stream. He timed his arrival with that of the tiresome woman's weak-willed lover, George Travis, who obligingly introduced the four fellows as Hank, Orin, Richard and Boy. The weak-willed lover identified him to them as "the man from Maryland. Or is it Massachusetts?"

Harris answered, "Both." Noting the one black face among the four, he did not make the mistake of looking at the big Negro when the name Boy was mentioned. He sorted out the individuals as best he could and gave a terse, "Howdy."

He was not the immediate focus of attention of the men hanging about the barrels. The weak-willed lover had to withstand a good deal of teasing for having danced thus far only with old, married ladies. It was pretty obvious that he was fortifying himself with more cider, for the time had come to choose between the tiresome woman and her rival as his next dancing partner.

When the weak-willed lover had departed, with the cowardly intention of waiting out one more dance "before taking the plunge," Harris noticed that the probable leader of the group was looking him over critically, in particular eyeing his moccasins.

"You an Injun?" the man asked.

"In part," Harris replied.

"Which part?" the Leader asked. His grin was cheeky.

"From the waist down."

The big Negro and the Stomach looked impressed with that response. The yellow-haired boy looked puzzled. The Leader whistled softly and said, "In that case, you'll be wantin' sump'n to drink."

Harris was handed a wooden mug, the contents of which had been scooped from the cider butt the Stomach was lounging agains.. He knew what was up and was ready for it. He downed the contents of the mug in one long draught. He said, "Thanks."

"Another?" the leader prompted.

"Only if you'll join me."

Three of the four fellows exchanged looks and accepted the counterchallenge with a nod. The big Negro declined. Harris handed his mug over, had it refilled and bent his elbow in concert with the three men. So it went for several more rounds, until the Stomach began to look woozy. He blinked and attempted to focus his eyes. To Harris, he said, "For an Injun, you drink purty good."

Harris stepped over to the Stomach and, in a gesture that spoke its own threat, placed a strong and very chummy arm around the burly man's shoulders. "From the waist up, I'm Welsh, and I can drink you deaf and blind any day of the week."

The big Negro thought this a wonderful joke and laughed heartily. He asked, "What's your name, Welshman?"

"Laurence Harris," he replied, releasing Orin, who hiccoughed in surprised relief and approval.

"What'cha doin' in Hillsborough, Laurence Harris?" Hank asked.

"Heading west."

"Like what'cha see?"

He nodded. "And what I drink." He held out his mug.

The four men nodded wisely. The Welshman had passed the initial tests, and the opening animosity converted to casual friendliness. The talk turned this way and that, skimmed a few surfaces, turned earnest on the subject of hunting, then inconsequential again at mention of the festival.

"Any purty ladies present you're interested to know about?" Hank asked.

Harris followed the direction of Hank's gaze to where Miss Cathy was standing with her girlfriends on an adjacent side of the square. He saw his opportunity to learn more about her and said idly, "Miss Cathy."

"Miss Cathy ain't purty," Boy countered, completely baffled by this Injun-from-the-waist-down-and-Welshman-from-the-waist-up.

Until that moment, Harris had paid no attention to the physical attributes of the Woman Who Fell From the Sky. Boy's comment caused him to focus his attention on her and to take stock of the particular woman who was Miss Cathy Davidson. He saw that she was no beauty, it was true. No, Miss Cathy was not the kind of woman a man ever looked at twice in that way. And now that he *was* looking at her twice, and in that way, he had the vague sense that her brownish hair was arranged more for utility than for effect and that her blue dress, though neat, was not particularly flattering.

Just then, she glanced around the square to observe the dancing, and he caught the flash of a twinkle in her hazel eyes. It reminded him of the lilting note he had heard in her voice when she had launched her frontal attack on the swaggering braggarts that morning in the marketplace, snowing them with a blizzard of fancy words. He remembered, as well, the final exchange. When they were about to leave, one of the braggarts had complained that she was making him look foolish. Miss Cathy had replied, in tones of withering amusement, "You need no help from me, Matthew Watts, to make yourself look foolish!"

Recalling that remark, he felt something heavy in his breast lighten again, as it had earlier in the day. Watching her laughing and gossiping with her friends, he was able to perceive, at third look, soft golden highlights in her nondescript brown hair and a sweetness in the curve of her generous smile. These observations unexpectedly triggered the memory of her body against his when she had fallen from the tree. Upon greater reflection, he decided that there was more to her as a woman than met the eye.

Harris glanced back at Boy and said, "No?"

"I don't see her as purty, that's for shore," Boy insisted.

"How do you see her?" he asked.

"Bossy."

The others chimed in. "She tells us what to do. Why, shoot, she tells *everyone* what to do."

"She won't let me have none of her bread puddin'."

"She runs things around here. Just the way her mama did years ago."

"Miss Cathy is mayor?" Harris asked, straight-faced.

Orin, Richard and Boy exclaimed at the same time, "Shoot, no!"

"Might as well be!"

"Rufus Cameron takes her advice, of course—has to, 'cuz she's got all the good ideas!"

Hank, who was in particularly fine form this evening, smiled cheekily again and said, "I dare you to ask her to dance, since you like her so much."

Harris's expression did not change. "I'll take that dare, if none of you are equal to it." He paused and looked at each one in turn, even Richard. "Well, men?"

"We're called the Boys," Boy informed him unnecessarily, given the level of their conversation.

"Oh, we're equal to it," Orin replied for the group, "but we don't wanna spoil yer fun."

"You scared, Welshman?" Hank asked, baiting him.

Harris had had no intention of dancing this evening, and he thought it inappropriate, disrespectful even, to have the Woman Who Fell From the Sky as a dancing partner. However, he saw that it would cause him far less trouble to accept the challenge to dance with Miss Cathy than to decline it.

He turned and began to make his way toward the ladies. With an odd turn of mind, he decided that dancing with Miss Cathy would surely have no more extraordinary consequences than those incurred by following her trail to the base of an apple tree and looking up.

The Boys watched his progress closely.

After a moment, Richard observed, "She's gonna turn him down."

"Ooohh-eee!" was Boy's considered opinion. "She's gonna send him off like she did them Watts brothers!"

"Nah, she's acceptin' him," Hank said, a note of faint surprise in his voice.

Orin perceived the advantages of the Welshman's success. "In that case, I'll get me some of that bread puddin' whilst she's not a-lookin'."

The Boys watched as the Welshman and Miss Cathy took their places among the dancers in the square, and Hank's surprise grew. "Why, she jes' smiled at him."

"A real purty smile, too," Richard opined.

"Ooohh-eee!"

Chapter Five

During a pause between dancing tunes, Cathy happened to glance to the side. Her eyes widened in surprise when she saw Laurence Harris walking around the edge of the dancers, heading toward her group. Although he seemed to be looking straight at her, Cathy did not imagine that he was coming to speak to her. Instead, the thought flitted through her head that he was coming to ask Miss Ginger or Miss Sylvia to dance.

Looking at him now, she realized that Mr. Harris was an attractive man, tall and dark and rangy. She admired the set of his muscular shoulders and the way he carried himself, displaying control and confidence without being either stiff or cocky. She admired as well the sharp cut of his high cheekbones and other features, finely chiseled by the light of the lanterns.

In imagining that he was coming to ask Miss Ginger or Miss Sylvia to dance, Cathy derived an amused satisfaction that George Travis, the poor fellow, would have his problem solved so neatly: whichever of the ladies Mr. Harris asked to dance, George could ask the other, without being perceived as having chosen between them.

Then Mr. Harris was standing in front of her and was saying, "Dance with me, Miss Cathy, if you please."

She was so surprised that she almost refused him, out of sheer lack of practice at receiving such offers. However, she was instantly nudged into accepting by her girlfriends, who giggled their delight that a man—a young and very intriguing stranger, no less—had asked Miss Cathy to dance. They knew it was more usual for Cathy to arrange for her own dancing partners, always choosing among the old codgers.

Her hand in his, Mr. Harris was leading her out among the couples drifting into position. The fiddlers played the signature notes of a quadrille, and the pairs of dancers began to form themselves into a square. For no reason that she knew, Cathy felt her courage fail and wished to return to the sidelines before the dancing began. She looked up at her partner, about to beg off. However, her eye was struck by the liquid sheen of his brilliant, black hair, which was pulled into a thick queue at his nape, and she was momentarily dazzled by the understanding of why at the market that morning she had thought Mr. Harris to be a poor Indian. She was suddenly more diverted by her corrected perception of him than by her lack of courage to dance with him.

"Your hair was *wet* this morning," she said impulsively, realizing now that he had been far from dirty and greasy. "You must have just washed it."

He looked down at her, his face straight, and replied, "Yes, when I arrived here last night, I made camp by the river. This morning I took advantage of the water." He did not alter his expression when he asked, "What makes you mention it?"

She was beginning to know that look. Although not a muscle in his face had moved, she caught the hint of a warm flicker in the depths of his dark eyes. She laughed and said, "Because when I saw you from behind this morning, I thought you some lost, ragged soul in need of saving from three bullies."

"Which I am not."

"I'll concede that you are not ragged," she said, "and if you follow nonexistent trails as well as you claim to, then I would say that you are not lost, either."

"I am never lost," he said. "But do you still think I needed saving from the bullies?"

The question put her on the spot. Standing next to him, she was aware of his quiet strength, and that awareness gave her a passing, but unmistakable vision of herself as a busybody. It was a disagreeable image, for she was used to thinking herself efficient and effective and, above all, necessary. She was also sorry she had given him the opportunity to consider himself indebted to her and heartily disliked the idea that he thought she, somehow, needed saving by him.

She puzzled out her rather tangled position and hit on what she thought would be the perfect response. "Let me say, sir," she began confidently, "that it was far less trouble for me to help you in the marketplace with a few well-chosen words than it would have been for you, as someone new to town, to—how shall I say?—have put your muscle to work. So you must not think you need continue to repay some imagined debt to me, because the exercise was no doubt more entertaining to me than useful to you. Although there was little *challenge,* all in all, in besting three such well-known half-wits! There now," she concluded, satisfied, "that explains quite nicely why I acted as I did and why you, sir, stand in no debt to me."

The first eight bars of "Darling Nellie Gray" cut off what might have been his response to this speech. The music also made her realize that it was too late for her to beg off now. So she addressed her corner, as was expected, then her partner, and joined hands with him, right over left.

When the steps started, a hideous thought occurred to her. To cover her embarrassment, she asked, suspiciously and with a hint of belligerence, "Is dancing with me part of your imagined debt to me? Did you ask me to dance as some misguided effort to save me from being a wallflower, perhaps?"

"No."

At this bald response, her suspicion abated, along with her belligerence. "Oh! Then why did you ask me?"

"The Boys dared me."

They moved to form a square with three adjacent couples. His response dissolved her embarrassment. She laughed. "How absurd! Do you mean to do everything they dare you to?"

"Up to a point."

"Well, *that's* a handsome concession," she said. "But why did they dare you, I wonder? Were you discussing with them your encounter in the marketplace this morning?"

"No, and I do not think the Boys realize that I was the target of the swaggering braggarts' harassment."

Cathy laughed again. "You mean the Watts brothers. But I still don't understand. Did the Boys dare you to dance with me for no reason?"

"Not for no reason. I asked them about you."

She harrumphed. "What did they say?"

"That you are bossy."

"That I'm *bossy*—" She looked him straight in the eye, noting the warm twinkle lighting the depths of his black, black eyes, but determined to resist it. With cool dignity, she asked, "Anything else?"

"That you tell the Boys and everyone else what to do, and that you run the town just the way your mother did."

"I might have known!" she exclaimed, a note of disgust in her voice.

"Yes," he agreed, "I suppose you would know your position in town."

She lost her dignity and retorted with some heat, "No, I mean I might have known that the Boys would say such impossible things about me. And," she continued, fixing him with a kindling eye, "I might have guessed that you would answer my questions pointblank and without an ounce of tact!"

"Yes," he agreed again, "you might have guessed that." His expression turned curious. "Do you wish for me to answer your questions indirectly and dishonestly?"

He had her there, so she took refuge in paying attention to the figures of the dance. "I am speaking of tact, Mr. Harris, and tact does not necessarily imply deceit," she said, defending herself. "Tact is a useful quality for a person to cultivate, and I would like to think that when I tell people what to do or how to behave, I am able to do so with great tact. The fact of the matter is that the reason I tell people what to do is because I can *see* what they should do, and they obey me because I am right. I do not mean for that to sound *self-righteous,* mind you, but it is simply the case in the town of Hillsborough that—"

He broke into this high-minded discourse with the simple statement, "You have not answered my question."

He'd caught her up short a second time. It was fortunate that at that point the dancers broke into four-couple groups to form a basket. She had time to recruit her forces. When she returned to his side, she said, in her best managerial tone, "In your case, Mr. Harris, I think it best for you to continue to speak your mind directly and honestly, just as you have been doing."

His voice was serious when he asked, "How am I to know whether your advice is sound?"

"You will simply have to take it on faith that I have very good judgment concerning how people should act."

He said meditatively, "And yet you admitted just now, in commenting on your own actions of this morning, that you were wrong to interfere, since I did not need your help."

"I admitted nothing of the kind!" she retorted, again making the mistake of looking him straight in the eye.

There he was looking *smug*—and it made no difference to her that he did not wear his emotions all over his face. She could see what he thought, plain as day. He did not even have to say it.

"I admitted that you are neither ragged nor lost," she said, with what she thought was truly admirable self-control, "and as for the matter of your needing my help, I argued a perfectly respectable middle ground. So you need not think that I have been *hedg-*

ing, or trying to put myself in the right when I am in the wrong."

He did not respond to that. Now came a half promenade. Because she knew the dance steps by heart and did not have to listen to the calls of the dancing master, Cathy continued to look at him. As they made a chassé toward the opposing couple of their foursome, she noted that his expression shifted from understated smugness to spuriously polite interest. She redoubled her efforts to justify herself.

"And I can see very well," she continued, "that you think that even if *I* do not need saving, my argument does! But if—*if!*—you did not precisely need my help this morning, then neither do I need yours now, and I am becoming increasingly convinced, sir, that you are pursuing this absurd idea of indebtedness in order to amuse yourself at my expense—for reasons best known to you!"

Pleased with herself, she took a half turn away from him. She engaged in half-right-and-left with the three other gentleman until she had once again put her hand in his. This time his hand came down on her hip to turn her.

She lifted her chin, then challenged, "Now, what do you say to that, Mr. Harris?"

He paused for a long, thoughtful moment. "I'd say, ma'am, that you just had an argument with yourself and lost."

She laughed in spite of herself, unable to prevent her bubble of self-righteous indignation from being pricked by mirth. She mastered herself well enough to ask with dry irony, "Do you think yourself terribly amusing, Mr. Harris?"

"Not at all," he replied. They parted for the ladies' and gents' chains, and when he had her again in his arms, he added, with no change of expression, "But I do find the discussion amusing."

"Well, I do not!" she exclaimed, a little breathless now from the exertion. She could not recall the last time she had come off this badly when speaking to a man and suggested that they change the subject.

He agreed, but made no mention of the fact that the music had ended and that the dancers were regrouping themselves in preparation for what was to be some version of a reel. He asked, "What do you want to talk about?"

It was only when the fiddlers announced the opening notes of "Devil's Dream" that Cathy became aware that one dance had ended and another was starting. Mr. Harris was taking his place opposite her in the line of men, so she had little choice but to take hers in the line of ladies. Then came the call, "Gents bow and the ladies know how," and the two lines stepped toward one another to bow and curtsy. She replied, "I want to talk about you."

He nodded, but moved away from her before she had a chance to ask him any questions. The first time he took her hands to swing her, she commented, "You dance well."

To this, he merely nodded, and she realized her mistake in not asking him a direct question. Although their lively movements did not allow for a smoothly sustained verbal exchange, she did piece together a conversation, the form of which fit the constraints of their dance. Between the brief touchings and long separations of the do-si-dos, swing-your-partners and chains, their exchange went something like this:

"Where did you learn to dance?"

"In Maryland."

"How long were you there?"

"Ten years."

She was surprised by this, although she could not have said why. She asked next, "And before that you lived in Lower Canada?"

"Yes. Quebec, as I have told you."

"Who taught you?"

"Who taught me what?"

"To dance."

"Barbara."

"Who's Barbara?"

"Morgan's wife."

"Who's Morgan?"

The answer to this question seemed to be longer in coming than the previous answers, and not because of the steps in the reel. At last he replied, "My father."

"Did you move from Quebec to Maryland with Morgan and Barbara?"

"No."

She had time to consider this. "So you did not grow up with your father?"

"No."

"Who raised you?"

"Attean."

"Well, who's Attean?"

"My grandfather."

"Morgan's father?"

"No."

"Your mother's father?"

"Yes."

"Did your mother help raise you?"

"No."

"So you did not live with your father, then, as a child?"

"For my first year only."

"How long did you live with Attean?"

"Fourteen years."

She calculated rapidly. "Are you twenty-five years old, then?"

He did not answer that, merely lifted one black brow.

She had no difficulty interpreting that look. At her next opportunity, she demanded, "Well, have *you* never asked such an obvious question?"

"Never."

It was their turn, then, to dance down the line under the arch formed by the other dancers' raised arms and locked hands. "I don't believe it," she said, "but never mind! Let me see now—where were we? Oh, yes! So how was it that you lived with Attean only until the age of, what, fifteen? Did Morgan fetch you away?"

"No."

"How did you come to live with Morgan, then, these past ten years?"

"I went looking for him and found him."

Cathy was not sure that she understood this rightly. They were at the end of the line, so they stopped to join hands and to become part of the arch under which the other dancers passed. Looking at him over their interlaced fingers, she asked, "You mean that you did not know where he was exactly?"

"That's right."

"Surely Attean helped you find him, no?"

"No."

Putting all this together, she asked, amazed, "You left Quebec as a boy of fifteen and found your father in—in Maryland?"

"Yes."

"Did you have any idea that he was in Maryland?"

"No."

"Were you even sure that he was alive?"

"No."

"Then how did you do it?"

The look on his face was as expressive as she had ever seen it. His dark eyes were hard and lit with confidence, and the curve of his black brows seemed touched with arrogance. His cheekbones, thrown into high relief by the light of the lanterns, cut stark shadows across the planes of his face as he moved through the steps of the dance. His finely sculpted mouth curved upward, but she did not count it a smile. Despite the civilizing effect of his clean white shirt and European-style jacket, she saw standing before her the Iroquois hunter he must have been for the first fifteen years of his life.

He replied simply, "I always find what I look for."

She did not doubt it, and she felt her eyes widen at thoughts of a mere boy setting off alone on a long journey, the destination of which was unknown. She said slowly, "Yes, you have said that you are never lost."

The archway of couples broke apart, and it was time for the grand allemande. They passed one another several more times in silence, and she used these moments to compose another question for him. She had decided that it would be only polite at this point to ask him less-probing questions about his past or more neutral ones about the present.

Thus, when they came together to form the final arch, she asked with what she hoped was friendly distance, "So, tell me, when did you leave Maryland?"

The look he bent on her was again unusual. At different points throughout the day—in her orchard, for instance, and in her side yard—he had seemed absent and aloof. Now, at this moment, she could only describe him as being completely *present,* for she could find no other word with which to capture the effect his focused attention had on her.

With his gaze steady, he replied, "I left the day I understood that Morgan had suffered in his life more than I had."

The reel came to an abrupt end, and they were left facing one another. She held his gaze, which was dark and impenetrable, but she was not embarrassed or self-conscious as she might have been under other circumstances with a man looking at her so. She was, however, taken aback by his response, and she did not want him to think she had taken unfair advantage of her recommendation that he speak his mind directly and honestly.

She explained hastily, "I meant, how long ago did you leave Maryland?"

"Ten days ago."

"Oh," she said, almost relieved by the normal response.

She took time, then, to examine the statement about Morgan's suffering, and his own. She turned it over several times in her mind, looking at it this way and that. She wondered briefly whether she should question him further about this remarkable admission, but decided against it on the grounds that he had probably said about as much as he cared or needed to on that subject. For a man of so few syllables, she noted, he managed to say quite a lot.

Indeed, Harris had divulged more to Miss Cathy than he normally revealed in a year. He had learned to dance from his father's wife, Barbara. She was the woman who had forgiven him his young warrior's rage and had called him son. She was the woman who had taught him English and many of white man's ways, but she had not been able to teach him twenty-five years' worth of American customs in only ten. Laurence Harris did not know that a young man was not supposed to ask a young woman to dance twice, much less three times in a row.

He had not at first wanted to dance with Miss Cathy, but once he began, he wished to continue and knew of no reason why he should not. He wanted to dance with her because she was a surprisingly good dancer, light on her feet and subtly graceful. He wanted to dance with her because he liked the sound of her voice, which was melodious and pleasant to his ears. He wanted to dance with her because he liked seeing her reactions, which were vivid and various. He wanted to dance with her out of sheer amazement that the earthly embodiment of the Woman Who Fell From the Sky would talk so much to so little purpose and be so lacking in restrained hauteur.

He wondered what Attean would think of such an ungoddesslike goddess. He imagined he would agree that she was woven tight in a web of difficulties and did not even know it.

He heard the opening notes of a slower, old-fashioned fancy. He held out his hand to her for this third dance. He saw her eyes widen. She looked ready to turn him down, just as she had almost balked before the first dance.

He did not want to lose his opportunity to discover more about that web of difficulties, so he said, with a hint of challenge, "It's my turn to ask the questions."

To his satisfaction, he saw her expression change from surprised hesitation to curiosity, then acceptance. She placed her hand in his, and they found their places, once again, among the dancers. When the music began, he asked, "What have you discovered about the letters?"

Her face was blank. "What letters?"

This slow couples dance required him to hold her in a partial embrace. His right arm rested firmly behind her back, his hand lightly riding her hip, while her right hand lay open in his left. He felt her body absorb his question, then register comprehension on her face. He was not disappointed to see the shifting array of emotions cross her mobile features as her apparently scattered thoughts came into order.

"Oh, *those* letters," she replied, her hazel eyes sparkling. "And you need not look so superior, Mr. Harris. Your question took me off guard, you see, for I imagined that you were going to return my interest in your family by asking me all about the history of my family in Hillsborough, which is exceedingly interesting. I was preparing to tell you all the best bits."

He had no intention of asking her about the history of her family and so said nothing.

He heard a sharp edge in her musical voice when she continued. "But I see now that you will neither ask about my family nor...insult me by repeating your original question, so I will simply say that what I discovered about the letters is that there are not two more of them, as you suggested, but four more."

Interesting enough. "Four more, then."

"Yes. That is to say, that in addition to the ones George and I received, you rightly remembered that Miss Ginger and Clive Smith, the postman—"

"I know who he is."

"Yes, well, Miss Ginger and Mr. Smith also received letters. Those were the other two you mentioned to me before you left my house this afternoon. And what should I discover on my way here this evening but that Richard Freeman received a letter. He is one of the—"

"I know who he is."

"You know everyone, it seems."

"I am beginning to."

"Yes, well! So, Richard received one, and the three other Boys also received one, collectively. Which makes six letters in all." She slanted him a sly glance. "That is, if you will permit me to make the *obvious* statement of the total."

He returned her look. "I will."

Her hazel eyes danced. "Thank you! I am much obliged! So that is where we are now—six letters, two lines each, by my reckoning."

"And they are all from the uncle?"

She sighed. "I suppose they must be, but not a one of them makes any sense!"

"What do the others say?"

"Let me see ... Richard's has something completely nonsensical to do with salvation that lies in a box, and the Boys' lines seem to refer to a still, although I cannot vouch for it." She added, obviously pleased with herself, "I have it on the best authority that Old Hitch had one of the best stills in the county."

"The contents of which are in one of the cider barrels?"

Her smile was rueful. "Most probably!"

"And what do the other two letters say? The ones to the postman and to that tiresome woman?"

"That tiresome woman's name is Miss Ginger Mangum," she informed him loftily, "and she is considered to be quite the beauty. Do you not think so?"

He gazed in her direction. "Yes," he said without interest, then returned to the point. "Now, what does that tiresome woman's letter say?"

Her reply was cool. "I do not happen to know the contents of *Miss Ginger's* letter."

"Why not?"

"Because I have not yet asked her."

"And the postman's?"

She hesitated. "I have not asked him, either."

"Why not?"

"Well, you see, I meant to ask them. I had it in mind to do so, in fact, when I arrived this evening, but then I got involved with other things." Her musical voice swelled with importance.

"You have been busy?"

"Very," she replied, a little haughtily.

He wondered whether she would be able to confine herself to such a brief response. A pause fell. He let it stretch out.

Sure enough, she proceeded to ruin her dignified effect by continuing. "Yes, I have been *very* busy, for I am in charge of the festival, if you must know. There are a thousand and one details to be seen to with an affair of this size—the food, the music, the decorations. Through it all, there have been endless problems to solve, not to mention that the entire town is in mourning over Old Hitch's death!'' Here she paused and looked straight into his eyes.

"But, of course, *dancing* does not normally make up a part of Hillsborough's mourning customs. If you want to know, Old Hitch insisted that the festival proceed tonight. We will bury him tomorrow. You need not laugh at us, sir! Not that anyone cares what you think. But the long and short of it is, I have had too much on my mind to bother myself with discovering the contents of several more extremely odd letters!''

"No? Would it have been so very difficult to ask the tiresome woman and the postman what their extremely odd letters said?''

"As to that, sir, let me say—''

He discouraged her irrelevant excuses with a silencing shake of his head. "A man prepares six letters and rises from his deathbed to post them,'' he said. "Now, no letter by itself makes sense. However, all six letters together may carry a message. Of the many things that needed attending to this evening, I would say that the question of the letters is the most important.''

She opened her mouth to retort, then closed it again. He saw the internal struggle that played itself out on her face. He had a pretty good idea that she did not really appreciate his advice, but she did not resort to petty carping. She managed to smile and say compliantly, "Perhaps you're right, sir! But you need not *smirk,* you know. What do you think I should do?''

"Before the evening is over, you should ask all parties to bring their letters to tomorrow's funeral. After the burial, you may determine what sense can be made of the whole.''

"All right, fair enough. Anything else?"

"You should not mention anything to anyone who did not receive a letter." He let her assimilate this, then remarked blandly, "And to imagine that you think you do not need my help!"

Her expression flashed from ungrudging complaisance to sparkling indignation. She retorted with spirit, "Let's imagine that this advice fully repays your debt to me, sir! Surely, at some point, you will feel that your services must come to an end."

He was looking beyond her. Just to see her react, he said, "They will certainly end soon for the time being, for here comes Young Cock."

Chapter Six

"Mr. Harris!" Cathy reprimanded him, exasperated with him all over again. "I wish to tell you that his proper name is—"

Harris looked down at her, and she saw that his black eyes were warm with unreleased laughter. "Shh." He hushed her, putting a finger to her lips but not quite touching them. "I know what you call him, but I believe in truth in naming. He and his uncle shared the name Hitchcock. If his uncle was known as Old Hitch, then it is only a question of symmetry how the nephew should be called."

There was time for no more. A moment later, she heard at her side a honeyed voice say, "My dance with the lady, stranger."

She turned to see Young MacGuff tap Harris on the shoulder and wave him away with an insolent nod of his head. Then he bent a smile on her.

"But the dance isn't over," she protested, confused.

"I'm cutting in," MacGuff said smoothly.

She felt like an inexperienced fool. "Oh."

She was aware that Mr. Harris released her. He bowed minimally and retreated. As she watched him depart, the memory of her first encounter with him sprang to mind, unbidden. Suddenly, she had a vivid recollection of being flattened out on top of him, with her cheek against his chest and his strong arms settled heavily around her. She did not know why she should remember that unexpected embrace now, when his arms no longer encircled her, comforted her, provoked her. Yet the effect of that initial contact washed over her. She caught his eye before he dissolved into the crowd of townspeople and felt herself flush at what she read in their dark depths.

Having no experience with this sort of thing, she decided that the look in his eyes was perhaps a trick of the light, enhanced by the effect of his remarkable cheekbones. Or that her senses were still scrambled from the fall from the tree this afternoon. She imagined, whimsically, that the impact had jolted her consciousness into a body she had long possessed but never inhabited. She felt both disordered and curious, like a new tenant in unfamiliar surroundings.

When she turned back around, she instantly forgot Mr. Harris, his arms, her fall, her newly inhabited, unfamiliar body. She forgot everything, for she was looking into the face of the man who had long been her ideal.

Her ideal took her in his arms.

She forgot her ability to dance and missed steps as easily as she dropped stitches from knitting needles.

Her ideal spoke.

She forgot her ability to converse.

Her ideal spoke again.

This time she heard a fragment of the question he posed her. The whole might have been, "And what was it, Miss Cathy, about Harris's conversation that kept you so well entertained during almost three dances?''

His manner was slick. Her thoughts slid past the memory of what Mr. Harris had just said to her. What was it now? Something about Old Hitch's letters. Something about not mentioning anything to anyone who had not received one.

She was aware that her hands were sweaty. They had been warm and dry when she'd danced with Mr. Harris.

Her ideal tried again. "Now, correct me if I'm wrong, but I don't think we've ever before had the pleasure of dancing together, have we, Miss Cathy?"

This time MacGuff's words and tone penetrated the disorder of her senses. She could not tolerate acting the fool for long. Only twice over the years had they danced together, and she had treasured those memories in her secret woman's heart. Whether he had forgotten those dances now or was teasing her, she did not know, but she had recovered sufficiently to prevent herself from blurting out, "Oh, no, MacGuff, this is not the *first* time!" It struck her as odd to consider that she had danced as much with Mr. Harris.

She chose the cautious path of truth. "I do not recall that we danced at last year's festival."

"Last year at this time I had already decided to leave Hillsborough for Raleigh," he said, smiling with a nice mixture of nostalgia, ambition and hinted regret, "to make something of myself." His smile deepened with unspoken meaning. "I was of no mind then to create attachments that would only be broken."

Did she dare turn that smooth phrase over to see what lay behind it? Did she dare hope that MacGuff had spurned her at last year's festival not because he was not interested in her, but because he had to leave town in order to prove himself? She wanted so badly to believe his smile and his hint that she felt her heart melt into a puddle and her eyes grow mistily unfocused. Then, through her haze, she managed to see that his smile had become a little fixed, in a way that had always made her remember her plainness. Simple pride helped her to untangle her feet and her tongue and to restore her eyesight.

"It seems you have made something of yourself in Raleigh," she said. Her comment was banal, but at least it was better than gushing absurdities or laying her heart out on a table for him to slice. "Or so you suggested when I saw you this afternoon."

His smile became jaunty. "I did more than suggest."

"So you'll be returning to Raleigh as soon as the funeral is over, to continue your successful business?"

His smile turned mysterious. "I don't know. It depends on what there is for me here."

She had never been able to resist his smile, and tonight its effect was particularly powerful. He had cut another man out to be at her side. He had just hinted that he had not danced with her the year before in a gesture of noble chivalry. He was holding out the possibility that he might return to Hillsborough. And he was smiling at her now in a way that did not become fixed.

She felt herself falling for him, for his smile, for the same ploy twice—or maybe it was a hundred times by now. She forced herself to look away from him into the nighttime darkness, and still she felt herself falling. However, just then she happened to dance past where Mr. Harris was standing on the sidelines and to catch his eye, and instead of falling freely, she landed on earth with a thud. She realized that she had fallen, figuratively speaking, smack against the hard reality of the quiet man. She looked quickly away from him and stifled a laugh of amused vexation. Well, I certainly won't give him the satisfaction of letting him know that he's saved me *again!* she thought.

She gave herself a mental shake, pulled herself together and turned back to her dancing partner. "What could be here for you, after all?"

"I don't know," he said again, hinting once more at mystery. "That remains to be seen."

"Do you think Old Hitch has left you something in his will?"

His smile carried an edge of derision. "Did my uncle even have a will, I wonder?" he countered.

"You would be the one to know whether he had a will, I suppose," she said, reasonably enough. With her feet on the ground and all her senses in order, she was at last able to concentrate on the topic at hand. "I had always imagined that you were his only living relative. Or could Old Hitch possibly have had a surprise heir that no one knows about? A son, perhaps?"

"That *would* be a surprise!" MacGuff exclaimed softly in accents of spurious reprimand. "My uncle was never married."

"I mean, of course, from some marriage that we never knew of. Why, Old Hitch could have been married fifty years ago or more without our knowing it—or anyone else in town remembering it! And he might have had a son, one who...who was raised by his mother when she left Old Hitch, because even as a young man he was an impossible curmudgeon!"

MacGuff laughed. "How likely is that?"

"Not very," Cathy admitted, "but possible."

He glanced down at her, his warm brown eyes turned curious. "I had no idea, Miss Cathy, that you harbored a romantic heart."

You didn't know even that about me? she thought, and missed her cue to be coy. "I am only trying to consider what I had not thought of until this moment, namely Old Hitch's will. If there are no other relatives in the MacGuffin family—and I believe that there are not!—then are you not, in fact, the only one to know whether or not he has a will?"

"The problem, my dear Miss Cathy," he said with charming irony, "is not whether there is a will or even a surprise heir, but whether there is anything at all to inherit."

"His house," she suggested, "and his land."

"*Worth* inheriting, I should have said."

Cathy did not dispute his implication. Old Hitch's house was best described as a shack built at the beginning of time and certainly not repaired since. His land was more of a scraggy patch that had no merit beyond the fact that it held up the other side of the hill crowned by her orchard. An unpromising inheritance, all in all—if inheritance it was.

Something about the trend in the conversation struck her as odd and unnatural, as if an unripe apple had fallen prematurely from the tree. She did not have long to consider what it might be that was out of place, or why she should think of apples in this context, for the dance had come to an end.

MacGuff bowed low and thanked her for her delightful company.

Cathy, still diverted by thoughts of Old Hitch, did not return the conventional compliment. She asked instead, "Did you receive a letter from Old Hitch today?"

"How could I have?" he answered, with exaggerated surprise. "I left Raleigh yesterday morning."

"That's true, but..."

"But?" he prompted, eyes shadowed.

"I thought, perhaps—" she began, then broke off. "No, of course you could not have received a letter from him today." She shrugged. "I don't know what I was thinking! But I suppose you received a letter from him last week, no?"

The slight shadow in his eyes lifted. "Two," he said with an amused, reminiscent smile. "Both of which I received upon my return from Sanford. The vigor of his attack on me in the first one made me doubt that he was truly on his deathbed. The second one convinced me to take him at his word that he was dying. So I returned as soon as I could to Hillsborough, as he requested of me." He assumed a properly mournful mien. "However, I was too late, as we all know."

Cathy considered this. "And all he wrote to you was a scold?" she queried.

"What else should Uncle have written me, after all?" MacGuff replied smoothly. "Did you imagine he would acknowledge that I had made a success of myself when he had predicted I would fail?"

"Unlikely," Cathy admitted, "if not impossible."

"Then I'll bow again and thank you a second time," MacGuff said with punctilious courtesy, "for it is not in my manner to damage a lady's reputation by asking her to dance twice in a row."

Cathy was thrown into acute embarrassment, and not only because he had cast her dances with Laurence Harris in a bad light. He had also made her see how she must appear to him, detaining him with pointless questions about Old Hitch's last letters in the hopes that the next dance would begin and he would have to ask her again.

She opened her mouth to begin a babble of self-effacing apologies. Hardly had she uttered more than a heartfelt, "No, MacGuff, really, I did not mean—" when she was interrupted.

A nervous man at her side was speaking to her, and Cathy was never more surprised to turn and see Mr. Lex Kenan, attorney-at-law, standing before her, asking her to dance. Although she had no desire to dance a fourth time in a row, she regarded Mr. Kenan as her savior from humiliation in MacGuff's beautiful eyes, and accepted him readily.

MacGuff moved away and threw a final glance at Cathy over his shoulder. His liquid brown eyes had turned a little hard, and a tiny frown marred the space between his brows.

When Harris ceded his position on the dance floor to Young Cock, he did not immediately return to lounge at the cider butts, but remained on the sidelines, idly watching the dancers. He did not have his eye out for Miss Cathy, nor had he set his thoughts on her. Rather, his eyes and his attention hovered around her, circling, not in a protective manner, but more in a wary and exploratory survey.

When, just before Young Cock took Miss Cathy in his arms, she had glanced back at him, Harris had felt something stir in his body. That feeling was not the

result of the little man in his breeches strutting to life—
or more accurately, not *only* the awakening in his
breeches, for the little man was admittedly part of the
stirring but not the origin of it. The physical stirring
surprised him as much as it annoyed him, and it distracted him from what he believed to be the purity of
his mission. It put his body and his soul at odds.

He tossed half his mind up to straighten out his soul
and pushed the other half down to tame his body. He
had more or less succeeded in achieving peace when
Miss Cathy and Young Cock chanced to pass in front
of him, and his glance happened to intersect with hers.
Then, without warning, it was as if he had arrived
again at the base of the apple tree and had looked up.
Once more he felt flattened.

The figures of the dance moved on, and Miss Cathy
was no longer in his line of vision, but he remained
dazed and winded. The various parts of his body and
soul felt alternately fused, then dislocated, then fused
again. He felt emotionally crushed, as he had been
physically crushed earlier in the day, but he could not
identify the emotion. It was unknown to him.

He recovered his breath. He realized then that this
second jolt had produced in full dimension a strong,
boyish *wanting,* a young man's hunger for a woman.
He had certainly felt such a wanting before, but he had
never acted on it, never surrendered to the hunger that
had caused his mother to betray her people. He—
nameless outcast, barely tolerated by his tribe, the
physical embodiment of his grandfather's shame—had
never wanted to diminish the monstrous anger that
was born of the flames and abandonment of his infancy and the shame of his fatherless, motherless
childhood.

That pure and undiluted anger had carried him through all the most rigorous tests of a warrior. Had fashioned him into the best hunter in the tribe, as well as the youngest. Had made him feared by rival tribes, of both the red men and white. Had made him desired by women, even before his fourteenth summer. Had helped him resist all womanly advances, even those of the most desirable. Had carried him, cherished him, nourished him during the long journey from Quebec to North Point, Maryland. Had kept him toiling side by side with Morgan in the fields of Barbara's farm until the moment, ten days ago, when he had learned what he had needed to learn.

He had always been able to summon his monstrous anger, to let it prowl through him when he needed it. But where was it now? he wondered. Had his youthful rage and violence dissipated through the years of Morgan's patient fathering and Barbara's faithful mothering? Or had it merely retired to some hidden cave within him that he could not find, leaving him prey to this boyish hunger?

Dissatisfied and, for the second time this day, unable to find what he was looking for, he fell to contemplating the Woman Who Fell From the Sky. Inevitably, his vision blended with his perception of Miss Cathy Davidson.

It dissatisfied him further to see that Miss Cathy was not engaged in activities of mythic proportions. She had finished dancing with Young Cock and was presently partnered by some ridiculous-looking, bespectacled young man, thin and nervous. The man's hair did not, apparently, submit easily to the discipline of a comb and brush. His spectacles sat at a slight angle across his nose. His coat fit him ill. His tie was half-undone. His shirt looked as if it had been misbuttoned, and even if it was not, his vest was. Half of one shirttail hung out below, suggesting that one side of his suspenders had come unhitched.

Throughout the dance, Miss Cathy was clearly giving the man some tips. When the dance came to an end, Harris was not surprised to see her straighten the messy man's coat and tie, with additional gestures indicating that he should tidy his shirttail and trousers. Harris felt his dissatisfaction fade into something lighter, more palatable, that seemed, oddly, to appease the hunger.

After that, he watched Miss Cathy make her way to the sidelines, waving away not one, but two other offers to dance. With a further lightening of his dissatisfaction, he saw her seek out first the postman and then the tiresome woman. She spoke to both of them as if giving them instructions, and they nodded their heads obediently in response to what she was saying.

He noticed that Miss Cathy spent a good deal more time with the tiresome woman than she had with the postman. It looked to him as if she was attempting to soothe the woman's feelings. He had noted earlier that the weak-willed lover had asked some other woman to dance at the precise moment he himself had stepped up to Miss Cathy.

Perhaps it was because of this that the tiresome woman had later refused her weak-willed lover when he asked her to dance. The fellow, looking abashed, had made his way over to the side of a wispy-looking, older woman seated in a rocker—his mother, no doubt. Harris himself had no interest in the tiresome woman, her weak-willed lover or his mother. Miss Cathy seemed to take great interest in all three of them, however, and spent a deal of time ferrying back and forth among them.

The evening was wearing on. He wandered into the vicinity of the cider butts, drifting here and there, shadow boxing with his old monsters, who were fighting shy. The atmosphere around him continued to be jolly, but some of the younger and older festival goers had had enough and were returning home. With the thinning crowds, the pleasant warmth of the air carried a deepening night fragrance.

At one point, he cast his eye routinely around the square, and his attention was caught by the sight of several new faces in the crowd. He stood up straight and alert. His old anger prowled out of its cave, fresh from its retreat, and he was pleased. His hunter's senses were sharpened. His hunter's appetite was whetted. He withdrew farther into the shadows, but he knew the precaution was unnecessary, for the new-comers had not seen him.

He walked up behind Hank, who was presiding at the cider butts, entertaining a group of men with apocryphal stories of heroic deeds. He said, "See the men across the square, next to the musician's platform? Do you know who they are?"

Hank broke off his story and gave his attention to the Welshman, who had earned his respect with a few words and hard drinking. Hank looked across the square and dismissed them as merely "The Watts brothers," but when he saw the group of men who stood next to them, he added consideringly, "And they come with a couple of them Duke boys. A rough lot, and that's for shore."

"Do they usually come to the festival?" Harris asked quietly. "The Watts brothers and the Duke boys?"

Hank scratched his head. "Don't think so. Cain't recall seein' 'em here last year." He consulted the group around him, and it was agreed that, no, the Watts and the Dukes from East Orange County did not have the taste for an event as genteel as the Apple Blossom Festival.

Harris knew how to ease Hank away without arousing suspicion. When they were about five feet from the cider butts, and the other men still drinking amicably, Harris asked, "And do the Watts and the Dukes know where Miss Cathy lives?"

"Everybody knows where Miss Cathy lives," Hank assured him.

"What do they know about her?"

Hank shrugged. "Ever'thin', I suppose."

"Do they know that she has an orchard, for instance?"

"Shoot, everyone knows that, too! She sells her apples in a good three or four counties." Hank shrugged again. "But men like them Watts brothers ain't generally interested in a woman like Miss Cathy."

"They are interested in something tonight, I would say."

Hank cast an inquisitive glance back across the square. He knew enough about looking for trouble himself to recognize the signs of it in another man. "Mebbe so," he said.

But when Harris told him why he thought the men from East Orange County were here, he was not quite sure he agreed. However, he liked the sound of the Welshman's plan. He tried to improve on that plan by suggesting that he could fetch his gun in five minutes flat, but the Welshman stated simply, ''No guns.''

Hank took himself off to find the Boys, while Harris, keeping his eyes on the men across the square, made his way over to Miss Cathy. She was standing next to the tiresome woman and not far from the weak-willed lover's mother.

Chapter Seven

Cathy's evening was a success. The festival was going smoothly. She was pleased—if puzzled—by her unexpected popularity as a dancing partner, although she could have done without dancing with messy Mr. Lex Kenan. She had succeeded in placating Ginger, who had neither nobly nor silently suffered the slight of George asking Sylvia Lee to dance first. Cathy had soothed George's lacerated feelings as well, for Ginger had flatly refused him when he had finally asked her to dance.

Standing at one end of the now-ravaged food tables, Cathy was chatting with the ladies and savoring her diplomatic triumph that had brought Ginger into discussion with Mrs. Travis on the subject of backyard drainage. Cathy knew there were few subjects that roused Mrs. Travis more than that of the runoff from the slope on Joe Whitey's property, which washed away half her flower beds every summer during the torrential July rains. Cathy had prompted Ginger beforehand on the subject, and she was sure to hear later from Mrs. Travis that "Miss Ginger has more good sense than one would expect, looking at her pretty face."

Ginger and Mrs. Travis presently concluded their conversation and joined their voices to the ongoing discussion of the most burning civic issue of the past several years, namely the fate of the Market House spanning the intersection of King and Churton. The ladies were firmly divided into two camps: those who thought the structure should remain for no better reason than it had been there forty years and might as well stay, and those who thought it an old-fashioned nuisance that should be torn down without delay.

Cathy was about to offer her opinion to keep the building standing when, without quite knowing how it came about, she found herself a good ten feet from the ladies' group, under a tree to which no lanterns had been attached. She blinked and looked up into the sharp, shadow-sculpted features of Mr. Harris. His hands held hers in a light grip.

When her eyes found his in the darkness, she read the look on his face. She smiled with satisfaction and said, "Don't worry, sir! I have already spoken with Miss Ginger and Mr. Smith, just as you told me to do, and we are all set for tomorrow. They will be bringing their letters to the church."

"I guessed as much," he replied. He did not immediately release her hands, and she was still too surprised by the encounter to withdraw them. He asked, "But do I look worried?"

"No," she said, then scanned his expressionless face again. "To me you do." She tugged at her hands, but he did not let them go. Because she nursed the hope that MacGuff might ask her to dance again, she protested, "Let me go back to my friends. I wasn't finished speaking with them, and I don't think it's proper that I dance with you again."

"I don't want to dance with you," he said bluntly. Then, just as bluntly, he stated, "The swaggering braggarts have returned."

"The— Oh!" Her expression cleared and she broke into a broad smile. "You're trying to *save* me again!"

"It is necessary."

"Nothing could be *less* necessary, sir, I assure you!" Looking about, she asked, "Where are they?"

"Across the square. At the far side of the musicians' platform."

"Ah, yes!" She gave the Watts brothers a quick once-over, then asked archly, "Since they are standing about, bothering no one, why is it necessary to save me from them?"

He did not answer that.

"Doesn't it seem likely to suppose that they have come to take part in the festival?"

He shook his head slowly. "They do not look as if they have come to take part in the festival."

Cathy laughed. "They always dress like that! A more ragtag assortment of ruffians than the Watts brothers I have yet to see!"

"I was not speaking of their dress. I was speaking of their manner." He asked, "'Ragtag' means badly dressed?"

She nodded.

Harris cast a glance over his shoulder. "If you wish to see more ragtag ruffians," he said, obviously liking this new word, "look at the men the braggarts brought with them this evening."

Cathy's gazed followed his. Her eyes widened. "The Duke boys are here? All four of them?" She considered the implications, then shook her head. "No, you cannot be right about what they mean to do!"

"I have not yet said what they mean to do."

"You think they have come to make mischief—"

"To do you harm."

"*Mischief,*" she repeated firmly, "and I tell you that such a thing is not possible!"

"Why not?"

"Why not?" she echoed, at a loss. "Well...well, because things like that don't happen to me. That's why not."

"There is always a first time."

She opened her mouth, then remembered that he had said the same thing to her this afternoon when she had fallen from the tree. "And all of the things happening for the first time seem to be happening today," she remarked. "Now that I come to think about it, I wonder if you are not the one to be causing all these strange things to happen!"

"I do not have such power."

She had to laugh at his solemnity. "No, I must suppose that you don't!" she conceded handsomely. "But certainly your arrival here in town has coincided with all my troubles, and so it occurs to me that they might go away when you do. Please don't take this amiss, but I would like to know, sir, how much longer you intend to stay."

"Until I am finished."

"Finished with what?" she asked. "Saving me?"

He did not respond to her prim irony, but said simply, "Which will soon be beyond my abilities if we stand here speaking instead of doing what needs to be done."

He turned then, deftly retaining his grasp on her hands, which he now held behind his back. She had no choice but to follow him as he led her away from the festival.

He angled toward the courthouse, moving them deeper into the shadows. "The swaggering braggarts did not see you before I took you away from your group, so they cannot know whether you are still at the festival or have returned home. That is good."

"Did they see you?"

"Their eyes passed over me without recognition," he replied, "and the look in them told me all I needed to know about their intentions toward you."

He made his way through the thicket of trees to the side of the courthouse, stopped at one tree in particular and released her hands long enough to reach up into some low branches. She was mighty surprised when he brought down a bow and a quiver of arrows, both of which he slung over his left shoulder. He took her hands in his again and, securing them behind his back, pulled her along the front of the courthouse, which faced King. He kept close to the building, away from the light of the lanterns that had been strung across the front lawn to the intersection of Churton and King. Then they stole into the street and slipped into the darkened center archway of the Market House.

When Hank and Boy materialized in front of her, Cathy asked, logically enough, "What are you doing here?"

"We're here to help you, ma'am," Hank whispered in the grand manner of an accomplice. With a jerk of his head toward the Welshman, he informed her, "He's got a plan to protect you from the Watts brothers and them Dukes they brung with 'em. The Boys and I are helpin'."

"I don't need pro—" she began in her normal speaking tones, but Harris's hand came down firmly over her mouth. Indignation swept through her, for no one had *ever* prevented her from speaking before. She glared at him, summoning all her authority and pouring it forth through her eyes.

He simply shook his head, indicating that he was not about to free her mouth. Then he cocked his head, warning of a noise. A moment later she heard the sound of men's boots and low, rumbling laughter, and then, from her position in the archway, she could see first one, then another, then the third Watts brother walk around the Market House. They were going up Churton, away from the festival. Cathy reasoned that they could have been headed any number of places, but certainly one of those places could have been her house. Matthew Watts seemed to be carrying some sort of club. Right in her line of vision, she saw him stop and shove the end of it into the last lantern on King, ripping the Chinese paper. When he drew the club back, its tip was aflame.

She heard the men say "That woman needs a lesson!" and "She cain't treat the Watts brothers like that!" and a strong, corroborating "Noo, sireee!"

Feeling a trace of panic, she looked back at Mr. Harris, her eyes wide. She nodded acquiescence, and he removed his hand from her mouth.

Hank, who had been closely watching this byplay, whispered, impressed, "Never would of thought of it myself. Put a hand over her mouth. Shut her up. Simple as that. Good idea, man!"

Harris promptly muzzled Cathy again, thereby stifling the hot retort that sprang to her lips. All this was too much for her dignity, so she sniffed majestically and let him understand with a dismissive toss of her head that she had no intention of lowering herself to the level of Hank Wilson by responding in kind.

Next the Duke boys straggled past, single file. The last one was shouldering a rifle. Hank looked pointedly at the bow and arrow slung across the Welshman's shoulder, but Harris merely shook his head. When the Duke boys had moved along, Harris motioned Hank and Boy out of the archway. They scurried across Churton and were swallowed by the darkness along King.

Harris and Cathy waited a few more moments in the archway, then set out, hand in hand, behind Hank and Boy. As they crossed Churton toward King, Cathy asked, "Where are Orin and Richard?"

"I sent them on to your house before I came to get you."

"What are they doing there?"

"Waiting by the well."

"By the well?"

"A precaution."

She looked up Churton. She could see the outlines of the seven men in the light of the torch carried by Matthew Watts. "Do they mean to burn down my house?" she asked, her voice wavering.

"If they do, Orin and Richard mean to douse their fun," he replied. "But I don't think your house is their target."

She asked, curious now, "How did you know what the club was intended for?"

"I know a lot about fire," was all he said.

Instead of following the footpath along Churton, as she had expected, he led her up King behind Hank and Boy. When they had passed the first house, he moved into the side lawn, then into the backyard gardens between King and Tryon. They were immediately surrounded by redbuds and dogwoods and pines and the pulse of the night. The air was dewy and fragrant and feminine. They crossed a clearing, bathed by the light of the round, milky moon riding high above, and a carpet of pink oxalis spread out underfoot. Harris cut a path through the tangles of laurel and great rhododendrons as if he had lived his entire life in Hillsborough. Quickly they emerged onto Tryon Street, crossed it and just as quickly moved into the gardens between Tryon and Queen.

"Where on earth are we going, sir?" she asked.

"I told Hank and Boy to meet us at your orchard."

"My orchard?"

He stopped abruptly and turned, causing her to stumble against him. He grasped her by the shoulders and held her close. His embrace was loverlike. His words were not. "Do you never think before you speak?"

Stung, she retorted, "Well, it would certainly help if you explained yourself in more than two or three words! Although I admire your habit of answering a direct question with a direct answer, I find your conversational style somewhat limited for the long run. If I must *guess* at each of your meanings, the possibilities for misunderstanding increase enormously and—and... No, sir, do not look at me like that! I can see very well that you think I am wasting words now. For your information, I can easily read on your face what you are thinking most of the time, so—"

"If that is the case," he broke in, "then why do you ask me the most foolish questions?"

She had no idea why she should be arguing, nose to nose, chest to chest, with a man she had not known more than a few hours. She did not even question the circumstance. Instead, she answered him in a voice that she hoped nicely blended imperiousness and long-suffering patience, "I can neither read your mind, Mr. Harris nor construct your grand scheme from the very spare information that we are going to meet Hank and Boy in my orchard. What I should have said that I *can* do, sir, is interpret the emotions on your face. I can see not what you are thinking, but I can see very well what you are *feeling*."

He challenged, "Tell me what I am feeling now."

He was keeping his face deliberately impassive, she could tell. She considered the stark planes silvered by moonlight and framed by the bow slung over his shoulder. She was not embarrassed either by the scrutiny that he was returning or by their embrace. She was so close to him that she could detect the lingering scent of warm sun on his cotton shirt. That new-tenant feeling came to her again, making her aware of her body. This time it was coupled with the long-forgotten, little-girl pleasures of traveling barefoot through squishy, springtime gardens. She had not experienced that lovely sensation in years. The curious and the new combined with the remembered and the familiar to make her feel very much alive.

Looking him straight in the eye, she said, "You are as plainly irritated by me as I am by you, sir, but for different reasons that I will not bother to explain at the moment. In addition, you feel confident about beating the Watts brothers at their own game, whatever it may be, and are eager to get on with it instead of standing here speaking to me! Aha! Yes, now I can see that you are surprised by what I have just said.'' She cocked her head. ''And I would say that you are even amused by it. Well, now, am I right?''

''Mostly,'' he admitted. He released her and turned back around. He took her hand again and proceeded to wade through the profusion of flowering bushes. ''Except that I am not amused.''

''You *are* amused,'' she insisted, adding on an inspired note, ''but perhaps you just don't know it yet. Now tell me what your grand scheme is.''

He countered, ''Name your most valuable possession.''

She had to think about that, then said, still weighing the matter, ''Either my mother's earrings or my father's Bible.''

He did not turn back to look at her when he said, curtly, ''Guess again.''

''I don't know what you mean.''

To that he stated, ''You are hopeless.''

He had been moving swiftly through the gardens, not hurrying, but not dallying, either. She was panting a little by now and did not want to waste breath on a retort that he was bound to ignore; and she was surprised when they reached the edge of her property, for he had certainly found the shortest of shortcuts. He led her up the grassy slope behind her house. She looked in the direction of Queen Street, where she could tell that the Watts and the Dukes were approaching her house by the flicker of the torch moving along beyond the thick filigree of foliage.

She suddenly understood what Mr. Harris guessed of their intentions. In a low voice she exclaimed, ''They wouldn't dare!''

He said, "I don't know what they would dare, but they could damage a major portion of this year's apple crop with little effort and no one being the wiser."

"I won't let them get to my root sprouts," she vowed fiercely. Her voice turned anxious when she said, "And my grafts have never before produced so many blooms!" Fierce again, she added, "I can't let them get to my grafts, either. I won't let them!"

"Neither will I," Harris assured her.

"But there are more of them than of us, and they are armed," she said in some alarm.

Harris cast a glance at her over his shoulder. The look on his face reassured her, as did the calm strength of his hand holding hers. Then she heard him produce a sound between a whistle and a birdcall, and to her amazement her mangy old hound, Black Twig, shambled across the slope and stopped at their feet. Harris squatted down, and with his free hand he stroked the hound between the ears. He had quite a lot to say to the hound in a language Cathy did not recognize. Black Twig wheezed his understanding, then loped off toward the house.

Harris took Cathy's hand again and with long strides covered the distance up the slope, making his way around her garden and the hog pen. They arrived at the orchard only a little behind Hank and Boy, who were waiting for them at the first row of trees. From their vantage point on the rise, they could see the flicker of the torch approach the front walk of Cathy's house.

Hank eyed Harris skeptically, then shook his head and said, "Richard and Orin ken dump their buckets of water on the torch, but I'm powerful put out not to have my gun. I'm thinkin' a bow and arrow jes' ain't no match for that Duke boy's rifle."

Boy seconded mournfully, "That's for shore."

Harris flicked a glance over Hank and Boy, then around the shadowy orchard. When he saw something that interested him about twenty feet off, he shrugged his bow off his shoulder and caught it deftly in his left hand, then reached behind into his quiver in a fluid movement and withdrew an arrow. He cocked the arrow, took aim and said instructively, "We don't want the swaggering braggarts and their friends to know we're waiting for them in the orchard. Now, what do you think would happen if I was to shoot that thing—"

Here he released the arrow. It flew straight and low and reached its goal with a muffled *thwack*.

"—with a gun?"

"What thing?" Boy asked. He began to walk curiously in the direction of Harris's target.

"Why, I guess it'ud make a noise," Hank responded slowly, "and let 'em know we was up here." He squinted into the darkness and cracked a challenging smile. "But what was yer point in shooting a stick?"

Boy bent over the object in question. "It weren't no stick," he called back. With hushed reverence, he added, "It was a copperhead."

Cathy shuddered and began to look about anxiously.

"Got 'im right between the eyes, too," Boy said with relish.

Hank was liking the Welshman more and more. "Well, now," he said, "let's get to work on that plan of yers."

Hank and Boy parted ways and disappeared into the orchard.

Still looking about, Cathy asked, "Do you see any other snakes?"

Harris shook his head, shouldered his bow and took her hand.

Making their way through the orchard, she asked, "Do I have a part in the plan?" and would have been quick to protest if she did not.

"Of course," he said and led her straight to the Nickajack tree she had fallen from that afternoon. "Up you go." He laced his fingers together to hold her foot, then hoisted her up to the first branch.

"What am I to do?"

"Jump down on anyone who passes underneath, wrestle them to the ground, call out and wait for me to help you."

She nodded and he left. It was only after she had climbed high up into the tree so that she could get a better view of the orchard and her house that she realized he had neatly gotten her out of the way. He had put her in the most central tree in the orchard, and thus the safest. She would have climbed back down to engage in more active protection of her property if it had not been for the thought of snakes, which had never before bothered her. Then it was too late to do anything useful anyway, for she was witness to an extraordinary scene unfolding before her eyes.

The light of the torch allowed her to easily trace the progress of the Watts and the Dukes. They had already made their way around her house, and from what she could see, they had set fire to neither her house nor her storeroom. The seven of them were on the grassy slope, headed straight for her orchard. She did not think their object was to burn the orchard, for the weather had been too moist for much to catch fire, but they could certainly char a lot of blossoms off the established trees. They could also easily trample the precious seedlings she had been so carefully nurturing for the past several years.

They were a rough and cocky bunch, she could see. They swaggered up the slope, speaking loudly and laughing among themselves, unconcerned that they might be detected. Alone now in the tree, without the comforting presence of Mr. Harris, she began to doubt whether the quiet man with his bow and arrows and the Boys would be any match for the men from East Orange County.

Then she caught sight of two shadowy figures creeping along behind the seven men, crouching low, carrying what looked like buckets, hiding behind every bush along the way. She smiled to see Orin and Richard engaged in clumsy stealth, which was succeeding only because the men they were trailing were so arrogantly ignorant of being followed.

Nevertheless, she did not understand why the men were proceeding unopposed or why they were able to get so close to the edge of her orchard. Now they were only about ten feet from her beautiful trees thick with blossoms. When the seven men began to fan out, her heart began to beat faster and with a sickening thud. When it looked as if they were within striking distance of doing damage to the first row, her heart quailed. Then it jumped into her throat as a chilling war whoop rent the night air.

Everything happened at once. She saw Orin and Richard slosh their buckets of water over Matthew Watts, causing both him and his torch to sputter. Boy and Hank fell down from trees atop the other Watts brothers, causing two balls of interlocked bodies to roll down the slope, away from the orchard.

Running wildly, yipping and yapping and generally causing confusion, Black Twig entered the fray. Incredibly, so did Smokehouse, her mannerless billy goat. Cathy clapped her hands in glee to see Smokehouse trot, head down, straight at the Duke boy who had been carrying the rifle and who was now aiming it straight at Mr. Harris, who was running toward him. The rifle went off the second after Smokehouse butted the man, causing the bullet to shoot harmlessly up into the air and the rifle to fly out of the man's hands.

Hank and Boy, having knocked two of the Watts brothers flat, scrambled back up the slope and turned their attention to the Duke boys. Orin did his part to keep Matthew Watts slipping and sliding in the water that had been thrown over him, while Richard and Harris scrapped with the remaining Dukes. The area was becoming good and sloppy, what with the water and the hound and the billy goat and twelve men swinging with wild abandon. One of the men peeled off from the group and scrambled over to where the rifle had fallen.

Cathy's heart stopped cold to see that it was one of the Duke boys. Before he picked up the rifle, however, she saw Mr. Harris dive for his bow and quiver, which were laying at the edge of the scuffle. Lying on the ground, Harris shot an arrow at the man going for the rifle. The man did not seem to have been hit, but he looked down at his rifle somewhat oddly and did not fire it. Then another chilling war whoop cracked the air, and Harris let flash in the light of the moon the blade of a very thick knife. He tossed another knife over to Hank. Its blade traced an arc of liquid silver in the moonlight.

She heard some grunts and calls of "Shoot!"

"I cain't!"

"Shoot the damned rifle!"

"I cain't!"

"They's got knives!"

"They's *big* knives!"

And finally, "Let's git out of here, boys!"

Then she saw the Watts brothers and the Duke boys scrambling inelegantly down the slope away from her orchard, with Black Twig and Smokehouse harassing their retreat.

When all was quiet, Cathy began to climb down from her high perch. When she reached the branch from which she had fallen that afternoon, she heard the sound of footsteps below her. She quickly arranged her skirts for modesty. She peered down and saw Mr. Harris. He was alone.

He held out his arms, as if he intended to catch her. "You can come down now."

Did he really mean for her to jump into his arms? She felt surprised and shy at the thought. "They're gone?" she asked, stalling for time.

"They're gone."

"They won't be coming back?"

"No."

"Are you sure?"

"Very."

"And the Boys? Where are they?"

"I sent them home."

"Oh." She did not wish to jump into his arms, and she certainly was not going to climb down on her own with him watching her. She asked, "What did you do to that Duke boy's rifle?"

"I shot an arrow through the trigger, and it stuck into the stock, making it impossible for him to shoot. The arrow can be dislodged, but it will take some doing."

"That was some fancy shooting on your part, Mr. Harris."

He did not respond to that, merely held out his arms to her.

She still did not move from the branch. "Are you the one who emitted that strange and bloodcurdling yell?"

She felt rather than saw his smile. "Works every time," he commented. "Now, come. I'll catch you," he coaxed. Although she could not see the expression on his face for the deep shadows under the tree, she distinctly heard the provocative note in his voice. "I want to get it right before the day is over, you see, and it's not often a man gets a second chance."

She looked down at him and said, equally provocative, "Are you sure that I am not too *heavy* for you, sir?"

"I'm prepared." When she did not immediately move, he added the interesting threat, "If you do not let me catch you, I'll come up and get you."

Her dignity was at stake. She took a deep breath and pushed herself off the branch.

He caught her securely in strong arms and set her gently on the ground. His arms remained around her waist a moment longer, while hers encircled his neck.

She felt breathless, as if she had jumped out of her thoughts and into her body. The new-tenant feeling was vivid. She was aware of him and of her and of the tiny space between them. She took a step back from him, and he let his arms fall away. She asked cautiously, "Are you finished saving me *now?*"

He shook his head.

Her eyes widened. "You mean there will be more threats to my property?"

"No, but I think that you still need my help."

She thought it better not to ask what further help she needed. More than enough had already happened this day. "I suppose I will see you again tomorrow, in that case?"

"Yes."

Then he disappeared. Truly vanished. As if into thin air.

Cathy walked out from under the shadows of the tree into the bright, flooding moonlight, darting her glance here and there, looking behind this tree and that for traces of him.

Suddenly she stood absolutely still. She recalled Old Hitch's dying words, whispered to her yesterday afternoon: "He'll come tomorrow. He'll take care of you." They had made no sense to her at the time. She had not even thought he was addressing them to her. But now she understood, and she was transfixed by the idea.

Old Hitch had sent her a guardian angel!

She shook her head, attempting to clear it of its moonstruck fancy. She had always thought a guardian angel would be light and ethereal. She would have never imagined a guardian angel to be as dark as Mr. Laurence Harris, or as solidly, intriguingly physical.

Chapter Eight

Cathy's impression of Mr. Harris as her guardian angel was reinforced the next morning, but was to wear off during the course of the day and vanish by evening.

She did not at first see him among the mourners gathering before the Presbyterian Church, and it was only when she gave up trying to find him and turned to go on into the church that she noticed him. He stood not more than ten feet from the walkway, in the wooded patch of the old town cemetery crowded between the entrance to the church and the side yard of the Nash house. He was almost indistinguishable from the moss-flocked stone statues of lambs and cherubs surrounding him and seemed to be part of the old weathered cross marking the grave next to which he stood.

How perfect, she thought, and went straight over to him. "Do you wish to worship with us, Mr. Harris?" she invited.

He had been gazing into the middle distance and did not immediately answer her. Then his eyes came down on her and focused slowly, as if he were returning from a great distance.

He said, "No."

"You're welcome to join us," she continued. She noted with relief that she was not aware of his body as she had been the night before. She decided that last night's aberration had been due to the strange events of the day, and to the moon, which had made her think that he was flirting with her and had caused her to respond so readily to his physical presence. "We would be pleased to have you as part of our congregation today, I assure you. It's a rather special day, you know, since we have come to eulogize and bury Old Hitch."

He said, "I am not a Christian."

She was fascinated by this new dimension to his role of guardian angel, but was not able to pursue it. Behind her, she heard the creak of hinges, suggesting that the door to the church was being closed. She realized that Mr. Harris was better off outside and said quickly, "I'll see you after the service, then."

He nodded.

She hurried to the front entrance of the church, where stood the Reverend Lee. Seeing the worry on his face, Cathy smiled and said reassuringly, "I'm sure it will go well enough."

The reverend adjusted the spectacles on his nose, reached into the folds of his black serge coat and withdrew a thick bundle of sheets, folded and sealed with a blob of red wax. "Well enough?" he repeated in repressive accents. "I would be most content if it were to go 'well enough.' But I can hardly be sure even that modest hope will be realized, since Old Hitch insisted that we not read his final statement before this morning. It is most irregular, not to mention entirely disconcerting!"

"It is unusual," Cathy agreed. She eyed the packet of papers with some misgiving. "We know that Old Hitch was working on his final statement this past week, most secretively, indeed." On a more cheerful note, she added, "But how bad can it be, after all?"

They were soon to find out.

Cathy preceded the reverend into the tiny church, and he closed the wooden door behind them. She took her seat in the third pew from the front, nodded to Mrs. Travis on her left and leaned forward to nod, as well, at George, who sat at his mother's left.

Mrs. Travis bent her head toward Cathy and whispered, "I must tell you, dear, that Miss Ginger is well-informed on the subject of backyard drainage. I am pleased to discover that she speaks more good sense than one would expect, looking at her pretty face."

Cathy smiled with amused satisfaction and patted the matron's hand. She followed Mrs. Travis's gaze across the aisle and up a row to where Ginger Mangum was seated. The midmorning sunlight was streaming through the tall, narrow panes of stained glass, gilding the golden curls that escaped her Sunday bonnet.

The same light that fell on Ginger fell on MacGuff, seated ahead of her in the front row. He sat still, properly looking straight ahead, and Cathy thought she had never seen a man who so perfectly embodied her ideal. Her heart fluttered to think he might wish to take up residence again in Hillsborough—if there were something to keep him here. Her spirits rose to think that Mr. Harris might be able to rearrange her face so that she had a more beautiful nose, sculpted cheeks and a pretty, pointed chin. Her spirits sank when she decided that any such transformation would be more in the line of work of a fairy godmother than of a guardian angel. Her attention returned to the business at hand.

Reverend Lee walked down the short aisle. He approached the altar, passed the closed casket—giving it a wide berth, as if it were an animal known to bite—then climbed the few steps to the pulpit. He adjusted his spectacles, cleared his throat and looked up to face the expectant congregation.

He said in his thin, carrying voice, "We have come today to eulogize Hitchcock MacGuffin, lifelong resident of Hillsborough, honest farmer and faithful friend. However, since, as we all know, Mr. MacGuffin was given to doing things his way—"

Audible coughing interrupted the reverend's voice.

"—he prepared his own fond goodbye to his dear friends." Under his breath, the minister added, "Let us hope." He held up the sheaf of paper. "It was Mr. MacGuffin's—Old Hitch's—dying request that I read this final statement to you on this occasion when we have come to mourn his passing and to celebrate his life. The statement was prepared by his own . . . loving hand during his last week of life on God's earth, and on his very deathbed he made me promise that it should be read to you this morning."

Cathy thought that the reverend might as well have come out and said that he had granted Old Hitch's last request against his better judgment. After breaking the seal and spreading out the crackling pages, he absolved himself of any further responsibility by insisting, "No one, save the dear, departed Mr. MacGuffin knows the contents. They are being read for the first time."

He cleared his throat again and readjusted his spectacles. He opened his mouth to speak, but the reedy timbre of his voice did little to mask the irascible effect of the opening lines.

"'Now any of you Methodists,'" the reverend read, "'who have come to send me off can get up and leave right now. I don't hold with Methodists, and I don't want 'em at my funeral.'"

The reverend looked up abruptly. His very soft "Dear me!" could be clearly heard above the titters of laughter that turned to hasty fits of coughing. He put the pages down a moment, smiled nervously and said, "Well! Isn't that just like our Old Hitch! Always joking! Now, in my capacity as shepherd to this flock, I would like to extend a personal welcome to any Methodists who have come to join us today and invite them to stay as honored guests. I will now continue with Mr. Hitchcock's statement."

The generous shepherd adjusted his glasses and returned his attention to the pages in his hand. "'And don't listen to a word that namby-pamby reverend of ours says,'" he read in a tone of increasing astonishment, "'for I've a strong notion he'll invite the lot of you to stay, and there's not a curst thing I can do about it, 'cept tell you to git! So you can see already that I've no mind to restrain myself today.'" Here the poor shepherd uttered, "Dear, *dear* me!" in a heartfelt voice before he continued, "'And I don't have to, 'cause I'm dead. Not that I'm happy about the circumstance with y'all alive and me dead. Why, if the devil gave me *my* way, I'd be alive and y'all would be dead!'" The page was turned to reveal Old Hitch's next comment, delivered as a very brittle, "'Ha, ha.'"

The now-beleaguered shepherd commented austerely, "I do not find that remark the least bit amusing." His opinion was not entirely shared by his flock, quite a portion of whom had to wipe irreverent smiles off their faces as well as looks of eager anticipation for what would come next.

The reverend ran a finger inside his stiff white collar and read dutifully on, "'I shouldn't have to go through all this now when I'm such a sick man, and I wouldn't have to if any of you twiddle-poops had had the sense to consult my advice when I was alive! So there you have it. It's Old Hitch's last moment in the sun, so to speak, before you put me six feet under, and there's more than one amongst you happy to see me go. The first, no doubt, is Ida Witherspoon. Her wretched coleslaw chews as good as wet wood and tastes about the same. If she can't learn to put a proper amount of vinegar in it, it ain't my fault! Now Gladys Travis, on the other hand, puts enough sugar in her molasses cookies (not to mention her tea) to rattle a strong man's teeth. When it comes time to stick *her* spoon in the wall, she won't need to be embalmed 'cause she's just about preserved herself already. Then there's Sally Lee and her soggy ham biscuits, and I don't care if she is the reverend's sister. Well, I didn't have to taste any of that mess this year at the mutton-headed Apple Blossom Festival, and it's highly likely I won't have to endure it next year neither!'"

By this time, three very indignant voices had been heard to utter, "Well, I declare!"

The reverend, exercising what he thought was severe restraint, smiled tightly and informed the congregation, "Sally's platter of ham biscuits came home quite empty last night, I don't mind telling you." He added, graciously including the other two offended ladies, "And I am sure that Miss Ida's tenderly spiced coleslaw and Miss Gladys's excellent cookies were greatly enjoyed by the festivalgoers, as well."

Then, apparently realizing that these interpolations were only prolonging the awkward unpleasantness of Old Hitch's final statement, he turned the page and read on through the next four, not stopping until the end. The trend, well established in the opening paragraphs, continued.

"'That gapeseed Jack Richards who calls hisself a farmer don't know nothin' about plantin' and I told him and told him and now I'm tellin' him what's what for the last time. If he's gonna plant corn, it better be Bloody Butcher. If he's gonna plant peas, it's only Ripper. For watermelons, the Lord knows and so does the devil that it's Moon and Stars what got the best juice. As for peaches, it's Greensboro, and it goes against the grain to say so, for if there's people I like less than Methodists, it has to be them 'snickety peach growers in Greensboro!

"'I've said my piece on that, and now I'd like to declare that Allen Lloyd robbed me blind when I swapped my perfectly good milch cow for his broken-down old nag that was a good five years older at the time than he would admit! And I'm not referrin' to his wife, Octavia, neither, and a more horsey-faced woman I have yet to meet! Why, that swaybacked nag Lloyd swapped me for was a prettier sight to behold than Octavia Lloyd and had a more genteel neigh. Now, that incident was forty years ago, and I didn't want to go to my grave with bloodsucker Lloyd thinking I'd forgotten it!

"'And another thing, speakin' of nags, is I can understand why Joe Whitey has been diddlin'—'" here the reverend's voice broke pitifully "'—Mary Stevens all these years, seeing what *his* wife looks like and all, but I'm tellin' you it fair maudles a man's innards to see Joe and Mary makin' sheep's eyes at one another and then slippin' off to satisfy theirselves, as if no one were the wiser. And wouldn't you know they'd choose a place at the edge of my property to do their business, with me able to see 'em, too, only by walkin' out my front door and down the path to the stream and then around the bend to the left, and lookin' straight into the thickest part of the blueberry bushes!'"

This last, public declaration of Hillsborough's least-secret secret, along with the identification of the trysting place, was either the high point or the low point—depending on the point of view of the listener—of Old Hitch's final tirade. It brought the reverend's handkerchief out his back pocket and to his brow, where it stayed during the reading of the next three pages. These went on in a similar vein, spared no one, were amazingly accurate and turned the tables so fast that the person most likely to laugh at a description of his neighbor was sure to be the next target of Old Hitch's crabbed invective.

When the reverend came to the end of this painful recital of his fellow citizen's foibles, along with his own, quite a few members of the congregation remained red faced. These included Young MacGuff, who had not only been blistered on the subject of his supposed elegance, but also dismissed as a silly whippersnapper, an epithet he had detested since boyhood.

When it came time to bear the casket out to the cemetery yard, an enthusiasm not usually characteristic of funerals animated the congregation. It lightened the load of the pallbearers and the steps of the mourners toward the newly dug grave. Not a heart bled nor an eye wept for the passing of Old Hitchcock MacGuffin as his casket was being lowered, and Cathy supposed that such might have been his intention. Suddenly Old Hitch's scold from the grave, combined with the general delight taken in burying him, struck Cathy as unutterably funny. When the first clods of dirt hit the top of the casket, she began to laugh.

Other mourners found her laughter contagious, and pretty soon almost everyone—except Mrs. Joe Whitey—found one of Old Hitch's phrases worthy of repeating and laughing over. Hank and Orin found the funeral highly entertaining and were trying to decide whose would be the next, so they could have another good laugh. Boy was quite sure that he still had his *whole* brain in his head and was telling anyone who would listen that he had never left any of it, so far as he knew, in the bottom of a moonshine bottle. Ginger Mangum seemed to enjoy repeating Old Hitch's comments about Sylvia Lee almost as much as Sylvia Lee seemed to enjoy repeating his comments about Ginger Mangum.

Sally Lee, the reverend's sister, was heard to declare in a rather spirited voice that the party—but then corrected herself in a more dignified tone to say the solemn funeral dinner—was to take place immediately in the rectory. Cathy stopped by there briefly for the sake of form and to remind Ginger, George, Clive and the Boys to meet her at her house as soon as they could get away.

She left the rectory by the side door and angled off across the cemetery lawn to skirt the Hooper house at the far corner. She emerged onto Wake Street, a pleasant little lane that intersected with Queen. She was almost to the corner of her street when she felt a presence behind her. Looking around, she saw Mr. Harris, who promptly fell into step with her.

She was dangling her bonnet in her hand by the strings. The warm, buttery sun on her face felt good. She smiled up at him because the day was fine, because she felt secure in his presence and because she felt like it.

He did not smile back with his lips exactly, but she thought he smiled at her with his eyes.

She said, "Have I thanked you yet for all you did for me last night? I would like to, you know."

He did not encourage her thanks. "Tell me instead whether the practice of laughing at funerals is customary to North Carolina or particular to Hillsborough."

Cathy's eyes lit up. "You must think us very odd! First we dance on the eve of the old man's funeral, then we laugh during the mournful service."

"And at the graveside," he added. "I have attended funerals both in Quebec and in Maryland, but I have yet to encounter the strange laughing custom you practice here."

"Not a strange custom," she explained, "but a very strange man." She proceeded to explain Old Hitch's final statement and its effect.

Harris listened with interest. When she was finished, he asked, "What did the uncle say about you?"

Cathy laughed and said without embarrassment, "That anyone with such a bleeding heart and romantic turn of mind would do better to have a face like Ginger Mangum's. Oh, yes, and that mooning around, dreamy eyed, made a plain-Jane miss like me only look more foolish than I already do."

Harris asked, with a slight inflection of surprise, "How did you feel about that?"

"To tell the truth," she said reflectively, "I was disappointed, because I was already well-informed of Old Hitch's opinion of me. Why, I probably spent more time with him than anyone else in town, so he had plenty of opportunity to tell me what he thought of me. More than once! So while I was listening to the wickedly funny things he was saying about everyone else before he came to me, I had been relishing a rather more imaginative complaint for him to lay at my address. Something with more bite."

"Perhaps he was trying to spare your feelings."

"What a lowering thought!"

"You wanted him to say something wicked about you?"

Cathy laughed again. "Wickedly *funny*. Some of his observations were good as gold, and they were usually right on the nose! But, no, I don't like hearing mean things said about me. However, today I would have enjoyed a better laugh at myself."

They turned the corner onto Queen and passed a vacant lot that was thick with crabgrass and broom sedge and gaily colored by scatterings of wild carrot, wild daisy and some late-blooming honeysuckle.

"At first, in the church, I was deliciously scandalized like everyone else to hear Old Hitch's final statement," she continued, "but then, in the cemetery, I began to think that he wanted us to be laughing at his passing, rather than mourning him. Now that I give his motives a second thought, it's just as likely that he wished to thumb his nose at his friends and neighbors for the last time.'' She laughed. ''Either way, his statement was highly effective.''

After a moment, Harris asked, ''What would the uncle have said about me?''

She appraised him critically. Then, affecting Old Hitch's creaky voice, she said, ''It's no good for a grown man to career around the countryside with a bow and arrow, wearing moccasins! Settle down, young man, and make something of yourself. Wear decent clothes. Not these animal skins! And cut your hair, son. You don't look proper!''

''And if I did not heed his advice?''

''He'd give you a week or two, and if you didn't shape up according to his specifications, he'd fix you with an eagle eye and snap, 'Dummy!' ''

Harris looked taken back.

''I *did* say that he was the man who defined the word *ornery.*''

''You also said that his observations were generally correct.''

Cathy met his eye and thought of him as he'd been last night, blazing a trail through the backyard gardens, shooting arrows, whipping and whooping it up. ''He was *often* right, I should have said, and he would have been dead wrong in your case.'' She cocked her head and considered him. ''There won't be any settling down for you, I think—or at least, not soon. You're more comfortable traveling the gardens than you are the streets, and my guess is that you like the forests even better. But Old Hitch never met you, so I don't know what he'd say about you except, perhaps, that you're doing a good job of taking care of me—not that he would admit that, exactly! Oh, we'll miss him, there's no doubt about it. Well, here we are.''

They had arrived at her pretty blue clapboard house with the red shutters and the inviting porches. Harris put his hand on the gate, but did not push it open. Instead, he paused and leaned against the fence.

''You live here alone?''

She looked down the street. Since she saw no sign of Clive or George or Ginger or the Boys, she was in no hurry to get inside to prepare for receiving them. ''Yes.''

''You've lived here all your life?''

''Yes.''

''How long have you been alone?''

''About ten years,'' she said. ''Since I was fourteen.'' She could not resist smiling provocatively and batting her lashes at him. ''But I am not going to tell you how old I am, because that would be obvious.''

He smiled at this. Or, rather, he smiled again with his eyes but not his lips. ''You've been alone for the past ten years, then, in charge of both the house and the orchard?''

She nodded. ''Mama died ten years ago. Daddy died when I was five.''

''How did you do it, living alone since age fourteen?''

For some reason, the question annoyed her. ''Well, when you were only one year older, you rode alone over a huge distance to find the father you did not know was still alive.''

''In my case, I had a hunter's skills by the age of twelve and was considered a man by my tribe at the same age. You, on the other hand, were still just a girl at fourteen. So my question is, how did you do it?"

She looked at him curiously. "What tribe?"

He returned her regard pointedly and spoke as much as she had ever heard him say at once. "I am from the Tohontaenrat, or Deer Tribe, which belongs to the Wendat. My grandfather, Attean, was chief. My first language was what the white man calls Huron, and my second was French, so I could trade with Breton trappers. I did not know more than a dozen words of English ten years ago when I came to Maryland, and I am still learning.

"The reason I set out to find Morgan was that I could no longer live with being a disgraced and nameless member of the tribe, for my mother dishonored her father, Attean, when she ran off with Morgan. She died when I was still a baby, and I was returned to my tribe, where I grew to manhood.

"Morgan's second wife, Barbara, took me into her heart. I have a stepsister named Sarah, who is eleven, and two younger half sisters named Martha and Helen."

Without stopping for breath, he continued. "Now I've told you everything that you could ask that would divert you from answering my question, and I will ask it again. How did you do it, a girl alone, running a house and an orchard at age fourteen? Or were you already running the town by then?"

She was so amazed that her mouth hung open a moment, before she exclaimed, "You leave me with nothing to say!"

"That's a change," he returned easily.

"Are you suggesting that I talk too much?"

"I'm not suggesting it," he said suggestively.

"No, you're *telling* me as much," she said in something of a huff, thinking, Isn't it just like Old Hitch to have sent me a decidedly unangelic guardian angel? "You are a very irritating man, Mr. Harris. Did you know that?"

Not a muscle in his impassive face moved, but there he was, looking *smug* again. "So you told me last night," he said, "and in the spirit of the or-ner-ee uncle who has died, I can tell you that you are equally irritating, mostly in your habit of asking foolish questions and of avoiding reasonable ones."

He was not lounging against the gate anymore but was standing straight and looking down at her. She, too, had straightened and was literally standing up to and almost against this unangelic angel. There was nothing angelic about her feelings, either. Sure, she was feeling all spiky and irritated, but the irritation had an attractive edge to it that rounded into a heightened physical awareness of the sheen of his black hair, the snap in his black eyes, the sun-dried cleanliness of his white shirt, the line of his neck and shoulders, the memory of his strong arms catching her securely last night, the feel of his body stretched out beneath hers yesterday afternoon.

"You want to hear my life story?" she queried, her tone as spirited as it was defensive. "There is nothing to tell! I've had no adventures like you. Why, I've hardly been farther away than Pittsboro, which is only down the road past Chapel Hill. And you know almost everyone in town by now, so there is nothing to tell on that score, either. As for being on my own in the early days after my mother died, I can tell you that I was not left to myself much because Old Hitch took it into his head to stop by every day."

"To help you?"

"Rather to vex me to death! He would come by to say that a corner of the roof needed repairing or that it was time to paint the trim or to slop the hogs or to dig up my root sprouts or to gather and sort my seeds! He must have thought I didn't know the least thing, when it was perfectly obvious to everyone else that I did." She reflected on those days and had to smile fondly. "It was reassuring, nevertheless, to know that he was looking out for me."

"You have lived alone in the house ever since?"

"Yes."

"You own it, then?"

"I suppose I must, because after Mama died, no one ever threw me out, and I learned how to pay the taxes." She pulled a face. "Or, rather, Old Hitch badgered me into putting money aside from my apple profits every month for the taxes and even harassed the tax collector so that he would come to my house first!" She lost her fond smile and expostulated, "Ornery old man!"

"What about your orchard? You own that property, too?"

She smiled again, this time with great pride. "It's mine and no one else's! And if I *don't* own it—for I've never seen the deed to it, nor that to the house—the true owners'll have to take it from me over my dead body! I have vivid memories of being in my daddy's orchard with him, doing whatever I could to help him, which was probably not much, since I was little more than a toddler then! I remember him out on the hill with his two-mule team, furrowing deep, because this is clay soil, and grafting our trees on seedling rootstock.

"That was twenty years ago, and so by the time I was on my own, the main trees were already bearing plentiful fruit, since a tree takes eight-to-ten years to produce apples. Why, I've grown up with the trees, I guess you could say. They're my hobby and my livelihood and my friends."

With a little prodding, Cathy was encouraged to talk about her apple-growing practices, the range of her business and her relationship to the Lindley nursery in Chatham County. She was most keen to discuss the varieties of apples she grew and the uses to which they were put, from those trees destined to bear poor fruit, which would be fed to the hogs, to those best for stewing or for cider or for keeping through the winter like Hall, Shockley and Winesap. She conveyed her professional enthusiasm for her experiments in grafting, both piece root and whole root, which every now and again would grow into a tree with a fruit worthy of further consideration.

"My most successful varieties," she explained, "are the local favorites of Red June, Nickajack, Magnum Bonum, Black Twig, Hunge, Smokehouse, Aunt Rachel and Summer Orange." She laughed at Harris's expression and said, "Yes, all my animals are named after apple varieties, along with my hogs and chickens and the guinea fowl that I let roam the orchard to eat the insects that damage the fruit. Why, I've even named some of my best-loved furniture after my trees." She pointed to the porch. "You see the swing? I've named her Sally Gray."

Harris, who had been asking questions to keep her going, smiled a little at that.

Finding herself talked out, she asked, "Have you heard enough, Mr. Harris?"

He nodded.

She looked down Queen Street, then back at him. "Good, because here come the others now. And we have work to do."

Chapter Nine

Harris stood on the street to the side of the gate as Ginger Mangum and the Boys passed through it, followed by George Travis and Clive Smith.

The postman took one look at him, uttered a startled "Eh?" and asked of no one in particular, "What's he doing here? Saw him last night at the festival and heard his name was Harris. Heard he was a Welshman, too, but didn't expect to see him at Miss Cathy's again."

George cast a disinterested glance at the quiet man. His thoughts were dwelling darkly on spurned love and his ruined life, for Miss Ginger still refused to speak to him today. He said colorlessly, "He was sent to Miss Cathy by the Lindleys. He's from Maryland, if you're wanting to know, but is no kin to the Lindleys there."

"Oh, I see!" the postman replied, completely satisfied by this explanation. In a vague, negative sort of way, he would forever associate Laurence Harris with the Lindleys by the very fact that he was not related to them.

Harris, who had taken no part in this exchange, followed the two men through the gate and closed it behind him. He found his place at the side of the walkway, next to the pillar post at the bottom of the porch steps.

From this vantage point he watched the activities of Miss Cathy and her friends and contemplated his mission in Hillsborough. He centered his thoughts on Attean's voice intoning the story of the creation of the world, how the daughter of the chief of the Sky People had fallen ill, and how a wise man had told the chief to dig up a tree and lay the girl beside the hole. The chief and his people began to dig, but as they did so the tree suddenly fell right through the hole, dragging the girl with it.

The chief's daughter fell down toward the endless waters that lay below the sky, where two swans floated. The Great Turtle had told the swans that the appearance of a woman from the sky would foreshadow future good fortune. The swans, not wanting the girl to drown, swam toward her to save her, but first they had to fight the muskrat, beaver and otter who were enemies of the Great Turtle. After many trials, the swans reached the Woman Who Fell From the Sky and supported her upon their backs. From her body and the clumps of dirt that clung to the roots of the fallen tree, the earth was made.

Harris was satisfied that he had met and defeated the muskrats last night in Miss Cathy's orchard. He cast about for the likely incarnation of the beaver and figured it to be the uncle and his mysterious chain of letters. As for the slippery otter, he had no trouble identifying Young Cock. More to the immediate point was the uncle and his letters, but, strangely enough, Harris did not think that the otter meant to threaten the Woman Who Fell From the Sky, and so he was puzzled to know how he could endanger her. His puzzlement was compounded by the fact that he had learned nothing from his engagement with the muskrats, as a great warrior was supposed to do from an exalted test. Last night's romp in the orchard had been more playful than it was challenging. He was, furthermore, disturbed that he was losing the vision of his goddess's heavenly spirit and was, instead, becoming more and more aware of her earthly body.

This shift in his vision was all the more inexplicable because he had imagined a strong, avenging goddess who would put him through tests of raw courage and trials of great skill. The goddess of his imagination was silent and commanded him to do her bidding without speaking. Instead, what he got was a woman who had resisted his help, did not think she needed it, ran the whole town and seemed to think of him as one of the Boys. And she talked too much.

Or rather, she talked more than he thought a goddess would. She talked more than any other earthly woman he had known, too—more than Morgan's wife, Barbara. He vastly preferred womanly silences. Or so he had thought, for he could not deny that he felt something happen inside him whenever he was with Miss Cathy. He felt something strange and new, like the lightening of a dark and shadowed space within his breast. He was at a loss to know exactly what it was.

Nor did he know why she should have that effect on him, but he guessed that it might have something to do with the way she moved. He watched her now. She had brought out a pitcher with glasses and a large tray holding small, white disks. While she was pouring drinks and passing the tray, he could not help but compare her to the tiresome woman, who sat on the swing and who seemed most suited to whimpering and sniffing. By contrast, his talkative, earthly goddess was competent and good-natured. She laughed with the postman, joked with the Boys, swatted Orin's hand away from the tray when he had taken too many disks, sympathized with the tiresome woman and humored the weak-willed lover, who languished on the other side of the porch.

She was affectionate, too, and generous with her affection. She touched her friends liberally and often. She put her arm around Ginger, leaned into Richard, poked Orin's stomach and stroked the cat mincing daintily along the railing.

He imagined her doing all this for the past ten years and realized that no one—not the postman, nor the tiresome woman, nor her weak-willed lover nor the Boys—noticed what an extraordinary young woman she was. They took her for granted, which both surprised him and did not surprise him. If they took her for granted, it was because she herself took what she was doing for them for granted.

She did not ignore him, either, and treated him exactly as she did the others. She handed him a glass of something that he discovered was lemonade, and she brought the tray over to him and told him that the disks were dried-apple slices. She pointed out the two kinds—one perfectly white, from the Maiden Blush apple, and the other, Rose Sweet, which she said was her favorite. Those she dried specially on a tin roof and with the peeling on, and she told him she often carried them in her pocket and ate them like candy.

He helped himself to one slice of the Maiden Blush, and she pressed two slices of Rose Sweet into his hand.

She took a slice of Rose Sweet herself and bit down on it, smiling with satisfaction.

By that time, discussion of Old Hitch's "final scold," as his statement was now being called, had exhausted itself, and Cathy declared that they needed to put not only their heads together but the old man's letters. "The only ones I have not heard are Ginger's and Clive's, so we'll hear Ginger's first, Clive's second. Then I want to see the exact wording of the Boys' letter, because I'm not convinced it has anything to do with a still."

After sniffing theatrically once or twice, Ginger opened her letter and read her two lines.

Cathy struck a hands-on-hip attitude and exclaimed, "What a puzzle!" Then she shook her head and said, "I just can't think with my shoes on!" She stripped off her shoes and stockings and wriggled her toes on the warm bricks of the front walk. "I can think much better now." She asked Ginger to repeat her lines.

Ginger read aloud:

"The key to it all you hold in your hand
And others. To find them, then, is your task."

She shook her pretty head. "What do you suppose it means?"

"I suppose it means that we are to make something of all these clues," Cathy ventured.

"Yes!" Clive said, enthusiastically seconding Cathy's interpretation. "And we're supposed to find the others who have clues. But that's easy enough, because we're all here, and after all, I ought to know. I delivered all the letters."

"And were there only these six?" Cathy asked.

The postman confirmed this was so. "Of course, I know Old Hitch sent two off to Young MacGuff last week, but they were telling him to come home, as we know from the young man himself."

Cathy was satisfied. "All right then, we have the six all together. So what does yours say, Clive?"

"Old Hitch is teasing me about his watch, the stingy you-know-what!" Clive said. "It's a beauty, too. He knew I had my eye on it these many years, and it's a dang sight better than the one my pappy gave me, which don't keep time anymore the way it should. Now, you know the next thing in importance after the satisfaction I get from hand delivering the mail is my desire to stay on schedule!"

"The lines, please."

Recalled to his purpose, the chatty postman uttered, "I'll get right to it!" He opened his letter to read:

"Watch out! Watch out! There's a face that unlocks
At the fall of noon, en route to the chime.

"See there? It's about his watch, no doubt about it."

Cathy had some doubts. "And you think that means he's giving you his watch?"

"I don't think he's *giving* me his watch, but teasing me with it, the old so-and-so! What else could it mean?"

"Almost anything," she replied. "Or nothing."

"Jes' like he's teasin' us about his still," Hank insisted.

"That remains to be seen," Cathy said, "and may—or may not!—become clear when we've read your lines. Do you have the letter, then, Hank?"

Hank handed Cathy his letter. She opened it and read with the usual puzzlement:

"And speaking of wills, there might be one still.
This sonnet tells you to see what you see."

She drew a breath. "Well, I don't know if he's teasing you about his still," she said. "He might be saying instead that there really is a will. But does anyone else's lines say something about wills?" She pointed to the page. "He says here 'speaking of wills.' And does he mean for these letters to go together to make his will?" She shook her head. "I am seeing what I am seeing, but it makes no sense."

Richard stepped forward at this point and said thoughtfully, "But you see, Old Hitch says in *our* letter that he's written us a sonnet. That must be an important clue."

Knowing exclamations peppered the group. "Yes, a sonnet!"

"Well, who would have guessed!"

"Yes, an important clue!"

Finally, Boy relieved everyone's mind by asking, "What's a sonnet? Does it have sump'n to do with stills?"

Richard informed Boy that a sonnet was a poem. "And this here being a poem will make everything easier."

Boy did not know what a poem had to do with stills or how it could make anything easier, and he said as much.

"In a poem," Richard explained, "the words at the end of every line rhyme."

Boy was struggling to keep pace. "Rhyme?"

Cathy illustrated the concept. "Like *cat* and *mat*," she said, pointing first to Aunt Rachel, then to her front doorstep.

"That's right," Richard said, "or like *house* and *mouse*."

Orin caught the spirit of the lesson. "How 'bout *candy* and *brandy!*" he offered brightly and received a friendly poke in the stomach from Cathy.

"I *knew* it had sump'n to do with a still," Boy said, nodding with satisfaction.

"Well, none of them lines rhyme," Hank said in disgust. He quoted by heart: "And speaking of wills, there might be one still. / This sonnet will teach you to see what you see. Now, *still* don't rhyme with *see,* and nothing you ken say will change my mind."

"The two lines together don't necessarily rhyme together," Richard said, "but mebbe do with the *other* lines, so's the whole poem is linked together."

Hank scratched his head. "Oh."

"That's not a bad idea, Richard," Cathy said. "So let's see if the lines *are* linked together." She gathered up the six letters and laid them out next to one another on the top step. Then she stood on the walkway at the bottom of the stairs in order to survey the whole.

Richard came to stand next to her. He bent over the stairs and reread to himself Clive's, Ginger's and the Boy's lines. Then he read aloud the three other letters that the group as a whole had not yet heard. The first happened to be George's:

"Together you'll see but mostly you'll ask:
What did Old Hitch have but a scrap of land?"

Then came his own:

"Between time and water, water and time,
The way to salvation, which lies in a box."

And finally came Cathy's:

"Apples don't fall very far from the tree,
Try as you might, say and do what you will.

"Aha!" Richard exclaimed. "There is mention of 'will.'"

"'Say and do what you will'?" Cathy quoted skeptically. "That has nothing to do with a written will."

Richard dismissed her objection. "That's beside the point. This is poetry."

Cathy objected again, "Old Hitch didn't have a poetic bone in his body."

"I didn't claim it was *good* poetry," Richard said. His reply seemed to call for a fair amount of commentary, except from Ginger and George, both of whom were sullen and sulking, until Richard commanded, "Now let me think!"

Everyone fell silent. Richard began to arrange and rearrange the letters to see if he could find rhymes that would fit it all together, muttering to himself all the time. Eventually, he looked up and pronounced, "Miss Cathy's lines must be the first, seein' how partial Old Hitch was to her. So if'n we put hers first, then the Boys' lines come next. All together they make what's called a stanza." He looked over at Boy and said, "That's four lines together, and here they are—

"Apples don't fall very far from the tree,
Try as you might, say and do what you will.
And speaking of wills, there might be one still.
This sonnet tells you to see what you see."

Cathy nodded slowly. "I think you're right, Richard."

"It makes good sense that the lines concernin' apples should be addressed to Miss Cathy," Clive pointed out.

"Which means that the still concerns us!" Orin and Boy cried in unison.

"But I'll be blamed if he means to tell us where it is," Hank said.

Richard was deeply absorbed in the technicalities of the rhyming scheme. Once he perceived the pattern that *tree* and *see* and *will* and *still* rhymed, he put the other lines in place with ease. Within a few minutes, he was able to read what he figured was the second stanza:

"The key to it all you hold in your hand.
And others. To find them, then, is your task.
Together you'll see but mostly you'll ask:
What did Old Hitch have but a scrap of land?"

Everyone agreed that Old Hitch must be hinting that he had more than just a scrap of land, and even Cathy was beginning to think that perhaps the still was involved. Hank pointed out slyly that Ginger's and George's lines went together to make this stanza, making it kinda cozy for them, poetry-wise. At that, the two of them cast soulful eyes at one another, then quickly looked away, but no one was paying attention to them because Richard had put the rest of the poem together.

Excitement was high when he began to read:

"Watch out! Watch out! There's a face that un-
locks
At the fall of noon, en route to the chime,
Between time and water, water and time,
The way to salvation, which lies in a box."

Excitement was low when Richard finished. They had expected to discover the meaning of the poem by the end of the twelfth line, but that expectation was clearly dashed by the enigmatic ending.

Cathy passed around more apple slices. Everyone munched and mulled thoughtfully, but no one had a solution to the problem at hand. After much discussion, they all agreed that the poem did mean something, but they did not know what; and they concluded that, yes, it had something to do with a will and, yes, the twelve lines formed the essential clues.

"Ornery bugger," Hank muttered, adding a hasty, "Beggin' your pardon, ladies. He's teasin' us with the still," he continued, "jes' like he's teasin' Clive with the watch. I knowed it yesterday, and I know it now, putting all this mess together. The cussed old coot hid that still years ago. No one's ever been able to find it, and it ain't been for lack of tryin'. Now he writes us a blessed poem—him knowin' some of us cain't read— and expects us to makes sense of it. Ornery bugger!"

he repeated with some heat and did not excuse himself a second time.

They agreed that the problem lay in what Richard referred to as the "pesky third stanza." Disappointment gathered and hovered among them.

Harris chose his moment. He did not shift his position, but suddenly he was part of the group, whereas the moment before he had not been. "Read the poem to me all over again," he requested.

Richard obliged him, and Harris listened impassively. When Richard came to the end of his recital, Harris asked, "And where did the uncle live?"

The glum mood of the group was now in tune with George's current disposition, so he felt moved to participate. "On a scrap of land," he said morosely, "just like he said in his lines to me."

"In a tumbledown shack," Richard added.

"A sorry shack," Orin agreed.

"Even sorrier'n where Boy lives," Hank informed him.

"But he had a good still," Orin mentioned, not for the first time.

"And a fine watch. Oh, yes, a very fine watch," Clive put in. "You see, my lines say, 'Watch out! Watch out!' Old Hitch is teasin' me with his watch."

Harris summed up the information he had assimilated so far. "Miss Cathy has the reference to apples, the Boys have the still, Miss Ginger has the key, George Travis has the scrap of land, Clive Smith has the watch and Richard Freeman has salvation in a box." To the nodding heads, he asked next, "Where is the uncle's scrap of land?"

He was informed that it was over yonder behind Cathy's orchard and down the slope.

"I think we should visit the uncle's property," he said.

"Visit Old Hitch's shack?" Hank asked. "But there ain't nothin' there!"

"I won't know that until I see it," Harris replied.

Something in his calm manner made his absurd idea to go to Old Hitch's seem reasonable. They all looked at each other, then at Miss Cathy.

Cathy was far from enthusiastic, but could not think of a reason why they should not go. "I was with Old Hitch until the end on Friday morning, and I don't recall seeing anything unusual, so I didn't have a thought to return to his place since," she said. Then she shrugged. "But why not? Perhaps one of you will find something there that I missed."

At that, they began to clean up after themselves. Ginger gathered the lemonade glasses and stacked them on the window ledge beside the front door. The Boys took the pitcher of lemonade and distributed the remains into the bowls for Aunt Rachel and Black Twig that were stationed permanently on one of the side porches. George shoved his hands into his pockets and walked down the steps in the company of the postman, who declared himself the leader. Cathy took up the tray of apple slices.

Harris followed Miss Cathy, catching up with her when she was halfway around the house. "Are you taking this to the uncle's?" he asked with a nod at the tray.

She shook her head. "I'm taking it to the storeroom around back."

They turned the corner of the house, and Harris saw a rough, narrow wooden structure that ran the length of it to the back door. Cathy explained to him that this was her special room. Because her hands were full with the tray, Harris unbarred the planked door and opened it for her.

He stepped behind her into the little windowless storeroom, which was fresh and fragrant with the smell of apples. He watched her empty the apple slices from the tray into a wooden box lined with cheesecloth. While she slid the tray onto a shelf above the box, he looked about with great interest.

She turned back to him and smiled. "When you asked me last night to name my most valuable possession, I should have said this storeroom. It's more important, in a way, than my orchard, because this is where I keep my apple seeds." She pointed to the rows of burlap bags on the rough shelves, each bag sitting above a neatly written note card stating the variety.

She continued, "Now, here are the barrels of apples for eating raw and for frying and for making pies. Here are some kegs of cider pressed last fall and siphoned off in March. And, of course, this is the best feature of this room," she said. She was pointing to a row of slatted wooden vents that lined the wall that was adjacent to the house. "If I think there is a hard freeze coming in the winter, I open these vents so that warmth from the kitchen seeps into this room. At the same time, the perfume from the storeroom comes into the house, and it is heavenly."

"And what do you do with the seeds?" he asked.

"I sell some, I give some away to children at Christmas and I plant some. Mostly I store them." She laughed at herself. "I must have a hoarding streak, because I measure my wealth by the size of my apple-seed bags."

He nodded and commented, "You're rich."

She nodded in return. "I am."

She sighed, and they left the storeroom. Harris barred the door behind them, and they set off across the backyard, trailing along behind the others.

From their position at the rear of the straggly procession, they witnessed a little drama going on ahead of them. George, who was walking in the lead with Clive, would turn his head every now and then to look at Miss Ginger, who was walking in the company of the Boys. George's face was a study in pain and indecision. He clearly wished to be beside Miss Ginger. He clearly feared making the attempt to drop back to speak to her. He even more clearly desired to hide his feelings, evident from one glance at his expression. He was looking back with increasing frequency, increasing indecision, increasing desire to be with his beloved.

Cathy started forward. Harris guessed what she intended to do and put a restraining hand on her arm.

She looked up at him in surprise.

He shook his head. "You must let them work the problem out by themselves."

Her expressive face registered comprehension. "But it will be so much easier," she explained, "if I simply bring them together, which is what they both so obviously want.''

"Just as it was easier for you to rid me of the swaggering braggarts than it would have been for me to take care of them myself?''

She made a face of displeasure. "Do you mean to throw that wretched incident in my face at every moment?''

"No, only when it is relevant.''

"This is different! George and Ginger are so . . . so helpless and so made for one another. It is more than I can stand for them to be miserable, you see.''

"Their misery won't hurt them,'' he said. He derived a curious pleasure from witnessing his ungoddesslike goddess attempt to manage everything and everyone in her earthly realm, and so asked in his gravest tone, "Now, what do you plan to do about the tiresome woman's rival?''

"Miss Sylvia?''

He nodded. "That is the one. Do you mean for her to be left . . . what is the word?''

"Jilted?"

"Yes, *jilted.*'' He looked down at her. "Have you considered her feelings, then?''

"I have,'' Cathy said seriously, looking up at him. A frown of concentration marred her brow. "And it is a difficult problem, I assure you, to know what to do with her. Last night, I was considering several eligible men who might replace—'' She broke off, and her serious expression was transformed into an extremely knowing one.

He felt again that lightening in his breast when he looked at her, and he wondered why she was popularly considered plain. She was no beauty, but her expressive face was anything but plain. "You were considering several eligible men?" he prompted politely.

She would have none of it. Instead, she accused, "You're trying to *save* me again, aren't you?"

Chapter Ten

Cathy was not fooled by his look of innocent denial. Although she thought he did a remarkably good job of keeping his face straight, she did not miss the twinkle deep down in his eye.

"Oh, yes, you are," she insisted. "You're trying to save me from myself, I suppose, and reform all of my interfering ways." She quickly held up a hand to stop him from speaking, although it was pretty clear to her that he had no intention of opening his mouth. "Not that I am admitting that I interfere in other people's lives. Not at all! Rather, I make their lives easier, you see, and—and facilitate what would happen naturally anyway." She was rather pleased with that turn of phrase. "Besides," she went on, somewhat spoiling her effect, "it just *slays* me to stand by, doing nothing."

"You'll get used to it."

"How is that?"

"Look ahead."

She directed her attention to the rise of the slope, where George had stopped to wait for Ginger to catch up. It looked as if Ginger was going to pass by him without deigning to notice him, much less speak to him, but then he said something to her, and she checked her step. She cast him a glance—the exact character of which was not discernible at such a distance—but she did not pass him with a flounce or seem as if she objected to what he had said. Neither did she linger at his side, but turned away to continue her progress up the slope. However, only a fool would have failed to recognize in that turning away an invitation to follow. George was certainly lovesick, but he was no fool. He followed.

"Good boy!" Cathy said approvingly, when George began to walk several respectful paces behind his ladylove. She turned to Mr. Harris. "But don't think that my work is finished! There is still Mrs. Travis to be won over."

"And the problem of the tiresome woman's rival," he added.

"Much you care about Miss Sylvia," she reprimanded him, "and I am finding it very difficult to ever have a serious conversation with you, sir!" She tapped him playfully on the arm. "Since you care nothing for the tender emotions of my dearest friends—and, in all fairness, why should you?—let us turn our attention to the more-immediate puzzle of Old Hitch's letters. Now, here is what I am thinking he probably had in mind and what we should do—"

He interrupted with a very definitive, "We will know what he had in mind once we've solved the puzzle, and we will know what to do once we are on his property."

Cut off midsentence, Cathy had to catch her breath. Then she swallowed his meaning, and the next breath of air up from her lungs was accompanied by a puff of self-deprecatory amusement. "You really *are* trying to reform me, aren't you? I imagine that you are guessing that I would like nothing better just now than to run through all possible interpretations of Old Hitch's poem along with our various options for action. Well! Let me tell you, sir, that I refuse to give you the satisfaction of proving you right! So I will say nothing more on the score of Old Hitch. Nothing!'' She paused and added for good measure, ''Nothing at all!''

She folded her lips together so that she could not speak and looked up at him. She tried to look triumphant, but was unable to maintain any sort of dignified expression because of the laughter bubbling up her throat and the unspoken words dancing devilishly on her tongue. The look in his eye as he watched her struggle did not improve her composure.

Finally, she had to gasp for air and to laugh. ''Oh, you!'' She reprimanded him again with another playful tap on his arm.

This time he caught her hand in his larger one and diverted their course up the slope. Guiding her along behind him, he headed straight into a thicket of pine trees scattered liberally with dogwood and redbud. Although the day was not particularly hot, it was fresher and more pleasant among the trees than it had been on the open slope. The mat of pine needles on the forest floor felt very good to the soles of her bare feet.

She looked up into the green canopy above their heads, where the branches of the tall pines intersected at odd angles and where thistle birds, redstarts and squirrels pitched jovially. The sun broke through in places and cast mottled patterns of gold against the greens and browns.

"Dare I ask where we are going?" she wondered aloud, then debated the point with herself. "Now, if I ask, I will be told that I pose a foolish question. If I don't ask, I deprive myself of hearing the explanation of why we are traveling this unusual route."

Harris did not turn around. "If you must speak, tell me where your property ends and the uncle's begins."

She had never thought about the question of property lines. When she answered, "I don't know," she felt the pressure of his hand on hers. She thought, How remarkable it is that I can tell what he thinks just by his altered grip. "Of course, you think my ignorance is absurd, but I don't know simply because the lines between Old Hitch's property and mine have never mattered one way or the other. Now to answer my own question about where we are going, I suppose you never take an established route when you can blaze a trail of your own. I do hope you know where you're going, but I don't know how that would be possible."

She could have commented liberally on any number of topics just then: The gentle loveliness of the afternoon; the way he was making her see her native ground in a wholly new way; why she really was not as talkative as he thought; the unusual effect his guardianship was having on her. She did not feel like speaking, however, for she was settling into the pleasurable silence of their togetherness as they traveled through the trees. She was aware of him, companionably so. She felt comforted by him, too—by the strength that communicated itself through his hand. It was a further pleasure to her to sense that he was happy in his element and at one with his surroundings.

Then two things happened at once. He stopped abruptly; she stumbled against a tree root hidden beneath a mound of pine straw and collided with his back.

He turned and automatically caught her forearms to brace her against a possible backward fall. The intimacy of the embrace and the rush of feeling it caused from her knees to her neck made her instantly forget the pain of her stubbed toe. She also forgot the sense of companionable comfort in his presence. She felt instead a heated flush of a new kind of awareness of him and his body. It was that new-tenant, half-moved-in feeling come to life. The warm breezes lazing through the trees became suddenly very warm.

His gaze came down to focus on her slowly, as if he had been looking far away. His features registered at first mild surprise that he was holding her in his arms, then shaded into something entirely different, and a look came into his eyes that she had never seen in a man's eyes before. Despite her inexperience with such looks, she did not have to be told that he desired to kiss her. In the dark mirror of his eyes, which gave back the reflection of her face in miniature, she was almost able to see herself as he saw her.

She lost the ability to breathe normally. Her heart misbehaved. Excited, frightened, confused and certainly not mistress of the occasion, she did the only thing with her lips that she knew to do.

She spoke. "Why did you stop just now?" Her voice was shaky. She hoped he did not notice.

He might have been bending his head down to kiss her. Then again, he might not have been, and she might have imagined that he checked slightly in his movement. His brow furrowed minimally, as if he was having difficulty recalling, then smoothed again. He cocked his ear. "I heard a new bird," he said. "I was interested to learn its call."

He continued to hold her next to him, not moving. The smile deep down in his eyes seemed to touch his lips. The sounds and silences of the forest embraced her as thoroughly as his arms. She heard the scurry of squirrel paws on the branches, the flutter of bird wings and the whispered shifting of small animals burrowing in the earth. She could almost hear his heart beat against her breast.

There came another call, high up and far off. The answer was closer by but still high up.

He put his lips together and whistled in imitation. He was dissatisfied by the result. "Do you know the bird?"

She waited a few more moments until the bird sang again. "That's the yellow warbler. It loves orchards and upland groves and comes from the south in the middle of April. Around these parts it's called the apple-blossom bird."

He tried the call again, with enough success to receive another bird's response. He quirked his brows with satisfaction, and his eyes held the glint of smugness that she was beginning to find irresistible.

What kind of heavenly angel is this, then, to make me feel so much of this earth? she wondered dreamily. The answer, dispelling her dream, was that he was no angel, but a man of flesh and blood. One who had both a history and a past. One who spoke the languages of man and of animals. One who wished to kiss her. One who—

He bent his head toward her again, a minimal movement, almost inquisitive, certainly seductive.

One who had no real business being here in Hillsborough, holding her in his arms, wishing to kiss her.

"Who are you?" she asked, breathless, fearful, wondering. She felt as if she were back with him in the orchard, at the beginning—but not quite where they had started.

He was so close to her, she could see the way his dark eyes came back into focus. "I have told you," he said slowly, not quite understanding.

She drew away from him a little. "You must have another name. A Huron name," she said.

"It is Tohin-ontan."

"What does that mean?"

He had difficulty interpreting the question.

"In English."

"Ah. It means—" he searched for the word "—Bird of Fire. Fire bird."

Her eyes were drawn to the old copper scars at his neck that slid into the collar of his shirt. "You are not an angel, are you?"

He had no difficulty with that one. He shook his head and said, "No, I come from hell."

Her first thought was, So Old Hitch *did* send him! Her second thought was, That's crazy! Despite his dramatic statement, she still did not fear him or think that he would do her harm. She feared, rather, how she felt next to him like this, surrounded by his arms and the warm forest breezes and the sounds and silences of spring. She feared her desire to yield to temptation, to taste the fire he apparently knew so well.

Caught between temptation and fear, she drew back from him a little more. At the same time, he must have realized what he had been about to do, because he drew back, too. A look of defenseless surprise came over his face, and that was just as quickly replaced by a look—she might have been wrong—that suggested he wished to kiss her still. She was confused and did not know whether he meant to release her or draw her closer.

However, before he made a definitive gesture either to end the embrace or to complete it with a kiss, they heard a volley of human calls coming from just beyond the edge of the woods.

"Are they behind you?" hollered Hank.

"Don't see 'em!" returned a voice from farther away, probably Clive's.

"Well, where in the blame world could they have gone?" Hank asked.

"Disappeared, seemingly!" Clive called back.

"Gotta protect our womenfolk from strangers!" Orin said. His voice was nearer. "Hank! Boy! Come with me to find 'em!"

Boy had something to say about that. "No, siree. That man can shoot a copperhead between the eyes at twenty paces in the dark!"

No immediate response to that statement was audible.

After a lengthy pause, Hank pointed out, "He ain't carryin' his bow and arrows now!"

"We'll wait for 'em!" Orin suggested cheerfully. "They'll be along!"

Cathy looked up at the expression on Harris's face and suppressed a laugh, but she could not contain a smile. She was glad for this absurd passage, because it seemed to break the uncomfortable tension that had arisen between them.

With a bemused shake of his head, Harris dropped his hands from her forearms and took her hand again in his. He did not say anything, merely looked around to get his bearings, then forged on in the direction of the voices.

Not too many paces later, they emerged from the woods onto a scruffy meadow that sloped up and away to Cathy's orchard and down toward another group of trees bordering a stream. Dotting the slope were the rest of the reconnaissance party. Orin was standing near the edge of the meadow nearest the woods. Hank and Boy and Richard had almost reached the meadow, and Clive was behind them. Still only halfway down the slope came Ginger, walking in as grand a manner as if she were strutting around the main square in Raleigh, with George following behind her like a faithful, chastened puppy.

In the center of the meadow stood as rickety a shack as anyone was likely to see. Cathy had been reluctant to return to Old Hitch's. Now she was heartily sorry she had come. When her friend had been alive, the shack had certainly been a disgrace, with its sagging tin roof and droopy front porch, its cockeyed chimney and weather-scarred boards, its rotten shutters and curtainless windows. However, the shack had suited him, had seemed to her as cantankerous a structure as the man who inhabited it. Now it looked deserted and desolate. Dead.

It was at this moment that Old Hitch's death sank in. She felt the loss of her crusty old friend, which she had been deferring since the moment he had died. He had still seemed so alive this morning during the reading of his final statement!

Harris had dropped her hand and was moving forward across the field. She was grateful to be left to herself for a few moments to contemplate her loss and to say a prayer for Old Hitch. She was not left to herself for long. Orin saw her, called to her and waved to the others. She waved back and waded through the weeds to walk with the Boys to the shack. Clive came along with them. Ginger and George brought up the rear.

They approached the shack from the side. When they rounded it to the front, Harris was already there at the first broken step to the porch. He walked up without hesitation, his moccasins making no sound on the floorboards, and strode back and forth across the porch. Then he went to the front door and gave it a creaking shove open. He walked in, then walked out a moment later and gestured for the others to enter.

Since they each privately interpreted Laurence Harris's movements in the light of ghost chasing, they were able to approach the house with easier minds. Their boots clattering on the squeaky, loose boards, the Boys climbed up the steps, speaking in hushed tones so as not to raise the dead and uttering shuddery phrases like "It shore is spooky" and "Do y'all think Old Hitch's spirit has truly found its final resting place?" and "He didn't never like visitors." Clive followed apprehensively, but his concerns were more for this world. He cast eyes upward, as if worried the roof were going to cave in on him.

Cathy hung back a moment, feeling sad, and went over to the ancient sundial, which had sunk unevenly into the clay earth so that it stood at a drunken angle. She absently traced the weathered cracks in the dial's face as she screwed up courage to enter the shack.

Ginger came into view. She was walking around the other side of the house, and Cathy saw her stop near the old well, just visible past the corner of the front porch. Cathy leaned against the sundial, witness to an interesting interaction.

George had come up behind Ginger. His ladylove was still majestically ignoring him and turned away when he approached her. Nevertheless, he addressed some words to her and gestured toward the shack. Ginger looked over her shoulder at the building, shook her head, then turned away again. George shrugged and walked on, coming around the house to the front.

Cathy moved forward to meet him at the front steps. "Making any progress?" she asked.

"She's allowing me to hover within five feet of her," George said, "and that is considerable progress since the festival."

"As good as could be expected," Cathy said. Her smile was kind. "She's coming around."

"But only so far. She wouldn't come in the house with me," George said forlornly.

"Who can blame her?" Cathy replied reasonably. "Watch the second step here. It's broken."

"Thunderation," George complained. "What a mess!"

She and George entered the gloom of the one-room shack, the inside of which perfectly matched the outside. In a far corner was the lumpy old cornhusk-mattress bed in which Old Hitch had died. Cathy had stripped its linens, washed and dried them and put them away, but that was the only change she had wrought in the room. Next to the bed was a night-stand on which stood an oil lamp. In the other corner, next to the fireplace, were some open shelves holding a mishmash of pots and pans and cracked pottery and threadbare dish towels—which Cathy had washed for the last time the week before—along with a table for eating and one chair. To the left of the door was a snarl of rusted farm equipment, hoes and plows and shovels. To the right of the door was an old trunk. There were no other objects in the room.

The Boys, uncertain and certainly uncomfortable, stood in the center of the room, their backs to one another as if they were forming a charmed circle for protection. Clive had gravitated toward a dirty window and was basking in what sunshine penetrated the filthy panes. He was gazing out the window, clearly wishing himself someplace else. Cathy could not blame him. The room felt as lifeless as a corpse and just as inviting. George did not seem to notice a thing. His hands were in his trousers pockets, his head was down and he was scuffing at the dirty floor with his shoe.

Harris had prowled the room and had stopped, finally, at the trunk. Looking down at it meditatively, he asked, "Does anyone know the contents?"

Cathy volunteered the information that she had never once during her lifetime seen Old Hitch open that trunk and surmised that it was empty. Neither George nor the Boys had anything at all to say about Old Hitch's trunk. Clive asked whose idea this had been, anyway, to come to this tomb.

"Mine," Harris replied easily.

"Creepy place," the postman said, muttering something that sounded like "no accounting for the tastes of a man from Maryland."

Harris applied himself to the catches of the trunk. He discovered that they were locked, but also old, and he had them jimmied open in no time. When he lifted the lid, a vast colony of moths escaped, along with enough of a musty odor to make him take a step back. He fanned the air a bit before he moved forward to peer into the trunk. His very long and thoughtful "Hmm" brought Cathy to his side.

She looked down into a trunkful of old clothes. Very old clothes. From the previous century, in fact. She reached out and with two fingers lifted the item on top to inspect it. It was an old-fashioned coat, long and whaleboned in the skirts, of a now-very-ragged mulberry velvet. Harris extracted a once-white shirt, severely yellowed, with a froth of lace at the wrists. An extravagant lace jabot, in tatters, hung around its collar. He next pulled up a box, opened it unsuspectingly, and fell to coughing from the cloud of fine white powder that escaped.

When he recovered, Cathy said, "That's a pounce box, I suspect. Hair powder."

He put the box back, while Cathy examined a pair of old buckled shoes that were wrapped in cloth and resting atop a pair of mulberry velvet knee breeches and small clothes. She put the shoes back and rummaged through the rest long enough to confirm her suspicion that clothes, and only very old clothes, filled the trunk.

"These are the uncle's?" Harris asked.

"They must be," Cathy said. "They are at least fifty years old, if not more, and were probably his as a young man."

Harris reached for the coat that Cathy had originally handled and held it up next to his frame. "He was tall?"

Cathy nodded. "Yes, about as tall as you, I would say. When he was younger, that is. He was stooped over in the last years, of course."

Harris eyed the garment critically. "A taste for finery runs among Hitchcock men, it seems."

Cathy frowned at the comment. "Excessive frills were the style at the time, you know." She considered the coat and the shirt in the trunk. "Although I think that even for those days, these must have been fancy clothes indeed. It is hard to imagine Old Hitch all dressed up!"

Harris put the coat back and flipped through the deeper layers, as Cathy had done.

When he was finished, Cathy said, "No clues here."

He straightened and dusted his hands. "Not to the mystery of the letters, at least," he agreed, closing the lid.

The moment the musty, moth-eaten past was shut away, a spine-tingling jingle-jangle rippled through the room. The eerie tinkling suggested a moody ghost's harp or the uncanny clink of chains, ones that might be worn by an unhappy, restless spirit.

When the open door creaked and swayed as if with the passing of an unseen force, someone whispered in a wavery voice of terror, "Old Hitch has come to git us!"

Chapter Eleven

The Boys bolted, as one, for the door. Clive was not far behind. It took some squeezing and pushing before all five men tumbled through the door, whereupon they shot across the porch and did not stop until they were beyond the sundial in the meadow. George, roused from his abstraction by the clattering of boots, looked up and figured it was time to go. He, too, left the shack.

Harris saw that Miss Cathy was looking at the door and wearing an expression of wry amusement on her face. She put her hands on her hips and said, "Wouldn't Old Hitch have relished this moment! I am *truly* sorry he was not here to see it. To imagine grown men frightened by a bunch of old spoons hanging from the porch!"

"Old spoons?" he echoed in interest. "I thought I saw some pipes hanging from the edge of the porch roof when I first came."

Harris led her outside to the porch and glanced over at the group gathered around the sundial, which now included the tiresome woman. He could see that she was being regaled by the Boys with vivid accounts of the haunting of the uncle's shack. He noted with faint contempt that her weak-willed lover was standing next to her, supporting her in her emotion and holding her parasol. He himself would not stoop to such tactics to win the woman he wanted and did not think he would desire a woman who would respond to them.

His immediate goal, however, was the inspection of what he had thought were pipes. He walked to the edge of the porch and looked up at the old spoons that were hanging from the metal rim of a small wheel. He gave them a tap so they tinkled again softly, reproducing the sound that had been heard in the shack. Then he turned his head to the right, toward the group gathered around the sundial in the meadow, to the left toward the well, then back to Miss Cathy, who was eyeing the dangling spoons speculatively.

With a note of hushed excitement in her voice, she smiled and said, "Why, the *chimes!* But of course!"

Suddenly he *knew,* and it was a rich, double knowing. He knew why a plain, talkative, bossy young woman should be turning him upside down and inside out; he knew the solution to Old Hitch's poem.

He had been confused by the recent, brief episode in the woods, when his mission in Hillsborough had lost focus, when he had wanted to kiss his ungoddesslike goddess more than he desired saving her from any danger. Holding her in his arms, he had felt that boyish wanting again, the young man's hunger for a woman that he had felt the evening before. This second time, however, it had been stronger and was leavened by the feeling of lightness he felt when he was with her. With her arms on his, with her body standing fully against his, her lips close to his, that lightness had expanded into an enchantment. A liberation.

He felt freed from the old anger that had always kept him strong with men and aloof from women.

He was surprised by the absence of the anger and, at the same time, had felt frighteningly defenseless by its absence. He had wanted to draw back from the potent new emotions he was feeling but could not name, but the wanting was still stronger than the surprise or fear. He was struck by the realization that if the protection of his anger was not there, then neither was the barrier of it. For the first time in his life, he might have acted on that wanting, to see where it would take him.

Then the Boys had started yelling something absurd, Miss Cathy had smiled and the moment had been lost. He had not understood that episode any more than he had understood why his faithful, monstrous anger should have deserted him at so critical a moment. Now, however, at Miss Cathy's exclamation, his confusion was swept away as easily as a cobweb. His mission became clear again, as clear to him as the message in the uncle's mysterious poem. *See what you see,* the old man had recommended. *Keep it simple!* his own instincts advised.

"Didn't the chimes figure in Old Hitch's poem?" Cathy was asking. Her eyes were still fixed above his head. Her brow was furrowed in concentration. Her lips—which smiled easily and often—were pressed into an unlovely line.

He applied the uncle's recommendation and his own advice to the mystery that was Miss Cathy's effect on him. So he saw what he saw, and discovered—keeping it simple—that he liked her. Just that. Only that. Particularly that. Liking.

It was a wholly new experience for him.

"Yes," he said. He gestured toward the sundial. "There's the time, and there—" he gestured toward the well "—is water."

Cathy's face lit with comprehension and appreciation. "And you are standing under the chime, between time and water, water and time."

He nodded. "Now all that remains to be verified is the probable direction of the sundial's shadow at noon, for that must be 'the face that unlocks'."

"Very good!" Cathy exclaimed enthusiastically.

They walked together toward the group gathered around the sundial and swept them aside unceremoniously. They proceeded to discuss the path of the sun, which indicated that it was far past noon, and came to rapid agreement that, yes, of course, the shadow at noon would point straight at the line of the chime and then on to the well.

Their audience had ceased speaking and were understandably drawn to ask what in the world the two were talking about.

Cathy gestured toward Mr. Harris with a flourish and said, "He is the one who had the idea, and he is the one who should get credit for explaining."

Harris replied simply:

"Watch out! Watch out! There's a face that unlocks
At the fall of noon, en route to the chime,
Between time and water, water and time,
The way to salvation, which lies in a box."

Richard understood immediately. "The pesky third stanza! Why, I'll be durned, you're right!"

The others, not as quick, required a fuller explanation. When they got it, Boy fixed his line of sight on the corner of the porch and the well yonder. He shook his head and said, "I don't see no box."

"We'll have to dig it up, I reckon," Harris said.

"That's forty feet to dig," Orin objected—naturally enough, for he was in a weakened state from not having eaten in nearly an hour.

"The uncle was not a complicated man," Harris replied. "My guess is that he made the exact location of the box as simple as his poem. Let's pace off the distance between the sundial and the well and begin to dig at the midpoint."

It sounded like a good plan to the Boys and Clive, and Harris led the way back into the shack for some shovels he had seen by the door. George offered to fetch Miss Ginger a seat and put it on the edge of the porch so that she could watch the proceedings. He even volunteered to hold her parasol in case the sun should shift and shine on her as she watched. He pointed out, apologetically, that he was still wearing his church clothes. He did not need to add that he wanted to spare himself the good scold he would receive from his fond mama if he returned home with dirt on them.

Not too many minutes later, the distance had been paced off. Harris, Hank and Richard, shovels in hand, proceeded to dig at the midpoint between the sundial and the well, which was not too far from the side edge of the porch.

Cathy hovered near them, excited by the prospect of solving the mystery, and felt her romantic heart racing at the prospect of discovering a hidden fortune in jewels or the diary of a life's lost love. She was also looking forward to the end of this odd adventure, because that meant Mr. Harris would be moving on and she could go back to her normal, peaceful life. As much as he had been helpful to her, she was beginning to find his presence distinctly uncomfortable.

Presently the sound of a shovel chinking against wood claimed everyone's attention and brought George from Ginger's side to where the men were by then digging the dirt away from a buried box with their hands.

Richard liked the symmetry of "burying Old Hitch in a box this morning and digging up one he buried this afternoon."

Orin, for his part, noted with disappointment that the homely little box was "way too small to contain the still."

The rough box was raised and placed without question in Harris's hands. With an understated sense of the dramatic, he held the box up briefly and paused just long enough for his audience to catch its collective breath and for Hank to urge, "Open the durned thing!"

He opened it and ended the suspense by laying it on the ground for all to see its contents.

There were two items, individually unremarkable, but together unexpected and rather touching, in an ornery sort of way.

The topmost item was, sure enough, Old Hitch's fine gold watch. Clive came over and held it up by its thick gold chain. There was a note with his name on it attached, which he read aloud: "'Since you've been all-fired itchin' for me to turn up my toes and push up the daisies so as you ken have my watch, here it is.'" Clive choked up and tears came to his eyes when he said, "That's the nicest thing Old Hitch ever said to me or did for me." He hugged the watch to his breast, and Cathy hugged him.

Next came a book, bound in sober black leather. It was, apparently, the Hitchcock family Bible. Richard's eyes widened when he saw it. Reverently, hesitantly, he stretched his large hand down toward the volume and drew it to him. Then he passed it to Clive, who was standing next to him. "Open it and read what it says inside," he requested. "I cain't bear to look."

Clive opened the cover and read: "For Richard. 'Cuz he ken read and them other Boys cain't, and 'cuz I won't be needin' this where I'm goin'. Ha, ha.'"

Clive handed the Bible to Richard. He hugged it, and Cathy hugged him.

"Well, that's right nice, Richard," George said and shook the big Negro's hand. "You wantin' to be a preacher and all."

Richard, speechless at first, smiled broadly. "It's why I learned to read! And now I have the Good Book!" He raised his eyes heavenward. "Praise the Lord!" he exclaimed in rich, round tones. He looked down at the ground. "And bless Old Hitch—wherever he is!"

There was one more item that was now uncovered by the removal of the Bible. Harris reached down and took that out, too. It was a plain sheet of paper, unfolded. He passed it to Clive.

Clive scanned it, then looked up. "Well, don't that just beat everythin'! Old Hitch jes' couldn't be content with a nice gesture. Noo. He's had to scold us one more time." The postman did not have to be invited more than once to read:

"Roses are red. Violets are blue,
If you came here first, I'm smarter than you.
Roses are red. Your poem's a sonnet.
Now don't that just put a bee in your bonnet?"

The Boys, Clive, Ginger, George and Cathy greeted these four lines with exasperation, puzzlement, downright irritation and a good deal of criticism for Old Hitch's wretched poetry. Harris remained thoughtful. Richard began to laugh.

"What's so durned funny?" Hank demanded.

"It's a *sonnet!*" Richard exclaimed, still laughing. "Old Hitch *is* smarter'n us! I cain't believe it."

Hank was more than fed up and not only because Old Hitch had given away his watch and his Bible but not his still. "We know it's a durned—no, a *gol-durned* sonnet, gol-durnit! And I *won't* be excusin' myself to the ladies. What's so gol-durned funny?"

Richard had to wipe the merriment from his eyes. "You see," he said to his quite-captive audience, "a sonnet has *fourteen* lines, and we've been working with only twelve. Old Hitch is tellin' us that we're missin' the last two lines!"

Back on Cathy's porch, the afternoon shadows had lengthened and speculation was deep about who had received the other two lines. With Ginger and Cathy seated on Sally Gray and the menfolk lounging at various places along the porch railing, many names were advanced, but only one kept reappearing: Young MacGuff.

Cathy was listening in silence to the arguments for and against Young MacGuff being the seventh recipient of the verses from Old Hitch. Of course, Clive's testimony that Old Hitch's nephew had received two letters from his uncle the week before was compelling. The first was surmised to have been the call to return to Hillsborough. The second must have contained the sonnet's final lines. It was, furthermore, fitting that Young MacGuff should receive the final lines, being Old Hitch's rightful heir and all.

"That is, if'n there *is* anything more to inherit," Hank interpolated glumly, "other than the watch and the Bible."

Harris had been quiet during this discussion. Now he said, "The uncle did not go to all this trouble for nothing."

That observation perked everyone up and fired the group with a determination to seek out Young MacGuff at the first opportunity—why, now was a good time, what with the funeral being over and the reception at the rectory no doubt finished as well—and ask him whether he had received two strange lines in the mail from his uncle.

The question arose whether Young MacGuff still had his rooms with Mrs. Hortense Smith, who had always treated him like the son she had never had. Clive confirmed that this was so. Hank volunteered to head the party that would wander on over to Granny Smith's.

Harris entered the discussion again. "I think he should be asked, of course," he said, "but perhaps not by a whole group. He should be approached in a gentle manner, this being a grievous time for him."

Orin began, "Why, shoot! Young MacGuff didn't give a hoot—"

"Yes, a grievous time," Harris continued serenely, "when he would wish for his feelings to be consid-

ered, to be handled delicately." He turned to Hank
and smiled slightly. "Do you think that you could
manage it?"

"Ask him delicate? Considerin' his feelin's?" Hank
echoed skeptically. "Don't think so, and don't see yer
point, seein' as how Young MacGuff was a care-
for—"

Again he was cut off. "No matter what his manner
was before his uncle's death," Harris said, "I certainly noticed how sober it was this morning. I think,
under these unusual circumstances, that we should
approach him . . . delicately, as I said."

No one had paid much attention to Young Mac-
Guff's manner this morning. Richard was frankly
uninterested, more concerned about thumbing
through the Good Book and moving his lips as he read
his favorite passages. Clive, too, was preoccupied with
snapping open and closing the lid on his watch, listening to the steady *tic-tic* at his ear, rubbing his chin
against the smooth gold of the back and playing with
the chain. Ginger still felt too sulky to care.

George and the Boys, on the other hand, had great
interest in figuring out the rest of the sonnet. Each
agreed with Harris that Old Hitch must have had a
reason for setting up this strange scavenger hunt. Each
entertained some mighty unpleasant thoughts concerning Young MacGuff. Each gave serious consideration to Harris's suggestion that the direct approach
was hardly the best where the wily Young MacGuff
was concerned.

Cathy's thoughts concerning the young man were
not unpleasant, but she, too, was beginning to see the
quiet man's ploy. She recalled her conversation with
Young MacGuff the night before, after they had fin-

ished their dance. He had acknowledged receiving two letters from his uncle. The first had made him doubt that Old Hitch's death was truly imminent, he'd said; the second had convinced him he should take his uncle at his word. If MacGuff had wished to confide that the second letter was an odd one, consisting of only two lines that were impossible to interpret, he would have done so most naturally at that moment. Thus, she did not think he would divulge the contents of it now, simply by being asked.

She felt uneasy at the trend in her thoughts. However, she could not locate the source of her unease, for beyond the Bible and the watch and possibly the still, nothing in particular seemed to be at stake. "I think that Mr. Harris is right," she said.

"You think Young MacGuff is holding out on us, too?" Hank asked.

"Not exactly holding out on us," she said, trying to convince herself that MacGuff was interested only in preserving his privacy. "But I agree with Mr. Harris that it would be...impolite to simply up and ask him, direct, the contents of his personal correspondence from his uncle."

Hank cracked a knowing smile. "Then have Miss Ginger ask him indirect. Real nice and sweet," he drawled, batting his eyelashes.

The Boys thought that Hank's wiles were mighty funny. They hooted and hollered raucously, elbowing one another suggestively.

Harris nodded, straight-faced, and said that Hank's suggestion was, in fact, pretty much what he had in mind. The feminine touch, he declared, was precisely what was needed in this instance.

All eyes turned to Miss Ginger.

George now came alive, fired by a cause. "Well, I won't have it!" he said with force and authority. "I won't have Miss Ginger making eyes at MacGuff and talking nice and pretty to him! Why, everyone knows what a ladies' man MacGuff has always been, and he's liable to take advantage of Miss Ginger's—" here he cast a dramatic and fiercely protective look at the love of his life "—undeniable beauty and sweetness of disposition."

Ginger returned his regard with a glow of happiness at seeing her love take such a strong-willed position.

"Take advantage?" Hank queried, baiting him.

George straightened and said chivalrously, "I will not stoop to describe the precise liberties MacGuff might take, seeing as how we are in the presence of a virtuous young lady."

"We're in the presence of two virtuous young ladies," Boy observed, somewhat hesitantly, because he was not quite sure about this turn in the conversation.

"Why, thank you, Boy," Cathy said with gentle irony, and at that moment all eyes shifted from Ginger to her.

She looked around and her eyes narrowed as she read the frank speculation in the faces of those who studied her, considering her chances with Young MacGuff. Doubt was plain on everyone's face—except Mr. Harris's. He wore a look of faint amusement and challenge. She glanced away from him in order to focus on the rest of her audience. "I see what it is! You're wondering if I am capable of speaking nice and sweet?" She smiled and showed her teeth. "Please, don't spare my feelings!"

They didn't. Serious discussion ensued on the subject of whether Miss Cathy was capable of properly charming young Mr. Hitchcock MacGuffin into revealing the contents of the letters he had received from his uncle. They considered her from this angle and discussed in embarrassing detail her attributes and lack thereof. They were about to abandon the idea when Ginger unexpectedly entered the lists.

Ginger had been warmed by George's spirited and manly defense of her tender virtue. She thought it augured well for a newfound fighting spirit in him that could apply to his future dealings with his mother. In this hopeful mood, she said, "I think Cathy has wonderful possibilities!"

This exclamation was met with unflattering silence.

"Well, I *do!*" she insisted, casting a critical eye over her friend. "Why, her hair could be changed, and only for the better, I think," she continued, speaking as if Cathy were a statue on exhibit, "and her dress...well! I think the material is quite fine, knowing as I do how she bought it at Travis's Dry Goods." She cast a sweet and forgiving look at George, then turned back to Cathy. "Nevertheless, the style does not suit her, and now that I am considering the matter, I must say that blue is not her color! Why, if I take her in hand right now, I am sure to achieve creditable results in no time." She furrowed her pretty brow. "Not *no* time," she corrected judiciously, "but with a little work!"

No one knew whether Cathy's hair could be rearranged for the better or whether or not blue was her color. However, they felt confident that if anyone could achieve results with such unpromising material, Miss Ginger could.

Ginger took her friend by the hand. Speechless for the first time in many years and out of her element, Cathy rose meekly from the porch swing and followed her.

"Now you men wait here while we're busy inside," Ginger said, adding with a flourish of generous hospitality, "but since we might be a while, I suggest that you entertain yourselves with cider and ham and whatever else you want. You know where it all is."

Before the two women disappeared into the house, Hank had a recommendation to make. "While you're at it, Miss Ginger, show Miss Cathy how to make them eyes you just cast at George here when you was talkin' about the merchandise in his store."

Ginger acknowledged Hank's remark with a saucy wink, then crossed the threshold and led Cathy down the wide central vestibule that ran the length of the house, from which radiated the sitting room, dining room and kitchen on the left, and two bedrooms plus a sewing room on the right. Cathy's was the second bedroom.

Once inside, Ginger shut the door behind them and had Cathy strip down to her chemise to reveal her large and generous figure, which was unusually well proportioned. Then she sat her down before the little mirror at the dressing table next to the window. She pulled the pins from the bun at Cathy's nape, coiled the thick, brown length around her arm. She held her hair this way and that, aiming for the most flattering framing of her friend's round face.

Finally, with a cry of inspiration, she retrieved the scissors from the sewing kit atop the chest of drawers, waved away the gulp of protest from her victim— who closed her eyes—and snipped a fringe across her brow. Delighted by the spring of shortened hair, Ginger snipped a few more wisps around the ears. Then she decided to braid the rest and have Cathy wear it over her right shoulder.

When she was finished, Ginger commanded, "Open your eyes, you coward."

Cathy obeyed. When she saw her reflection, she realized that she had been hoping for a miracle. But, no, her nose had not miraculously straightened, nor had her mouth drawn into a Cupid's bow. Nevertheless, she was modestly pleased by her reflection and thought that maybe this was not such a bad idea, after all. Perhaps MacGuff would notice a difference.

"Now for your clothes," Ginger said with determination, drawing Cathy to her feet.

She opened the wardrobe, only to close it again and ask if she owned any clothing that was not blue or pink. "Greens and golds are what you need, to bring out your eyes. Don't you have anything in one of those colors—even a shawl or a ribbon?"

The question jogged Cathy's memory. She remembered her mother's shawl, fringed in gold, and how pretty her mama had always looked in it. Cathy had put the shawl, along with the rest of her mother's clothing, in a box and had stored it under her bed ten years ago. It was easy enough to get the box out and open it to reveal old-fashioned, but otherwise perfect clothing for Cathy, who took after her mother in coloring and size.

Ginger sorted expertly through the gowns, trying various ones on Cathy until she achieved a look she liked. "Perfect," she finally said. "The soft moss green dress with the tiny yellow print is perfect. Now, we'll tie this green sash just so, to give you a waist, and drape the gold-fringed shawl across your arms. Oh, the entire line is lovely! The soft shape becomes you and so, I must say, does the neckline. Now, it's time we went outside to judge the effect of our work.''

Ginger did not belabor the point about the neckline, for it revealed far more of Cathy's full breasts than Cathy herself was aware. Indeed, she was more concerned about her hair and the altered effect it had on her face.

Since she did not own a full-length mirror, she had to content herself with taking one last, critical look at herself in the little mirror at her dressing table. She wondered aloud, "What will they think of my hair?"

Ginger was surveying her friend with satisfaction and replied, "Cathy dear, I predict that they won't even notice your hair."

Chapter Twelve

Ginger was right. At her earlier suggestion, the men had found some hard cider in Cathy's storeroom, using the cups stacked on the window ledge, and had helped themselves to a side of ham—which Harris refused—from the smokehouse. They were noisily discussing the finer points of horses and carriage wheels and loudly disputing various techniques for tossing horseshoes and rolling balls down greens when the two women stepped back out onto the porch. At that moment, the discussion stopped dead, for a full minute at least. Not one of the men noticed Cathy's hair.

Harris's attention perched long enough on Miss Cathy for him to receive forcible impressions of early autumn green and gold and ripe harvest. Beyond those images, however, he could not have described the details of her clothing: Not the wide sash at her waist; the flattering drawstring bodice that gathered softly over ample breasts; the puffy sleeves that buttoned just below the elbows, leaving rounded forearms exposed; the shawl that softly framed the whole, draping over her wrists to grace strong, capable hands.

The feeling of lightness inside him suddenly glowed bright and combined with a hunger that was not restrained. The feeling solidified into something strong and strangely rumbling, tightening his muscles everywhere, particularly those at the corners of his mouth. He felt the familiar wanting, but this time with an intriguing new dimension. He did not know what that new dimension might be, but it was tantalizing enough for him to want to find out. His original mission in Hillsborough expanded to incorporate a goal that would have been unthinkable as recently as the night before, when he had thought it inappropriate, disrespectful even, to imagine the Woman Who Fell From the Sky as a dancing partner.

But that was last night; this was today. His newly defined goal did not seem inappropriate or disrespectful but entirely natural, and Cathy Davidson was the woman he wanted.

A new logic surged through his veins. It was the logic of the wanting without the restraint of the old anger and shame, for a new flame had been struck inside him and was burning clean and bright. It was an extraordinary logic, one of the whole body, that allowed him to dismiss thoughts of the purity of his mission. It was a crafty logic, one bent on seduction. After all, what else was a man to do with an ungoddesslike goddess who fell out of the sky straight into his arms?

He thought it wise, for the moment, to set his attention on a strategic, mid-distance flight. He was in no hurry to pursue his new goal, for he had waited this long—the whole of his adult life, in fact—and he was a man who knew how to bide his time.

Hank was the first one to find his voice. In a hushed, almost disbelieving tone, he said, "This plan jes' might work."

His comment was followed by others of a more directly flattering sort. George complimented Ginger on her good work, and Ginger cast him a shy and extremely effective glance of thanks. Clive said that Cathy looked "fine and just like a lady."

Boy summed up his thoughts with a succinct, expressive, "Ooohh-ee!"

Orin was of the opinion that she did not look so much like a dead fish anymore, but more like an overcoddled.

"An overcoddled?" Hank queried. "You think Miss Cathy looks like a cooked egg?"

Orin looked disgusted. "Not a cooked egg! An overcoddled," he explained with great authority, "is green and tastes buttery. Miss Cathy looks peeled and ripe, just like one of them things." He traced a rounded pear shape in the air with his hands.

Orin's idiocy restored Cathy's wits, which had momentarily fled in the face of so much unaccustomed —and unflatteringly surprised—male admiration. "You mean *avocado*," she corrected, then asked sweetly, "and did you enjoy the ham, Orin?"

"Not salty enough," he replied, licking a greasy finger.

Cathy was about to retort, but then she glanced at Mr. Harris. He was leaning against the corner railing and looking away over her side yard. He was in one of his absent moods. Oddly, she was both relieved and vexed, and the comment she'd been about to make to Orin flew out of her head. The lapse allowed Ginger to take control.

Ginger was pleased with the results of her work and was eager to proceed with Cathy's transformation. "My dear," she said, pointing to the swing, "you will sit down and receive your first lesson in how to speak to a man when you want something from him."

Cathy was still having difficulty taking orders instead of giving them. "I know how to do that," she objected, a little grumpily. However, given the reaction of the men to her new look, she was willing to submit to Ginger's lessons, thinking, Maybe, just maybe, I'll learn how to keep MacGuff in Hillsborough. So she went ahead and sat down.

"You know how to *tell* a man what to do," Ginger said, "which is not at all the same thing. This will be a lesson in speaking nicely and gently. Now, let me see," she said, looking around. "We need a likely man for you to practice with." Her eye first stopped at Hank.

Hank, looking horrified, declined the office. "This plan may work 'n' all, but I'm not a-goin' to give my head to *her* for washing! Why, what if'n she don't take to them lessons, and ends up by tellin' me what to do anyway, without being nice and gentle about it? And I don't care if'n she *does* look better'n I ever seen her!"

"Why, thank you, Hank," Cathy said dryly.

Hank appealed to Ginger. "See what I mean?"

"I said thank-you," Cathy pointed out.

"It was the *way* you said it, Miss Cathy," Hank said. "Made me feel as if I'd said somethin' wrong!"

Ginger silenced Cathy's retort with the brisk comment that she obviously had a lot to learn. "Who's next?" she then asked, but did not find any volunteers.

Boy ducked at her glance.

Richard, feeling her eyes upon him, looked up from his Bible and said, "It wouldn't be right, ma'am," and left it at that.

When she came to Orin, he belched, bringing a swift, "I don't think so!" from Cathy.

Next came Clive, who said a little nervously that he might be more useful timing the lesson. He held up his watch. "To see how quickly she learns and all!"

That left George. From Cathy's point of view, he would have been the most-agreeable and least-embarrassing partner to help her practice unfamiliar feminine wiles. However, just as George had protested Ginger's role in wheedling the letter out of MacGuff, so it was apparent to her that Ginger would object to George playing the role of stand-in lover to another woman, even if it was only to plain-Jane Cathy.

Cathy was partially relieved that the lessons were to come to nothing. "Well, that's it then," she said, about to rise from the swing. "Since there's no one suitable, we may as well just call the whole thing..." She trailed off, seeing the direction of everyone's gaze.

The Boys and George, who were most interested in retrieving the last two lines of the sonnet, were looking at Harris. Apparently feeling all eyes upon him, Harris turned away from the side yard and toward the group. His face was impassive, except for the slight arch of one black brow in response to the speculative gazes upon him. "I was not listening," he excused himself. "Did you want something from me?"

"Mr. Harris," Ginger said as she swept forward. She took his arm and led him toward the swing. Smiling up at him and batting her misty blue eyes, she said in sugared tones, "You've been so helpful to us thus far. Do you think you could exert yourself just a little more with some lessons we're wishing to give Miss Cathy?''

Feeling vulnerable and unsure of herself in this new role, Cathy uttered weakly, ''I don't think Mr. Harris is interested in helping us that far—''

Harris did not apparently hear her, for his voice cut across hers. ''What would you have me do, ma'am?''

''Nothing too difficult,'' Ginger assured him. ''Just sit on the swing next to Miss Cathy.''

With no change of expression, he repeated, ''Just sit on the swing? No, ma'am, that's not too difficult.'' He looked down at Cathy and said politely, ''I like your hair. Did you do something to it?'' Without another comment, he shooed Aunt Rachel off the swing and sat down.

Cathy decided that Mr. Harris knew exactly what was going on, but she was hard-pressed to define the look in his eyes. She knew his smug expression, but this was beyond smug. Eager, maybe. But for what?

She was similarly perplexed by the effect of his presence. The moment he sat down next to her, she noticed that he filled the space in a way that no other man sitting with her on the swing had ever done before—not Old Hitch, certainly, nor Clive, nor George, nor any of the Boys. His immediate effect was to make her aware that the neckline of her dress was far lower than any she had ever worn. She decided that she needed to rearrange the shawl so that it might cover her better.

Harris offered to help, and without waiting for her response, put an arm around her and gently arranged the shawl around her shoulders. Her own fussing with the wrap had caused her bodice to gape forward slightly, and this gave the man seated next to her an excellent view of the expanse of her breasts. She looked up quickly to see him looking down her bodice. Although his eyes did not linger, she felt herself flush.

Hank admired the pink in Cathy's cheeks and said with more conviction now, "Yes, ma'am. This plan jes' might work!"

Cathy pounced on Hank to vent her confusion and embarrassment. "If you don't watch yourself, Hank Wilson," she said, "you'll find yourself seated next to me on this swing, and then you'll be sorry!"

Hank said, "Ouch!" and won an appreciative laugh from the Boys.

Clive held up his watch and said to Ginger, "You've got your work cut out for you, because it took less than fifteen seconds after Harris sat down for Miss Cathy to file her tongue on poor Hank here."

Ginger ignored Hank's and Clive's provocative remarks as well as Cathy's unfeminine outburst. She instructed, "There was your first opportunity, Cathy. When a gentleman helps you with your shawl, what you need to say is 'Thank you kindly, Mr. Harris.'"

Cathy knew she was behaving badly in her embarrassment, but could not help herself. Her response was an immediate and none too kind, "What?"

"'Thank you kindly, Mr. Harris,'" Ginger repeated slowly, as if her pupil had not understood.

"I don't need to say anything like that," Cathy grumbled testily.

"If you choose not to say anything," Ginger continued in an instructive spirit, "you could just give him a look of thanks. Something like this." She fluttered her eyes and composed her beautiful features into a look of melting gratitude.

"You expect me to do that?" Cathy demanded.

"Well, you have to do something," Ginger said reasonably. "You can't just sit there."

"I don't have to do anything!" Cathy replied huffily. "And you're right, I don't have to just sit here, either." At that point, she began to rise.

After helping with her shawl, Harris had settled his arm across the back of the swing. Thus, at Cathy's slightest movement, he was able to grasp her shoulder and keep her seated. "It's for a good cause," he said, unperturbed.

"A lot you know about it," Cathy snapped.

"I am here to help, remember?" Harris said.

Cathy's eyes narrowed. "I know why you're here, and it's...it's absurd! I should have known yesterday afternoon where all this would lead, which is precisely to making me look like a fool, not to mention act like one! Putting on airs! That's what this is all about! And I am beginning to think this is a plot to undermine my authority! I'd like to point out to you, sir, that *I'm* the one who calls the shots around here! Which is something that you had better learn, Mr. Harris, if you're wanting to get along in these parts!"

Ginger looked deeply dismayed and was clearly unable to handle such an unruly pupil.

Boy voiced the thoughts of the men present. "I'm shore glad it ain't me."

Richard muttered a heartfelt, "Amen!"

Harris took the verbal lashing without a blink and even maintained the straightest of straight faces. When Cathy had finished berating him, he said solemnly, "I do not think that this is strategy Miss Ginger had in mind when she suggested that you thank me.''

"Oh, no?" Cathy cried, regarding with him a fiery eye. She was working herself up to a pretty thorough condemnation of his character and his motives since arriving in Hillsborough the day before. "I suppose *you* know what Ginger had in mind—"

She was cut off midsentence when he leaned over and said, "I do, and it is this." Then he put his lips on hers.

She was momentarily incapable of speech. She was surprised, too, for this was the first time, yes, the very first time that she had been kissed *like this,* with a young man's lips upon hers warm, touching, pressuring, inquiring. Before she could register a further reaction, however, Harris moved away from her. Her first, sweet kiss was over.

Hank commented appreciatively, "Never would have thought of kissing her to shut her up."

"Hush, now!" Ginger told Hank. She covered the charged moment for Cathy by saying with a professional air, "Yes, Mr. Harris, that is what I had in mind—*eventually.* I think, however, that you have been too forward for the occasion—not *this* occasion, certainly, for you were merely demonstrating! I commend you for your ready understanding! Now, my point is that, in the right situation, *you* are not supposed to initiate a kiss, but only to react with one if Miss Cathy is sweet enough to you to draw you into it.''

Harris considered this instruction gravely. "Only if she is sweet enough? How do you know that I don't have more of a taste for tart than sweet?"

Ginger took that as a little joke and laughed. "I don't, of course, sir! But just now you are playing the role of Young MacGuff, and *everyone* knows what he likes!"

"I am not so well-informed," Harris said.

"Ah, but that's what we're here to show you," Ginger replied reasonably, "or, at least, we're here to teach Cathy to show you what MacGuff likes."

Boy raised a moral objection. "I thought we weren't s'posed to discuss the liberties MacGuff might take, much less *demonstrate* 'em, seein' as how we're in the presence of two virtuous young ladies."

This comment caused considerable consternation. Hank, with his thoughts on the still, did not want to lose his chance to get at the last two lines of Old Hitch's poem. After giving the matter some thought, he replied, "But that was when George here was referrin' to Miss Ginger. When it comes to MacGuff takin' liberties with Miss Cathy, she ken take care of herself."

Ginger had warmed to her new role as teacher to Cathy and did not want to see it end. She said to Hank, "What we're trying to do is to teach Cathy to make it not so obvious that she can take care of herself." To Boy she said, "You're quite right. We should not take our lessons too far or make Cathy too desirable, so that MacGuff forgets himself and takes those liberties."

No one except Harris really thought there was much danger of that. Then Clive complained that they had wasted a good two minutes on this pointless discussion, and everyone agreed that the lesson should be allowed to continue.

"Now, you're going to begin again," Ginger said.

Cathy was startled. "Begin again?"

"Yes, you need practice thanking Mr. Harris for helping you with your shawl," Ginger explained. "You get no credit for having lured him into that peck—it was not really a kiss! He only did that to keep you quiet. So let's start over. Mr. Harris, please take your arm off the back of the swing." Ginger bestowed a very cordial smile on him when he readily obeyed. "Now, Cathy, you have to try and arrange your shawl again. You see, it is necessary to do so anyway, because it has gone quite askew."

Cathy went through the motions, steadying herself with the practical thought, What can it hurt to learn a few tricks that might keep Young MacGuff in town? She felt Mr. Harris's hand at her shoulder, helping her with the edge of her shawl as he had before, leaning toward her solicitously as he did so. She felt her bodice gape slightly. She felt him looking down her dress. She made the mistake of glancing up at him and was unnerved by the subtle and fleeting look that crossed his features.

Was it eagerness she saw? Then his eyes moved to hers, and her gaze was arrested by his. She felt herself flush again. The flush deepened when she realized how much she *liked* him looking down her bodice and how intriguing she found the look that came over his face. It was like issuing an invitation to a special guest and being sure that he was happy to accept.

Ginger clapped her hands together. "Cathy, the look on your face is perfect! Now what do you say to Mr. Harris, my dear?" she cajoled, as if speaking to a little child.

"Thank you," Cathy said a little breathlessly, feeling herself sinking into the depths of his black, black eyes.

"You are most welcome, ma'am," he replied. "I am here to help, as I have said." Without breaking his regard, he stretched his long legs out in front of him and let his arm rest along the back of the swing so that his hand grazed the shawl at her shoulder.

Cathy had no more doubt about the effect of his presence next to her. She felt herself falling, falling, and when, in her mind's eye, she reached the earth, Laurence Harris was there, lying beneath her, holding her in strong arms. And they were both naked.

She squirmed and uttered in a small voice, "To help?" She faltered. "How kind." She knew that she should have stopped there, but somehow, in her embarrassment, her tongue started running away with her and prattling foolishly.

When she started to dither, Harris leaned over and said that she was wasting a lot of time—that a simple, "How kind" would have done the trick. To demonstrate what he meant, he put his lips on hers again and let them linger. She was surprised again and responded to his eagerness. His arm came around her shoulder, holding her to him, and she could feel his vitality against her breasts, which were pressed to his chest. She was amazed by how very pleasant was the sensation of his lips on hers, of his arm around her. How very pleasurable and intriguing it was, this touching and wanting more....

She heard Hank say, "Well, that shore shuts her up, I declare! Never would have thought of kissing her to shut her up. Never would have tried it, even if I had thought of it!"

... How very public ...

Clive seemed to be timing the proceedings. "Fifteen ... twenty ... twenty-five ..."

Hank again. "You're a brave man, Welshman."

Aunt Rachel yowled.

Then Clive. "Thirty seconds and counting!"

"Ooohh-ee!"

... How very amusing to be kissing a man she hardly knew, to be able to feel the curve of his smile and the unreleased laughter rumbling around inside him. She could not help it. Her lips trembled against his, and she started to laugh, thereby breaking the kiss.

"Thirty-five seconds!" Clive pronounced.

Ginger was frowning. "You are not supposed to laugh, Cathy."

"No?" she replied unsteadily, merriment shaking her. "How could I not laugh?"

"Well, Mr. Harris is not laughing," Ginger pointed out.

Cathy looked into Harris's eyes and saw his laughter, but the rest of his face was remarkably straight. "How *do* you do it, sir?" she wondered.

"Do what?" he returned.

"Not laugh at the most absurd things!"

"I have much more self-control than you do."

"He apparently does," Ginger said, "while you, Cathy, are going to have to learn to control yourself if you want to sweet-talk Young MacGuff. Really! What do you think would happen if you were kissing Young MacGuff, about to have him yield the last two lines to you, and you started laughing? Then where would we all be?"

The thought sobered Cathy enough to make her stop laughing.

Ginger added severely, "I'd ask you to try it again, but I don't think you're in the proper frame of mind." To Cathy's partner, she nodded and smiled. "However, I must compliment Mr. Harris for his fine cooperation. It isn't every man who would step into this awkward situation and take to it so easily! Well! Let us turn our attention to more practical matters and determine how Cathy will get MacGuff to give her his letter, or at least tell her his lines."

Orin offered the obvious plan. "She has to butter him up first," he said confidently. "She should make him supper tomorrow evening—roasted duck and snap peas and mounds of mashed potatoes. My, my, yes, and after serving several helpings of chocolate pie—out on the porch here, with her all-cozy next to him—she should ask him, real sweet, jes' like she was talkin' now to the Welshman before she started to blabber, what Old Hitch wrote in his last letter, and did it say anything about the whereabouts of that still."

George was nodding in approval, up until the final point. "She can't ask him straight out about the still."

"Don't you think of nothin' but food?" Hank demanded.

"Nah."

"But Orin's idea is a good one," George seconded. Because he was feeling guilty about having defended Miss Ginger's virtue, but not Miss Cathy's, against the possible advances of Young MacGuff, he added, "But I don't think she should invite him to supper. It's too forward. Just the midday dinner. It's more proper."

So it was decided. Cathy was to ask MacGuff to her house for dinner on the morrow, and she had to practice the invitation on Mr. Harris several times before she got the right amount of bashful sweetness into her voice. When it was decided that Ginger had done all she could on such short notice and that Cathy would just have to do her best tomorrow, the men began to take their leave.

Cathy got up from the swing, and Harris rose with her.

Upon parting, Ginger instructed, "Now, link your arm through Mr. Harris's as you accompany him to your front gate. You should work it so that you end up holding hands before he leaves." She waved them a cheery goodbye.

Alone now on her front porch with Mr. Harris, Cathy somehow found her hand in his. Following Ginger's instructions, they strolled hand in hand down her walk, under the dogwoods and the spreading veil of the evening. At the front gate, Harris paused and turned toward her. He was looking down at her, his expression less impassive and more lively than she had ever seen it.

Black Twig whisked up to them then, but Harris did not let the dog distract him. He issued a few authoritative commands, causing the hound to sit and thump his tail obediently, and had a few choice words to say to Smokehouse, too, who wandered over in Black Twig's wake. Then, looking over Cathy's shoulder and acquiring a very creditable expression of surprise and opportunity, Harris said seriously, "Here comes Young Cock. It would probably be best to work up his jealousy and give him a bit of an appetite to accept your invitation."

So saying, he gathered her into his arms and kissed her. This was a much different, a more intent and passionate kiss than the one he'd bestowed upon her in front of an audience—or in front of the human audience, anyway, for both Black Twig and Smokehouse were making odd noises, whimpering and bleating at the sight of their mistress in a man's arms.

Soon enough she forgot the presence of her animals and was aware only of the delicious taste of the lips of a man who never ate pork, the strength of his arms, the ripple and shifts in his muscles as he moved this way, that way, blending himself to her, drawing from her a moan and a desire for more. She felt a pleasurable weakening inside her as she caught the scent of his shirt, his hair, his neck. She even became a little tipsy. If it's this good kissing Mr. Harris, she thought, think how wonderful it will be to kiss MacGuff.

The kiss might have gone on for quite a while, except for the fact that Cathy became aware of footsteps approaching—MacGuff's, presumably—then stopping on the other side of her front gate. When she heard the deep and disapproving clearing of a throat, she didn't think the sound belonged to Young MacGuff. She broke the kiss to look beyond Mr. Harris and discovered that Old Man Lloyd was standing there, his expression stern.

She jumped guiltily away from Mr. Harris and wished Mr. Lloyd a too-bright "Good Evening!" Old Man Lloyd grunted and walked on, casting disapproving glances over his shoulder at her every few yards.

Cathy put her hands on her hips. "You mistook Old Man Lloyd for Young MacGuff?"

Harris seemed surprised. "Apparently I did. My eyes must not be as good in the dark as I had thought."

She said, "They are not? Then how was it that just last night, when it was even darker, you were able to shoot a copperhead right between the eyes at twenty feet?"

He shook his head sorrowfully and ventured the explanation, "I suppose that twilight can play more tricks on a man's eyes than darkest night."

Cathy had to shake her head, too, but suppressed a laugh. It was impossible to be angry with a man who smelled so good, who kissed so nicely, who looked so boyishly eager and who told such outrageous lies.

"You're a devil," she said.

He did not dispute the statement. He simply bowed minimally, gave her a look that caused her eyes to widen, and left.

Chapter Thirteen

Cathy awoke the next morning to the faint, promising glow of daybreak. Soft May breezes lifted the wispy lace curtains at the half-open window by her bed. The gentle zephyrs came to curl around her, to caress her, to persuade her to snuggle into pillows scrunched up under her head and breast. She tangled herself further in the sheets and light cotton cover already twisted haphazardly around her legs and waist.

Although those same breezes carried the crow of every rooster in Hillsborough, she ignored the raucous alerts and snuffled sleepily, half dreaming of guardian angels and devils and a feeling of delicious tension. In her semiconscious state, the tension was tightening inside her, and she felt as if it needed to be released by a laugh—a long, glorious laugh that began in the belly and traveled slowly up the throat so that she would have to throw her head back to allow it to escape. Mmm, yes, such a laugh would be wonderful now, as the perfect end to sleep and the perfect beginning to wakefulness. The laugh would have to begin low, in the belly. But, no, not the belly. It would have to begin farther down, below the pit of her stomach. Just a little farther down. Right at the most exquisite spot, such a rare and unexpected discovery. . . .

She awoke with a start and sat up. The glow of daybreak had leapt to full sunrise, and she realized that she had overslept. She lumbered out of bed, feeling languorous, as if her legs were full of honey. Normally, she would dress first, but today she did something different. She felt the short hairs at her forehead and went to her dressing-table mirror to see if yesterday had, indeed, happened. Verifying the existence of her newly cut bangs, she nodded and turned away from the mirror. With her fingers, she combed the bangs back so that they stuck up at odd-angled points. In her thin cotton night rail and barefooted, she proceeded to wander through her house, as if seeing it for the first time.

She was certainly seeing it through new eyes, although they were still groggy and slightly puffy from sleep. She went first into the wide central vestibule that ran the length of the house, admired its proportions and thought, It's odd how I feel that this is the first day of my new life, with Old Hitch dead and buried. She drifted into the sitting room, which welcomed so many friends during the winter months. She glanced out its front window to the front porch, the gathering place of her friends in spring and summer.

She moved on into the dining room, surveyed the generous oval oak table and thought involuntarily, This is where MacGuff and I could serve our friends dinner every Sunday. She shied away from that idea for a variety of reasons and entered the kitchen, where she discovered she was ravenously hungry. This was fortunate, since she had a special midday meal to cook up. She whipped up batter for bread, right there in her night rail, and left it to rise. Then she fixed soda biscuits and apple butter for a makeshift breakfast that she ate while she gathered together her dinner fixings.

When she returned to her bedroom to dress, she wondered why she felt in such an unusual state of transition, as if she could not determine whether she was moving into her house or out of it. Since she had no reason to move out of her house, she decided that she would feel more settled come nightfall, after MacGuff had taken the midday meal with her and she had discovered what she could of the last two lines of Old Hitch's sonnet. That is, *if* she were able to discover anything about them from MacGuff. . . .

The thought led her to consider her choice of dress for the day. All right, she admitted to herself, she had *liked* the sensation of Mr. Harris looking down her bodice. And if she had relished that pleasantly shivery feeling through his eyes, she decided that she would like it all the more through MacGuff's. So she discarded the idea of wearing the more conservative blouse and skirt that Ginger had unearthed from her mother's old wardrobe and pronounced to be "pretty enough." Instead, she opted for the green dress with the low-cut bodice.

When it came to tying the drawstring, she thought, Now what would be the harm if I left it just a little looser than yesterday? She had to laugh at herself and rephrase her question: Now, what would be the *effect* if I left the drawstring just a little looser than yesterday?

She donned her dress, tied it as loosely as she dared and fit the wide sash around her waist. She was about to leave the room when she ran her fingers through her hair and realized that she had not yet combed it. She recalled Ginger's wisdom from the day before that she should try to cultivate a little vanity. She would have to remember to look in the mirror more often, though it had never before been her friend.

Cathy brushed out her bangs, feathering them around her forehead, arranged the springy curls at her ears and experimented with the long fall of hair over her right shoulder. The effect was not bad. She felt emboldened, given Mr. Harris's reaction to her on the swing, to try her wiles on Young MacGuff.

After attending to a variety of light chores in the house, Cathy put her coin purse in her market basket, slipped the handle over her left arm and left by the front door. It was a lovely Monday morning, her spirits were bright and her thoughts raced ahead to weave a variety of charming stories that ended invariably with a kiss from beautiful lips. She harbored a not-so-secret hope that those kisses might be accompanied by several good laughs. She bit her lip and flushed at the thought.

At the corner of Churton and Tryon, heading toward Granny Smith's, where she hoped to find MacGuff, she passed in front of an establishment with a bow window, on the panes of which was painted Lex Kenan, Attorney-At-Law. On an impulse, she entered, and the little bell above the door jingled when she opened it. Although Mr. Kenan's habits were well-known to her—and everyone else in Hillsborough—she had to stifle a gasp at the disorder that surrounded her the moment she stepped into his office.

Cathy eyed askance the half-closed cabinet drawers spitting forth foamy waves of paper, the gateleg table that ran the length of one wall, groaning under the weight of folders and documents, the floor piled with haphazard towers of more folders and books taken down from the shelves. And those shelves! The bookcase on the wall opposite the table had not a single row of books in place. Instead there were gaping holes, like missing teeth, on all the shelves, where legal tomes should have been. Those tomes seemed to be here, there and everywhere, opened at random or buried under further papers.

At the jingle of the bell, a bespectacled head raised and a pair of curious eyes looked up over the rolltop desk. The thin man rose and came out around the desk, an inquiring look on his nervous face. He squinted at his visitor, and when a surprised and admiring recognition dawned across his features, Cathy felt a burst of confidence for the outcome of the day.

"Miss Cathy?" Mr. Kenan queried in a hesitant voice. "Is that really you?"

"It is I, Mr. Kenan," she answered pleasantly, liking the way his eyes ran over the details of her dress, then ran over them a second time.

"Did you come..." he began, forlorn and hopeful, his tongue tying itself piteously into knots. "Did you come to see me again, after our dance, Miss Cathy?"

Cathy momentarily forgot her resolve not to be so bossy for the day. She walked up to him, straightened his shirt and jacket and pointed at his waistcoat. "Misbuttoned," was all she said on that score. Then answered, "I've come to you for legal advice."

Mr. Kenan's spectacles had slid down his nose. With one long finger, he shoved them back into place. He gabbled that he would be glad to help her, glad to help her in any way.

"My question is simple," she said. "Did Old Hitch leave a will? You see, I never thought about it until yesterday, and so I was wondering..." She smiled sweetly, charmingly, she hoped.

Mr. Kenan's long face took on a disapproving cast, but not because Cathy's smile had missed its mark. He said, with great professional disapproval, "I urged Old Hitch time and time again to write a will, but he would not listen to me. When I brought up the matter—oh, two weeks ago was the last time I discussed it, I recall, when he was first taken so sick!—he just laughed and called me a pettifogger!" He drew a shallow but nonetheless indignant breath. "Pettifogger! Me! With a degree from the University of North Carolina at Chapel Hill!" He gestured with his long finger to the framed parchment, hanging askew on one wall. "I studied with Professor William Graham, too!"

"And that's all he said on the subject of his will?" Cathy pressed.

"Well, he told me to clean up my desk," Mr. Kenan added. He looked around the room and said vaguely, "Perhaps I have let things go a bit in the last few days, but as for my desk, I know where every paper can be found!"

Cathy thought, rather, that the wreck of his office was more the product of several years. She was able to peer around the side of the desk to ascertain it matched the general state of the rest of the room. She was justifiably skeptical that Mr. Kenan knew where every paper could be found.

"If he filed no official will with you," she asked next, "could some other document serve as such?"

Mr. Kenan nodded brusquely. "Any document—signed by him in sound mind, of course—that a reasonable person could interpret as a will, would have legal status," he explained. "Although Old Hitch could not have had much, I still deplore the carelessness with which he approached the entire matter!" Aggrieved, he added, "And he did not have to insult me into the bargain, or say what he did in his final statement yesterday! Why, I wouldn't have charged him a third the amount he claimed I would." He considered that statement briefly, then amended, "Well, *half,* anyway."

Cathy forbore to comment on the subject of carelessness, as she cast her astonished eye, once again, around the office. She made some soothing remarks to the effect that everyone had been insulted at the funeral, so that Mr. Kenan should not feel particularly wounded. Then she smiled, thanked the legal eagle for his time and left on her next errand.

Mr. Kenan returned to his desk. In the general confusion of his thoughts, he entertained the scribble of an idea that he might be in love.

Cathy proceeded to Granny Smith's, down Churton and around the corner on Margaret Lane. The closer she came, the more her soaring spirits dipped and the more she had to buck herself up. She said to herself, "You can do it, girl. It's only an invitation to dinner, and he knows you're the best cook in town. And think of serving him dessert on the porch swing. One sweet bite just might lead to one sweet kiss—or more!"

Cathy was apprehensive about the awkwardness of having to call on MacGuff, but when she turned the corner, she saw that she was in luck. MacGuff was in the side yard next to Granny's porch. He was half turned away from her and standing next to his showy roan, suggesting that he was either coming in or going out for a ride. She liked the fact that she would be able to cross his path naturally, strike up a conversation and then ask him to dinner.

As she came closer, she saw to her surprise that Sylvia Lee was standing on the other side of the horse, stroking the roan's coat and apparently cooing to it.

Because of the direction of Cathy's approach, Sylvia saw her first. Her eyes widened a trifle, then narrowed slightly, and Cathy was pleased to think that Sylvia found her new dress and hair arrangement becoming. Then Sylvia said something to MacGuff and nodded, taking her leave of him. She moved away with only the most casual wave at Cathy and a trilled greeting.

MacGuff turned slowly and looked at Cathy. His beautiful eyes were assessing, but were they appreciative? She could not determine. However, she was sure that he had noted the changes in her appearance.

Courage! she told herself, and *don't,* whatever you do, talk too much! She fought against the fuzziness that always seemed to veil her wits when she looked at him and to set her tongue prattling uselessly.

"MacGuff," she greeted him. "Hello."

"Hello, yourself," he said with a lazy smile. His eyes lingered. "What brings you to this corner of Hillsborough?"

"You," she replied directly, for she had already determined that coyness could never be her style. "I've come to ask how you're doing since the funeral."

MacGuff's smile was a blend of the sad and the seductive. "Well enough, I suppose," he answered, "but I was surprised that you did not stay long at the rectory after the burial, where we could have discussed the matter on the spot.''

''I had things to do.''

''Like what?''

Behind his question she was able to hear another: ''And what would there be to do in Hillsborough on a Sunday afternoon?'' She decided that he meant it less as mockery and more as a challenge. ''Like begin to prepare a fine dinner for today,'' she said. ''Are you interested in sharing it with me?''

His brow quirked speculatively. ''Only the two of us?''

She nodded, hoping she looked neither too eager nor too apologetic.

Both eyebrows rose. She inwardly cringed to think that his speculative gaze might turn derisive. It did not. He asked instead, ''And what if I already have an invitation for today's dinner?''

With Sylvia Lee? she wondered. In her relief that he had not turned her down flat, she said, ''Refuse it, because mine will be better.''

His speculative gaze turned amused—not derisively, but appreciatively. His eyes traveled over her altered appearance. They paused at the drawstring of her bodice. She waited for the pleasurable feeling to come over her at him contemplating her womanly charms, but it did not, and she decided that she must be too nervous to perceive it.

At last, he drawled, ''I'm sure it will, Miss Cathy.''

''So, then, you'll come at one?'' she pressed. ''My house.''

He was not so easily persuaded. ''Just dinner?'' he pressed in turn, as if still considering whether or not to accept her invitation.

She said with what she hoped was appropriate mystery, "There might be things we need to talk about. Things pertaining to Old Hitch's death."

"But didn't we discuss that at the festival night before last, at the very end of our dance together?" His teasing drawl was thick as molasses.

Something in his manner reminded her that he had thought she was trying to lure him into dancing with her again by making him dally at her side, answering pointless questions. Embarrassed, she bit her tongue before it could flap away, out of control.

"We began to discuss it, as I recall," she replied, and saved face by adding, "but did not quite finish, for Mr. Kenan approached me then for the next dance."

"Is that how it was?" he queried, teasing still.

She made no answer.

"The way I recall it," he said, "was that we had, in the end, little to discuss on the subject."

"Maybe, since Saturday night, I've learned something that might give us something to discuss on the subject."

A subtle but unmistakable look of interest suddenly lit the depths of his otherwise uninterested eyes. Seeing his change of expression, she realized that he had been intending to turn her down.

The next moment he fixed her with a smile that made her think she was the only woman alive. "Do you want to tell me about it?" he asked.

She felt herself weakening. Before she crumbled completely and began to dither, she said, "Yes, at dinner."

His smile remained in place. "One o'clock, then," he said. "Your house."

Her brain fuzzed up and rendered her feet immobile. Missing her cue to depart with grace, she simply stared back at him.

His smile seemed to set in the way that had always caused her a pang of humiliation. He moved toward his horse and said, nice and smooth as you please, "Well, I must be off, to give another pretty lady my regrets for her dinner plans."

"One o'clock, then," she repeated, stupidly now, for it was a few moments too late. "My house."

He nodded at that and turned away. However, he let his guard down too soon, and Cathy saw a look of boredom bordering on disgust touch his features. She turned away, too, feeling something curl and shrivel inside her. A sadness came over her when she realized that it was her newfound sense of attractiveness that shrank at her knowing MacGuff was not looking forward to sharing a cozy meal alone with her.

Her native optimism combined with a touch of willful delusion to recall that he had said he was off to give "another pretty lady" his regrets. She reasoned that he would not have said *another* pretty lady unless he had not thought that she was one. Would he?

Somehow, this line of logic did not raise her spirits, and she returned to Churton Street with a heavy heart and her old, dull sense of plainness. She made the few purchases she needed at the Market House, put the items in the basket on her arm and was about to return home when she caught sight of Mr. Harris, way off, disappearing into the woods beyond the lawn of the courthouse.

Curious to know what the quiet man was up to and possibly desirous of distracting herself from her misery, she left her basket in the care of a friendly vendor and went to follow Mr. Harris. She hurried across the courthouse lawn. She entered the woods at the precise point he had, hardly the minute before, but she had difficulty spotting him among the greens and browns into which he seemed to have melted. Then her eye caught a trace of movement off to her left. A form seemed to have disappeared over the high bank that led to the river.

She started in that direction. Realizing that she was making a good deal of noise by cracking branches and crunching pine straw underfoot, she stopped to take off her shoes and stockings. Holding her footwear in one hand, raising her skirts with the other, she proceeded to tiptoe, as soundlessly as she was able, through the woods. When she came to the riverbank, she spotted Mr. Harris not too far ahead, threading his way nimbly along the rocks. She scrambled quietly down the bank, and when she came to the water's edge, hitched her skirts up into the sash at her waist, so that she would not wet the hem.

At the place where he'd slipped up the bank on the opposite shore, she did likewise. She was able to keep her eye on him as he made his way through the woods, but when she came to the edge of a clearing, he was suddenly nowhere to be seen. She stopped near a large oak, looked around and listened intently. She was mystified by his disappearance.

The next moment, she nearly swooned in fright to feel a strong arm clamp around her waist and a large hand encircle both wrists. She dropped her shoes and stockings when she found herself suddenly in Laurence Harris's embrace, held tightly against his chest and legs. That extraordinary sensation of jumping out of her thoughts and into her body flashed from the soles of her feet to the tips of her ears and up her scalp, causing every point in between to flush.

She was looking into black, snapping eyes that made her bodily flush deepen. No warm twinkle of unreleased laughter lit their dark depths, but something far more intense. She strained away from him, but he did not release her.

In an attempt to recover composure, she aimed for a light touch in her voice. "My, sir! You frightened me!" What came out was breathless and throaty.

"When you are following someone's trail," he instructed, "it is best not to announce yourself at every footfall."

"I was being very quiet," she returned with a sniff of indignation.

The quality of his silence told her what he thought about that statement. Then he asked, "Why did you follow me?"

"I wasn't *following* you, exactly," she said. "I was coming to tell you . . ."

She floundered when she realized that her legs had been partly bared by the tucking of her skirts at her waist, and that they were intertwined with his. The buckskin covering his knees rubbed against either side of one of her thighs. It was a delicious sensation, having that of his buckskins against her own flesh. It was alarming, too, to become aware of the stirring of his desire.

"I was coming to tell you," she managed to blurt out, "that I was successful."

"Successful?" he queried.

"In executing the first part of our plan," she said. "MacGuff has accepted my invitation to dinner today."

"Did you have any difficulty," he asked, lowering his eyes from her face, "interesting him in your invitation?"

Her eyes followed the direction of his, and she saw that he was looking straight down into her bodice, which was fully agape from this rough handling. Her thin chemise did little to cover the peaks of her breasts. She should have been embarrassed, but she was not. Instead, she felt the return of the confidence she had lost after her encounter with MacGuff. She felt a surge of feminine power that allowed her to resist her attraction to the dark devil who held her, even as she acknowledged it to herself.

"I got his attention, all right," she said in a provocative manner she had needed no lessons to learn.

"And you have told the others of your success with the first part of the plan?"

She squirmed again in his embrace. "I'm on my way to tell them now."

"Ah," was all he said. He released her slowly, with a look in his eyes that warned her he was not a man to be toyed with for long. He bent to retrieve the shoes and stockings she had dropped and gave them to her. He reached for the drawstring of her bodice, pulled gently, gathering the material together for modesty, and tied it firmly. He patted his handiwork. The feel of his hand against her breasts produced a shivery sensation inside her that felt like a promise.

"Consider me informed, then," he said, a hint of steel in his voice, "that you'll be dining this afternoon with Young Cock."

Chapter Fourteen

Cathy returned home feeling, paradoxically, both chastened and emboldened, and more curious than ever. She made what repairs she could to her dress by brushing off the forest debris that clung to her skirts and by wiping the dirt from the hem. She decided not to overplay the point of her bodice and so left it tightly drawn, the way Mr. Harris had tied it. And as for young Mr. Hitchcock MacGuffin, his boredom and his beautiful eyes . . . well, she'd show him!

And show MacGuff she did, although she did not fully realize it until after he had left.

He arrived at her front door at the appointed hour. She had left the door open so that she could hear his arrival. When Black Twig barked ceremoniously in the yard and MacGuff announced himself with a carrying "Hello," Cathy called him back to the kitchen, where she was still busy with preparations.

When he appeared at her kitchen door, she looked up from the bowl in which she was mixing a savory blend of spring greens and bitters. She had to admit that he looked mighty fine in his store-bought suit, with his chestnut curls tamed to regular waves around his handsome features, his familiar smile spreading slowly over his face as if it came to exist because of her. She hoped that, as his eyes dwelled on her, his smile would not become fixed, giving that lovely curve a practiced look.

What she did not know was that she was at her attractive best. After her orchard—where MacGuff was unlikely to ever see her—the kitchen was where she was at her most comfortable, and therefore at her most naturally graceful. When MacGuff stopped at the kitchen door and leaned against the jamb, Cathy was cradling the large bowl in the crook of her arm and plucking the leaves rhythmically as she tossed her salad. She looked up and bestowed on him a smile that was cordial but nothing more, for her thoughts were focused on her dinner and the orchestration of her meal. She told him that he could put his hat down on the closest counter. He did so, then let himself be surrounded by the inviting smells of fresh-baked bread and biscuits and pie, roasted chicken and steamed vegetables.

Cathy had been cooking contentedly for the past hour, and her cheeks were pink from her light exertions. The moment before MacGuff appeared at the kitchen door, she had blown a hearty gust of breath to cool her face. The puff of air had lifted the feathery bangs above her eyebrows, causing several strands to stick up straight. The disarray created a charming effect, and for someone disposed to the unusual charms of Cathy's person and personality, it would also have been endearing.

MacGuff's eyes settled contemplatively on her for a few minutes. He did not speak beyond the conventional greetings and a few extraneous comments. He was more interested simply to watch this woman he had known his entire life, one who had never entered his thoughts at any moment when she was not in his direct line of vision. He watched her move unself-consciously through routines she obviously knew well: bending at the oven, stretching for something on a shelf, sprinkling salt, dipping a finger in a sauce to taste, stirring this, mixing that, pausing to think what she should do next.

At one moment, she nodded definitively and un-tied the apron at her waist. She smoothed her skirts with several sensual gestures, but forgot to tidy her hair, and pronounced the dinner ready to be served.

She was in perfect command. She informed her guest that they would be eating on the side porch, just beyond the dining room, and she handed him a tray set with steaming bowls of mushroom soup, to open the meal. She preceded him through the house and to the double doors of the dining room, thrown open to reveal a small table on the porch draped with an ele-gant white cloth. It was already set, with two chairs placed opposite one another. At the table, she fussed agreeably with the pouring of the water and the tea and the scuppernong wine. And so the cozy meal be-gan.

MacGuff, initially reluctant when the invitation was first issued, became a willing participant in this obvi-ous feminine play for his affections. He thrived on at-tention from women, angled for it and accepted it regularly as his due, but he had never particularly valued Miss Cathy's adulation.

Until this dinner. She was a good cook, a confident hostess, and she had a fine house. A mighty fine house, comfortable and neat and well maintained, with a porch looking out over a grassy expanse of land that sloped down into luxurious gardens and up into a profitable orchard. The kind of house he had never had, growing up as he did without parents. The kind of house to which he could invite the riff and raff of his business acquaintances and show them a thing or two. The kind of house a man with his talents and attributes naturally deserved. The kind of house he had with Granny Smith only on sufferance and by the unspoken contract that he fawn over the old ninny in a manner somewhere between that of adoring son and eunuch lover. The kind of house he had always felt was too good for a bumptious woman like Miss Cathy Davidson.

This afternoon, feeling replete and relaxed, he was less resentful and more opportunistically aware of her and her house than he had ever been before—as a smart businessman should be aware of offers that came his way. It amused him to speculate how far Miss Cathy might go in demonstrating her devotion to him.

He imagined—perhaps for the first time—an entertaining interlude that might find the drawstring of her primly tied bodice loosened, as it had been earlier in the day when she had come to Granny's to tempt him to her house for dinner. At least she had the figure for such a ploy, but she had been so pathetically obvious about it that it had bored him to imagine spending even half an hour alone with her. Now he had reason to revise his negative opinion—or at least saw a reason to rouse himself to make the kind of moves that would put a plain woman like her in the palm of his hand.

And it just might be true that since Saturday she had discovered something concerning the old geezer's death that might interest him. In any case, that part of her bait had worked to hook him into dinner, and he was not about to ignore the possibility that his uncle's repeated hints of hoarded wealth had come to her ears, as well. Even if the old man's hints proved to be only half true, that half could still ease the constant financial pinch in his life.

Then, too, Miss Cathy had been more than casually interested in questions of inheritance on Saturday night, and it occurred to him that if anyone could help him interpret those two cryptic lines he had received from the old geezer the week before, it would have to be Miss Cathy. He would take care, however, not to tip his hand to her too soon or to anyone else's advantage.

It was time for dessert, and he had properly impressed her with his tales of sales and contracts pending. She suggested they take dessert on the front porch swing. He readily agreed, recognizing an opportunity. He helped her tidy up the dishes and the glasses and the serving plates. When she sent him off to the front porch with the dessert tray, saying she was going to fetch her shawl, he sent her a smile that was calculated to melt her vulnerable heart.

Cathy went to her bedroom for the shawl, puzzled and dissatisfied, and puzzled all the more by her dissatisfaction. She had expected the dinner to be both more nerve-racking and more exciting. It had been pleasant, certainly, but not much more. Her food had been tasty enough, the talk had run smoothly enough and the setting had been fine. Yet the merely "good enoughs" had left her dissatisfied. Added to which was her puzzlement over a strange tension in the air, one she could not quite define. Draping the shawl across her elbows, she laughed inwardly at herself and thought, If I could define the strange tension, I would not be puzzled by it.

Once out on the front porch, however, she began to feel better. She was coming to the twin and intertwined goals of the occasion, which were to try her wiles out on MacGuff and to learn what she could of Old Hitch's correspondence with his nephew. She settled herself on the swing next to her guest and was pleased to feel a little spark in the atmosphere. She began to perceive that the strange tension in the air was due to the fact that they had been hovering around the unspoken topic uppermost on both of their minds. Realizing that, she felt her puzzlement begin to resolve itself.

She cut MacGuff a piece of warm chess pie, making sure to bend and move her arms for maximum exposure of her breasts, making sure, as well, that he followed her movements. When she set the tray aside without helping herself to any, MacGuff turned to her, his brows raised.

"You're not having a piece?" he inquired, taking a healthy bite. He continued, a little thickly, "It's delicious."

She knew just what to do. She smiled, looked wistful and said, "I'm glad you like it, but I don't have room for a whole piece."

MacGuff slanted her a glance. "A bite, then?" he offered, holding up his fork.

"Mmm, please," Cathy said, leaning forward to accept the piece that he fed her. A crumb tumbled off the fork and caught in the folds of drawn material curving over her breasts. She looked down at it, then at MacGuff, without attempting to brush it off her bodice.

It was left to MacGuff to perform that tender office for her. He laid his plate aside and put a hand to her breast. He flicked the crumb with two fingers. When it was gone, his hand remained. He spread his fingers across a generous handful of her feminine flesh. She found that she liked his touch, but not because it produced a delicious weakening inside her, as she had thought it would. Rather, she felt strengthened by it. Powerful.

She met his gaze and did not flinch or look away. She saw something very gratifying in the depths of his beautiful, amber eyes: the tiniest flicker of surprise. She shifted so that his hand slid down the side of her breast to her waist. She moved up next to him. She noted the scent of his hair oil and shaving soap. She liked their spicy tang, but decided she preferred the smell of clean, sun-dried cotton. She was not sure, but she thought that MacGuff might be wanting to kiss her. Or at least, might be wondering what it would be like to kiss her.

She said, "Let's talk."

"About what?"

"Old Hitch."

"Is that why you invited me here today?" His hand moved back over her breast, then up to her shoulder, where it rested.

She liked that she was not losing control. "Sure," she said. "And that's why you came."

"I came for dinner," he said, adding meaningfully, "and dessert."

"You've had both," she said, pushing him away slightly, and relishing the look that came over his face.

He straightened fractionally and slanted her another glance, this time an almost-appreciative one.

"What about the old geezer, then, now that he's dead and buried?"

The old and familiar part of herself—the one that had longed for him to admit to having received the last two lines from Old Hitch without her asking—had vacated the premises. The new tenant, the one who had just moved into her young woman's body, was happy to try to entice the clue from him.

She looked up at him through her lashes and raised her hand to toy gently with the lapel of his spruce, store-bought jacket. "When a man is dying," she said, "he sometimes wants to make all right with the world before he goes. It occurs to me that Old Hitch was in such a frame of mind last week."

MacGuff did not resist her touch. The hand at her shoulder slid down her arm to draw her closer to him. "And just what makes you think that he was in such a frame of mind?"

"He told his neighbors off, one and all," she said thoughtfully, "in a statement that a weak man with little energy could not have written without a good deal of inspiration."

MacGuff's beautiful lips set in a slightly cynical line. His hold on her relaxed. He was clearly unimpressed with this argument. "Inspiration," he repeated. "Is that what you call it?"

"And he was in a giving mood last week," she went on. She was pleased that his hold tightened again. She tugged on his lapel, drawing him closer.

"Giving?" he repeated in a murmur. He seemed to think this observation was more interesting, and he brought his lips down closer to hers. "What did the old geezer have to give?"

"His watch and the Hitchcock Bible," she said softly, "among other things, I suppose."

He checked his movements. "His watch and the Bible?" His voice was clearer now and inquiring.

"Why, yes, he gave his watch to Clive and the Bible to Richard," she said, then added artfully, "hadn't you heard?"

He did not look pleased, but she did not know whether it was because a costly watch had slipped through his hands—never mind the Bible—or because he had not heard the news. "He gave them away," he asked on a rancorous note, "before he died?"

She shook her head and continued in her role of innocent temptress. "No, he willed them, I suppose you might say."

"Ah, so that's what you've discovered, then," he said, smiling. "He did leave a will."

"I don't know about that," Cathy said. She was still in control, even with MacGuff's arms around her, his lips but a few inches away, his smile in existence for her and her alone. "He left them two lines each," she explained, "and when the two of them put their letters together, the four lines as a whole told them where to find their treasures."

His beautiful, amber eyes were focused on her. She could nearly read the thoughts that turned in their depths. "Two lines, you say? Put together with two other lines?"

She nodded slowly. "Um-hmm."

"And the four together told them where to find their treasures?"

She nodded again.

He considered. "Not much as far as treasures go," he commented. "A watch and a Bible."

"Enough for Clive and for Richard."

His smooth smile, his lips coming closer and closer to hers, turned cagey. "I wonder if it's legal, that four lines can will a valuable family watch to someone who's not a relative." A moment passed. "And a Bible, of course."

"As for legalities, you'd have to ask Mr. Kenan."

"Maybe I will," he said, taking her chin in hand and angling her lips to his. "But you said that he gave his watch and Bible away 'among other things.' What other things?" Then his lips touched hers.

The touch of his lips was pleasant. She liked the taste of her good cooking on his lips. She liked the feel of his fingers curled around her chin, holding her lips to his. She liked the way his other hand caressed her shoulder, then trailed along the expanse of bare skin above her bodice to fondle her neck. But she was waiting for something more than mere liking. She was waiting for that pleasurable weakening inside her.

She could feel the cocky smile of his lips against hers, but no trembling of unreleased laughter. He broke the light kiss in order to press his lips first to one corner of her mouth, then the other. "What other things, Miss Cathy?" he repeated huskily. "Did you receive two lines from Old Hitch, then, that you're wanting to match with two others?"

The pleasurable weakening did not come. Instead, she still felt strong—strong enough to want to experiment with this kiss. Before she increased her interest and affection, however, she countered with her own question, "Did you?"

"What difference would it make, since my uncle lived like a pauper?"

She pressed, "But was he one?"

He permitted himself a more intimate embrace by sliding his hand down her bodice and caressing her breast, boldly. He put his lips back to hers. "This is where we started, my dear," he said, but his honeyed drawl had an edge, "and I want to know if there is something you know."

She felt a jumble of emotions. Surprise mixed with a return of her puzzlement, then blended with a sense of disappointment, with even a twinge of violation at his hand on her breast. She pushed it away, broke the kiss abruptly and sat up. She was about to switch tactics and tell him the truth about the six letters, sure now that he had received the seventh. However, she was not going to tell him because she had been weakened by his touch or his kiss. Rather, she was going to tell him because this false enticement did not feel right, and she simply could not continue.

She sighed and pushed her ruffled bangs back off her forehead. "Let me tell you what this is all about," she began. But the sweet experiment on the swing turned suddenly sour.

MacGuff did not like the rebuff. There was an unpleasant glint in his eye. Before she could launch into her explanation, he said, "I'll tell you what this is about. This is about a pretty story you have concocted of two and two equaling four." He touched her lips, then his. The honey of his voice was laced with vinegar. "You went to a lot of trouble for a kiss, but found you weren't woman enough for more."

She was trying to adjust to the abrupt change in mood. "You think I've done all this so that you would kiss me?"

He stood up and looked down at her. "Why else would you have gone through this elaborate scheme?"

"Maybe I wanted to know what your uncle wrote you at the end of his life," she said.

"Maybe," he said, "Clive opens everyone's mail, and he told you about the old geezer's letters." His eyes raked her hair and her dress. "Then you cooked me dinner and tried to trap me with the bodice of an old-fashioned dress."

She was stung into replying, "How do you know I did not receive a similar letter? One with the lines to match yours?"

He smiled a tight, confident smile. "Because if you did, you would have told me by now."

She was surprised. "I would have?"

His smile spread but did not reach his beautiful, amber eyes. "Well, honey girl," he said, "I kissed you, and asked you, and kissed you again. You didn't tell, because you didn't have anything to tell." He cast his eyes over her again, once, contemptuously. "Don't you think that I know you've been sweet on me for more years than I can count?" Then he turned his back to her and walked away.

Cathy sat stunned, speechless. She watched his swift departure down her front walk and through her front gate, which he left stuttering behind him.

The first feeling that penetrated her numbed shock was humiliation, an old and shabby humiliation. However, that familiar feeling did not last, because a stronger force rose up inside her, new and pungent and bracing as fresh-ground mustard.

The first words to leave her lips were low and hissing and heartfelt. "Silly whippersnapper!"

She stood up from the swing, shoulders back, head erect, and repeated louder, "Silly whippersnapper!" Then, with throbbing relish, "Vain puppy!"

She swept toward the front door, opened it dramatically, flounced across the threshold and shut the door smartly behind her. She announced to her vestibule, as she strode toward her bedroom, "He thought he could get me to tell him anything he wanted just by peppering me with a few paltry kisses!"

She stepped into her bedroom, pausing a moment to strike a righteous pose. "And they were *very* paltry! No heart! Even worse, no soul!"

Then she whipped the sash from her waist and dropped it on the floor. As she walked to her bed, she untied the drawstring of her bodice, wriggled out of the sleeves and pulled the dress over her head. She heaved the formless material atop her bed covers, sat down and stripped off her shoes and stockings, tossing them across the room. "Silly whippersnapper!" She relished the taste of those tart words on her tongue.

She stood up again and declared, "I am going to spend the rest of the afternoon in my orchard, climbing happily in my trees!" She was about to leave her room, when she stopped and held up a hand. To the audience of her bed and dresser and dressing table, she said with great dignity, "But I am not going to the orchard in my chemise and pantalets, much as I would like to!"

She decided to scorn her old brown work dress along with every blue or pink dress she had ever made. So she retrieved the trunk of her mother's clothing and rapidly chose the skirt and blouse Ginger had rejected yesterday with the words, "These would be service-able for everyday wear around the house, Cathy dear, but not for the present occasion."

She put them on. They were a perfect fit and so comfortable that she did not bother to tuck the blouse into the waistband. She left her bedroom with as much energy as she had entered it and made her way through the house to the kitchens. There she confronted the piles of dirty dishes, pots and pans and serving pieces—and MacGuff's hat perched on a counter.

With a flippant, "He'll be back!" she marched through the room, without the least grain of guilt that she would be leaving her kitchen dirtier for longer than she had ever left it before. She let the clatter of the back door state how she felt about that!

The afternoon sun on her head and face felt great, as did the bristling grass warming her bare soles as she climbed up the slope. Even better was the indignation surging through her veins, cleansing her of the old, making ample room for the new. At this powerful housecleaning, she felt the spirit of her dead friend perch on her shoulders. She had never before felt in such glorious sympathy with dear, crabby Old Hitch.

"Ah, but 'silly whippersnapper' is far too good for him, my friend!" she told the spirit. "'Vainglorious pretty boy' is nearer the mark! Or 'puffed-up cox-comb'!" She laughed triumphantly. "Or just plain 'cock'!" She was put in mind of Mr. Harris's apt phrase and opined, "He was certainly right about that!"

"Right about what?" came a provocative voice at her side.

Cathy was completely surprised to see Mr. Harris appear from behind the old garden shed as she rounded the slope to her orchard. She was further surprised to see him surrounded by the unlikely combination of Aunt Rachel, Black Twig and Smokehouse. However, her surprise hardly dented her indignation.

Instead, without checking her step, she cast him a withering look of contempt. She tossed her head and uttered, "Men!" The word rang with condemnation.

Harris had either dull wits or exceptional fortitude. He asked, politely, "Did you have continued success with Young Cock?"

Her jaw dropped, and she swerved her head to look him square in the eye. "Silly whippersnapper!"

Apparently assuming that her invective referred to MacGuff and not to himself, he continued unperturbed. "I was expecting to hear the good news that he had revealed the final clue to you. I've been restraining the animals," he said, apparently hoping to please and indicating the menagerie around him, "so that they did not bother you during dinner." He paused delicately. "Or afterward. Black Twig doesn't like Young Cock, you see, and I thought he would get in your way."

She was in no mood, really *no mood,* to be diverted by the light of unreleased laughter warming the depths of Mr. Harris's black, black eyes. "Continued success, sir?" she said with icy dignity. Her effect was somewhat spoiled in that she stumbled against Smokehouse, who was capering about. She spanked the dratted animal on his rump and sent him off. "I have learned nothing from the dinner that I didn't know before, except that I've conceived a decided dislike for young Mr. Hitchcock MacGuffin! Never have I met a more disagreeable, conceited creature!"

Harris took this commentary in stride. "I could have told you that, ma'am," he said, very agreeably.

She stopped and put her hands on her hips. He stopped with her. They were standing in the shade of the first row of apple trees. He was looking down at her, his face an impassive mask, except for one cast of expression that she had no difficulty interpreting.

"Allow me to amend my statement, sir," she said in full-blown bossiness. "I *have* met one more disagreeable creature in this world, and it is you! So I would appreciate it if you were to take your very smug self away from me now and let me go about my business. And take my animals with you, if you please!"

She turned and stalked off into her orchard.

Chapter Fifteen

Harris knew just how to respond to her pique and high-handed command. He sent the animals off with a clap of his hands, then followed her down the row of trees.

If he had not already had a hankering for her, her flushed cheeks, sparkling eyes and indignantly swishing hips would have inspired him with one. But he already desired her, and he had come with the purpose of nudging her natural affection toward an equally natural sexual response. He judged his timing, deemed it good and began figuring the angle of his approach.

Young Cock might be a fool. He was not.

He easily caught up with her and was able to keep his face perfectly straight when she favored him with a look that could kill. But she did not speak, and he took that as a good sign.

He asked, as if half confused, half wounded, "Did you really mean to compare me to Young Cock?"

Her eyes narrowed to hazel green slits. "Indeed I did, sir, and I said that you were *more* disagreeable than that—that vainglorious pretty boy!"

He nodded thoughtfully. "Now there you have me, ma'am, for I have never thought of myself as a pretty boy." He paused, then added, "Of course, I would not know whether or not I was vain-glor-i-ous, since I am not sure what it means."

"It means," she began with a swell of her chest, but then let her breath out in a whoosh. "Oh, never mind what it means! I imagine you have a fair-enough idea. Anyway," she snapped, "I said that you were *worse* than he is!"

"I may be far worse than he," Harris agreed easily, "on any number of scores. My dress, for instance." He was ready to receive her look of daggers drawn and was not disappointed. He continued with bravado, "But I can think of three ways in which I am far different, and perhaps better, than Young Cock."

Cathy harrumphed.

"With respect to you, that is."

That did it. She stopped. She turned to look and him. Her mouth was open.

They were standing in the shade of a graceful, mature tree. He took advantage of her speechless surprise to ask, "What is this variety?"

She looked up into the branches, then back down at him. She was too surprised by the question not to answer it. "Magnum bonum."

He nodded. "Magnum bonum. It will do."

She eyed him suspiciously. "What three ways?"

He was happy to tell her. "First, I like you. Second, I acknowledge your faults and appreciate your qualities. Third, you were mine from the moment you fell on top of me, into my lap."

"Into your arms," she corrected.

"Into my lap," he repeated.

Her mouth fell open again, and the color that came into her cheeks was as appealing as the skin of the tenderest apple variety she would ever grow. Rose Sweet, perhaps. Or, better, Maiden Blush. Watching her reaction, he found his boyish wanting increase, as did the lightness he always felt when he was with her.

She was not at a loss for long. "I don't have any faults," she said testily, "except perhaps—in your opinion—my tendency to boss people around."

That strong and strangely rumbling feeling came to him, the tightening of his muscles everywhere, particularly those at the corners of his mouth. He knew that to smile now, however, would be a disaster. He controlled himself enough to say, seriously, "That's not the worst of them."

"Oh, no?" she queried with snapping eyes, obviously working herself up to quite a speech about *his* faults.

"No, your worst fault is a tendency to talk too much," he said, knowing that he was pushing his luck a little. However, given the change he felt in the relaxation of her crackling indignation to a mood less brittle and more elastic, he was encouraged to think he was on the right track. A fine tension was arising between them that he knew was worth nurturing.

Before she could deliver herself of the speech that was bubbling to the tip of her tongue, he continued. "But we've been over that ground before, and we've both agreed that we irritate one another, although in different ways. So I would appreciate it if you could hold whatever you were going to say for a time when I'm not so much in the mood to kiss you."

"You would appreciate it—!" She choked. "When you're not so much in the mood—!"

"That's right," he said. "To kiss you. I have the feeling that Young Cock did not do the job right."

He had backed her up, by small degrees, to the trunk of the thick-branched, thick-leaved magnum bonum tree. He put one arm up against the trunk above her shoulder and defined the space of their intimacy with his body. Both her hands were behind her back. He had not put his other hand on her, for he had not quite completed the tricky, teasing task of both gentling her and arousing her.

His eyes traveled first over the spiky fringe of hair at her forehead, sticking out here and there in the heat of the afternoon. He looked down into her wide, hazel eyes, over her flushed cheeks, sprinkled with freckles that bridged a blunt nose, and paused to contemplate her parted lips, so generous with smiles, so ready to speak. He looked farther down to her full breasts, rising and falling rapidly under a thin blouse the color of late-harvest wheat, which blended with the sun-gilded skin of her neck and arms.

He had first seen her through a shower of apple blossoms. Now he wished to touch her with his hands and lips and chest and legs, and to bring the blossoms to life on her body.

She said, a little shakily, "And you said you *like* me?" Her voice was gruff, as if she were still trying to hold him off. "Is this how you treat a friend?"

He put his chin lightly and experimentally on the top of her head. She accepted his touch. He felt his muscles smile. He bent his lips down to her ear and said, "I never said that I like you as a friend."

"You don't?"

He added, deliberately provocative, "And to prove to you that I do like you, I won't ask you to explain what you meant when you exclaimed, a few moments ago, 'He was certainly right about that!'"

"I did?" she asked vaguely.

"Just before you saw me by the garden shed," he explained.

"Just before you jumped out at me," she complained. "You are always appearing and disappearing when I least expect it!"

"I don't know who 'he' is," he continued, unperturbed, "or what he was right about. I'm curious to know, of course, but I don't think this is the moment to press you for an answer."

"If you do," she said, "I'm more likely to tell you exactly what I think *your* faults are."

"Which is why," he answered easily, "I do not intend to give you the opportunity to speak at all."

She was still determined to be grumpy. "For a man who seems more accustomed to silences," she objected, meeting his eyes directly, "you sure have become pretty glib."

He couldn't help it. He smiled. He was not sure what *glib* meant, but he had a pretty good idea that she was giving him back some of his own and suggesting that he was talking too much. He was not going to wait for a further invitation from her to shut up and kiss her, and he had nothing more to say to her in words, anyway. He bent his head.

"And smug," she managed to say before his lips made contact with hers.

As Harris kissed her, he felt very light. His old anger rolled away, like the tide out to sea, creating neither protection from her nor barrier within him to keep his desire in check. He kissed with a feeling of openness inside himself that he had not felt to this degree the evening before. He pressed his lips to hers, this way and that. He experimented, tasted and kissed each corner of this mouth that smiled so generously, wanting to make her smile his.

"But you've been smug from the beginning." Her whisper was something between a complaint and a sigh.

The beginning. The beginning was when his un-goddesslike goddess had landed in his lap. He had felt her weight stretched out on top of him before he had seen her full face. He remembered the force of her body against his. Then, lying on the ground, he had looked up and seen her through a fragile cloud of drifting apple blossoms. He had been stunned into remembering the teachings of his youth, and he had realized, with pride and confidence, that he had followed the right trail to the base of the apple tree. He realized now that he had been stunned into fusing two halves of his life together—the years with Attean and the years with Morgan; the body that Attean had trained and the soul that Barbara had returned to him.

He had always been good at finding things, and that stunned moment of fusing had opened onto the further trail of his desire. His desire. Deep dwelling. Well hidden. Fragmented in disparate parts of himself. He had found it. He had put it together. But he had not put it together all alone. He preferred to be alone, but he could not have put it together without her. He felt proud and confident that he had found his desire. She called that "smug." His pride and confidence swelled when he realized that the next challenge, the true test of his hunter's powers, would be to find hers. That would make him even more smug. Her, too, perhaps. He would see about that.

He was patient, as well. He had waited this long. He would wait until he had helped her find her desire.

With a leap of his blood and a happy tightening of his muscles, he realized that hers might not be as well hidden and fragmented as his had been. As he kissed her and felt her reaction, He Who Was Good at Finding Things guessed that her desire lay closer to the surface, waiting, expectant almost and breathless. Hidden, but not deeply, in the soft folds of her natural affection.

But where was it? he wondered. Or, rather, where was it the most? He would have to find out. He tested with his tongue and met the tip of hers. He liked the sensation that produced in him, and he more than liked her reaction. He more than liked her. It was a good start. But, perhaps, only a start.

The beginning. He liked beginnings. Beginnings were, for him, secret openings onto hidden trails in thickly wooded forests. Beginnings were first movements of instinct.

She had fallen on top of him. She was his. Her body was his to explore. The open fields. The thick woods. The hidden trails.

Cathy could not have said just then how it came about that she was backed against the trunk of her oldest, fullest magnum bonum tree, within the circle of Laurence Harris's arms—or almost within the circle. She could not have said just then why it seemed perfectly natural that his arm was raised above her shoulder and that he was leaning into her, against her, putting his lips to hers with sweet contact.

These were not his first kisses—those had come the evening before. But these were his first serious kisses. Well, not serious exactly, because she felt like smiling. Still, she could tell the difference.

He had appeared from behind the garden shed, and she had been angry at him. He had followed her, and she had been glad. She would have been disappointed, even sure-fire angry at him, if he had *not* followed her. And he *knew*. He knew—or guessed well enough—what had happened with MacGuff on the porch swing. So he followed her into the orchard and caught up with her. And suddenly the quiet man was not so quiet anymore, and she was not so talkative.

They resolved their differences, it seemed to her, by putting their lips together and kissing. She was touching him with her lips only. Her hands were still pinned behind her back and rubbing against the rough bark of the trunk. Kissing was a good solution, she thought. It seemed to calm her outrage and indignation, as the pleasurable weakness it produced spread through her body.

But there was more. His arm slid down from the trunk of the tree to settle at the crook of her neck and shoulder. His other hand came up to the top button of her blouse. When his fingers slipped the first button from its buttonhole, she began to feel her calm disturbed and to become aware of new disruptions beginning to take place. But these were not accompanied by outrage or by indignation or by a desire for anything other than for him to continue.

He continued. First one button was dislodged, then the next, then the next. Slowly. Respectfully, in a strange sort of way, as if he intended no damage with his exploration and would halt at the slightest hint of resistance from her. Then her blouse was sagging open, and her thin chemise was exposed. He pulled the ribbon, undoing the bow, and pushed the light material aside so that his whole palm and fingers could spread and graze across her flesh. The sensation was glorious. She felt beautiful. She felt his desire to touch her breast and shifted slightly to make herself generously available to what he wanted.

She luxuriated in the gentle movement of his fingers on the tip of one breast and felt her quick response in the fine peak that budded under his fingers. Then he slid the hand at her shoulder down to her other breast and stroked it to a quicker, more titillating response. His lips were against hers, and he slid his tongue into her mouth and teased hers until she had to bring her arms around from behind her back and raise them to his shoulders, clasping her hands behind his neck. She decided she liked him best when he was speaking to her in this most-direct, most-silent, most-effective way. So much to say. So little room for misunderstanding.

She liked having her bodice open and her chemise shoved down so that her breasts moved against his chest. She was aroused by the feel of his buckskin vest and shirt beneath, but she thought she would like the feel of his skin against hers even better. The day was warm, the breezes were sweet and his skin against her skin could only make the day warmer and sweeter. She wondered, hazily, whether she would be able to open his vest and shirt as easily as he had opened her blouse and chemise.

Before she had a chance to act on that thought, he broke away and kissed his way down her neck and throat to her breasts. Any hazy musing fled when he put his lips to the tip of one breast, twirled it with his tongue, tasted it and teethed it lightly, causing heat to flash along her skin and streak along her nerves. He cupped her breast, propping up its heaviness, so that he could kiss and tease and taste and twirl the tip to his content. He raised his head and gently caressed that breast with his hand, smoothing his palm against its hard bud. Then he kissed his way to the other breast, parting the material of her dress further, shoving the chemise farther down. She felt magnificently exposed, magnificently unashamed and just plain magnificent. She wondered what could possibly come next.

She was to find out. When he had finished teasing that breast to a taut peak, he paused and looked up at her. His eyes were black on black, with desire, with question, with intention. She looked at the top button of his shirt. He nodded minimally, then pressed his lips to the crook of her neck as she parted his shirt and vest—inexpert, impatient and unprepared for the shock and warmth and feel of his skin flush against hers. She must have groaned. Or else he did. Or they both did, and the sounds of their satisfaction were indistinguishable.

Then the flat of her hands touched his chest, gently, and she tried to ease his shirt off him. But he did not let her. Somewhere during her tentative, hesitant exploration of his muscled ribs and his broad shoulders, his arms had traveled down to her hips, pressing her buttocks so that she was more fully against him. His hands were bunching up her skirts and grasping at the hem. His legs had intertwined with hers, and then his hands were on the bare skin of her thighs.

She started. She tried to draw back. The moment she did, he relaxed his hold, but then she did not feel as intensely the press of her breasts against his chest. She moved against him once more. He continued to touch her thighs. She attempted to adjust to the next

sensation, more intense, more exciting, more dangerous. The drawstring on her pantalets must have been
loosened, for she felt his hand on the inside of her
thigh. His fingers moved up the back of her thigh to
her buttocks. He pressed her to him. She felt his fullness. She began to feel a fullness of her own, very different from his but complementary.

His hand moved around to the inside of her thigh
again, moved up, across the apex, grazing lightly as it
passed, to the other thigh. Just the topmost top of the
other thigh, where fold met fold upon fold. He was
seeking, exploring, testing.

He put his lips back on hers and possessed her
mouth fully. If she had wanted to retreat, she could
not now. She could feel his fullness and his confidence and his desire and his goal. He shifted his fingers, drawing them again across the apex of her thighs,
back and forth, then circling. Her legs spread a little
wider, either from the pressure of his thighs easing
hers apart or by the stretching of tense muscles whose
widening smiles she could not prevent. The new-tenant
feeling she had with him heightened to full occupancy. Fully inhabiting her body now, she became
aware of new rooms inside her, small and secret and
unexplored.

The tips of his fingers pressed at her body, spread
tender lips gently and touched—to her surprise and
gasping delight—a seed. Just a little pip. Very promising. Well planted in moist soil. It was a new variety,
unknown to her. Certainly interesting. Well worth examining. To her continuing surprise and delight, the
little seed seemed to grow with the sliding, circling
pressure of his fingers. She was full and surrounded by
him, his lips, his arms, his chest, his abdomen, his

thighs. And his fingers were bringing a sprouting seed to blossom.

The day was very warm and very glorious. Birds sang. Bees buzzed. Breezes wafted the scents of earth and apple blossoms. Her world turned on an angle, and she felt herself falling into the arms and across the body of a stranger who was passing beneath her tree, passing through her town. He was a quiet man whose silences were eloquent. He was a smug man who said he liked her. He was a strong and desirous man—

—Who was breaking his passionate kiss, stilling his hands, pushing her skirts back into place and moving away from her.

"Miss Cathy!" she heard a voice call from below the orchard. "Halloo! Miss Cathy!" The voice was coming closer. It was Clive's. "Are you there?"

The quiet man had apparently heard it before she had and was already putting himself to rights. Cathy looked into his black, desirous and highly frustrated eyes. He nodded toward her bodice, indicating that she should be quick and button herself up.

"Miss Cathy!" Clive insisted. "Where are you?"

To Harris, she whispered, "I'll call out in a second." Her hands were shaking with haste and a frustration to match her partner's. "He's at the first row, now."

Harris's face was a study of thinly veiled emotions—a rich array that included a twist of fugitive humor. He said, "I remained the first time the busy man came by. I will not remain the second time."

Cathy felt anxious. "Are you going?"

He nodded. Before he left her side and vanished, he remarked, "I now know the feeling of or-ner-ee."

She should have laughed at that, or at least smiled, but she did not. When he slipped behind the magnum bonum tree and out of sight, she waited for a sudden wave of embarrassment at what had just transpired between them, but it did not come. She did not have much time to wonder at her lack of maidenly modesty.

She managed her last button and called out, "Over here, Clive! But, wait, I'm coming to you!"

She looked down at her dishevelment and pulled herself together as well as she could, but forgot—as usual—to do anything to put her hair in order. She hurried out from under the tree, but could not resist looking back over her shoulder at the strong trunk and spreading branches, studded with blossoms, and the spot where she had stood in Laurence Harris's arms, intertwined with his body, almost joined with it.

A wave of remembered, unreleased desire washed over her. Her gaze remained on the spot a moment longer, and she was overwhelmed by emptiness and loss. What if he decided to leave town now as suddenly as he had come? But, no, she thought, he will not leave until the mystery of Old Hitch's letters is settled. Then came the next, inevitable thought: And after that? He would surely leave town then.

He was not a man for a place with streets laid out in rows. He was not a man for houses and food and clothing the way she understood them. He was not a man who would stay put, once and for all, in a town, even a town as agreeable as her birthplace.

But that emptiness and loss would be for later. Right now, this second, she feared the emptiness and loss that might come from not completing what they had just started.

Her thoughts and limbs were still in a tangle of passion and anxiety. In her clumsiness and perceptual fog, she nearly ran straight into Clive.

The postman had to steady her with hands on her shoulders. He took one look at her and asked, "What's wrong, then, Miss Cathy?"

She gathered her wits, looked up at him and, with a pitiful attempt at nonchalance, said, "Why, nothing. What should be wrong?"

"I don't know," the postman said frankly, dropping his arms. He looked around, peering suspiciously among the trees, as if searching for something or someone. "I don't know," he repeated, "but you never know who or what might be lurking about such a fine orchard." He glanced back down at her, frowned in puzzlement.

Cathy began to walk with him, out of the orchard. "You're imagining things, Clive," she said. Her voice was a little steadier.

"Imagining things, my foot! Remember the last time I came to the orchard to deliver your mail? There was a strange man!" He shrugged and laughed. "It turned out to be only the Welshman, but I'm telling you, Miss Cathy, now with Old Hitch dead and you being such a fine young woman, I'm thinking the men of Hillsborough had better keep a proper eye on you."

She nearly groaned and could not meet his gaze. She said, "But why did you seek me out in the orchard in the first place?" She saw that he was not carrying his mailbag. "It doesn't appear that you've come this time with the mail."

Clive looked a little surprised by her question. "But have you forgotten, Miss Cathy? We all agreed to meet after MacGuff had taken dinner with you, to hear the news. George saw MacGuff walking down Churton Street, awhile ago it was already, and he rounded up the rest of us. We're all waiting for you now on your front porch!" He amended his statement. "All of us except the Welshman, of course. No one could find him!"

Chapter Sixteen

Cathy walked with Clive back to her front porch. There she saw Ginger and George seated on the swing, making eyes at one another and speaking softly, though not yet intimately, still negotiating the terms of their reconciliation. The Boys as a whole were ignoring them, each for a different reason. Richard was engrossed in his Bible. Hank was whittling. Boy had brought his banjo and was strumming and humming and breaking into occasional snatches of song. Orin had found the remains of the dessert tray and was polishing off the chess pie, perfectly content to swat the flies swarming around it.

Cathy took one look at the assembled group and knew just what to do with six pairs of idle hands. However, she had a number of questions to answer before she could put her plan into effect.

"You got his lines?" Hank asked straight off. He looked up from his whittling, closed his knife and pocketed it.

"I couldn't tell from the look on MacGuff's face when I saw him on Churton whether he had coughed up the clue or not," George offered. "I engaged him in conversation for a minute or two, but he was cagey. A real cool customer.''

Cathy was not sure she agreed that MacGuff was a real cool customer, but she did think that he was, among other things, cagey. Unbecomingly so. She shook her head. ''No, I didn't get the clue. MacGuff was playing it coy. Cagey, as you've said, George.''

''Did you tell him you had two lines to match his?'' Hank demanded.

Cathy nodded.

''And that Clive and Richard here put their four lines together which won for them the watch and the Bible?''

Cathy nodded.

''Well, shoot, mebbe he doesn't have the last two lines,'' Hank said. ''If he did, why should he hold back?''

''Oh, he has them,'' she assured him. ''As for holding back, he thought that I was making up a story about my lines, just to find out about *his.*''

The Boys thought this pretty clever on MacGuff's part.

George, however, asked how on earth MacGuff imagined that Cathy would ever think that Old Hitch had sent his nephew just a two-line letter. ''It's not a common thing for someone to do, so MacGuff could hardly have imagined that you *guessed* Old Hitch wrote such a one.''

Cathy cast an apologetic glance at Clive and said, ''Well, MacGuff was persuaded that Clive opens everyone's mail anyway, and figured he told me about the two strange lines.''

All eyes turned to Clive. The postman held up his hands in innocence. ''The quality of envelopes being what it is,'' he explained chattily, ''you can't imagine the number of letters that just fall out and get separated. So I have to read them to figure out who they're to and what envelope they belong in! Now, in the case of Old Hitch's letters, I've been mortal busy these past ten days and didn't have a chance to read any of—that is, his *envelopes* were so well sealed that I didn't worry about them falling apart and losing their contents!''

''Even so, why did MacGuff think you cared whether he had two lines, if'n he thought you had none?'' Hank asked Cathy, a puzzled frown on his face.

Cathy just shrugged her shoulders, unwilling to divulge the embarrassing truth—that MacGuff had thought she was merely making a play for his affection. Hank's question stirred up the feelings she had had prior to her encounter with Harris in the orchard. The old humiliation was there, but more as a distant memory.

Hank's question demanded an answer, and Cathy stated the truth as she now understood it. ''Because MacGuff thinks he's pretty smart, but what he is is greedy. I think he's holding out because he doesn't want to share any possible inheritance with the rest of us.''

Everyone was too absorbed in considering the truth of that statement to notice the edge in Cathy's voice. They fell to pondering exactly what might be in it for each of them. It occurred to each, in various degrees of clarity, that MacGuff's reluctance to divulge his clue was a sure sign that Old Hitch had left something worth inheriting.

''We've got to think of another plan, then,'' George said.

"Let's think of one," Cathy suggested, wily in her own way, "in the kitchen."

Orin was the first to agree to that suggestion, and when they all trooped back into the kitchen, Cathy put them to work cleaning up the magnificent mess that her excellent midday dinner had created. Of course, they all benefitted by sampling the leftovers, which were plentiful, and since the afternoon had slid into evening, the occasion turned into an informal supper, which meant more plates were dirtied.

Throughout the cleanup, the supper and the further cleanup, discussion was spirited and directed toward devising a plan to weasel the clue out of MacGuff. However, the suggestions were, for the most part, either absurd or unworkable, and the group hit on nothing that seemed effective.

The only fragment of an idea concerned MacGuff's hat, which Hank picked up from the kitchen counter. What they were to do with it, they did not know.

"It might come in handy," Cathy said, "because he has to return for it. Tomorrow, I would guess." She asked Hank to hang the hat on the clothes tree by the front door.

When Hank returned from that task, he had formulated the perfect plan. "We'll ask the Welshman," he said. "He'll be able to think of sump'n."

"Say, where is he?" George asked.

The Boys shrugged.

"Do you think he's left town?" George asked next. For some reason, he turned to Cathy to address the question.

Cathy could only gulp and say, "I hope not."

* * *

Harris had not left town, but he had left Cathy's property, entertaining some violent thoughts about Clive Smith. He derived a certain satisfaction from thinking of shooting an arrow deep into the postman's neck. However, he knew that his murderous intentions were misplaced, and killing the postman would not really improve his condition. Nor did he think it would improve if he were to send his thoughts on a transitory flight high in the sky. It seemed, somehow, better to wait out his wanting and to remain in his body—as uncomfortable, even painful as that was for him.

He had tasted fire and tasted it still, for he was still half ignited. He had told his ungoddesslike goddess that he knew a lot about fire, and he did. He respected it for its terrible beauty and feared it appropriately. He had made it his business to learn its secrets, first from Attean, then from the white men in North Point, who knew the magic of chemicals. Yet the fire he had tasted today was new and different and very good and, he suspected, of a kind that would not destroy and disfigure, but would rather give life.

Now, he knew that he had not yet fully experienced this new fire—and was physically suffering because of it—and when his murderous impulse faded, he was left only with his suffering. For the first time in several days he became aware again of the dark heaviness inside that had been so much a part of him before he'd met Miss Cathy Davidson. He disliked that black weightiness more than his suffering and tried to find a way to relieve himself of it, but he discovered no strategy that seemed to work.

He made quick work of the distance between the orchard and his camp by the river, feeling dark and heavy and knowing nothing more to do than wait for the afternoon to dim to evening and then fade to night. He felt better under the warm black of the sky and the distant silver of stars.

He lit a small fire and made a leisurely meal, feeding himself off the land and from the river. Then he bathed in that same river, immersing himself in the shivery coolness of the water, liking the clean flow running over him and the feeling of ritual purification. But no water would ever wash away the stained, crabbed skin that spilled from his neck to drape over one shoulder, front and back, like an old copper cloak.

He thought many long thoughts, about the fire that had taken his mother's life, about his two fathers, about his two childhoods and how experienced they had been, but how he remained an inexperienced adult. He thought about his approaching adulthood, and the boyish wanting he intended to satisfy no longer felt so boyish. He attempted to poise himself on the edge of his physical state, midway between exuberant urgency and necessary restraint. What he felt mostly was exuberant urgency.

He put on the clothing he had washed out the day before and dried in the field. He laced his moccasins, shouldered his bow and arrows and set out on a trail that he no longer needed to blaze. His feet knew the way, the dark protected him and he set his memory free.

He recalled the anger that had fueled him for so many years of his life. It had taken him far from his Iroquois home and driven him to the doorstep of the man his mother had married, to the disgrace of her tribe. That man had robbed him of his name and his dignity—or so he had thought at the time—and his Iroquois honor required that he kill him. He had tried to kill him, and Morgan now wore his son's anger in a scar across his shoulder and arm.

He had been the young warrior named Tohin-ontan then. Yet even as he grew into the young man named Laurence Harris, he had never once regretted attacking his father and having him feel the bite of his anger. Of course, in retrospect he was glad that he had not killed him. However, his anger had kept him at bay and camped out on the edge of Morgan and Barbara's farm for over a year after that first, violent meeting, until Barbara had gentled him into accepting a meal in their home. His anger had fueled him in the fields, as he toiled next to Morgan, for nine long years. His anger had continued to drive all his emotions and perceptions until two nights before, at the unlikely event of the Apple Blossom Festival.

Now another force, as strong as anger, fueled him and drove him. He was aware that it had been there all along—or at least for many years—but it had been indistinguishable from his anger. He and Morgan had never discussed the ways in which a man could be with a woman, and his father had commented only once on the subject of women. Not too many years ago, Morgan had, apparently, noticed that a young beauty from Baltimore had taken to hanging about the farm and the nearby meetinghouse, and he had guessed that she was interested in his son. His brief comment on the subject indicated that his own passion for Barbara was sacred and that no other relationship was worth the pleasure.

Laurence had felt attracted to the Baltimore beauty, but he had restrained himself. However, he had not restrained himself because of Morgan's wisdom, for he resented it more than anything else. Rather, he had not been attracted enough to the beauty to wish to lose that private and pure space within himself that had kept him alive.

Tonight, as each step took him closer to the house on Queen Street, he justified his own actions by reasoning that Morgan could have known what qualified as a sacred relationship only by experiencing the profane. Furthermore, he liked his unsacred Cathy, the music of her voice, the music of her movements, the music of her response to his kiss and his touch. And he was not planning to stick around much longer.

He hurried his step. He crossed the grassy slope behind her house, awash in silver splendor, vaulted lightly over the railing of her side porch and came to the window of the room he had determined was her bedroom. The sash was raised enough for him to slip under it and through the light fall of lace covering it. Once inside, he paused and adjusted to the slight cramp he felt at being within four walls and under a roof.

He looked at the bed where she was sleeping. He had made no noise, and she did not shift. Her head was buried in pillows, and her night rail was visible above the bedclothes in which she was haphazardly wrapped. The bed seemed unnaturally soft, unnaturally complicated with its mattress and sheets and pillows and coverlet. Still, she looked mighty desirable, enfolded within the layers but still accessible, just as he had discovered that her sexiness lay lightly wrapped within the folds of her natural affection, available to the man wise enough to want to touch her with liking and desire.

He laid his bow and quiver of arrows by the side of the bed and quickly shed his clothes. He slid in next to her, and when she opened her eyes with a start, exhaled a frightened "Oh!" and moved reflexively to defend herself from an intruder, he simply propped his head on one hand and held up the other, showing himself to be weaponless and therefore harmless.

He let her blink away her surprise and allowed her to do whatever she wanted to next. He was prepared to listen to her chatter, to seduce her outright or to do anything else in order to remain in her bed. Thus, he was very happy that the first thing she did when she had registered his presence was to catch her breath. Then she chuckled. He thought she smiled, too, for he could feel but not quite see it in the darkness of the room.

"It is most disconcerting the way you appear, suddenly, out of nowhere and in the strangest places!" she scolded.

"Is this such a strange place?" he asked.

She did not answer that, but he heard the sharp intake of her breath in response to his bold question.

"And I did not come exactly out of nowhere," he continued.

"I thought you might have left town," she said.

He heard the note of relief in her voice. The lightness that had left him earlier was returning. "Why did you think that?" he asked.

"You left the orchard rather abruptly," she said, "and you seemed angry."

"Not angry," he replied with confidence, "although I admit to feeling violent. And as for leaving abruptly, I did not have much choice."

She harrumphed. "Well, there was another instance of you disappearing just like that! I did not have the luxury of such an escape, you realize."

He heard her huffiness and her sense of mild grievance against him and the gloriously awkward position he had put her in under the apple tree. His lightness increased. It came in the form of a now-familiar tightening of his muscles. He began to think of it as his body smiling.

"But now I've reappeared," he said.

"Which was my point to begin with," she returned, "and I must say again that your habit of doing so is most disconcerting!"

He was not going to encourage her to elaborate on that theme. Or any theme. He was more interested in her fully absorbing the fact that he was stretched out next to her in her bed and that he was naked. He recognized the moment when she realized he had returned to complete what they had started.

Not distracted by seeing her, he was able to fully feel the nuances of her bodily reaction. Given the way she shifted away from him, slightly, hesitantly, he realized that she might not be in as eager a state of exuberant urgency as he. He might have had the aftertaste of that new fire in his mouth the evening long, along with that partially ignited feeling, but she had not. She had accepted his presence in her bed, but she was not ready in the same way that he was. Her natural sensuality was there but still had to be sought.

To equalize the terms, he moved over her, deftly unwound the bed covers and slipped her night rail off before she could protest. This action brought her first active resistance: she put her palm flat against his chest and straightened her arm, holding him off.

"I don't know about this," she said, a little shakily.

He could feel the fullness of her nakedness more than he could see it. He contradicted, "I do."

"No, I mean that this might be unwise."

He could agree in part. Experiencing the powerful and the unknown involved risks. "It might be," he acknowledged.

"No, no, I mean that I've never done this before," she said, speaking the words in a rush and choking slightly.

This time he could agree fully. "Neither have I."

He read her silence and savored it. She was completely surprised.

She asked, carefully, "You have never before made love?"

"Never."

Her silence now encompassed awe. "You are sure?"

"Of course, I am sure. How could I not be sure?"

"I don't know, because it would be absurd, of course, not to be sure about a thing like that," she said, verging on prattle. After a tiny pause, she ventured, "How can I believe you?"

A fresh surge of power raced through his muscles. The corners of his mouth tightened and curved upward. "You can believe me," he said, "because I have never answered one of your direct questions indirectly or dishonestly."

His eyes remained fixed on the faint but luminous glow of her eyes, and she returned his regard steadily. Their eyes held in the dim room, and in the quiet, highly communicative silence, he knew he had won her trust, and that he had had it from the beginning.

The arm braced against his chest relaxed at the elbow. She was no longer holding him off. Now she was simply touching him. In a small, provocative voice, she asked, "Are you trying to *save* me again?"

He put his hand over hers at his chest. The smile of his body broadened. "Since leaving you in the orchard, I've been frankly more concerned with saving myself from prolonged agony."

"Prolonged . . . ?" she began, then uttered a knowing "Oh."

In an effort to bring himself some relief, he dared her with, "I could show you what I mean."

She did not flinch or draw her hand away from his, but neither did she accept his dare. "So, let me understand. I'm doing you a favor now? Saving you in return for the times you've saved me?"

He clasped her hand tighter and lightly caressed her fingers. "I had not figured it to be so one-sided, nor had I thought of it in terms of saving." He drew closer, his blood and muscles and skin straining toward her. He knew what he wanted. He knew what she wanted. He hoped he had the skill and the patience to bring the two wantings together at the same time. "If you think back to the orchard, you might remember that I was doing my best to ruin you."

"That's a rather tactless way of putting it!"

"I am merely following the good advice you gave me the other night—that I continue to answer your questions directly and honestly."

"I should have known that it would be my fault," she commented. Then, on a breath of wonder, she said, "And that's what I don't quite understand about the episode in the orchard. If you are as inexperienced as I am, how could you . . . that is, how did you know to, um . . . How were you able to make me feel the way I felt?''

The energies that had flowed in to fill the void of his retreated anger had pooled between his legs and taken root, filling him with more exuberant urgency than ever. It was becoming increasingly difficult to lie next to her, feeling the shape of her nakedness but a few inches from his, breathing in the scent of her sweet, earthy skin. In an unformulated way, he knew that this playful discussion was part of the rekindling of the desire in the orchard. He made an effort to respond in a manner that would help her accept his touch and be fired by it.

"I am very good at finding things," he boasted. "You can call me smug."

She groaned, then accepted his invitation, with an inflection of humor. "You are smug. *Very* smug."

He drew her next to him completely, so that he luxuriated in the feel of her skin. He let his hands explore her generous contours, the back of her knee, her thigh, the curve of her hip, her breast, her neck. She resisted a little at first, for his grip was forceful, but when he put his lips to hers as gently as he could, he breathed in her sigh and was inspired to bring her to a pitch equal to his own.

Their kisses moved swiftly from sweet to fiery, and the great new fire was flaming through him. He retained enough of his senses to know that he did not want to burn without her, but he wanted her now, and she was not yet burning. He moved over her, finding the fit of every curve and crevice, nudging her legs apart with his own. But the position was not right, and he could not touch her in the way that would make good his boast. He moved off of her and drew her slightly across his chest.

An ingenious solution to his problems presented itself in the most natural way. He lay on his back and drew her across him, still kissing her and caressing her, and positioned her so that she straddled him. It felt so good to him that it was all he could do to pull her up slightly across his chest, so that he did not enter her on the instant.

"I'm not sure..." she said, hesitantly. "This isn't right."

"I'll have to hurt you," he said, "either way. This way might bring you pleasure."

He kissed her deeply, then grasped her shoulders and pushed her away from his chest, so that her back arched. He slid his hands down and caressed her breasts fully before he slid his hands farther down to her waist, then her hips. He held them firmly, pushed her back against him, but before he entered her, he slipped one hand around and touched the little seed of her desire. He was further inflamed to find that it had taken root in moist soil, and he found satisfaction in stroking the seed, nurturing it, imagining it flowering into a ripe fruit. As he stirred her fertile soil, stroked and nurtured, he nestled himself closer and closer so that he could plant himself inside her.

He nestled and nudged until he met with the resistance of her innocence. He guided her hips with one hand, pressed her back against him and stroked her budding fruit with the other, and she gratified him by helping him in his struggle to enter her. His bones and muscles and emotion and attention were focused on one goal, his body drenched in pleasure. He was blazing virgin territory, dark, unknown, unexplored. Just the way he liked it.

The journey did not end there. As he moved forward by degrees, he felt himself enter a ring of fire. He had feared fire and respected it. He had been burned and disfigured by it. Suddenly he no longer feared fire, no longer respected it, and if this was hell, he never wanted to leave. But it was a different kind of hell. Its fire was liquid and tasted new to him. His mouth burned with flaming blood and new fire. His body became saturated with the liquid fire. He was surrounded by it, encircled by it, wanted it to flame forever within him, around him. Wanted it to make him soar.

His ancient, flame-scarred soul felt young again. He was the firebird. He had lived through fire, and he lived for flight. When he was ready to take off and leave the earthly realm to shoot to the sky, he made sure to bring his round, green-and-gold bird, his apple-blossom bird, with him.

Chapter Seventeen

Cathy was returning home from an extraordinary voyage. Or perhaps, she thought drowsily, as she lay lightly wrapped in white cotton and copper skin, she had never left home. Or perhaps again, the voyage itself was actually a *coming* home.

Now there was an appetizing thought—that of coming home. But it was strange, too, and made no sense. Hadn't she lived in this town and in this house her entire life? How could she be coming home, when she had *been* home all that time?

She snuggled against the warm, soft cotton and the warmer, less-soft skin. So now she knew the proper conclusion to the episode begun in the orchard, when that new-tenant feeling of being in her body had heightened to full occupancy. She had become aware, then, of small and secret rooms inside her, unexplored and pulsing with mystery. Those secret rooms were no longer unexplored, and the body that she now happily and fully inhabited had received its first guest. Hardly a gentle guest, but certainly a considerate one. And most welcome.

From somewhere deep inside her emerged a little prayer to Old Hitch. She sent it on its way—perhaps it rose to the sky, perhaps it sank into the ground—and when she received the answer, she discovered that her old friend was not precisely disapproving of her actions.

She allowed herself to gently float in the thick aftermath of affection and intimacy, with her blood and muscles and desire both alive and exhausted. Well, maybe not her desire. Although physically exhausted, she could easily imagine trying to bring her desire alive again soon, in order to experience this wonderful new, paradoxical experience of traveling and homecoming and receiving guests in her special, secret home.

And that reminded her. Just where was her embarrassment? She reflected on what she had done, how she had been with him, over him, around him, with him, a part of him. Strangely, and again, appetizingly, the image evoked in her lazy brain did not cause her to wince, but rather to widen her eyes—metaphorically speaking, of course, for her eyes were closed, and even if she opened them, all she would be able to see would be the dark velvet of deep night. So where was the embarrassment a virginal young woman should feel when she was no longer so virginal?

Or even married.

That consideration held so little importance to her that it did nothing more than flit through her brain and flit out again. She supposed that wondering or worrying about marriage did not stick because she had the blessing of Old Hitch. No, not his blessing, but at least not his disapproval.

She heard the echo of his crotchety old voice asking, "Well, Cathy gal, do you know what you're doing?" Then his own cackling answer to the question: "I suppose that you do! It was bound to happen sooner or later. I'm glad it was later, rather than sooner, for your first time!''

Her first time. It seemed like forever, or maybe just a day, that she had been waiting for her first time.

That reminded her of something else. Something far more important than trivial considerations of her nonexistent embarrassment or flitting, unfitting thoughts of marriage or modesty. She was reminded that it had been *his* first time, too, and that she could be absolutely sure that he had told her the truth.

Why had he waited so long? she wondered. However, that question was not nearly as intriguing as the next one, which was, Why had he chosen her? That question was followed by an even more compelling one, namely, Was he as profoundly happy as she that he had waited so long and chosen her?

She smiled and snuggled deeper. He had chosen her because he liked her. Well, she liked him back. A lot. She liked his clean smell, the cut of his shoulders, his black hair and black eyes, his lips, his hands and his legs. Even more, she liked his dependability, his quiet sense of what needed to be done, his noble and misguided sense of saving her, his less-noble and more-focused desire to ruin her, his strength, his eagerness. To the top of this lovely and loverlike catalog of virtues rose his most outstanding quality: his honesty.

She could not resist. She raised her head and shifted her arms so that she could cross them over his chest, propping her chin at the intersection of her wrists. She looked up at him, peering through the darkness, and had a perspective on his face similar to the one she had had when she'd first fallen on top of him from the apple tree. From this angle, his face was mostly chin. Although he lay perfectly still and his breathing had returned to a steady rate, it seemed that he was awake. She determined that his eyes were open and that his gaze was, most likely, trained on the ceiling.

"So," she whispered, "what do you think?"

He did not answer or indicate that he had heard her.

She was not discouraged. "For your first time, that is." She teased, "Or were you telling me what I think the gentlemen call 'a pretty line'?"

Still he did not answer.

"Answer honestly, now," she persisted.

That got his attention. He raised the hand that had been wrapped around her shoulder and groped awkwardly for her head. With his fingers, he brushed back her hair.

"You take unfair advantage of the moment," he murmured with a half groan, "now that I am so completely at your mercy."

"You have always been completely at my mercy."

He rolled over quickly, turned her on her back, grasped each of her wrists and had her pinned beneath him almost before he took his next breath. "Do you want to discuss that statement further?"

She lost her drowsy contentment in a flash of surprise and excitement. "No," she said a little shakily, "I simply want your answer." She caught her breath and waited, ready after he answered her to pour out in words what she was feeling.

He did not answer her in words, and the quality of his silence was rich and complex. He had her caught beneath him with one strong arm across her breasts and one knee over her thighs. He shifted over her, then shifted back. He put his head down to the crook of her neck and breathed deeply. He began to caress her lightly, not with purpose, but with attention and affection.

Until he put his hand to her skin, to her curves, to the crooks and not-yet-sufficiently-explored places of her fully inhabited body, she had felt like speaking. Now she did not. She felt like feeling his touch, and the words inside melted on her tongue to murmurs, then pooled and slid down her limbs in long and lovely stretches of liquid, filling her knees and hip joints, her elbows and her wrists, her neck and jaw, then her eyelids. She felt like being silent with him, though perhaps not yet again a part of him. She felt like sleeping next to him, cradling and caressing him, as he was cradling and caressing her.

"I will let you know when I am ready to answer your question," he said, just before she dozed off.

It must have been several hours later when her eyes fluttered open, then closed, then fluttered open again. The room was barely, but perceptibly, lighter. She could just discern the faintest outlines of furniture emerging from the gloom, but dawn was still a comfortable distance away.

She was lying completely exposed on top of the covers, no modest, wrinkled sheet or light blanket shielding her newly inhabited, uninhibited body from peering eyes or probing hands.

Probing hands. She sighed once, deeply, and rolled onto her side. As she did so, she discovered a trapped hand between her thighs. Before she was fully aware of the implications of that hand, she was rolled onto her back again. Another hand kept her there, then moved to her breast, where it began to tease her nipple.

His lips came to her ear. "I am ready to answer the question now."

"Are you?" she said weakly. The hand at her thigh was grazing the inside of one, then shifting to the other. "Remind me what the question was."

"What I thought about making love for the first time."

"Oh, yes," she breathed. "That's a good question." She sighed. "And the answer?"

"It is like having been hungry your whole life," he said, "so that not only is your body starved, so is your appetite. Then, suddenly you have a real meal. It is not just that the body is fed. It is more important that the appetite comes alive."

She was following this explanation drowsily. She had always had a healthy appetite, and she had not been starved her whole life. Perhaps that was why she fell so easily into his arms or, at least, why the transition from touching to making love had seemed so smooth and natural to her.

"Your appetite has come alive?" she asked, turning toward him slightly, luxuriating in his continuing touch.

He said, "Yes," into her neck. "I was starved, and I didn't even know it. Now that I have had a taste, I don't think I'll ever have enough. Of this. Of you."

His appetite, long starved, had come alive. Her appetite, well nurtured, had simply added a dimension of which she had not previously, before she had met him, been aware. In his arms, she felt well up deep reserves of affection and caring that no other man had bothered to tap. At his touch, she responded with the healthy, unapologetic appetite that had always been hers, and that no man before him had liked her enough to notice and to enjoy.

"Could it be," he asked, "that, for once, you have nothing to say?"

She had the perfect retort, one she had not thought she'd ever have the opportunity to say to him. She responded quietly, with great enjoyment, against his lips, "You talk too much."

She was more than rewarded for this impertinence by a lover who was hungry, ardent, insatiable.

She pushed to the back of her mind the fact that he would take his insatiable appetite with him when he left Hillsborough. She easily ignored the whispering sense that he would be happier making love out in the woods, on a firm bed of pine straw, rather than on a soft bed of feathers. She barely perceived the thin yet durable barrier within him that would keep him from requiring that he be with her, remain with her, always, irrevocably.

She easily blotted out visions of the end, for she was saturated in a limitless present, intent only on responding to his lips and his arms and his legs and his hands. He was such a hungry and appreciative guest, and she had so much to give him and to take from him. She was stingy neither with her hospitality nor with receiving offerings from her guest that made him feel welcome, that gave him further pleasure, so that pleasure was heaped on pleasure.

So, then, where was her embarrassment? How could it be that she could lie naked and completely exposed and submit to the most intimate exploration of his hands without a moment's hesitation, a maiden's breath of protest or a moral woman's demand for commitment? She felt too delicious, she supposed, to feel embarrassed. When he touched that remarkable spot between her heavy, pleasure-filled limbs and she felt the fruit of her desire blossom and grow, she who had worked with apples her whole life could not feel that this blossoming and ripening was forbidden. She had lived and worked for ripe, red apples. Planting and cultivating them was her life. Their harvest was her livelihood. She could never be embarrassed about wanting to eat delicious fruit, coming alive in various shades of pink and red; about feeling the sweet juice dribble down her chin, or inner thigh. She could hardly move for the pleasure.

Then his hand came away and was replaced by his own immediate desire. At first, she was entwined with him in the deep, dark earth. Then they sprouted out of the ground together, still entwined, and she felt as if they were climbing a very lovely apple tree, broad and leafy and bright with fruit. They were hugging the rough bark and shimmying past smooth leaves, tasting the fruit along the way, little bites, big bites, satisfying bites, wanting more. Insatiable.

In the twining, shifting, forking branches of the tree they explored the crook of an arm, the bend of a neck, the joint where leg met body. Every touch, every kiss, every breath exchanged was of the orchard, rich in rows of many such trees, all broad and leafy and bright with fruit. She caught the faintest hint of apple-blossom fragrance in his hair.

They came to the top of the tree together, but it was not yet finished. More tendrils stretched and reached for the sky, and they climbed those together, too, happily. Finally, nearly exhausted, when the tendrils could go no farther, they flung themselves off the tip with abandon and fell to the ground. She caught him.

He caught her. She gave him her love and received his strength. She, who had never been light or airy, was scooped up in his arms, and she soared with him like a bird, streaking through the sky on wings of fire.

Then they shuddered together, as if releasing a flock of fire birds. When she could give and receive no more, when she could fly no higher, when she had no strength left, she let him lie, happy and exhausted, within her.

The next thing she knew, the room was perceptibly lighter, and he was shifting away from her, untangling himself from the sheets that also entangled her. It seemed that he was preparing to leave the bed.

She stretched her hand to grasp his arm. The sheet fell from her breasts and pooled at her waist. "You're leaving?"

He paused at the edge of the bed, ready to sit up. "The day is coming."

"That does not mean you have to leave," she protested.

He did not answer, merely rubbed his face with his hands and combed his tangled hair with his fingers.

She felt a touch of desperation. She sought for some way to keep him near her and thought, forlornly, that his insatiable appetite must be, in part, appeased. She did not realize that he was feeling as confused and desperate as she.

Because his nature was not naturally affectionate, his response to his confusion and desperation was to leave her house and plunge into the woods, to surround himself with a dense forest. There he was familiar with blazing unfamiliar new trails alone. What he had experienced with Cathy had opened up a new kind of forest, one he had never encountered, with none of the familiar markers or signs. He had no skills to help him move through it, for neither Attean nor Morgan had taught him those ways. It suddenly seemed to him the most complicated, incomprehensible thing in the world to walk a path, side by side, in company with a woman.

"I must tell you what happened after Clive came to get me," she said quickly.

He turned to look at her over his shoulder. She felt a rush of relief that his interest was caught, if only minimally.

It was then that she noticed his skin. The light in her bedroom was sufficient now for her to see the drape of crepey, cracked skin spilling from his neck over his left shoulder and down his back. He had been burned as a child, it seemed—most probably as an infant, before conscious memory. But he wore the experience of it on his body, like a cloak.

The damaged skin had stretched and pulled unnaturally. It had shrunk from the task of growing with the growing body it encased. She could only imagine the pain and the physical conditioning he had suffered in order to make his arm and shoulder usable, much less so skillful. She remembered feeling and stroking patches of rough skin, but she had not perceived them to be so tortuously wrenched. Now she knew that he had, indeed, come from hell.

He must have noticed her eyes on his skin, for something in him drew away from her. It was nearly a physical drawing away, and she wondered how he could make himself so physically absent, when his body was present. It was as if, before her eyes, she saw him take flight. Without her.

Her feeling of loneliness and abandonment was acute and was all the more powerful in that his body was still next to her. She wanted to draw him back.

"Clive brought me to the house," she continued, speaking against the possibility of silence and his departure, "and the porch." She nodded toward one wall, indicating that direction. "They were all there. You know—the Boys, Ginger and George." She paused. "They wanted to know where you were."

"Did you tell them?"

"No, because I did not know, and because it didn't seem to be their business. Anyway, they had come to find out whether I'd been successful with MacGuff."

He repeated flatly, "MacGuff," as if the name sounded vaguely familiar to him and he was trying to place it.

"About retrieving the last two lines of the sonnet," she reminded him. Although solving the puzzle would mean his departure from Hillsborough, she hoped that the reminder of his original purpose would bring him back to her now, while he was still in her bed.

To judge from his expression of mild disinterest, her ploy hadn't worked.

"Of course, I had to tell them that I was not successful," she pursued. "So we spent the rest of the afternoon and most of the evening attempting to devise a plan to finagle the two lines out of him."

He nodded slowly.

She said with a tentative half smile, "We finally decided that you would think of something."

That snagged his interest. His attention came back, and his eyes focused on her. He thought about it for a moment—or at least, he thought about something for a moment, but he did not speak.

She rushed on. "Yes, we decided that you would think of something, but we had no more specific ideas than that. You see, the only possible prop we have is MacGuff's hat, which he left here at the house yesterday, but we could not imagine that it would help us in any way, except maybe to make him return here. So..."

She was about to launch into more empty speech to fill the emptier silence, when she realized that they had reverted to their old habits: she was talking too much and he was talking too little.

"So what do you have to say say to that?" she asked, resorting to direct questions to make him answer her.

"Nothing."

"Oh. Well, do you think you'll be able to think of a plan?"

"I might."

"Any ideas yet what it would be?"

His eyes focused on her more intently. A speculative light lit their dark depths. "Make sure he comes to the uncle's house tonight. After dark."

"How do I do that?"

"I don't know."

"So it's my problem, then, making sure he comes to Old Hitch's?"

"Yes."

"You mean, alone?"

"You can come with him, if you want."

"Where should he—or we—show up?"

He considered the question. "By the sundial."

"What do you intend to do?"

He did not answer that.

"You're not going to tell me?" She was frustrated, but wanted to keep asking questions so that he would stay.

He shook his head slightly. Then his expression shifted almost imperceptibly. His eyes roamed her face, then dropped to her breasts, which she had not modestly covered when the sheet fell to her waist. His eyes came back to her face, where they rested. He hesitated.

She thought he was about to speak. "Yes?" she said, anxiously, hopefully.

He shook his head again.

"Were you going to say something?"

"No."

"Do you want to say something?"

"No."

"Really, it looked as if you were going to speak." She felt ridiculous, persisting like this, but could not contain herself, not with that irresistible look in his eyes, as if he could feed his insatiable appetite again and still want more. Then she thought, Make it a direct question! Otherwise he won't answer!

"What is it that you were going to say?" she asked as calmly as she could.

A very subtle expression came over his features. He shook his head a third time, declining her invitation to divulge his thoughts. Rising from the bed, he said, "You said I talked too much."

In front of her very astonished, admiring eyes, he dressed, picked up his bow and quiver from the floor at her bedside, noiselessly crossed the room, slipped out the half-open window and vanished into the gray dawn.

Chapter Eighteen

She plopped back against the pillows, filled with strong and rich emotions, mostly delicious, but cut with irritation and indignation, as well. With a further swirl of those delicious emotions, she had to admit that the irritation and indignation felt good, too.

The man had been *smug!* She had seen it as clearly as she could read any emotion on his maddeningly expressionless face. Well, it wasn't expressionless to her. Not by a long shot! No, she had read his emotions plainly, and he was feeling both superior and amused. Now, what had he said to her when they had been mock kissing, but then again, not-so-mock kissing, on the swing? He had said, straight-faced, that he had more self-control than she did. Ha! He hardly had any more self-control than she did, and she was glad of it, too.

The man had an unexpected and unpredictable sense of humor, that was for sure, and it scarcely mattered that she had never heard him laugh or even seen him smile, really. But she knew. She knew that his humor—for all that it was subtle and nearly imperceptible—was there, coasting just below calm waters, like a fat fish whose tail would occasionally ruffle the surface.

It was arousing, too, his superior amusement and reference to their passion. Why, he had actually been *flirting* with her! He had made her want him again, had made her want him more, had made her wish she had never taunted him with the words *You talk too much.* He made her think that perhaps he had been about to say something lovely and loverlike. Instead, he'd chosen to tease her and arouse her, rather than to satisfy her with sweet words or kisses.

What had he said at that most passionate moment when she had told him words were no longer necessary? He had said that he'd been starved. That he now had an appetite. That he did not think he could ever tire of their passion or of her. It roused her own well-nurtured but underexplored and underappreciated appetite just to think of that moment, and the next. And the next after that.

If he walked back in the room right now, she would know what to do, and she would not show a shred of self-control. She would feed his appetite, knowing as only a well-fed, well-nurtured person knew, that appetite came with the eating. She would make his appetite grow and flourish. She would fill his starved soul so that it would only want her more, the more she filled it. She would make that thin yet durable barrier within him vanish, the one that kept him from being able to fully accept her nourishment, the one that kept him from being able to fully enjoy her love.

She sat up. Barrier? She ran her fingers through her knotted hair, causing the fringe at her forehead to stand up in spikes. Where had that thought come from?

She had no earthly idea. He certainly had set up no barriers between his body and hers. He had shown no hesitation, no inhibition, no holding back in the expression or satisfaction of his physical passion. He had not doubted, nor had he failed to find, her own passion. And he had teased her upon parting, not cutting her off from him, but making her want him more.

Because lying in bed naked, surrounded by the sheets still warm from him and their lovemaking, and thinking of teasing and passionate barriers only made her quite definitely desirous of him, she decided that she had better get up. She swung her lazy, satisfied legs over the side of the bed, drew a deep breath and thought that every step forward during the day would take her a step closer to him.

Would she truly not be seeing him until tonight, after dark? What was his plan for Old Hitch's house? And what might they do, alone and together, afterward?

She tossed these questions around as she dressed for the day. She washed herself and put on the same pale gold blouse and skirt from her mother's trunk that she had worn the day before in the orchard. She made the bed, although reluctant to straighten the turbulent sheets and pull the covers over so memorable a scene, and tidied the room. She went to the kitchen and fed Aunt Rachel and Black Twig, and made herself a breakfast of grits and dried apple slices fried in butter. The apple slices tasted particularly good this morning, and she wished she could have fed some to her fiery bird, her fire bird.

Then she went through the rest of the house, doing a dozen chores or more that she had left undone in the past several days. In those same days, the house that had always been big seemed to have grown even larger; and it had grown strange to her, too, as if it did not belong to her. Or no longer belonged to her. Her odd sense of transition accelerated.

She decided that the feeling of transition came from the fact that she did not want Laurence Harris to leave Hillsborough, ever, but that she knew, deep down, he would never be contained by this house, no matter how large it grew. She was instantly saddened by the thought, but buffered herself against it by thinking back on the night before and forward to the night ahead.

She had this, that and the other thing to do, and then, midmorning, she heard a knock on her door.

She knew intuitively who would be standing on the other side. Without giving the least thought to her appearance, she crossed the vestibule to the front door and opened it.

She was right. MacGuff stood before her, all spruced up. Slick, really, now that she took a good, critical look at him. She was put in mind of Old Hitch's deathbed words concerning his nephew: *I'll be damned if he hasn't been spendin' his time preenin' before some Raleigh tailor's mirror!* And, of course, he was hatless, revealing hair that was carefully curled and pomaded. She admired, rather distantly, the way the chestnut color of his hair harmonized with his warm, amber eyes and his natty brown suit.

"Miss Cathy," he said. His drawl was just as honey toned as the rest of him.

"MacGuff," she replied, thinking that he was a pretty nicely put together package.

She noted that, today, the package had little effect on her. However, the presence of such perfection reminded her, belatedly, that she had not combed her hair. She imagined that it must be tousled to the point of dishevelment. A mere three days before she would have been hideously embarrassed to be seen like this by him. Now she was more interested in his reaction, then downright amazed to read the change of expression in his eyes as they touched her hair, her face, then ran over her blouse and skirt and back up to her face.

From that look, she knew three things at once: He saw her as sexually desirable and was again surprised, but even more so, pleased; he had seduced countless women with such a look; she would never let him touch her again.

When she did not immediately invite him in, he raised his arm to the doorjamb and leaned casually against it, striking a slightly aggressive, more than slightly suggestive pose. "It looks like you just got out of bed," he said in a way that made her think he was issuing an invitation to return to her bed with him.

She did not waste time considering how it was that he could tell just by looking at her that she was suddenly sexually available. Maybe it was a look of satisfaction in her eyes or on her face. Maybe it was a different way she held her body because she felt so good about it. Maybe it was a new, enticing scent she exuded. She should have felt more exultant about finally appearing more desirable to him than he was to her, but she didn't waste time considering that issue, either.

Her thoughts were more centered on conceiving her plan to get him to Old Hitch's tonight. What she said was, "I suppose you've come for your hat." She reached over, took his hat off the hall tree and extended it to him, dangling it on one finger. "Here it is."

His brows quirked at her provocative, dismissive gesture. He looked a little taken aback that she didn't use the excuse of his hat to draw him inside, fix him tea and biscuits, make him tarry. She was sending him on his way, just like that. She saw his desire for her jump up a notch, and she saw her plan for the evening ahead spinning itself out before her very eyes. She was no longer weak and fuzzy headed in his presence, but strong and clever. And that felt nice, too.

He drew the hat slowly off her finger. "Thank you."

"You left it on the kitchen counter yesterday," she said. She affected a pretty, unconcerned shrug. "I figured you'd come back for it today."

"Did you?" He was attempting to draw her out.

"Stands to reason." She was not going to give him an inch. She was going to make him work. "And to prove me right, here you are."

The slight cock of his head signaled appreciation of her remark. She saw him turn up the warmth in his eyes, ratchet up his charm a notch. "Here I am," he said, all honeyed smiles.

She thought, He's pretty good. To which she added, And I'm glad I'm immune. She leaned against the opposing jamb of the door. She folded her arms under her breasts. If that gesture shoved her breasts up in a way that was both offering and taunting, she was content to offer herself and to taunt him.

"Here you are," she repeated, "and now you have your hat."

There was nothing for him to do but depart. She was glad that he hesitated. He twirled the hat deftly around his hand. He said, "About dinner yesterday..."

She smiled knowingly and, she hoped, mysteriously. "What about dinner yesterday?" Then, boldly, "Or were you thinking about dessert?"

She leaned forward ever so slightly, so that her bodice gaped enough to reveal a hint of cleavage. She had generous cleavage, and now she had reason to flaunt it. The day before she had caught a crumb of chess pie in the folds of her bodice. Today she hoped to catch a crumb of a different sort.

"I was thinking about dessert," he admitted. He glanced down at her bosom. His gaze lingered.

Caught! "The pie was sweet," she said, "but you weren't."

He affected an artful expression of contrition. "I behaved badly."

"You did."

"But you teased me," he pressed reproachfully.

"I did," she admitted.

A hint of craftiness cut across his contrite and reproachful expression. "You mean that you were teasing me about wanting to know what Old Hitch wrote me?"

She smiled lazily and nodded. She could think of no better hook than to tell him what he wanted to hear. "You were right. Clive mentioned the strange letter you received from Old Hitch last week. Of course, your uncle was a little crazy at the end—"

"Well before the end," MacGuff interpolated. His eyes displayed a trace of relief. "So, Miss Cathy, what are you saying?"

"I'm saying that you were right that I went to a lot of trouble for a kiss," she said. She was amazed to feel nothing: no humiliation, no twinge of embarrassment at feeding him his own interpretation of the incident on the swing. "And if—as you said—I wasn't woman enough for more than a kiss yesterday, I might be today."

She wondered if a man's eyes could fall out of his head. Of course, MacGuff was not outrageously unsubtle in his reaction, but his eyes did widen perceptibly. Then they narrowed, warmly and seductively. He was obviously pleased, but was taking it in stride that she would be making up to him in such a fashion.

"Well, well," he breathed. He pushed off from his side of the door and leaned closer to her. "How do I know that you aren't leading me on again?" he asked. His question suggested doubt, but his tone was cocksure.

She forced herself not to draw away from him. "You don't," she said, matching him for warmth and seduction. "But you can find out."

He liked the sound of that. "How?"

"Tonight," she said.

He glanced at her swing and quirked his eyebrows, then looked beyond her, as if toward her bedroom.

Her immediate thought was, Hah! Not likely!, but she kept to her role of seductress. "I sure do like my porch," she said, "but I'm feeling bad about yesterday. You know." She shrugged again, revealing a pretty glimpse of breast. "And my house...well, it wouldn't be right to be *inside*. So I was thinking, for an exciting occasion, we should go to Old Hitch's."

He looked at first surprised by the suggestion, then puzzled, then intrigued. "Old Hitch's?" he echoed, as if tasting the strange possibilities of a romantic interlude with a woman he had known his entire life but whose sexual potential he had severely underrated.

"Not inside his old shack, of course," she continued, hoping to maintain her pose and tones of breathy anticipation. "Say, in the meadow, by the sundial."

"The sundial?"

"We wouldn't stay there, of course. We'd only meet there."

"And?"

She smiled very slowly and pretended that she was looking at her fire bird at the very moment of their joining. "And you'll see."

It seemed as if MacGuff might start panting. Really, this was too easy!

He pulled himself together to say, with hardly a crack in his voice, "At the sundial, then. When tonight?"

"After dark, of course," she said, "when the moon is halfway up." She added, for good measure, for she was liking this taste of power reversal, "It's going to be a full moon tonight."

He straightened up and said smoothly, "Well, then, in order to discover just how much woman you are, we'll have to find ourselves a cozy little spot that's sheltered from the moonlight."

"Then, again, bathing in the moonlight might be nice," she said brazenly. She took a deep breath, arched her back slightly so that her breasts were thrust out, then shut the door in his very handsome, very astonished face.

George Travis had reached a decision. He was a man who had come to the point where he could no longer let himself be ruled by his mother. Now, he loved his mama and respected her opinions, but he was not in love with Miss Sylvia Lee, and nothing in her father's healthy bank balance—well, hell, the man *owned* the bank!—could make him love Miss Ginger Mangum less.

That was it, pure and simple. He loved Miss Ginger and always would. Even if he married Miss Sylvia. Now, being in love with one woman and marrying another was not fair to either, and if one woman was going to be disappointed in all of this, it might as well be his mama. In having arrived at that conclusion, George's mind had taken a practical turn: his mama was not going to live forever.

In one small, well-concealed, unfilial corner of his soul, he hoped that his announcement to marry Miss Ginger just might send his poor mama's heart into a spasm and cause her to die. In another small, well-concealed, but equally unfilial corner of his soul, he doubted that the spasm of his poor mama's heart would cause her to do anything but make him suffer unbearably over his decision to follow his heart's desire, rather than hers.

The dialogue between the deep, unexamined corners of his soul hardly penetrated his conscious thoughts as he left Travis's Dry Goods for his midday break. He walked with purpose down Churton, turned up Tryon, crossed Wake and did not stop until he arrived at the front steps to the little humble house where lived the love of his life with her granny. He mounted the steps with confidence and knocked resolutely on the front door.

It opened to reveal an angel—one with beautiful blue eyes, a beautiful nose, a beautiful mouth and beautiful curls. Why, his angel was the most beautiful woman he had ever seen or ever hoped to see! Everything about her was...just beautiful.

"Miss Ginger," he said, taking his hat from his head and holding it in his hands, signaling his respect for her.

"Why, George," she said, "you surprised me. I was not expecting you." She looked down and said shyly, "You have never come calling before."

"Today is different," he said with the air of a new man, a forceful man. A man's man.

"Is it?" she said, raising her eyes to him, just as shyly. If George had not been so much in love, he would have seen the quick calculation behind the guilelessness. She, apparently, knew the import of this first call and had been waiting for it for a very long time. She was able to contain herself, however, for she merely smiled, came out the door and closed it behind her. They stood together on her little front porch. She looked up at the sky. "Why, to me, today seems just like yesterday."

"To me, the world is transformed," George pronounced.

"Oh?"

He took his love's delicate hand in his. "I *hope* the world is transformed," he amended, "if you will but answer yes to the question I have come to ask."

Ginger knew her lines by heart. She increased the pressure, ever so slightly, of her hand in his. She looked up at him with melting blue eyes. She asked, without a hint of coyness, "And what question is that, George?"

He did not immediately oblige her. He wished to explain himself first. "I have been holding off asking you this question for...a variety of reasons. Then, for the past several days, I have thought that, perhaps, Old Hitch was going to leave something to you or to me—something more than a scrap of land, maybe— that would justify me asking you this question, without concern for... for *practical* considerations.''

This was not exactly an opening to a declaration of love and a proposal of marriage that would warm most women's hearts. However, to Ginger's credit, her melting blue gaze did not freeze up or become fixed.

''So I woke up this morning,'' George continued with conviction, ''having come to a decision, and I waited for my first free moment—the break for the midday meal, right now, this very minute, and I must tell you that I have not yet eaten, nor could I reasonably think of food at a time like this!—to come and ask you the question.''

''Yes, George?'' Ginger said, with all the prompting encouragement any woman could muster.

''The question that a man who is a man must one day ask a woman, the question that fills the heart and mind of a man in love, the question that will affect the course of his life, the question that bears upon his whole existence, the question that—''

''And the question, George?'' Ginger pressed, becoming a slight bit impatient.

''Will you marry me, Miss Ginger?'' he said, coming at last to his point.

''Oh, George!'' Ginger breathed.

''Is that a yes?'' George demanded.

''Oh, George!'' she breathed again, becoming a little light-headed after all these months—and, indeed, years—of waiting.

''I'll take that as a yes,'' George said, liking the manly feel of making forceful decisions. ''Now, may

I kiss you?'' He decided that he would not accept no for an answer, so he took his love in his arms and bent his head toward hers.

"Oh, George!" Ginger sighed a third time, unutterably happy.

"Oh, George!" called a voice with a very different and commanding tone. "Ginger!"

Ginger and George broke their embrace with an almost-guilty jump away from one another. When they saw that Cathy was the one who had hailed them, they both relaxed—and each denied, privately, that they had imagined Mrs. Travis sneaking up on them.

Ginger left the porch and went toward the new arrival. She grasped her dear friend's hands and said, "Cathy, George has just asked me to marry him!"

Cathy's brows rose. "Did he?" She looked impressed. To Ginger, she said, "I'm very happy for you!" To George, she said, "Congratulations!"

"Yes, I am very happy that Miss Ginger has consented to be my wife," George said.

"There was no doubt about that!" Cathy said in her high-handed fashion, and George could see that she was in one of her bossy moods. "I'm congratulating you, rather," she continued, "on having finally screwed up your courage to ask her. It's about time!" She put her hands on her hips and smiled broadly. "So, then, when's the happy date?"

"We have not yet told Mama," George said, coming down the steps in his betrothed's wake, "and I think, under the circumstances, that we'll allow her to choose the date that best suits her." He was looking at Cathy and wondering what was different about her. He could not quite put his finger on it.

"Ah!" was Cathy's pithy response to that. "I'm happy for you, and I hope your mama won't delay the wedding for very long." She kissed both Ginger and George soundly on the cheek and said, "Well, I won't stay long, then, for I believe that I happened upon you just as you were going to seal your betrothal with a kiss. But I needed to tell you the news about Mr. Harris's plan."

"He has one?" George asked.

"Yes, he asked me to get Young MacGuff over to Old Hitch's tonight after dark."

"What does Mr. Harris propose to do there?" Ginger asked.

"I don't know," Cathy said, "but I have just seen MacGuff, and he has agreed to meet me at Old Hitch's tonight, after dark, when the moon is halfway up the sky."

"But why would MacGuff agree to do that?" George queried. It didn't seem a likely plan to him.

Cathy smiled in a way that George had never seen her smile before. "He thinks he is meeting me there for a little tryst."

"Miss Cathy!" he expostulated, quite shocked. "Don't tell me that you mean to compromise your...your maidenly virtue!"

Cathy's sun-kissed skin acquired a tinge of pink. "Not at all, George. MacGuff only *thinks* that I mean to compromise myself with him. I only intimated that in order to *lure* him there, I suppose you might say. Once he's there, Mr. Harris will get him to reveal his clue."

George, in his newfound manliness, decided that Miss Cathy needed protection from MacGuff's lecherous ways—and to think that Miss Cathy needed protection from *any* man's lecherous ways would have been unthinkable as recently as forty-eight hours ago. He said, "Although I appreciate your method, I am not sure I approve. I had better go along with you, so that MacGuff takes no undue liberties." To Ginger, he said masterfully, "You must stay behind, I am afraid, my dear. Old Hitch's shack after dark is no place for you."

Ginger smiled and breathed, "Oh, George!" and was more than happy to obey.

Cathy's response was more prosaic. "Suit yourself," she said with a shrug, "but for heaven's sakes, stay out of sight until we discover what Mr. Harris has in mind!"

Chapter Nineteen

Not much later, Cathy found the Boys lounging on the courthouse steps. Upon hearing the news of the evening's adventure, they informed her that they, too, wanted to go out to Old Hitch's after dark. She was not at all surprised to discover that their motives were not as noble as George's desire to keep a watchful eye on her virtue. Rather, they were curious to witness what the Welshman had up his sleeve for Young MacGuff's undoing.

"Did he tell you what he planned to do?" Hank asked curiously.

Cathy shook her head. "He told me only to make sure that MacGuff got out to Old Hitch's after dark."

Hank frowned. "So, how are you goin' to git him out there? It don't seem a likely idea to me, why a man would want to visit an old haunted shack."

Cathy smiled. "MacGuff's not imagining that he's going to visit the house or anything like that!"

Hank's frown remained. "No? Well, then, what would make him go out there?"

Cathy's smile became a smirk. "Maybe I was a better pupil than you realized for the lessons Miss Ginger gave me the other day."

Hank's frown vanished, and his eyes were measuring as he looked her over from head to toe. He pulled a thoughtful face and nodded. He said, not for the first time, since his expressive range was not great, "Your plan jes' might work."

"Why, thank you, Hank," Cathy said.

He was quick to respond. "Now, there you go again, Miss Cathy, saying thank-you like you don't mean it! Now, if that's the kind of sweet-talkin' you think will git MacGuff out to Old Hitch's, let me tell you that—"

"MacGuff's already agreed to meet me there," she interrupted, "so you can figure I asked him sweetly enough! And if I bait you continually, Hank, it's because you rise so beautifully to the fly."

The new sauciness in her usual bossiness affected each man differently. Richard thought that, although Miss Cathy's looks had improved in the past several days, she was still capable of handling any shenanigans Young MacGuff might dish out. Hank was inclined to think that, shore enough, Miss Cathy had learnt a thing or two from Miss Ginger. Orin thought, inevitably, of flies and fishing lures and fish, and announced that he was hungry.

In his own dim way, Boy happened to ask the essential question. "But jes' when did you have a chance to see the Welshman, I'm wonderin'? He weren't with us last night, and you said that MacGuff appeared on your doorstep first thing this mornin'. After that, you went to Miss Ginger's and found George, then came here and found us. It seems to me, if'n I understand it now—" here he furrowed his brow in deepest concentration "—that you had to've seen the Welshman *afore* you saw MacGuff. Otherwise, you couldn't have knowed the plan."

Cathy felt herself go pink at this line of reasoning and could think of absolutely nothing to say. Her thoughts were tangled in and around the memory of her merging and melting in the arms of her fire bird.

She pulled herself together and said a little lamely, "Well, I saw MacGuff *second* thing this morning, which means, actually, that I saw Mr. Harris *first* thing. Yes, that's it. He came by real early to tell me his plan." She gulped. "*Part* of his plan, anyway."

Looking at Cathy's cheeks, Orin's fantasy platter of fried fish acquired a side dish of poached peaches, glazed to a pink-gold perfection. "I'm mighty hungry, I declare."

When the talk turned to what the Boys were going to do about the midday meal, Cathy saw her opportunity to make a quick exit. "I'll see you tonight, then, *after* Mr. Harris's plan has been executed. Now, remember—MacGuff and I will be meeting at the sundial. So for heaven's sakes, make sure that you stay out of sight and be quiet! After all, if MacGuff thinks he's being set up, he'll bolt, and then Mr. Harris's plan—whatever it is—won't work!"

The Boys reassured her on that score, and Cathy returned home, thinking that she was not very good at dissembling. If she didn't watch out, she'd give her new and secret life away with more than a furious blush.

Thereafter, for Cathy, the day passed performing useful work around her house and garden and orchard. Part of her mind dwelled on her chores; part on her fire bird's mysterious plan for the night; part on what they might do afterward; part on what he would do the next day, assuming that he would be successful in coaxing MacGuff into coughing up the contents of his two lines.

She worked herself into a fine and dirty sweat, and when the sun was starting to sink after a long and lovely afternoon, she decided that she needed a bath. Nothing less than head to toe would do, and she washed her hair into the bargain and let it dry in the long rays and sweet breezes of the coming evening. She put on the flattering green dress with the drawstring bodice. She thought she would have to leave it pretty loose, once night fell.

Ginger stopped by the house right before supper, beaming with her good news and radiant with happiness.

Cathy hugged her dear friend. As she drew her over to the swing, she said, "Now, tell me everything!"

"Why, there is nothing to tell!" Ginger protested. "You know everything already."

"But not the date of the wedding," Cathy teased.

Ginger bit her pretty lip. "We haven't set that yet, Cathy dear. We told you this morning we would let Mrs. Travis—I suppose I should start thinking of her as Mother Travis now!—establish the day that would suit her best."

"Yes, but..." Cathy began. "Ah! I suppose that Mrs. Travis has not yet heard the happy news."

"She might be hearing it now," Ginger explained, "for George promised me he would tell her at supper-time."

Cathy considered dropping by the Travis's this evening. She wanted to make sure that all was well and that Mrs. Travis was responding to the—for her—catastrophically bad news without too much vaporish fuss. Cathy imagined soothing Mrs. Travis, talking her out of her vapors and generally making everything smooth at the Travis household. The thought felt not only very familiar, but also very appealing.

With effort, she banished the idea and firmly decided to let the Travises and the Mangums work out their problems on their own—but not without some afterthoughts about how much she would have liked to put everything in order, just the way she wanted.

Cathy turned to Ginger and said, "I am sure that George is doing a fine job of informing his mother of your betrothal, and I hope that Mrs. Travis will remember to pay a visit to Grandmother Mangum tomorrow, as she ought."

Ginger bit her lip again and said hopefully, "And if Mrs. Travis doesn't, you'll remind her, won't you, Cathy?"

After a deep breath, Cathy smiled and said, "I think *you* should remind her, Ginger dear."

Ginger shook her head, "Oh, no, I couldn't!"

Cathy's smile broadened. She took Ginger's hand in hers. She said, "On this swing, not two evenings ago, you told me how I was to talk nice and sweet to a man to get his attention. Well, you were an excellent teacher, and the proof is that MacGuff has agreed to meet me tonight at Old Hitch's! Now, I'm returning the favor and telling you that, beginning tomorrow, *you* will be the most important Travis female and must act the part! Oh, I'm not saying that Mrs. Travis will like it, but she'll simply have to learn to play second fiddle, just as you, my dear, will have to learn to take charge."

Ginger sighed and said, "I suppose you're right, but it won't be easy."

"You'll take one thing at a time," Cathy counseled, "and make one decision at a time."

"I'm already learning the business," Ginger said on a brighter note. "Why, I returned with George to the store, and he began to teach me about the stock and the ledgers and how to treat customers."

"And what did you learn that was most interesting?"

"I suppose it must be that the customer is always right," Ginger said, "which George is impressing upon my mind. No matter what odd request a customer makes, it is my duty to fulfill it. Why, take Mr. Harris's request, for instance."

"Mr. Harris's request?"

"Yes, he came into the store this afternoon and made the oddest purchases! Well! It was all I could do to talk him out of it, but George said I was to smile and sell him what he wanted!"

Cathy blinked. "What did he want?"

"Soda ash and salt," Ginger said. "Bags of it! It was very odd!"

"What did he want soda ash and salt for?" Cathy wondered.

"I don't know. George and I discussed it afterward, and I was of the opinion that Mr. Harris meant to bake something. George thought rather that Mr. Harris must have eaten something that did not agree with him. He told me he has heard that people sometimes put some soda into water to make it bubble up, and when they drink it, the fizzy water makes their stomach settle." Ginger smiled. "So, you see how much I've learned already. Why, the next time Old Man Lloyd comes into the store complaining of stomach cramps, I'll stir him up a glass of fizzy water and sell it to him!''

"So Mr. Harris has either a hankering to bake something or an upset stomach?'' Cathy repeated, still amazed. "I suppose we'll find out which one it is soon enough.''

They were to find out, and Laurence Harris's purchase of soda ash and salt had nothing to do with either baking or his diet.

The evening drifted gently into night, and the moon appeared on the eastern horizon. When it began to creep up in the sky, Cathy loosened her bodice, fetched her gold-fringed shawl, covered the expanse of her bosom with the ends of the large triangle and left her house by the back door. The grass was damp, so after a few paces, she returned to her back steps, stripped off her stockings and unbuckled her shoes. She left these items behind.

She started out again for Old Hitch's, liking the warm, squishy feeling of spring beneath her feet. She sighed and thought of Laurence Harris and the night ahead. She sighed again and thought, How ironic that I am finally meeting MacGuff for romance and can think only of the man I hope to meet afterward!

Because her night eyes were not, apparently, as good as Laurence Harris's, she did not attempt the shortcut through the woods. Instead, she traveled the safe, well-known path to Old Hitch's, climbing the hill and skirting the orchard. At the crest of the slope, she looked down. Below her, glowing ghostly gray in the moonlight, floated Old Hitch's tumbledown shack. It looked sad to her and utterly abandoned.

She descended the slope and waded into Old Hitch's meadow. She made her way over to the sundial, straining her eyes in the darkness for signs of either Young MacGuff or Laurence Harris. She saw neither and felt a shiver ripple through her at the thought that she was alone and standing not too many yards from a dead man's doorstep. She wrapped her shawl more tightly around her shoulders. She would have felt better to have received some kind of sign from Laurence Harris, signaling, if nothing else, that he was present.

The effect of the eerie setting skittered across her skin, raising bumps. The loneliness of the moment settled uneasily into her bones. The occasional hoot of an owl made her senses jump. She was so jumpy, in fact, that when a hand grasped her elbow and a deep voice whispered in her ear, "Have you been waiting long for me?" she clutched her heart in fear.

Before turning to her captor, she caught the familiar scent of hair oil and shaving soap. She scolded in a whisper, "Good heavens, you scared me, MacGuff!"

"I did?" he said smoothly, sliding his hand from her elbow to her shoulder. "Why should you have been scared? You were expecting me, weren't you?"

She gustily exhaled her relief. "Yes, I was expecting you." She wanted him to remove his hand from her shoulder, but she could not do that until Laurence Harris made his appearance—whenever and wherever that would be. She looked around and said, "If I was startled, it's only because this place is so...creepy."

MacGuff's hand caressed her shoulder. He moved a little closer. "I thought that was the idea," he said with relish, "to find a place that would stimulate our imaginations and appetites. Why, I rather liked your suggestion of coming to the old geezer's dump. I'm curious to discover where our imaginations and appetites will lead us.''

So saying, he moved in front of her and backed her against the sundial, pressing his length against her. The hand at her shoulder moved down her back. His other hand plucked at the place where her shawl crossed in front, and slid in under the material. His fingers spread over the bare skin of her neck and began to move downward.

He put his lips to her neck and began to kiss her. He must have noticed that she had become quite rigid, for he lifted his head and said into her ear, "If you don't put your arms around me, little lady, you'll have me thinking that you didn't really want to come out here."

Cathy lifted her arms, rather reluctantly, and put them around his once-beloved, once-desired neck.

"That's better. Remember that you promised to be woman enough for me," he said, "and I like my women to be women."

"Women?"

He laughed low. "You don't think you're the first, do you?" He put his lips back at her neck and nuzzled her.

No, she didn't. On the other hand, it struck her as rude—to say the least—or unnecessarily boastful that he should mention past conquests in the present context. "In which case," she said, "I assume you don't think you're the first for me, either."

He stopped his nuzzling and looked up, putting her away from him slightly. "What?" he asked. His voice was flat.

"I was simply wondering whether what's sauce for the goose is good for the gander."

His handsome face was high-contrast shadows and planes, and the brown warmth of his coloring was chilled to cool pearl in the flooding moonlight. "What are you saying, little lady?" he asked. His voice was as chill as the pale, white light. His grip on her became threatening and a little hurtful.

She hoped that Laurence Harris would show up soon. Or even George, who had declared that he would protect her virtue. And where, come to think of it, were the Boys? She had not truly believed they could keep themselves out of sight and quiet. Where were they now, when she needed them most?

"You said you liked your women to be women," she reminded him, stalling for time, "and so I assumed you meant them to be . . . experienced."

The narrowing of his eyes, so potentially seductive by day, took on a sinister cast in the moonlight. "I like them to be women," he said, moving the hand under her shawl to the drawstrng of her bodice, "and to be pure."

Her skin crawled. His hand was at her breast. "Just how I like my men to be," she said.

She thought of her fire bird's eager exuberance and his lavish affection. She thought of the strength of his fresh desire, the unselfish way he gave his body to her and his demand that she be as satisfied as he. He had given her the whole of him and cherished the whole of her, which she had given in return. By comparison, MacGuff's artful pawing and practiced nuzzling seemed shabby and threadbare. She wanted to push him away. Nevertheless, for the sake of the plan, she would try to hold him off for a few moments more.

"You must be joking, little lady," MacGuff said to her face as he tugged one end of the drawstring and loosened it. Then his hand closed over the thin chemise covering her breast.

She tried to jerk away from him, but his other arm held her firmly to him and wedged her against the sundial. She turned her head, feeling desperate now, aware of a male violence rising within him that could have extremely swift and negative consequences for her. She wished that she could whimper or play the little-girl innocent or truly sweet-talk him into letting her go, but she felt a feminine anger rise up in her that might only spur his further violence.

There it was, her feminine anger, and there was no denying it. She could not, would not, reverse the effects of what she had experienced in the course of last night and the past few days. She was living fully in her body now. *She* was the sole owner. *She* decided who she would invite to visit or would ask to leave.

"I am not joking," she said. Her voice was just as flat as his and far more authoritative. "You can let me go now, sir, and if you don't—"

Three things happened at once. She raised her leg to knee him in the groin. He gripped her tighter and said, "Why, you bossy bi—!" The sky flamed with fire.

She did not complete her action of hurting him. His grip slackened, and he never completed his ugly curse. He turned away from her to look, dumbstruck, at the fire in the sky.

With MacGuff out of her line of sight, Cathy could see that there was no fire in the sky. Rather, the fire was on the ground, and it was burning Old Hitch's rickety shack. But, no; she saw at second glance that Old Hitch's shack was not burning. It was encircled by a ring of fire that ran right up to the porch and around both sides. Leaping tongues of fire licked the air within a mere few feet of the dry old wood of the shack.

Hardly had she perceived the placement of the first ring of fire than a second ring sprang up from the ground. This second circle was farther out from the house than the first, but wider and with higher flames. Then, before her eyes, a third concentric and more terrible circle rushed up from the ground, as if shooting straight from the fury of hell.

She fell back and was supported by the sundial. MacGuff, having nothing behind to steady him, nearly stumbled and fell in his surprise and fear. She heard the exclamation, "Lord have mercy!" coming from behind her. The rich, round tones echoed in her brain, and she knew that they could have been uttered only by Richard Freeman. At the moment, however, she was completely unconcerned that the Boys would give their presence away.

In any case, it was equally likely that MacGuff had said those words. Or, perhaps, even she herself had said them, for the exclamation blended precisely with her own thoughts and her own gasp and her own words, either muttered or spoken aloud. "Good God! Good God in heaven!"

The three rings of fire had sprung up within the small space of three frantic heartbeats. MacGuff's reaction, her own, and the various words thought and spoken flashed within the tinier space of the third desperate heartbeat. Before she had fully registered the presence of the flaming rings, she was transfixed by a more-awe-inspiring, more-fearful sight.

A man was walking through the flames. Her eyes widened. Yes, it was a man. He was tall and lean and very old, and he was walking straight through the rings of fire, unflinching, unaffected. She could hardly believe her eyes. She dashed a hand across her brow and attempted to reconfigure the impossible image in her scrambled brain, but when she focused again on the circles of leaping flames, she saw that the old man was still there.

He had stopped walking. From where she stood, he seemed to be standing in the very middle of the flames, but he was not burning. Flames were behind him. Flames were before him. His long, white hair was flowing free around his shoulders. His dress was old-fashioned and elegant and glowed a deep, dull red in the firelight. He looked stately, even magnificent, standing there immobile in the midst of flames. His features were not precisely discernible, for his face was darkened and heavily lined. However, his expression was plain to see. It was one of furious displeasure and burning rage.

Cathy's immediate thought was that this apparition had come straight from hell.

The apparition spoke. Its voice was low and creaky and carrying as it intoned the spitting, spiteful words, "Silly whippersnapper!" The voice was ancient with age and suffering when it continued with, "Vain-glori-ous pretty boy!"

These hellish pronouncements turned Cathy's thoughts in a new direction. Her amazement did not lessen, but it grew now in earthly, rather than in otherwordly, proportions. She was regaining enough control over her chaotic reactions and emotions to perceive the effect of these words on the man trembling next to her.

"Good Gawd! Good *Gawd* Almighty!" MacGuff whispered in a voice of disbelieving terror. "It's the old geezer!"

Cathy knew what to do. In a voice that matched his for disbelief and terror, she breathed, "It's Old Hitch! But—but it *can't* be! We buried him on Sunday! You were there, MacGuff! We all were!"

MacGuff's eyes were wide. His knees were actually shaking. "Dead and buried, but not laid to rest. . . ."

Cathy thought it might be effective to grasp MacGuff's arm in terror. She did so, and he nearly collapsed in fear at her touch. "He's come back from the dead," she whispered in horror.

"He's come back from—from . . ."

She could not resist. She held up her arms before her, as if shielding herself from an evil force. Aloud, she exclaimed, in a wailing voice, "He's come back from hell!" Privately, she wondered how it was possible for Laurence Harris to stand in the middle of the flames and not burn up. Then she remembered he had once told her that he knew a lot about fire.

MacGuff had fallen to reciting, over and over, "Good Gawd! Good Gawd Almighty!" He was hardly in a condition to hear or understand the next words the apparition spoke.

The figure raised its arms and spread its fingers wide. The flames leapt higher, burned brighter. "You have been stupid and wasteful, Young Hitchcock MacGuffin!"

MacGuff made no response to this charge. He was, indeed, impervious to anything, even mild insult, for he was stiff with terror.

The apparition continued. "You have been self-serv-ing and un-trust-worthy!"

MacGuff was trying to pull himself together. He said the first thing that came to mind. His voice was as unsteady as his legs when he called back, "You sound different, Uncle."

Old Hitch's apparition spoke harshly and with supreme displeasure. "I am *dead,* you puffed-up coxcomb!" At a few more flicks of his fingers, the flames soared.

MacGuff stumbled back. "I can see that, Uncle!" he cried, hoping to appease him. "But what I want to know is why!" In his quaking fear, he proceeded to babble, "I mean . . . I mean, I know why you're dead. What I want to know is why you've come back! Why you've come back to haunt me! I haven't done anything wrong."

The apparition looked pleased. It said, "You have not done anything right, but it is good that you have asked! I will tell you why I have come all this way, overdressed puppy!"

The apparition also had a sense of timing. It paused dramatically, long enough for MacGuff's knees to buckle.

Standing next to him, Cathy was aware that MacGuff was about to fall. She reached out to steady him. She wanted him to be upright and in condition to hear whatever the apparition had come to tell him.

Chapter Twenty

Now that Cathy had overcome her astonishment and fear, she was determined to appreciate the fine points of this extraordinary drama.

She found Laurence Harris remarkably convincing as Old Hitch, dressed as he was in the clothing they had found the other day in the trunk. He had apparently drenched his black hair in the powder from the pounce box, rendering it white and fashioning it so that it looked stringy and lifeless. The old-fashioned, whaleboned coat fit him well enough, as did the knee breeches, stockings and shoes. The ragged condition of these items could not be discerned at such a distance at night and through flickering flames.

The mulberry velvet glowed a splendid dull red in the context of the surrounding fire. The lace at his neck and wrists, however, was the decisive touch to his ensemble. Whenever he gestured or tossed his head, the fragile wisps of lace leapt with firelight, as if woven of tiny yellow flames. The effect was nothing less than magnificent and terrifying.

Even better, he had captured all the color and choler of Old Hitch in his gestures and in his pronouncements. However, MacGuff was right: the exact quality of the apparition's voice was not her old friend's. But, after all, Cathy thought practically, what could one expect from a man who had been underground and burning in the fires of hell for the past four days?

And the apparition was plainly enjoying himself.

With the flames leaping around him, the ghost of Old Hitch stood unconcerned, confident that no fire on earth could harm a dead man. He gestured left. He gestured right. He drew flames from the ground, raised them up, sculpted them as he pleased. He looked up to the sky. He looked down at the ground. He fixed MacGuff with a quelling eye.

He said in a deep and commanding voice, "Tomorrow you will go to the Market House."

MacGuff nodded dumbly.

"Do you obey, silly whippersnapper?" the apparition demanded angrily. "Speak, so that I know you have heard me!"

MacGuff gobbled a marginally coherent, "Yes, Uncle! Yes! I heard you! I obey! I—I—I promise to go to the Market House! Nothing could be easier!"

"At eight o'clock!"

"Yes, yes, oh, yes! At eight o'clock! I'll be there!" An inevitable thought occurred to MacGuff. He must have been imagining a sleepless night ahead of him, and eight o'clock was mighty early. "But what if I am late? Even a minute?"

The laugh that rumbled up from the apparition's chest and out his mouth raised the hairs on Cathy's neck and arms. Fresh flames soared with the wrath of the aged and ancient voice. "You do not want to find out, my pretty boy!"

"I won't be late, Uncle! I swear it!"

The apparition did not deign to respond to that. It continued. "You will read aloud, to the entire town of Hillsborough, the words that I wrote you in my final letter!"

MacGuff was too amazed by this simple request to be suspicious of it. He was only happy to be able to fulfill it. "Is that *all?* Is that all, Uncle? Read aloud at the Market House your final letter to me?"

"That is enough!" the apparition scolded.

"But it's so long, your last letter," MacGuff protested, willful and whiny, even under these inauspicious circumstances, "and you've already berated me in public in the final statement that was read at church on Sunday!"

"Not the long letter, young fool!" the apparition cried in accents of terrible rage. "Two lines! Two lines only!"

MacGuff was plainly puzzled by this request and was again struck dumb.

"Say you will do it!" the figure intoned furiously. "Say you will read the two lines at the Market House tomorrow morning at eight o'clock!"

Quaking, shaking, half confused, half relieved, MacGuff exclaimed, "I'll do it, Uncle! I'll do it! I'll read the two lines tomorrow morning at eight o'clock at the Market House!"

The apparition stretched his hands forward, and it looked as if he plunged them straight through the third circle of flames. Thinking that his uncle's reach might extend as far as the sundial, MacGuff shrank back instinctively. So did Cathy—out of sheer amazement at Harris's daring.

Then the apparition said, with magnificent threat, "Do not plan to live a minute past eight o'clock if you do not do it!'' His ghostly, ghastly laugh cackled hideously above the crackling flames. "I almost hope you do *not!*" The last thing to be heard were the words, spoken as a curse, *"Silly whippersnapper!"*

"I *hate* it when he calls me that," MacGuff was able to mutter, angry and disgruntled.

Then, before Cathy's very surprised eyes, the flames were extinguished. She was blinded for a few seconds by the fiery afterimage, having stared too long at the light. When the sight of Old Hitch's front porch resolved itself again in her vision, she gasped. She rubbed her eyes and shook her head and peered into the darkness. The apparition had vanished as suddenly as it had appeared, along with the flames. Both were well and truly gone.

She turned to MacGuff, whose handsome face was ashen in the moonlight. "Is it possible...?" she asked hesitantly. She did not need to infuse her voice with an artful note of disbelief to sound convincingly astounded by what she had just witnessed. Even knowing that no ghost had stood before them, but the very live body of Laurence Harris, did not settle her shaking senses. She was inclined to think this the work of the devil. Or, rather, the work of a fallen angel, since the apparition had succeeded in wresting from MacGuff the promise to read aloud his two crucial lines.

MacGuff shoved an unsteady hand through his hair, disordering his perfectly pomaded waves. He was still muttering, but his articulations had reverted to the litany of, "Good Gawd. Good Gawd Almighty."

"But is what we saw just now what we really *saw?*" Cathy asked in wonder. "I can't believe it!"

"Neither can I," MacGuff said. "Neither can I."

Cathy discerned an edge of suspicion creep into his voice, now that the immediate danger from hell had disappeared.

"But can you afford not to believe it?" she asked.

MacGuff looked at her, then glanced away without answering. His breath was coming hard and heavy. She could see him, limp now with relief, struggling with the aftereffects of the fear, the meaning of the unusual request to read aloud the two lines in public and the mental dissonance created by the sight that his eyes had plainly seen but that his brain just as plainly rejected.

Cathy decided to leave well enough alone. She was not going to insist on the fact that MacGuff had promised to obey the instructions of his uncle's ghost. Laurence Harris had done his part, and MacGuff would have all night to decide what he wanted to do come eight o'clock. Her best course now was to remain amazed.

This was easy enough. Arranging her shawl comfortably around her shoulders, she began to move toward the house and the now-vanished rings of fire. She took two steps forward, as if compelled to examine the scene, then one step back, as if fearful. Her contradictory attraction and repulsion was not entirely feigned. The most primitive part of her feared the return of the flames from hell, although her rational self knew that it had merely been an earthly trick.

MacGuff followed behind her, more profoundly afflicted than Cathy and struck through and through by very real fear. When she stopped in front of him, he stopped, too, stumbling against her back, but moving quickly away, as if burned.

Cathy looked down at the scorched earth, whose fire scars were barely visible in the moonlight. Sure enough, there were three rings, each within several feet of the other, and each a good foot in width. It must have been devilishly hot for Laurence Harris within those rings. She felt the afterglow of the fire even now.

She stepped over the outermost ring and knelt down, keeping her skirts away from the burnt edges, although there were no embers left, only dead cinders. She touched first one ring, then the other.

She looked up at MacGuff and said, her voice realistically dazed, "It's still a little hot, but there isn't the least bit of fire in sight. But it was here. I saw it." She drew a breath. "Then it wasn't. Can you believe it?"

Again, MacGuff said nothing. He looked down, in blankest wonder, at the remains of the rings of fire. He looked at her, all amorous intentions evidently wiped away. He looked at his uncle's shack. He looked up at the moon.

From nearby came the eerie creak of a rusty hinge. Then the rippling, jingle-jangle music of an unsettled ghost shivered around their ears and down their spines. Startled, Cathy sprang up, her skin on tiptoe, and looked at MacGuff in time to see a tremor of real terror run through him. He took one last, horrified look at the cold, shadowy shack. Now at last, she thought, his eyes are going to pop out of his head. Without another word or glance, he turned on his heel and ran.

Cathy moved around the house so that she could watch his departure. She saw MacGuff stumbling through the overgrown meadow, scrambling toward the slope. His retreating form was etched black in the night, and his skitterish movements seemed scrawly, as if drawn by a child holding an unwieldy pen.

She heaved a sigh of relief and attempted to calm herself. She had not quite succeeded in recovering her good sense when the swish of tall grass came from behind her. A shiver raced through her again, and she sensed bodies moving up behind her.

She uttered a strangled cry, whirled and saw the apprehensive faces of the Boys and Clive and George.

"Good heavens!" she scolded. "You scared me, sneaking up on me like that!"

Not one of them was ready or able to speak. Finally, Boy said in hushed tones, "It shore won't be nec'ssary for the Welshman to try anythin' now. There's no way he kin top what Old Hitch just done, comin' back from the dead like that and all."

Cathy exhaled. She felt so much better that she wanted to laugh. She clasped Boy's hands in hers and said, almost lovingly, "Why, that *was* Mr. Harris, you see, Boy, and he devised that—that trick to make MacGuff believe he was Old Hitch!"

Boy looked powerfully skeptical. He withdrew his hands from Cathy's clasp, as if he did not wish to be sullied by such blasphemy. "That weren't no trick. Leastwise, no trick that I ever seen before."

Hank cleared his throat. He tucked his thumbs in his suspenders, puffed out his chest and sniffed. "Shore, I knowed that. It was the Welshman. I knowed it all along." He turned to Richard, whom he had to nudge. "You knowed it, too, didn'tcha, Richard?"

Richard's dark face was solemn in the moonlight. "Lord have mercy," he confined himself to saying.

"I knowed it, too," Orin confirmed with shaky confidence. "A trick by the Welshman."

"No accounting for the tastes of a man from Maryland," was Clive's opinion.

George said, taking a deep breath of obvious relief, "It was a mighty fine trick. Why, he had me going, he did. Thought it was Old Hitch, to the life! Well, not the life exactly! It beats me, though, how the Welshman could have made the fire go out, just like that."

"We will have to ask him, of course," Cathy said. She looked around. "Maybe we should go over to the house now. Mr. Harris was evidently last on the porch, since he rang the chimes a few minutes ago."

Boy was not yet willing to believe that what he had seen was an act of man. "I liketa died when I heard that noise just now. Kinda reminded me of when Old Hitch came the other day and spooked us out of his house!"

"The eerie noise you heard was made by the spoons hanging from Old Hitch's porch. It was the wind that rang them the other day," she said as matter-of-factly as she could, "and it was Mr. Harris who rang them tonight. Now, let's go over to the house and speak to him."

She took a step in the direction of the house, but no one followed. She really did *not* want to walk over there alone, but she had to show them that she, at least, was not scared. She took a second resolute step away from the group, then another and another. When she stepped into the darker shadow of the porch, a strong hand came out of nowhere and gripped her arm.

The sound of her strangled cry brought the Boys and Clive and George tumbling over to her. By the time they arrived at her side, the body attached to the hand had materialized. It belonged to Laurence Harris.

"I am sorry I frightened you," he said to Cathy, releasing her when the men arrived at her side. "I thought you knew it would be me."

"Oh, yes, I knew!" she said, clasping a hand to her racing heart, then arranging her shawl. "Or at least I thought I knew. In any case, I am glad that it *is* you! But where have you been?"

"Back of the house, changing my clothes," Harris explained. He gestured to his dress. He was wearing his customary buckskins. "And washing my face. I lined and blackened it with some charcoal."

"What about your hair?" she asked with a half smile. She could see now that it was still white and wispy.

"I'll have to wash it later. I brought water in a jug, but only enough to wet the uncle's old clothing and to wash my face."

"Is that how you did it, then—walking through the flames?" George asked. "You dampened the clothing?"

Harris said yes, he'd made sure it was thoroughly wet but not soggy. That had had the further benefit of causing the fire to sizzle whenever he gestured, casting droplets into the air and flames around him.

"But you walked straight through them flames, man!" Hank said. "Water or no water, I don't know how you did it!"

"One foot in front of the next," Harris said. He did not elaborate.

"And about that fire," Orin said, thinking that it had gone to waste by not having cooked anything, "how did you get it in them rings and bring them flames up, up in the air, when you wanted?"

"Oil," he said.

"Nut oil?" Richard asked.

Harris shook his head.

"Whale oil?" George asked next, highly skeptical. His merchant's mind was turning fast. Since he did not carry a large stock of it, he asked, "How did you find so much of it?" Then, the more pertinent question, "And what's more, how could you have afforded it?"

"No, not whale oil," Harris said, "but another kind. I forget the term the white man uses, but I call it wet fire. I learned about it in Baltimore."

"Ah, so that explains it!" Clive said, completely satisfied. "I've been thinking these past few days that the folks in Maryland are plumb strange!"

"It comes from rock," Harris continued, "and just a few drops can make a large fire. I brought a flask of the oil with me, and it should last me a very long time. I used only a small portion of it tonight to make the rings, and I carried a small bottle of it in each palm, so I could sprinkle the flames as I wished."

"Oil from rock?" George asked. It did not seem a likely proposition, but if only a little of it had made such a big fire, the marketability of this oil from rock might be enormous. Then again, so were its dangers, if so little could produce such a fire. He was, start to finish, a cautious soul. He did not think he would pursue the sale of it.

"We don't know a durned thing about this here oil from rock, and we all know how to get a fire *started*," Hank said, "but what I want to know is, how did you get them blazes to go out?" He snapped his fingers. "Just like that!"

''I had several bags of powder in my pockets that I call dry water,'' Harris said. ''The white man calls it so-di-um hy…so-di-um hy-dro…'' he trailed off and shook his head. ''A white man in England has discovered how to make it, and I learned about his experiments, again, in Baltimore.''

''Soda ash and salt?'' George asked. ''That's what you bought today at my store.''

''Yes.''

''That shore is strange,'' Boy said, shaking his head. He hardly knew what to think of this talk of wet fire and dry water, but then he had not understood much, anyway, of this Injun-from-the-waist-down-and-Welshman-from-the-waist-up.

Cathy didn't have a very clear idea, either, of how her fire bird had managed to do what he had done. However, she was sure of one thing. ''Whatever you did, Mr. Harris,'' she said, smiling up at him, ''you were certainly effective! Why, you had MacGuff—and most of the rest of us, including me at first, I confess!—believing you had come straight from the devil's quarters!''

Noises of agreement were made all around, along with further commentary on Harris's methods and techniques, disclaimers that any of the men had *really* thought they were in the presence of the devil and inevitable questions about what would happen come eight o'clock the next morning. That subject brought on Cathy's description of MacGuff's reaction to the whole, and finally the entire party was laughing and joking. In part from relief that Harris—and not the devil—had performed that trick, in part from the perceived success of that trick.

All were laughing, Cathy noted, except Laurence Harris. She cocked her head and looked at his face, strong and impassive, with only a hint of humor around his eyes. She thought, Is it because he has more self-control than the rest of us? Or, in fact, too much self-control? She wondered how she might test the limits of his self-control.

Harris must have felt her gaze on him, for he looked down. Responding to the speculative look in her eyes, he allowed the corners of his mouth to curve up ever so slightly. The look in his own eyes became quite clear to Cathy, and she felt a flush creep up her neck and cheeks. She was glad it was so dark and that none of her friends were, just then, concerned with her reaction to this most intriguing, most desirable man of fire.

Harris looked around the group and said, "Well, men, our work is done for the night. I will take Miss Cathy home." Before anyone could countermand him or offer to accompany them, Harris took her by the hand and started out over the meadow toward the woods. He tossed over his shoulder, "See you tomorrow morning."

"Yes, tomorrow morning!" several of them called back. "Eight o'clock at the Market House!"

George, remembering his mission, cried out, "Be sure you take good care of Miss Cathy, now! See her safely home."

"I will," Harris assured him.

As they moved away, Cathy could hear the men discussing whether they needed to follow the Welshman to make sure their Miss Cathy got safely home. However, since none of them knew the shortcut through the woods, and Harris was quickly putting distance between them, they resolved to think that the Welshman was a trustworthy human being. Good enough to fool Young MacGuff, at any rate—which was good enough for them.

The Boys, Clive and George started out across the meadow toward the slope. They stayed together in a close-knit group. Each one was thinking that Old Hitch's spirit just might decide to take a holiday from hell. Not one of them would admit it except Boy.

Cathy was glad to be rid of them. She was glad to be holding her fire bird's hand, being led along behind him, moving out of the moonlight and into the very dark woods, safe with him and—hopefully—not so safe with him.

A warm silence surrounded them, and it carried a hint of electricity. Cathy wanted to speak yet didn't want to break the exciting silence. Finally, she could stand it no longer. "You called me Miss Cathy."

He stopped, turned and drew her into his arms, almost before she knew it. "You called me Mr. Harris."

"What else was I supposed to call you?" she returned, yielding to his embrace. "In front of the others, I mean."

"I have a variety of names."

"Which one do you wish me to call you?"

He thought about it, then said, "I do not know."

Neither did he seem to care at the moment. Her shawl had fallen away from her shoulders and was caught in his arms, which he had wrapped around her to draw her close to him. Her bodice was still loosened from MacGuff's indelicate prying. She loved the feel of her bared skin near his. She didn't feel at all modest. She felt shamefully, shame*less*ly, forward.

She felt frankly desirous. She had only one idea in mind.

She asked, wrapping her arms around his neck, pressing herself to him, "Are you going to see me safely home and then come in?"

He shook his head. "No."

She nearly died from the sharp disappointment and the sudden shame that she would have been so bold to imagine he wanted her again, the way she wanted him. She tried to draw away from him, but he did not release her. She couldn't see his face for the darkness. She was close enough, however, to feel his breath and his heartbeat and the desire of his body against her. He was a man with a healthy appetite, a man who wanted her.

"I am not taking you home," he said, "but I am coming in."

She gasped and laughed and felt a further surge of desire. He bent and kissed her. She could smell the remains of the fire on him and could taste the fire in his kiss. She did not think his heat was produced entirely by the flames he had created this night.

"Where are you taking me?" she asked. She kissed him back fully, letting his tongue slip between her teeth, letting her tongue meet his. She was startled by the quick flash of her desire for him, how it seemed that rings of fire had sprung up around them, each ring more powerful than the last.

"Are you taking me here?" she teased.

Chapter Twenty-One

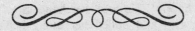

"Not here," he said, giving himself to the kiss, then drawing away. "That is, not here, unless we do not move on soon."

The imp in Cathy hopped with an urge to test the limits of his self-control, which she knew formed a part of the barrier she had perceived within him after he had left her bed that morning. She knew of no other way to test him than to tease and taunt him with kisses and to mold her body against his.

"If we do not move on *soon*," he repeated, now with some urgency, "we may have to linger here." His lips yielded to her sweet kisses, and his body was about to surrender itself to hers, as well. "Which was not what I had in mind."

"It was not?"

"No," he said, then again, with a groan, "no. I wanted to wash my hair first in the stream."

She could not help it. She laughed, causing her lips and body to ripple against his in a sketch of what was to come between them. "You wanted to wash your hair?" she mimicked lightly, moving very boldly against him. "Have you become the shy maiden that you say such a thing?"

Before he spoke, she felt his reaction and was deeply pleased.

"The shy maiden?" he returned. "Not hardly." Then he said, somewhat sternly, "It has been a long walk these past years, and I have learned the value of waiting for what I want, exactly as I want it." He broke their kiss and their embrace. "For which you should be happy." He took her hand in a firm, authoritative grip and pulled her along behind him. "And grateful."

"Grateful?" she mocked. "Mr. Harris, you rate your skills too highly!"

Without turning around, he said, "I have heard your challenge and accept it gladly. The aim of my arrow is true, especially at night, and a copperhead is not the only thing I can slay with my exceptional skills. I intend to make you wait, and then I will pin you, right between—" he paused "—the eyes."

His voice was hot and heavy with suggestion and caused her to think that her self-control was, indeed, not the equal of his. Still, she could not resist taunting him. "Your arrow must be mighty impressive. I recall that you shot the copperhead at a distance of twenty feet."

After a very long moment spent considering possible replies to that outrageous remark, he said, "Let us hurry."

And they did. He stepped up their pace and led her deftly through the tangle of trees and branches, the snarl of bushes and vines. They were at her house before the Boys and Clive and George had even topped the slope near her orchard. He hurried her across the grassy expanse of her backyard, bright with moonlight. He plunged with her into the dark and dewy shadows of the flowering backyards between Queen and Tryon Streets. Sneaking away from her house like this, she felt naughty, and the naughtiness felt nice.

He moved swiftly and surely, alternately helping her over the tricky spots and ignoring her difficulties in his haste. She breathed in the fragrance of the redbuds and dogwoods and pines. She inhaled the sweet scents of the laurel and rhododendrons and roses. She was glad that she was barefoot and that the warm, wet earth was in direct contact with her skin. She recalled that she had first traveled these backyards with him on the night of the festival, going from town to her orchard. She was glad that she was traveling now in the opposite direction with him, being pulled along behind him, her desire for him as fully in bloom as the blossoms all around them.

He zigzagged through town, cutting an unusual path around the courthouse and across Margaret Lane, leading them straight to the woods on the town's southern boundary. He entered those woods where he had the day before, when she had followed him and told him she was dining with MacGuff. He led her to the banks of the river and danced a deft pattern between the rocks and the shore. When he came to the wide bend, he stopped and released her hand.

"Bathe with me," he commanded.

Her mouth dropped open. "It must be cold," she protested. "The night is warm, of course, but the water cannot be!"

He stripped to his skin before she could close her mouth. He took her hand, as if he intended to pull her in fully clothed. "Have it your way," he said, "but it will be warmer without your clothes. You'll see."

She scrambled out of her dress and underclothes and followed him into the water. Since she had already washed her hair that afternoon, she piled it atop her head and held it there. The water was cool. At first it stung her ankles and calves and thighs, and she was vexed with him. However, after he had dunked himself fully and slid up next to her, wet and glistening in the moonlight dappling through the tress, she began to perceive the appeal of this activity. She had waded out waist deep, and the feel of his slick chest against her breasts was glorious. The feeling did not last, for he broke away from her and dunked himself again.

"The powder in my hair," he said when he rose once more from the water. "You would not like it." He touched her neck and shoulders. "And I would not like the scent of Young Cock on you."

"You could smell him?" she asked, amazed.

"Hair oil and shaving soap," he said fastidiously. He disappeared into the water. He reappeared. "Only faintly, of course, but I hardly wish to be distracted by his scent."

"It's your fault," she said, splashing herself in the places MacGuff had touched her. "You waited a frightfully long time before you began your performance, thus giving Young Co—Young *MacGuff* the opportunity to put his hands all over me."

She was having some difficulty speaking with a man who was bobbing up and down in the water, tossing his head back so that his hair was immersed and scrubbing his scalp. This last remark of hers brought him to his feet, dripping.

"All over you?" he queried.

"Well, not all over," she conceded.

"Good," he said. "I wanted him to be aroused enough to make him vulnerable to his fear, but not enough, of course, to have unpleasant consequences for you."

She smiled at him, her confidence and humor mingling with a hint of shyness and a good dose of desire. "I wanted him to stop touching me and I wondered where you were. Still, I wasn't really worried. You've long since proved that you would be there to save me, if I needed it."

His body went still as he contemplated her. Then he moved around her toward the bank where they had left their clothes and gathered them up. Holding them high above his head in one hand, he returned to her and took her hand in his other. Together they waded to the opposite bank and emerged onto dry ground. He wrung out his hair. She let hers fall down her back, which was damp.

The bath had been cleansing, and it was certainly refreshing, but almost too refreshing, with only the night air to dry her. She asked for her clothing.

He looked down at her and shook his head.

"But I'm cold," she said, reaching out for the bundle he cradled in one arm.

He shifted it out of her reach. "I'll warm you soon enough."

She looked at him and decided that he was probably right. They walked together, naked, across the clearing at the edge of which he had made his camp. He whistled to his horse, then sent the beast to the far side of the clearing. She had felt naughty, but nice, sneaking behind her house. She felt even naughtier, and a lot nicer, approaching his domain wearing nothing and having nothing to hide.

He made their bed under a friendly old tree. The pine straw beneath it was thick. The cover he spread out for them was soft, and like everything else that was a part of him, scrupulously clean. They tumbled down on it, instantly entwined, rolling together playfully and quite happily, kissing and shifting arms and legs for a different fit, a better fit, a different touch, a better touch. Their skin was almost dry, but not quite. The backs of their knees, the bends of their elbows, the crooks of their necks became places where they slid against one another and where they placed their mouths to lick. His long hair was not dripping, but it was still very damp. Its tendrils wrapped around her and stuck to her.

Cathy had never felt so frisky or desirous or alive. She had never felt so inviting or hospitable. When he rolled onto his back, positioned her hips firmly on his and entered her with one stroke, she had never felt so thoroughly visited. She leaned back, arching luxuriously to accommodate herself to his fullness, to revel in it. She braced her hands on his knees, then became interested in exploring the area of his thighs, knees and calves that were within reach. She found she liked stroking him lightly, just grazing his skin, almost tickling.

She found she liked even more how his hand came to the juncture of her thighs. How he began to stroke her moist little seed. How he grazed and tickled it. How he encouraged it to blossom and grow into the ripe fruit, the delicious apple it was meant to be. How he wrapped both arms around her and drew her down to him, bringing her breasts to his chest and her lips to his. How he gave himself to her. How he made himself a part of her, fully and completely. How he cherished her. How they climbed the scruffy, leafy tree of their desire together. How they came together at the top, soared, and floated to the earth in one another's arms.

She luxuriated atop him for a motionless eternity. Then she crawled off him and snuggled up next to him. She sighed. He sighed. They kissed once. They fell asleep.

She awoke some time later with a feeling that all was not right. Or, rather, that all was not yet complete. That she had not tested the limits of his self-control. That the barrier within him was still there.

She was puzzled. She reached a lazy arm across his chest to his opposite arm. She caressed the muscles, ran her hand up to his shoulder and contemplated the disfigured skin with thoughtful fingers. She passed in mental review everything she knew about her fire bird and realized that she knew a surprising amount from a man who spoke so little. She had guessed in a way that words could not describe how deeply the scars on his skin ran into his soul; and she had witnessed this night his fearless mastery over the fierce and frightening force that had seared him in his infancy.

The fiery trial he had endured as a child was significant, of course, as was the fiery defiance of his fear that he had performed this night. However, her mind fastened on one of his statements and would not let it go. She recalled vividly the look on his face and the tone in his voice when he'd said, "I left Maryland the day I understood that Morgan had suffered in his life more than I had."

That was it, then—the twenty-five years of his solitary suffering. It had made his face a mask, devoid of pleasure and every other emotion. Even now, as he slept the sleep that follows pleasure—and she knew, with confidence and pride, that he had experienced pleasure—his face was impassive.

The imp inside her suddenly sprang to life again. It jumped up and hopped around impatiently, wanting more from him, wanting to test his limits. It knew just what to do.

She propped herself up on his chest and addressed him. "Laurence Harris."

He gave a sleepy snort of acknowledgment.

She began to stroke the muscles and ribs of his chest, as if she were dipping her fingertips lazily in water.

"Laurence Harris," she said again. Then, imperfectly, "Tohin-ontan."

He mumbled something under his breath in a foreign tongue. Aloud, he said, "What do you want?"

She did not stop her gentle exploration and altered the pressure of her fingers when she came to the smooth, undamaged skin under his arm. She tickled him lightly. "You."

His eyes opened. They focused quickly on her, narrowed appreciatively and with intent. He took a breath and grasped her hand in his.

She shook her head. She wriggled her hand out of his clasp and returned to her grazing and occasional tickling. "Oh, no," she said. "I'm too sated at the moment for more."

"I'm not," he said, "and neither are you."

"You're greedy."

"I am."

When he made another move to satisfy his greediness, she moved away from him. "No, no and no."

"Then why did you wake me up?"

"To tell you a story."

He grunted in disinterest.

"On second thought," she said, considering her strategy, "it might be better if I were sitting on top of you again, as I tell it."

He grunted again, this time with approval.

"My mother once told me the story," she began, "of a young maiden who had never cried." She straddled him, but did not put any of her weight down on him and avoided any directly arousing contact. "Have you heard that story?"

He had not and added that he was not sure he wanted to hear it now. He raised his arms to embrace her.

She laughed, shrugged him off and began to tickle him. Under his arms. At his belly. "This young maiden was a princess, and she was as beautiful as her father, the king, was rich and powerful. Well, the king was distressed that she had never cried, *couldn't* cry, as if she were missing some very human part of herself. He decided that the man who could make her cry would win her hand."

Cathy stretched back awkwardly and tickled the soles of Harris's feet. "Now, of course, many princes from many kingdoms came to try for her hand. They told her many sad, sad stories. But none could make her cry." She leaned forward and tickled his ear with her tongue. "And do you know what happened to the princess?"

He did not know what had happened to the princess, and she could feel his bodily confusion, as well. Beneath her fingers, as she told her story and tickled him, his reactions were hesitant, his muscles tense with questions, as if he did not know what was happening to him. She guessed that, in fact, he did *not* know, as she had never seen him smile a real, broad, relaxed smile. And she had never heard him laugh.

"A man came one day—a plain, humble man, not a prince—and he made her cry," she said.

She continued to tickle him, lightly, teasingly. She would resort to sexual tickling, if all else failed, for she was determined to seduce him into laughter.

"Do you know how he made her cry?" she asked, tickling him still, feeling his strong resistance, feeling the even-stronger rumbling inside him that might break that resistance.

He groaned a "No" that hovered between pain and pleasure.

"He made her chop an onion," she whispered into his ear, tickling it with her tongue again, "and the tears began to flow."

She was searching his body boldly, trying to find his most sensitive, ticklish spot, but she was having difficulty. He did not seem to be vulnerable under his arms or at his sides or on his soles or under his chin.

"I am not trying to make you cry, Laurence Harris," she continued, "because you've wept inside for twenty-five years. Instead, I'm trying to make you laugh, and the only way to do that is to tickle you. I want you to laugh as heartily as you make love."

"But...but why?" he gasped.

"Because I don't think you've ever laughed before," she said, touching the taut groove that ran from his hipbones to his groin. As she did, she felt a perfect muscular quiver there that could only be released as a glorious laugh. "You've been a laughter virgin, Laurence Harris."

His voice was hot and strangled. "How do you know?"

"Because you were the only one who was not howling with laughter at the trick you played on Mac-Guff," she said, tickling him lightly and mercilessly at his most sensitive muscle, "and I have thought, from the minute I met you, that you had a very distinct sense of humor."

She felt him trembling on the precipice.

"But I've never heard you laugh. I want you to laugh, Laurence Harris," she breathed in his ear, hoping to push him over the edge. "I want you to laugh because of me, for me, with me."

He was back at the crossroads, where he had decided to take the trail to North Carolina, just like that. On a whim. Or so he had thought. It had been a magical turning at the fork in the road, he had realized early on, but one whose grand design had remained hidden from him until this moment. He recalled attempting to discover within himself a glimmer of urgency at that moment of turning south to North Carolina instead of west to Kentucky. He had found only darkness and had been puzzled, for he was good at finding things. But he was puzzled no more, and what he was finding now had been so well and so painfully hidden that even he had been unable to find it on his own.

At first, he had thought to be on an exalted mission in service of the Woman Who Fell From the Sky. He still wished to protect her, of course, but in the past several days, he had worked to alter his relationship with that ungoddesslike goddess and had redefined his mission in less-exalted terms. In her presence, he had been experiencing, ever more constantly, a lightness of spirit within him and a broadening smile of his physical body, particularly at the corners of his mouth. Last night, he had added to those spiritual and physical transformations an awakening of a sexual appetite for her that he suspected would grow both ever more satisfied and ever more ferocious at every union. Then, tonight, he had been nothing less than amazed and dazed and hungry all over again to have found a kind of heaven on earth in her arms and between her legs, one that he had not truly thought possible.

But this. This emotion was utterly new. And frightening in its strength and intensity, and in the light it was shining into his heart of hearts after so many years of darkness. She seemed to have lowered his dark defenses almost from the moment she had fallen on top of him from the tree, and in the following days she had breached them easily with the lightness of her presence. Now she was storming his barrier. Touching. Teasing. Tickling. Penetrating the heart of his darkness with the painful brightness of her light and her laughter.

It hurt to have his most secret emotional chamber so touched. It would hurt more if it could not be pierced.

He felt the power of his anger in this new emotion, but, incredibly, no anger. He had summoned his trusty anger for the fire drama in front of the uncle's house this night. He hoped he never lost that anger, that he would always be able to summon it at will and for his purposes. But he had never imagined he would feel that same power without the grinding, bone-deep, still-smoldering hatred against the world, for the shame he had endured because of his mother's betrayal of her tribe by marrying a white man. He had never imagined he would feel that same power with a corresponding amount of light. His most-secret, fire-scarred chamber rumbled open, broke wondrously open with light.

It was not a painful opening, as he might have thought, but a joyful one. He felt light flooding his entire body, then welling up deep inside him. He felt it pool in his legs, then begin to rise up, from his hips, through his belly, up his chest. Then it poured out his mouth in a great, forceful rush. He was laughing, shaking against the earth, happy, happily out of control, and the experience was nothing less than extraordinary. He felt nothing less than a man deeply in love. He wanted nothing more than to lodge himself deeply within this woman.

She was on top of him, but she did not remain there for long. Before she had the satisfaction of feeling his body shaking beneath her and of hearing his deep, rumbling, very masculine laugh, she had been flipped onto her back, and he had wedged his legs between hers. He caught her face in his hands.

The smile he smiled then was for her and because of her. His well-cut lips curved upward without restraint. His dark eyes shone with laughter. His high cheekbones were crinkled with merriment. The sight of his laughing face caused her to melt on the spot. The next second, he was within her, swift and strong, no longer a visitor, now the possessor.

She had only wanted to make him laugh. She had only wanted to give him the fun of it. She had not expected to enjoy his enjoyment so much. She had not expected to be rewarded with a glimpse of his beauty. She had not expected to be tossed with such strength and exuberance to the stars.

*   *   *

Cathy snuffled awake with a yawn, on a wave of remembered desire and a happy echo of nightlong laughter, as well as the odd sense that she had forgotten something. She burrowed closer to her man and snuggled under the light cover he had spread over them when they could love and laugh no more.

Then she remembered.

She sat bolt upright. She shook Laurence Harris's broad, scarred shoulder. "Wake up! Wake up! It's late."

He awoke with a very boyish, utterly masculine smile on his face. He said that she was pretty rude, but that he was willing to excuse anyone with such an inviting body. He reached for her.

She pushed him away. "No. It's almost eight o'clock. I'm sure of it!" She looked to the east and the bright sunshine breaking through the trees.

"I'm ravenous," he said.

"You'll just have to wait for breakfast," she retorted.

"I don't mean breakfast. I'm greedy, remember?" He reached for her again.

She wriggled out of his reach. "Are all men like this?" she wondered aloud, as she stood up and plucked at the bundle of clothes, selecting the items belonging to her. "You were also the one who commanded MacGuff to show up at the Market House at the ungodly hour of eight o'clock."

Harris was rising, too, but reluctantly. "I assigned the hour of eight only so that we would have the day to work through the clue, if need be."

She harrumphed. "It's your own fault, then, and the least you and I can do is to show up." As she slipped on her pantalets and arranged her chemise, a thought occurred to her. She clapped her cheeks with embarrassment. "But I have no shoes, no comb and brush, and I certainly can't show up in town coming from this direction, at this hour and in your company."

Harris considered this. "You can't?" He had succeeded in shrugging into his clothes far more efficiently than she. "Let's worry about it when we arrive in town. Everyone's attention is sure to be directed at Young Cock."

He took her hand and pulled her away from their cozy nest while she was still arranging her dress and trying to tie her bodice. She barely managed to drag the shawl along behind her.

They hurried through the clearing, across the river, through the woods, and came up on the courthouse by way of Margaret Lane. As Harris had predicted, everyone in town was gathering in front of the Market House, so no one was paying attention to Cathy, her dress, the direction from which she had come or her choice of companion. As the Market House clock began to strike the hour, she and Harris were making their way hastily across the courthouse lawn. By the seventh stroke, they had merged into the curious crowd gathered there. Panting lightly, both amused and excited, Cathy saw Young MacGuff standing in front of the center arch on Churton, facing the crowd in front of him.

On the eighth stroke, he looked nervously up to the sky, then more nervously down at the ground. He held

an unfolded sheet of paper in front of him. He cleared
his throat and read:

"Where there usually is, there is no mess.
Get keen legal help. It's your best guess."

Chapter Twenty-Two

Cathy put a hand on her hip, turned to Harris and remarked, "I don't know why I was expecting some fabulous revelation. Those two lines are no more comprehensible than the others."

Harris was smiling. He couldn't help it. His impulse just then was to drape his arm around his woman and draw her to him. He was glad that she was so naturally affectionate and was happy to have discovered a streak of affection in himself, but he thought it might not be appropriate in such a public place as the main square of town and in the middle of a rather large crowd. He would be sure to ask her about it later, and he was confident that she would teach him how to be comfortable with his newfound affection before he left town. On that thought, he decided that he might just wish to stay on a few more days.

She continued, "Legal help, indeed! I *did* ask the lawyer whether Old Hitch had made out a will, and he told me no." She stopped, then looked at him curiously, her brows raised. She demanded, "Did you figure out the two lines already? Is that why you're smiling?"

He shook his head. "No, I was thinking of something else. Could you repeat them for me?"

She made a noise of disgust and repeated the two lines. In the meantime, the Boys, Clive and George had made their way over to them.

Cathy took one look at George's face and realized that he was deeply troubled. She tried to catch his attention, and when she got it, he rolled his eyes in a beleaguered fashion. She looked around and saw Ginger standing to one side of the crowd, near the courthouse lawn. The poor girl, incongruously, seemed both triumphant and crushed. Cathy looked to the other side of the crowd, near the intersection of Churton and King, and saw Mrs. Travis. This fragile matriarch appeared to be on the verge of a nervous attack and, at the same time, in complete control of the situation. To Cathy's way of thinking, George was in a rare pickle and needed her help.

Wrapped in her own happiness and wanting to insure the same for others, Cathy decided to fix her friends' love life first before unraveling the meaning of the final two lines of Old Hitch's sonnet. She planned her strategy for approaching Mrs. Travis and started out in the direction of George's fond Mama, who loved her son almost as much as she loved wealth and status.

She was halfway there when her arm was grabbed from behind, and she was whirled around to face a very angry Young MacGuff. She had not been thinking of him, had not considered his part in all of this beyond his recital of the two lines. Now that she was looking at him, she wondered why she had not always seen the sly twist of his mouth, the what's-in-it-for-me gleam deep in his beautiful amber eyes.

He was holding her roughly and, she thought, possessively. She did not like it. She looked pointedly down at his hand and commanded, "Let go of me, MacGuff."

He did not let go of her arm. Rather, he gripped it tighter. "I'll let go of you when you tell what this is all about!"

She winced but forced herself to remain calm. "I have no idea what you mean."

He snorted. "I just heard from Boy that the old geezer sent around six pairs of lines and that mine made the seventh."

Her smile was saucy. "So?"

"So, Boy said that y'all needed my lines to figure out where the old geezer hid his will."

"So?" she demanded again, flippantly.

"So, you didn't tell me that you and everyone else in town had received two lines."

"I suggested as much."

"Suggested!" he echoed contemptuously. "You were suggestive, all right, when we were sitting together on your swing." His eyes narrowed with intention, in which desire for her body was mixed with equal parts desire for revenge, and both were tinged with violence. "You were mighty suggestive the next day, too, when I came to pick up my hat. You didn't own up to your two lines then, but suggested something else entirely."

She was feeling just as angry as he, but fought against her particular desire for revenge against his careless, casual dismissal of her lifelong, girlish crush on him. "You didn't own up to your lines either, as I recall, and I gave you plenty of chances."

"And you didn't deliver on your promise to be womanly."

She reverted to saucy flippancy. "So?"

"So I think I was set up last night." His expression became skeptical. "I'm supposed to believe that the old geezer came straight from hell to scare me into making a public spectacle of myself this morning? Do you think I'm a fool?" But he scoffed with just enough of an edge of fear in his voice for her to know that he was testing her.

Her arm was really beginning to hurt from the pressure of his fingers, and she was sure to have bruises there before he was finished. She would have loved to smile and say, "Yes, MacGuff, you were set up, and you played the fool beautifully." The words would taste sweet, and she might even savor the look of humiliation that would come across his face. However, she sensed that such an admission would be unwise, and it seemed beneath her, somehow.

She drew a breath and thought of Laurence Harris, his purity, his directness, his suffering. He'd said he had come from hell, and he had proven it last night. She had no reason to deny the magnificence of his performance, which, she imagined, had helped to win him release from that hell.

She nodded her head slowly and said, "Yes, I think you *are* supposed to believe that Old Hitch returned from the dead last night. He scared me as much as he scared you."

He frowned skeptically at the note of sincerity in her voice. He wanted to shake her. He wanted to harm her. He wanted her to adore him again, like she used to. He wanted her to become awkward in his presence and all misty-eyed. He wanted her to make him feel good again, cocky, how he used to feel around her before he left town last year. How he'd felt when he stopped by her house upon his return just a few days ago. Was it only Saturday?

"But why didn't the old geezer tell *you* to read your two lines this morning, in front of everyone?" MacGuff demanded.

"Because I already shared mine with the others," she said. "I was not keeping them to myself."

"Sharing!" MacGuff spat. "Why should I share?"

"Why shouldn't you?"

"Because I have nothing, as you well know."

His motives suddenly became clear to her. Without thinking twice, she said sadly and confidently, "No, that's not true. You didn't share with the rest of us because you thought that Old Hitch just might have something to pass on, after all. You wanted to find a way to have all of it yourself."

His violence finally broke through. "You who have everything," he said with rage, "dare to criticize me for wanting what is mine?"

Cathy did not know what he could do to her in such a public place, but she felt a shiver of real fear pass through her. Sharp pain shot up her arm. She was weak from it. She didn't know what to say next and was glad, a moment later, that she was spared the necessity of saying anything.

She heard Laurence Harris's voice state with cold challenge, "Let her go." Her arm was abruptly released. Harris was standing between her and MacGuff. He was holding MacGuff in a rough grip, ready to murder him at her slightest indication.

"No, don't, Laurence," she said, intervening quickly.

MacGuff's expression shifted from startled fear and impotent anger to derision. "Laurence?" he echoed, a note of dawning comprehension in his voice. He ran his eye over the details of her person—her bare feet, the clothing, crumpled now, that she had been wearing the night before, her disheveled hair.

Cathy looked away and felt a flutter of panic to imagine what would happen to her position in town if everyone came to know her as a fallen woman.

Then MacGuff spat a word at her that would have brought Harris's strong hands around his throat if Cathy's gaze had not just then fixed on the bow window of the lawyer's office not twenty paces away. Her attention was drawn to the name painted in neat, black letters: Lex Kenan, Attorney-At-Law. She cried, excited, "That's it! I've got it!" thereby drawing her lover's murderous attention away from MacGuff.

"What have you got?" Harris asked.

"The solution to the sonnet! 'Get keen legal help,'" she quoted. "Old Hitch is telling us to go to Mr. Kenan."

"I've already asked Lex about the old geezer's will," MacGuff said, reverting to his earlier derision.

"So did I," Cathy said swiftly, shooting him a glance that said he had just confirmed her suspicions about his motives. However, just now she was too excited to worry about MacGuff, his motives or his knowledge of her relationship with Laurence Harris. "But Old Hitch is telling us to look in a place that is usually messy. He must be referring to Mr. Kenan's office, so the task is to find where in that room there is no mess! Come on!"

Harris released his grip on MacGuff's jacket and followed her. So did MacGuff. Cathy called to the

Boys and Clive and George and commanded everyone to head for Mr. Kenan's office. She glanced
around and decided that Mrs. Travis, the old biddy,
would just have to wait to be gentled into accepting her
son's wedding plans. Cathy moved across the dispers-
ing crowd and collected Ginger with the words,
"Come with me, and we'll see what Old Hitch had in
mind for you, my dear!"

Ginger brightened a little and obeyed without
question.

Not too many moments later, Cathy and Ginger
jingled the bell above the door to Mr. Kenan's office
and joined Harris, MacGuff, Clive, the Boys and
George. Cathy saw that the office was as helter-skelter
as it had been two days before. The long gateleg table
was still piled high with books and folders. So was the
floor. The cabinets still spewed paper; the bookcase
had not been put to rights. The entire space swirled
with disorder, the chaotic energy of which seemed
drawn, with centripetal force, to the more compact
disorder of Mr. Kenan's desk.

MacGuff was standing by the door sulking angrily,
his arms folded across his chest. Boy stood next to
him, relating an imperfect version of the contents of
the first twelve lines of the sonnet. Boy was given to
repeating his sincere and unshaken opinion that if
MacGuff had not read out his two lines by eight
o'clock that morning, he would now be burning in fire
and brimstone right alongside Old Hitch.

Orin and Hank were poking around and wondering if Old Hitch could have "drug" that still over to
the office and hid it among the piles of papers and
books. Richard had been holding his Bible to his heart
since the hellish performance of the night before.

When he'd caught sight of Mr. Kenan's office, his earlier mutterings of "Lord have mercy!" had switched to ones suggesting that cleanliness was next to godliness.

George and Clive were following Harris, who was moving thoughtfully through the mess. Mr. Kenan himself was following along behind them, nervously demanding to know what was going on and squeaking every time one of his precious towers of paper threatened to fall over.

Cathy watched Laurence Harris do what he apparently did best, namely find things. She saw him move, deep in concentration, pacing slowly, looking here and there. He touched the frame of the parchment hanging crookedly on one wall. He lifted it, looked behind, then restored it so that the cerulean blue seal proclaiming *Lux et Veritas* was straight and upright. He continued to pace through the room, his retinue behind him.

He came to the lawyer's desk and stopped. He contemplated the center of the paper storm, which was not calm like the eye of a hurricane, but rather itself bursting with paper. He asked the lawyer several questions, thought about the answers, then looked across the room at Cathy. He smiled at her, a quiet, easy, genuine smile. He winked at her. His black, black eyes sparkled with good humor.

Cathy fell in love with Laurence at that moment. Or maybe she realized that she had fallen in love with him long since—when he had possessed her body with such passion this past night, or when he had brought Old Hitch back to dramatic life the evening before, or when he had made love to her the first time in her bed, or when he'd first kissed her on the porch swing in front of everyone. Or maybe even before that, when she had fallen from the apple tree into his arms.

She felt a deep and abiding love for this man, who was strong and quiet and had been willing to learn to laugh.

She saw him open the center drawer of the lawyer's desk. To everyone's surprise, including Mr. Kenan's, the drawer was nearly empty and held only one neat bundle of papers. He withdrew the papers and handed them to the lawyer.

"These are from the uncle," Harris announced with confidence.

"Wouldn't you just know it!" Mr. Kenan exclaimed with a kind of distracted delight. "I *never* think to use that drawer, always intending to keep my good pens in there, and the deed to the office and whatnot, but I never seem to be able to get—" he glanced nervously around the room "—organized, if you see what I mean!"

They did, and instead of encouraging the messy lawyer to expand on his intentions of getting organized "one of these days," they demanded, in one voice, that he read the papers in his hand.

"Well, yes! Let me see now!" He untied the little black band around the bundle, unfolded the sheets, adjusted his spectacles, and read.

"I, Hitchcock MacGuff, being of sound mind— and don't *none* of you say a *word* about the soundness of *my* mind, 'cuz it took you the blamed longest time to figger out where these papers were. And with no help from my nephew, the silly whippersnapper—"

"Is this a legal document?" MacGuff demanded from his corner.

The lawyer riffled through the pages, sought the signature at the end and said simply, "It is." He looked around and asked, "Shall I go on now?" Receiving a unanimous and unqualified "Yes!" he continued to read Old Hitch's irascible prose.

"And if you're wondering how I know how long it's taken you to find these papers, it's 'cuz I'm able to look down on you now. Yes, *down* on you. Although it seemed for a time that I would rot in hell, especially if you *didn't* find these papers, I'm up in heaven now and havin' a grand time tellin' off all them prissy do-gooders that irritated me whilst I was on earth. And there are a righteous fat lot of them up here, too! Now, the reason that I made it to heaven you'll be discoverin' soon enough, but in the meantime let me mention that the lawyer ain't gonna get a penny for this, 'cuz he didn't help me, not one little bit. I don't care if he does got some fancy sheepskin from that university down the road in piddlin' old Chapel Hill, he's got no more sense than them idiot Duke boys in East Orange County, and most likely a whole lot less!"

The lawyer put the papers down and was about to expound heavily on this comment from his nonclient, but Cathy cut him off. "You've already pronounced this document to be legal," she said, "and you did it in front of ten witnesses, so keep reading!"

The lawyer kept reading. In the least-gracious and thus, paradoxically, most-endearing way possible, Old

Hitch began to divide up his property. He said he hoped that Richard and Clive were enjoying the Bible and the watch, respectively. Richard and Clive assured everyone that they were.

To the Boys, Old Hitch left a sheet with strange pen scratchings on it. Mr. Kenan, who could make no sense of this document, knew only that it belonged to the Boys and so handed it over to Hank, whose eyes popped open upon taking one swift look at it. "I'll be durned! I'll be gol-danged! I'll be *goddamned!*" he whooped enthusiastically. "It's a map to the still! I knowed it! I just knowed it!"

Orin and Boy crowded around, studying the map, which to their otherwise illiterate eyes could not have been more plain in revealing the exact location of the hidden still. "Never would have thought he had it under that rock outcropping on Eagle's Hill. Would you have guessed it, Hank?" Orin demanded with a serious, professional air.

Hank had not guessed it, not in a million years. "We are gonna have a *good* time tonight!" he announced.

"And a headache tomorrow," Cathy predicted.

All this sounded mighty good to Boy, who said, "Ooohh-ee!"

Now came the good part. As certain old rumors had had it, Old Hitch was indeed a very wealthy man, both in land and in cash, and he set about answering the question he had posed in his sonnet about what he owned besides a scrap of land.

To Ginger, Old Hitch left the property around his house, which incorporated a good stretch of the river and included the rents on the mill. He also left directions to which file in which drawer of the "pettifogger lawyer's cabinet" the deed to such could be found and which, he informed them, was made out now in Ginger's name. In one stroke, Miss Ginger Mangum had become a rich young woman.

Old Hitch explained this action as a "desire to tweak Gladys Travis's nose by making Miss Ginger a better catch for her son than Miss Sylvia, and if George hasn't already done something stupid like marryin' Miss Sylvia, I'm givin' him a good reason to marry Miss Ginger. I never found that special woman in my own life—never wanted to, I reckon—but that didn't mean I was agin anyone else findin' and marryin' who they wanted."

Cathy clapped her hands with delight at this wonderful turn of events and smiled with real joy to see George cross to Ginger's side and take her hands in his. He said, "I was not as stupid as Old Hitch feared. I want everyone to know that I asked her to marry me yesterday. I broke the news to my mother last night and, again, I want everyone to know that I remained unmoved by her tears."

He kissed his bride-to-be and said, with something of an unloverlike anticlimax, "Although I will say that the scene she played me this morning was a severe trial to me, and I can hardly wait to tell Mama the good news, for her delicate nerves are likely to be pretty well soothed by the news of Miss Ginger's wealth!"

Ginger surrendered to George's kiss, and Cathy remarked that Mrs. Travis was likely to discover that she had thought "Miss Ginger the perfect wife" for her son all along.

To George, Old Hitch left half his cash, which was in a bank account in Greensboro, the old man not having been able to trust those shifty moneylenders in town. The numbers of the account, the exact and astonishing sum bequeathed, as well as the name of the man George was to contact at the Guilford County State Bank, were all written down. Old Hitch explained that he never did like that "pinch-penny banker, Josiah Lee" nor his daughter, Sylvia, whom he declared was a sight too sure she would marry into the security of the Travis dry-goods business. As far as he, Old Hitch, was concerned, Miss Sylvia could marry his worthless nephew and namesake. They were two of a kind.

"And speaking of findin' and marryin' who you want, to Cathy Davidson I leave—and this is agin my better judgment—her house, her orchard and the other half of my savin's account in Greensboro. Yes, I owned that lot and land when I was alive, but I've written the deed over to her now, and you can find it next to Miss Ginger's deed for the river land and the shack and the mill. Now, the reason that I say it's agin my better judgment is 'cuz I'm thinkin' that Cathy gal has been sweet on that puffed-up coxcomb of a nephew of mine, though she's never said yea nor nay about him when I've mentioned him. Nevertheless, I think he's a worthless good-for-nothing, and I say it now, just in case I never made my opinion of him clear when I was alive! Ha, ha. To him, I'm leavin' nothin'. But if Cathy gal loves that silly whippersnapper and wants him, I want her to have him and instead of snotty Miss Sylvia. So I can think of no better way for Cathy gal to git him than to give her the bait. I loved her like she was my own daughter, and I love her still, even from this distance.''

Cathy was so taken by surprise by the tears that pricked her eyes that she was unable to check them when they started to spurt out of the corners. Once begun, they flowed. She who was never prone to crying, who had not shed a tear since the moment the breath left Old Hitch's body, was crying now. She took one end of her mother's fringed shawl and began to dab her eyes, but the tears kept coming so that soon the fine old material was soaked.

'''And that's all I have to say to the lot of you,''' the lawyer said by way of finishing this astonishing document. '''Goodbye.'''

Cathy's sniffles turned to sobs. She ceased trying to stop the tears that were falling plentifully. She made inadequate attempts to speak.

Ginger came over to her side and put a very loving arm around her. She said, "Are you sad about something, my dear? I would think you would be happy!"

"He was my friend," she managed to blurt out, "my dearest friend, and now I've lost him! I had been denying his loss during the past several days, you know, and I—I was even *laughing* at his funeral—but it *was* funny! Now it's so final. He's gone. But at least he said goodbye."

Ginger smiled comfortingly. "He did say goodbye, and he did it as only he was capable of doing. And he took care of you—all of us!—didn't he?"

"Yes," Cathy sobbed, "and that's why I'm crying! He was such a—a *nice* man, wasn't he? So very nice and caring!" She gave a watery laugh. "Oh, he would just *die* to hear me describe him as such, but oh—!

How we shall all miss him! How much he has given us!''

She sniffed and tried to pull herself together. She looked around and smiled at her dear friends, who had received so much bounty from Old Hitch. She gazed fondly and at length at Richard, who was holding Old Hitch's Bible to his breast and smiling back at her with great serenity. She smiled at the Boys, who were embarrassed and uncomfortable with her tears and had taken refuge in studying the map to Old Hitch's still. She smiled at George and at Ginger and at Clive. She even smiled at Mr. Kenan, who was naturally vexed but happy to have been of service.

Her gaze moved on to MacGuff, and her smile fell a little. He was looking at her in a very inviting, very appreciative way, as if she were the only woman in the world. But she had already seen through him. She did not love him. She did not want him. Old Hitch had been right: He was a very silly whippersnapper. He was perfect for Sylvia Lee.

She did not yet look at Laurence Harris. She recalled Old Hitch's dying words to her: *He'll come tomorrow. He'll take care of you.* She considered the most evident possibility—that the old man had meant for her to marry his worthless nephew, if she wanted it that way. Then she considered the even more extraordinary possibility that Old Hitch had truly taken care of her after his death and had sent her Laurence Harris. Her fire bird. Her angel from hell. Her devil from heaven.

Cathy suddenly felt very free. Free of MacGuff. Free of the house and orchard that had never really been hers. Free of many of the routines she had upheld in Hillsborough these past ten years. The freedom felt great, but it was also scary, and she did not yet dare look at Laurence Harris.

"Mr. Kenan," she said through her sniffs and gulps, "if Old Hitch signed the deed to the house and property over to me, am I allowed to sign the deed over to MacGuff? And the money in the bank account?"

"Why would you want to do that?" the lawyer gasped.

"Because they don't really belong to me, and they never have," she said. "They should be MacGuff's, by right of inheritance."

She did not wish to see MacGuff's reaction. She did not want to see the satisfaction in his eyes at coming into a considerable inheritance. Neither did she want to see his displeasure at being rejected so easily by the likes of her.

Instead, she raised her eyes bravely to meet Laurence Harris's and walked over to him, not confidently, but at least without awkward hesitation. When she was standing before him, she asked directly, "You travel alone, don't you?"

"Yes," he answered, equally direct.

"Are you planning on leaving town soon?"

"Yes."

"Perhaps as soon as today?"

"Yes."

Although his responses might have discouraged her from her course of action, the light in his eyes was very encouraging.

"Will you let me come with you?" she asked next.

He said, again, "Yes."

Cathy was not exactly satisfied, then realized she had asked the wrong question. She quailed for a moment, then forced herself to ask courageously, "Do you *want* me to come with you?"

He placed his hands on her shoulders. He paused a long, loving moment. "Yes," he said, and she knew he meant it.

She smiled. "I'd like to call you Laurence, I think," she said.

"Please do, and I will call you Cathy."

Her smile became suggestive. "That is, when I'm not thinking of you as my fire bird."

Laurence seemed to like that. "Is that, perhaps, at the same time that I am thinking of you as my apple-blossom bird?" he returned.

Her eyes widened. Her smile became *very* suggestive. "No, really?"

He nodded.

Orin made a noise of distaste and said, "If you don't quit lookin' at each other with such goo-goo eyes, I'm gonna be off my food for the rest of the day!"

Ginger said, "We'll miss you, Cathy."

Cathy blinked back to the present and her surroundings. "Oh, I suppose that I *am* leaving!" She looked around her. "How will you go on without me?"

"We'll manage," George assured her. He added, almost shyly, "Although we'll miss you, we're happy for you."

"I can't believe it," Cathy said, "and the leaving will be so difficult! I've so much to do! So much to pack!"

Harris shook his head. "So little to pack, Cathy. But I'll ask you to take your seeds."

The leaving suddenly seemed much easier to her. Of course, she would take her apple seeds—her wealth—with her. She had a vision of a magnificent orchard, grandly blossoming with apple trees of all her favorite varieties.

"I'll want to take Aunt Rachel, too," she said.

"As well as Black Twig," Harris agreed, "but we'll leave the mannerless Smokehouse behind for Young...MacGuff."

Clive entered the discussion. "Say, just what were you two doing the other afternoon in the orchard?"

Cathy flushed. Harris draped his arm affectionately and possessively over her shoulder. He did not respond to the nosy postman's question. Instead, he said, "She'll need a horse. Can you provide her with one, Travis?"

George thought he could. Harris ushered Cathy out of the lawyer's office into the warm May sunshine flooding Churton Street.

"Where are we headed?" she asked, mildly curious about the direction of her new life.

"West." He kissed her, right there in the middle of town. "I've a lot to tell you on the way."

She nodded and smiled and did not feel the need to speak, only to listen.

He chuckled. The sound was deep and rich. Then he kissed her again.

* * * * *

Fifty red-blooded, white-hot, true-blue hunks
from every State in the Union!

Look for MEN MADE IN AMERICA! Written by some
of our most popular authors, these stories feature some
of the strongest, sexiest men, each from a different state
in the union!

Two titles available every month at your favorite
retail outlet.

In February, look for:

THE SECURITY MAN by Dixie Browning
(North Carolina)
A CLASS ACT by Kathleen Eagle (North Dakota)

In March, look for:

TOO NEAR THE FIRE by Lindsay McKenna (Ohio)
A TIME AND A SEASON by Curtiss Ann Matlock
(Oklahoma)

You won't be able to resist MEN MADE IN AMERICA!

⬧ Harlequin® ◇ Historical

**Why is March the best time to try
Harlequin Historicals for the first time?
We've got four reasons:**

All That Matters by Elizabeth Mayne—A medieval woman is freed
from her ivory tower by a Highlander's impetuous proposal.

Embrace the Dawn by Jackie Summers—Striking a scandalous
bargain, a highwayman joins forces with a meddlesome young
woman.

Fearless Hearts by Linda Castle—A grouchy deputy puts up a fight
when his Eastern-bred tutor tries to teach him a lesson.

Love's Wild Wager by Taylor Ryan—A young woman becomes
the talk of London when she wagers her hand on the outcome of a
horse race.

It's that time of year again—that March Madness time of year—
when Harlequin Historicals picks the best and brightest new stars in
historical romance and brings them to you in one exciting month!

Four exciting books by four promising new authors that are
certain to become your favorites. Look for them wherever
Harlequin Historicals are sold.

MM95

HARLEQUIN®

Deceit, betrayal, murder

Join Harlequin's intrepid heroines, India Leigh
and Mary Hadfield, as they ferret out the truth
behind the mysterious goings-on in their
neighborhood. These two women are no milk-
and-water misses. In fact, they thrive on

MISCHIEF & MAYHEM

Watch for their incredible adventures in this
special two-book collection. Available in March,
wherever Harlequin books are sold.

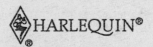

Harlequin invites you to the most
romantic wedding of the season.

Rope the cowboy of your dreams in
Marry Me, Cowboy!

A collection of 4 brand-new stories,
celebrating weddings, written by:

New York Times bestselling author

JANET DAILEY

and favorite authors

Margaret Way
Anne McAllister
Susan Fox

Be sure not to miss Marry Me, Cowboy!
coming this April

HARLEQUIN®

Bestselling Author

JoAnn Ross

Delivers a story so exciting, so thrilling, it'll have you begging for more....

Legacy of Lies

From the haute couture world of Parisian fashion to the glittering lights of Hollywood, Alexandra Lyons will find fame, fortune and love. But desire and scandal will shatter her life unless she can uncover her legacy of lies.

Look for it at your favorite retail outlet this February.

MIRA The brightest star in women's fiction

MJRLOL

HARLEQUIN®

Don't miss these Harlequin favorites by some of our most distinguished authors! And now, you can receive a discount by ordering two or more titles!

HT#25577	WILD LIKE THE WIND by Janice Kaiser	$2.99	☐
HT#25589	THE RETURN OF CAINE O'HALLORAN by JoAnn Ross	$2.99	☐
HP#11626	THE SEDUCTION STAKES by Lindsay Armstrong	$2.99	☐
HP#11647	GIVE A MAN A BAD NAME by Roberta Leigh	$2.99	☐
HR#03293	THE MAN WHO CAME FOR CHRISTMAS by Bethany Campbell	$2.89	☐
HR#03308	RELATIVE VALUES by Jessica Steele	$2.89	☐
SR#70589	CANDY KISSES by Muriel Jensen	$3.50	☐
SR#70598	WEDDING INVITATION by Marisa Carroll	$3.50 U.S. $3.99 CAN.	☐
HI#22230	CACHE POOR by Margaret St. George	$2.99	☐
HAR#16515	NO ROOM AT THE INN by Linda Randall Wisdom	$3.50	☐
HAR#16520	THE ADVENTURESS by M.J. Rodgers	$3.50	☐
HS#28795	PIECES OF SKY by Marianne Willman	$3.99	☐
HS#28824	A WARRIOR'S WAY by Margaret Moore	$3.99 U.S. $4.50 CAN.	☐

(limited quantities available on certain titles)

	AMOUNT	$
DEDUCT:	10% DISCOUNT FOR 2+ BOOKS	$
ADD:	POSTAGE & HANDLING	$
	($1.00 for one book, 50¢ for each additional)	
	APPLICABLE TAXES*	$_____
	TOTAL PAYABLE	$_____
	(check or money order—please do not send cash)	

To order, complete this form and send it, along with a check or money order for the total above, payable to Harlequin Books, to: **In the U.S.:** 3010 Walden Avenue, P.O. Box 9047, Buffalo, NY 14269-9047; **In Canada:** P.O. Box 613, Fort Erie, Ontario, L2A 5X3.

Name: _____

Address: _____ City: _____

State/Prov.: _____ Zip/Postal Code: _____

*New York residents remit applicable sales taxes.
 Canadian residents remit applicable GST and provincial taxes.

HBACK-JM2